Also from Cohesion Press

SNAFU: An Anthology of Military Horror
– eds Geoff Brown & Amanda J Spedding

SNAFU: Wolves at the Door
– eds Geoff Brown & Amanda J Spedding

SNAFU: Survival of the Fittest
– eds Geoff Brown & Amanda J Spedding

SNAFU: Hunters
– eds Amanda J Spedding & Geoff Brown

SNAFU: Future Warfare
– eds Amanda J Spedding & Geoff Brown

SNAFU: Unnatural Selection
– eds Amanda J Spedding & Geoff Brown

SNAFU: Black Ops
– eds Amanda J Spedding, Matthew Summers & Geoff Brown

SNAFU: Resurrection
– eds Amanda J Spedding & Matthew Summers

SNAFU: Last Stand
– eds Amanda J Spedding & Matthew Summers

SNAFU: Medivac
– eds Amanda J Spedding, Geoff Brown & Matthew Summers

SNAFU: Holy War (2021)
– eds Amanda J Spedding & Geoff Brown

LOVE, DEATH + ROBOTS

THE OFFICIAL ANTHOLOGY

LOVE DEATH + ROBOTS

THE OFFICIAL ANTHOLOGY

COHESION PRESS
THE BATTLE HAS JUST BEGUN

Mayday Hills Asylum
Beechworth, Australia
2019

LOVE, DEATH + ROBOTS
♥ ✖ ▦

Anthology © Cohesion Press 2021
Stories © Individual Authors
Cover design: Jennifer Miller/BLUR Studio
Amanda J Spedding/Geoff Brown (eds)

Set in Palatino Linotype

COHESION PRESS
THE BATTLE HAS JUST BEGUN

COHESION PRESS
Mayday Hills Asylum
Beechworth, Australia

TABLE OF CONTENTS

INTRODUCTION - Tim Miller xiii

SONNIE'S EDGE - Peter F Hamilton 1

THREE ROBOTS - John Scalzi 21

THE WITNESS - Alberto Mielgo 29

SUITS - Steve Lewis 41

SUCKER OF SOULS - Kirsten Cross 77

WHEN THE YOGHURT TOOK OVER - John Scalzi 105

BEYOND THE AQUILA RIFT - Alastair Reynolds.................109

GOOD HUNTING - Ken Liu...145

THE DUMP - Joe R Lansdale 165

SHAPE-SHIFTERS - Marko Kloos 171

HELPING HAND - Claudine Griggs 187

FISH NIGHT - Joe R Lansdale 193

LUCKY THIRTEEN - Marko Kloos 201

ZIMA BLUE - Alistair Reynolds 215

BLIND SPOT - Vitaliy Shushko 239

ICE AGE - Michael Swanwick 251

ALTERNATE HISTORIES - John Scalzi 261

THE SECRET WAR - David W. Amendola 265

FIRST APPEARANCES

DEDICATED TO:

Reed Hastings
Ted Sarandos
Cindy Holland
Peter Friedlander
Alison Engel

For creating a place where *Love, Death + Robots* could exist.

INTRODUCTION

Tim Miller

I feel so unbelievably fucking fortunate to have had the chance to make a show like *Love, Death + Robots*, and more fortunate still that folks seem to like it. Fans may assume that it's a love of animation that drives the show, and that's certainly a huge part of it. But for myself, it has always been as much or more about a love for the written word... for the stories.

Choosing the material for *LD+R* has been THE best job I've ever had. Searching for stories feels like walking along a beach in paradise filled with an endless variety of unique and beautiful seashells. All I have to do is pick a few up, brush the sand off and put 'em in my pocket. And the tide washes up more treasure every day.

Developing each story into a script is a stress-free pleasure because we already know they work! It's simply a matter of adapting them in the best ways possible to a new medium and focusing on the imagery.

Because we have so much respect for the authors and the source material we try very hard to stay true to the spirit of the original. We want the authors to feel that we're respectful caretakers of their work and to feel proud of the result. But it's not an exact science and there's always a bit of magic missing; small details lost, interesting moments cut for time, or scope sacrificed on the altar of budget. So we created this anthology to give fans an easy way to read the original, untamed stories - think of it as viewing the animals in the wild.

And we wanted to share the spotlight with the creators of the amazing work we've built the show upon. Hopefully, this will lead readers to other works by these authors; there are a lot more seashells scattered on the beach.

Tim Miller
Creator of *Love, Death + Robots*
April 2nd, 2021

SONNIE'S EDGE

Peter F Hamilton

I t was daylight, so Battersea was in gridlock. The M500 motorway above the Thames had taken us right into the heart of London at a hundred and fifty kilometres an hour, then after we spiralled down an off ramp onto the Chelsea Bridge our top speed braked to a solid one kph. Our venue was another three kilometres ahead of us.

We joined the queue of chrome-silver vehicles jamming the street, turning up the reflectivity of our own windscreen against the glare. Bikes slithered through the narrow gaps, their riders in slick-skinned kooler suits. Lighthorns flared and blared in fury as they cut through the two-way tailback, chasing after them like some kind of runway strobe effect. As if that wasn't bad enough, every vehicle on the road was humming urgently, hub motors and air-conditioning vibrating the air at a frequency guaranteed to induce a migraine. Three hours of that.

I hate cities.

Midday, and we rolled into the derelict yard like an old-fashioned circus caravan come to town. I was driver's mate to Jacob, sitting up in the ageing twenty-wheeler's cab, feet up to squash the tideline of McWrappers littering the dash.

Curious roadies from the arena were milling about on the fractured concrete, staring up at us. The other two vans in our team's convoy turned in off the road. A big pair of dilapidated metal gates clanged shut behind us.

Jacob locked the wheels and turned off the power cell. I climbed down out of the cab. The silvered side of the lorry was grimy from the city's airplaque, but my reflection was clear enough. Blonde bob hairstyle that needs attention; same goes for the clothes, I guess: sleeveless black T-shirt and olive-green Bermuda shorts I've had for over a year, feet crammed into fraying white plimsolls. I'm twenty-two, though I've got the kind of gaunt figure thirty-year-old women have when they work out and diet hard to make themselves look twenty-two again. My face isn't too bad; Jacob rebuilt it to give me the prominent cheekbones I'd always wanted as a teenager. Maybe it wasn't as expressive as it used to be, but the distorting curves of the lorry's bodywork made it hard to tell.

Outside the cab's insulation, London's sounds hit me square on, along with its heat and smell. The three major waste products of eighteen million consumers determined to preserve their lifestyle by spending and burning their way through domestic goodies and energy at a rate only twenty-first century industry can supply. And even that struggles to keep up with demand.

I can plug straight into that beautiful hive of greed; their need for a byte of the action. I know what they want best of all, and we provide it for them.

Excitement, that's how me and the rest of Sonnie's Predators suckle our money. And we've brought a big unique chunk of it here to Battersea. Tonight, there's gonna be a fight.

Beastie-baiting: the all-time blood sport; violent, spectacularly gory, and always lethal. It's new and it's happening; universes away from the sanitized crap of VR games consumers load into their taksuit processor each night. This is real, it ignites the old instincts, the strongest and most addictive of all. And Sonnie's Predators are the hottest team to storm ashore in the two years since the contests started. Seventeen straight wins. We've got Baiter groupies howling for us all the way from the Orkney Islands down to Cornwall.

I was lucky, signing up at level one, when all the rage was modifying Rottweilers and Dobermanns with fang implants and razor claws. A concept I bet poor old Wing-Tsit Chong never thought of when he invented the affinity bond.

Karran and Jacob were the team's nucleus, fresh out of Leicester University with their biotechnology degrees all hot and promising. They could have gone to any company in the world with those qualifications, plunged straight into the corporate universe of applied research and annual budget squabbles. It's an exchange millions of graduates make each year, zest for security, and the big relief of knowing your student loans will be paid off. But that was about the

2

time when the Pope started appeasing the Church's right wing, and publicly questioned the morality of affinity and the way it was used to control animals. It didn't take long for the mullahs to join the chorus. The whole biotechnology ethics problem became prime topic for newscable studios; not to mention justification for a dozen animal-rights activists to launch terminal action campaigns against biotechnology labs. Suddenly, establishment biotechnology wasn't so enticing.

If they didn't start paying off the student loan within six months of graduation, the bank would just assign them to a company (and take an agency fee from their salary). Baiting was the only financially viable alternative for their talent.

Ivrina was an ex-surgical nurse who had just started helping them with grafting techniques when I arrived. A drifter with little ambition, even less education, but just enough sense to realize this was *different*, something I could immerse myself in, maybe even make a go of. It was new for everybody, we were all beginners and learners. They took me on as a driver and general dogsbody.

Wes joined three months later. A hardware specialist, or nerd, depending on your prejudice. An essential addition to a sport whose sophistication was advancing on a near-daily basis. He maintained the clone vats, computer stacks, and Khanivore's life-support units, plus a thousand other miscellaneous units.

We were doing all right, Jacob's Banshees, as we were known back then, battling hard for cult status. A decent win ratio, pushing sixty per cent. Jacob and Karran were still massively in debt, but they were making the monthly interest payments. The purse money was enough to keep us independent while our contemporaries were scrambling for syndicate backing. Poor but proud, the oldest kick in the book. Waiting for the whole sport to earn cable interest and turn big time. It would happen, all the teams knew that.

Then I had my mishap, and acquired my killer edge.

The buzz from the hub motors on the other two vans faded away, and the rest of the team joined me among the weeds and cat pee of the yard's concrete. According to a London Administration Council sign on the gates, the yard had been designated as a site for one of the proposed Central-South Dome's support pillars. Though God knows when construction would ever begin. Central-North Dome was visible above the razor wire trimming the yard's wall. A geodesic of amber-tinted crystal, four kilometres in diameter, squatting over most of the Westminster district like some kind of display case for the ancient stone buildings underneath. The struts were tiny considering the size of it, a type of superstrong fibre grown in orbit, glinting prismatically in the achingly bright sun. Empty gridworks for the Chelsea and Islington domes were already splintering the sky on either side of it. One day all cities will be like this, sheltering from the hostile climate which their own thermal emission has created. London doesn't have smog any more. Now it just has heat shimmer, the air wobbling in the exhaust vents of twenty-five million conditioning nozzles. The ten largest ones are sitting on the Central-North dome, like black barnacles spewing out the surplus therms in huge fountains of grey haze. London Administration Council won't allow planes to fly over it for fear of what those giant lightless flames will do to airflow dynamics.

Karran came over to stand beside me, setting a wide panama hat over her ruff of Titian hair. Ivrina stood a few paces back, wearing just a halter top and sawn-off jeans; UV proofing treatment had turned her Arctic-princess skin a rich cinnamon. Wes snaked an arm protectively round her waist as she sniffed disapprovingly at the grungy air.

"So how's the vibes, Sonnie?" Karran asked.

They all fell silent, even Jacob who was talking to the roadie boss. If a Baiting team's fighter hasn't got the right hype then you just pack up and go straight home. For all their ingenuity and technical back-up, the rest of the team play no part in the bout. It's all down to me.

"Vibes is good," I told them. "I'll have it wrapped in five minutes."

There was only one time when I'd ever doubted. A Newcastle venue that matched us against the King Panther team. It turned into a bitch of a scrap. Khanivore was cut up pretty bad. Even then, I'd won. The kind of bout from which Baiter legends are born.

Ivrina punched a fist into her palm. "Atta girl!" She looked hotwired, spoiling for trouble. Anyone would think she was going to boost Khanivore herself. She certainly had the right fire for it; but as to whether she had the nerve to go for my special brand of killer edge I don't know.

4

SONNIE'S EDGE

It turned out that Dicko, the arena's owner, was a smooth organizer. Makes a change. Some bouts we've wondered if the place even existed, never mind having backstage gofers. Jacob marshalled the roadies, and got them to unload Khanivore's life-support pod from the lorry. His beefy face was sweating heavily as the opaque cylinder was slowly lifted down along with its ancillary modules. I don't know why he worries so much about a two-metre drop. He does most of the beastie's body design work (Karran handles the nervous system and circulatory network) so more than anyone he knows how tough Khanivore's hide is.

The arena had started life as a vast tubing warehouse before Dicko moved in and set up shop. He kept the corrugated panel shell, stripping out the auto-stack machinery so he could grow a polyp pit in the centre – circular, fifteen metres in diameter, and four metres deep. It was completely surrounded by seating tiers, simple concentric circles of wooden plank benches straddling a spiderwork of rusty scaffolding. The top was twenty metres above the concrete floor, nearly touching the condensation-slicked roof panels. Looking at the rickety lash-up made me glad I wasn't a spectator.

Our green room was the warehouse supervisor's old office. The roadies grunted Khanivore's life support into place on a set of heavy wooden trestles. They creaked but held.

Ivrina and I started taping black polythene over the filthy windows. Wes mated the ancillary modules with the warehouse's power supply. Karran slipped on her Ishades, and began running diagnostic checks through Khanivore's nervous system.

Jacob came in smiling broadly. "The odds are nine to two in our favour. I put five grand on us. Reckon you can handle that, Sonnie?"

"Count on it. The Urban Gorgons have just acquired themselves one dead beastie."

"My girl," Wes said proudly, slapping my shoulder.

He was lying, which cut deep. Wes and I had been an inseparable pair for eight months, right up until my mishap. Now he and Ivrina were rocking the camper van's suspension every night. I didn't hold it against him, not consciously anyway. But seeing them walking everywhere together, arms entwined, necking, laughing – that left me cold.

An hour before I'm on, Dicko shows up. Looking at him, you kind of wondered how come he wound up in this racket. A dignified old boy, all formal manners and courteous smile; tall and thin, with bushy silver hair too thick to be entirely natural, and a slightly stiff walk which forced him to use a silver-topped cane. His garb was strictly last century: light grey suit with slim lapels, a white shirt with small maroon bow tie.

There was a girl in tow, mid-teens and nicely proportioned, sweet-faced, too; a fluff-cloud of curly chestnut hair framing a composed demure expression. She wore a simple square-necked lemon-yellow dress with a long skirt. I felt sorry for her. But it's an ancient story; I get to see it countless times at each bout. At least it told me all I needed to know about Dicko and his cultivated mannerisms. Mr Front.

One of the roadies closed the door behind him, cutting off the sounds of conversation from the main hall, a whistling PA. Dicko gave me and the other girls a shallow bow, then handed an envelope to Jacob. "Your appearance fee."

The envelope disappeared into Jacob's sleeveless leather jacket.

Delicate silver eyebrows lifted a millimetre. "You are not going to count it?"

"Your reputation is good," Jacob told him. "You're a pro, top notch. That's the word."

"How very kind. And you, too, come well recommended."

I listened to him and the rest of the team swapping nonsense. I didn't like it, he was intruding. Some teams like to party pre-bout; some thrash and re-thrash tactics. Me, I like a bit of peace and quiet to Zen myself up. Friends who'll talk if I want, who know when to keep quiet. I jittered about, wait-tension making my skin crawl. Every time I glanced at Dicko's girl her eyes dropped. She was studying me.

"I wonder if I might take a peek at Khanivore?" Dicko asked. "One has heard so much..."

The others swivelled en masse to consult me.

"Sure thing." After the old boy had seen it, maybe he'd scoot. You can't really shunt someone out of their own turf.

We clustered round the life-support pod, except for the girl. Wes turned down the opacity, and Dicko's face hardened into grim appreciation, a corpse grin. It chilled me down.

Khanivore is close on three metres tall, roughly hominoid in that it has two trunklike legs and a barrel torso, albeit encased in a black segmented exoskeleton. After that, things get a little out of kilter. The top of the torso sprouts five armoured tentacles, two of them ending in bone-blade pincers. They were all curled up to fit in the pod like a nest of sleeping boa constrictors. There was a thick twenty-centimetre prehensile neck supporting a nightmare head sculpted from bone that was polished down to a black-chrome gleam. The front was a shark-snout jaw with a double row of teeth, while the main dome was inset with deep creases and craters to protect sensor organs.

Dicko reached out and touched the surface of the pod. "Excellent," he whispered, then added casually: "I want you to take a dive."

There was a moment of dark silence.

"Do what?" Karran squeaked.

Dicko beamed his dead smile straight at her. "A dive. You'll be well paid, double the winning purse, ten thousand CUs. Plus whatever side bets you care to place. That should go a long way to easing the financial strain on an amateur team like yourselves. We can even discuss some future dates."

"Fuck off!"

"And that's from all of us," Jacob spat. "You screwed up, Dicko. We're pros, man, real pros. We believe in beastie-baiting, it's *ours*. We were there at the start, and we're not letting shits like you fuck it over for a quick profit. Word gets out about rigged bouts and we all lose, even you."

He was smooth, I'll give him that, his cocoon of urbanity never flickering. "You're not thinking, young man. To keep on Baiting you must have money. Especially in the future. Large commercial concerns are starting to notice this sport of yours, it will soon be turning professional with official leagues and governing bodies. With the right kind of support a team of your undeniable quality can last until you reach retirement age. Even a beast which never loses requires a complete rebuild every nine months, not to mention the continual refinements you have to stitch in. Baiting is an expensive business, and about to become more so. And business it now is, not some funfair ride. At the moment you are naive amateurs who happen to have hit a winning streak. Do not delude yourselves; one day you are going to lose. You need a secure income to tide you over the lean times while you design and test a new beast.

"This is what I am offering you, the first step towards responsibility. Fighters and promoters feed each other. We always have done, right back to the days of the Roman gladiators. And we always will do. There is nothing dishonest in this. Tonight, the fans will see the tremendous fight they paid for, because Khanivore could never lose easily. Then they will return to watch you again, screaming for victory, ecstatic when you win again. Struggle, heartache, and triumph, that is what demands their attention, what keeps any sport alive. Believe me, I know crowds far better than you ever can; they have been my life's study."

"So has money," Ivrina said quietly. She'd crossed her arms over her chest, staring at him contemptuously. "Don't give us any more of this bullshit about doing us a favour. You run the book in this part of town, you and a few others. A tight, friendly little group who've got it all locked down. *That's* the way it is, that's the way it's always been. I'll tell you what's really happened tonight. Every punter has laid down their wad on Sonnie's Predators, the dead cert faves. So you and the boys did a few sums of your own, and worked out how you can profit most from that. Slip us the ten grand for a fall, and you'll walk off with the mega-profit."

"Fifteen thousand," Dicko said, completely unperturbed. "Please accept the offer, I urge you as a friend. What I have said is quite true, no matter what motives you assign me. One day you will lose." He turned to look at me, his expression was almost entreating. "You are the team's fighter, by nature the most practical. How much confidence do you have in your own ability? You are out there in the bouts, you have known moments of doubt when your opponent pulled a clever turn. Surely you do not have the arrogance to believe you are invincible?"

"No, I'm not invincible. What I have is an edge. Didn't it occur to you to wonder how come I always win?"

"It has been the cause of some speculation."

"Simple enough; although nobody else could ever use it. You see, I won't lose to the Urban Gorgons, not while they have Simon as their fighter."

"I don't understand, every bout cannot be a grudge match."

"Oh but they are. Maybe if the Urban Gorgons team fronted a female fighter I'd think about taking your money. But I'm virtually unique; none of the other teams I know of use a female to boost their beastie."

"This is your advantage, your legendary edge, women fight better than men?"

"Motivation is the key," I said. "That's why we use affinity to control the beasts. These creatures we stitch together have no analogue in nature. For instance, you couldn't take a brain out of a lion and splice it into Khanivore. For all its hunter-killer instinct a lion wouldn't be able to make any sense of Khanivore's sensorium, nor would it be able to utilize the limbs. That's why we give beasties bioware processors instead of brains. But processors still don't give us what we need. For their program a fight can never be anything more than a complex series of problems, a three-dimensional chess game. An attack would be broken up into segments for analysis and initiation of appropriate response moves. By which time any halfway sentient opposition has ripped them to shreds. No program can ever instil a sense of urgency, coupled to panic-enhanced instinct. Sheer savagery, if you like. Humans reign supreme when it comes to that. That's why we use the affinity bond. Beastie-baiting is a physical extension of the human mind, our dark side in all its naked horror. That's the appeal your punters have come to worship tonight, Dicko, pure bestiality. Without our proxy beasties us fighters would be out there in the pit ourselves. We'd kill each other, no two ways about it."

"And you are the most savage of them all?" Dicko asked. He glanced round the team, their stony faces, hunting confirmation.

"I am now," I said, and for the first time bled a trace of venom into my voice. I saw the girl stiffen slightly, her eyes round with interest. "A year or so back I got snatched by an estate gang. No reason for it, I was just in the wrong place at the wrong time. Know what they do to girls, Dicko?" I was grinding the words out now, eyes never leaving his face. His mask was cracking, little fissures of emotion showing through.

"Yes, you do know, don't you. The gang bang wasn't so bad, there was only two days of that. But when they finished they started on me with knives. It's a branding thing, making sure everyone knows how fucking hard they are. So that is why, when the Urban Gorgons send their Turboraptor out in the pit tonight, I am going to shred that bastard to pieces so small there's going to be nothing left but a fog of blood. Not because of the money, not even for the status; but because what I'm really doing is carving up that *male* shit Simon." I took a step towards Dicko, arm coming up to point threateningly. "And neither you nor anyone else is going to stop that happening. You got that, shitbrain?"

One of Khanivore's tentacles began to uncoil, an indistinct motion beneath the murky surface of the life-support pod.

Dicko snatched a fast glance at the agitated beastie and gave another of his prissy bows. "I won't press you any further, but I do ask you to think over what I proposed." He turned on a heel, snapping his fingers for the girl to follow. She scampered off through the door.

The team closed in on me with smiles and fierce hugs. Time for the bout, they formed a praetorian guard to escort me out to the pit. The air around the arena was already way too hot, and becoming badly humid from the sweat and breath of the crowd. No conditioning. Naturally.

My ears filled with the chants rising from the seats, slow hand-claps, whistles, hoots, catcalls. The noise rumbled sluggishly round the dark empty space behind the stand.

Under the scaffolding, reverberating with low-frequency harmonics. Then out into an unremitting downpour of harsh blue-white light and gullet-rattling noise. Cheering and jeering reached a crescendo. Every centimetre of wooden seating was taken.

I sat in my seat on the edge of the pit. Simon was sitting directly opposite me, naked from the waist up; lean, bald, and sable black. A stylistic ruby-red griffin tattoo fluoresced on his chest, intensity pulsing in time to his heartbeat. Big gold pirate earrings dangled from mauled lobes. He stood to give me the grand fuckittoyou gesture. Urban Gorgons fans roared their delight.

"You OK, Sonnie?" Ivrina whispered.

"Sure." I locked eyes with Simon, and laughed derisively. Our side's supporters whooped rapturously.

The ref bobbed to his feet halfway round the side of the pit. The PA came on with a screech, and he launched into his snappy intros.

Standard soundbite fodder. Actually, he's not so much a ref as a starter. There aren't too many rules in beastie-baiting – your creature must be bipedal, no hardware or metal allowed in the design, no time limit, the one left alive is the winner. It does tend to cut out any confusion.

The ref was winding up, probably afraid of getting lynched by an impatient crowd. Simon closed his eyes, concentrating on his affinity link with Turboraptor.

An affinity bond is a unique and private link. Each pair of cloned neuron symbionts is attuned to its twin alone; there can be no interception, no listening in. One clump is embedded in the human brain, the other is incorporated in a bioware processor. It's a perfect tool for Baiting.

I closed my eyes.

Khanivore was waiting behind the webwork of scaffolding. I went through a final systems check. Arteries, veins, muscles, tendons, failsoft nerve-fibre network, multiple redundant heart-pump chambers. All on line and operating at a hundred per cent. I had the oxygenated blood reserves to fight for up to an hour.

There wasn't anything else. Vital internal organs are literally that: vital. Too risky to bring into the pit. One puncture and the beastie could die. One! That's hardly a fair fight. It's also shoddy combat design. So Khanivore spends most of its time in a life-support pod, where the ancillary units substitute functions like the liver, kidneys, lungs, and all the other physiological crap not essential to keep it fighting.

I walked it forward.

And the crowd goes *wild*. Predictable as hell, but I love them for it. This is my moment, the only time I am truly alive.

Turboraptor was already descending into the pit, the makeshift wooden ramp sagging under its weight. First chance for a detailed examination.

The Urban Gorgons team had stitched together a small bruise-purple dinosaur, minus tail. Its body was pear-shaped with short dumpy legs – difficult to topple. The arms were weird, two metres fifty long, five joints apiece – excellent articulation, have to watch that. One ended in a three-talon claw, the other had a solid bulb of bone. The idea was good, grip with the talon and punch with the bone fist. Given the arm's reach, it could probably work up enough inertia to break through Khanivore's exoskeleton. A pair of needle-pointed, fifty-centimetre horns jutted up from its head. Stupid. Horns and blade fins might make for good image, but they give your opponent something to grab; that's why we made Khanivore ice-smooth.

Khanivore reached the pit floor, and the roadies hauled the wooden ramp away behind it. There was silence again as the ref stretched out his arm. A white silk handkerchief dangled from his fingers. He dropped it.

I let all five tentacles unroll halfway to the floor, snapping the pincers as they went. Sonnie's Predators fans picked up the beat, stamping their feet, clapping.

Turboraptor and Khanivore circled each other, testing for speed and reflexes. I lashed a couple of tentacles, aiming to lasso Turboraptor's legs. Impressed by how fast it dodged with those stumpy legs. In return its talon claw came dangerously close to the root of a tentacle. I didn't think it could cut through, but I'd have to be vigilant.

The circling stopped. We began to sway the beasties from side to side, both tensing, waiting for either an opening or a charge. Simon broke first, sending Turbo- raptor at me in a heavy run, arm punching the bone fist forward. I pirouetted Khanivore on one foot, whipping the tentacles to add spin-momentum. Turboraptor sliced past, and I caught it across the back of the head with a tentacle, sending it slamming into the pit wall. Khanivore regained its footing, and followed. I wanted to keep Turboraptor pinned there, to hammer blows against it which it would be forced to absorb. But both of its arms came slashing backwards – the bastards were pivot hinged. One of my tentacle tips was caught in its talon claw. I brought more tentacles up to fend off the punch from the bone fist, simultaneously twisting the captured tentacle. Turboraptor's punch slapped into a writhing coil of tentacle, muting the impact. We staggered apart.

The tip of my tentacle was lying on the pit floor, flexing like an electrocuted snake. There was no pain; Khanivore's nerves weren't structured for that. A little jet of scarlet blood squirted out of the severed end. It vanished as the bioware processors closed off the artery.

The crowd was on its feet, howling approval and demanding

vengeance. Slashes of colour and waving arms; the roof panels vibrating. All distant.

Turboraptor sidestepped hurriedly, moving away from the danger of the pit wall. I let it go, watching intently. One of its pincer talons seemed misaligned; when the other two closed it didn't budge.

We clashed again, colliding in the centre of the pit. It was a kick and shove match this time. Arms and tentacles could only beat ineffectually on armoured flanks while we were pressed together. Then I managed to bend Khanivore's head low enough for its jaws to clamp around Turboraptor's shoulder. Arrow-head teeth bit into purple scales. Blood began to seep out of the puncture marks.

Turboraptor's talon claw started to scrape at Khanivore's head. Simon was using the dead talon like a can opener, gouging away at the sensor cavities. I lost a couple of retinas and an ear before I decided I was on a hiding to nothing. Khanivore's mouth had done as much damage as possible, it wouldn't close any further. I let go, and we fell apart cleanly.

Turboraptor took two paces back, and charged at me again. I wasn't quick enough. That pile-driver bone fist struck Khanivore's torso full on. I backpedalled furiously to keep balance, and thudded into the pit wall.

Bioware processors flashed status graphics into my mind, red and orange cobwebs superimposed over my vision, detailing the damage. Turboraptor's fist had weakened the exoskeleton's midsection. Khanivore could probably take another couple of punches like that, definitely no more than three.

I slashed out with a couple of tentacles. One twined round Turboraptor's bone fist. The second snared the uppermost segment of the same arm. An inescapable manacle. No way could Simon manoeuvre another punch out of that.

I shot an order into the relevant control processors to maintain the hold. Controlling five upper limbs at once isn't possible for a human brain. We don't have the neurological programming for it, that's why most beasties are straight hominoids. All I could ever do with Khanivore was manipulate two tentacles; but for something simple like sustaining a grip the processors can take over while I switch to another pair of tentacles.

Turboraptor's talon claw bent round to try and snip the tentacles grasping its arm. I sent another two tentacles to bind it, which left me the fifth free to win the war.

I'd just started to bring it forwards, figuring on using it to try and snap Turboraptor's neck, when Simon pulled a fast one. The top half of the talon claw arm started to pull back. I thought Khanivore's optical nerves had gone haywire. My tentacles' grip on the arm was rock solid, it couldn't possibly be moving.

There was a wet tearing sound, a small plume of blood.

The tentacles were left wrapped round the last three segments of the arm, while the lower section, the one which had separated, was a sheath for a fifty-centimetre sword of solid bone.

Simon stabbed it straight at Khanivore's torso, where the exoskeleton was already weakened. Fear burned me then, a stimulant harder than any adrenalin or amphetamine, accelerating my thoughts to lightspeed. Self-preservation superseded reticence, and I swiped the fifth tentacle downwards, knowing it would get butchered and not caring. Anything to deflect that killer strike.

The tentacle hit the top of the blade, an impact which nearly severed it in two. A fountain of blood spewed out, splattering over Turboraptor's chest like a scarlet graffiti bomb. But the blade was deflected, slicing downwards to shatter a hole in the exoskeleton of Khanivore's right leg. It slid in deep enough for the display graphics to tell me the tip was touching the other side. Simon levered it round, decimating the flesh inside the exoskeleton. More cobweb graphics flowered, reporting severed nerve fibres, cut tendons, artery valves closing. The leg was more or less useless.

I was already throwing away the useless section of Turboraptor's trick arm. One of the freed tentacles wove around the sword hilt, contracting the loop as tight as it would go, preventing the blade from moving. It was still inside me, but prevented from causing any more havoc. Our bodies were locked together. None of Turboraptor's squirming and shaking could separate us.

With a care that verged on the tender, I slowly wound my last tentacle clockwise round Turboraptor's head, avoiding its snapping jaw. I finished with a tight knot around the base of a horn.

Simon must have realized what I was going to do. Turboraptor's legs scrabbled against the bloody floor, frantically trying to unbalance the pair of us.

I began pulling with the tentacle, reeling it in. Turboraptor's head turned. It fought me every centimetre of the way, straining cords of muscle rippling under the scales.

No good. The rotation was inexorable.

Ninety degrees, and ominous popping sounds emerged from the stumpy neck. A hundred degrees and the purple scales were no longer overlapping. A hundred and ten degrees and the skin started to tear. A hundred and twenty, and the spine snapped with a gunshot crack.

My tentacle wrenched the head off, flinging it triumphantly into the air. It landed in a puddle of my blood, and skidded across the polyp until it bumped into the wall below Simon. He was doubled up on the edge of his chair, hugging his chest, shaking violently. His tattoo blazed cleanly, as if it was burning into his skin. Team-mates were swooping towards him.

That was when I opened my own eyes, just in time to see Turboraptor's decapitated body tumble to the ground. The crowd was up and dancing, rocking the stand, and crying my name. Mine! Minute flecks of damp rust from the roof panels were snowing over the whole arena.

I stood up, raising both my arms, collecting and acknowledging my due of adulation. The team's kisses stung my cheeks. *Eighteen.* Eighteen straight victories.

There was just one motionless figure among the carnival frenzy. Dicko, sitting in the front row, chin resting on his cane's silver pommel, staring glumly at the wreckage of flesh lying at Khanivore's feet.

Three hours later, and the rap is still tearing apart Turboraptor's trick arm. Was it bending the rules? Should we do something similar? What tactics were best against it?

I sipped my Ruddles from a long-stemmed glass, letting the vocals eddy round me. We'd wound up in a pub called the Latchmere, local *it* spot, with some kind of art theatre upstairs where the cosmically strange punters kept vanishing. God knows what was playing. From where I was slumped I could see about fifteen people dancing listlessly at the far end of the bar, the juke playing some weird acoustic Indian metal track.

Our table was court to six Baiter fans, eyes atwinkle from the proximity to their idols. If it hadn't been for the victory high, I might have been embarrassed. Beer and seafood kept piling up, courtesy of a local merchant who'd been at the pit side, and was now designer-slumming at the bar with his pouty mistress.

The girl in the yellow dress came in. She was alone. I watched her and a waitress put their heads together, swapping a few furtive words as her haunted eyes cast about. Then she wandered over to the juke.

She was still staring blankly at the selection screen a minute later when I joined her.

"Did he hit you?" I asked.

She turned, flinching. Her eyes were red-rimmed. "No," she said in a tiny voice.

"Will he hit you?"

She shook her head mutely, staring at the floor.

Jennifer. That was her name. She told me as we walked out into the sweltering night. Lecherous grins and Karran's thumbs-up at our backs.

It was drizzling, the minute droplets evaporating almost as soon as they hit the pavement. Warm mist sparkled in the hologram adverts which formed rainbow arches over the road. A team of servitor chimps were out cleaning the street, glossy gold pelts darkened by the drizzle.

I walked Jennifer down to the riverfront where we'd parked our vehicles. The arena roadies had been cool after the bout, but none of us were gonna risk staying in Dicko's yard overnight.

Jennifer wiped her hands along her bare arms. I draped my leather jacket over her shoulders, and she clutched it gratefully across her chest.

"I'd say keep it," I told her. "Except I don't think he'd approve." The studs said Sonnie's Predators bold across the back.

Her lips ghosted a smile. "Yes. He buys my clothes. He doesn't like me in anything which isn't feminine."

"Thought of leaving him?"

"Sometimes. All the time. But it would only be the face which

16

changed. I am what I am. He's not too bad. Except tonight, and he'll be over that by morning."

"You could come with us." And I could just see me squaring that with the others.

She stopped walking and looked wistfully out over the black river. The M500 stood high above it, a curving ribbon of steel resting on a line of slender buttressed pedestals that sprouted from the centre of the muddy bed. Headlights and brakelights from the traffic formed a permanent pink corona across it, a slipstream of light that blew straight out of the city.

"I'm not like you," Jennifer said. "I envy you, respect you. I'm even a little frightened of you. But I'll never be like you." She smiled slowly. The first real one I'd seen on that face. "Tonight will be enough."

I understood. It hadn't been an accident her turning up at the pub. A single act of defiance. One he would never know about. But that didn't make it any less valid.

I opened the small door at the rear of the twenty-wheeler, and led her inside. Khanivore's life-support pod glowed a moonlight silver in the gloom, ancillary modules making soft gurgling sounds. All the cabinets and machinery clusters were monochrome as we threaded our way past. The tiny office on the other side was quieter. Standby LEDs on the computer terminals shone weakly, illuminating the fold-out sofa opposite the desks.

Jennifer stood in the middle of the aisle, and slipped the jacket off her shoulders. Her hands traced a gentle questing line up my ribcage, over my breasts, onto my neck, rising further. She had cool fingertips, long fuchsia nails. Her palms came to rest on my cheeks, fingers splayed between earlobes and forehead.

"You made Dicko so very angry," she murmured huskily.

Her breath was warm and soft on my lips. Pain exploded into my skull.

* * *

My military-grade retinas flicked to low-light mode, banishing shadows as we trooped past the beast's life-support pod in the back of the lorry. The world became a sketch of blue and grey, outlines sharp. I was in a technophile's chapel, floor laced with kilometres of wire and tubing, walls of machinery with little LEDs glowing. Sonnie's breath was quickening when we reached the small compartment at the far end. Randy bitch. Probably where she brought all her one-nighters.

I chucked the jacket and reached for her. She looked like she was on the first night of her honeymoon.

Hands in place, tensed against her temples, and I said: "You made Dicko so very angry." Then I let her have it.

Every fingertip sprouted a five-centimetre spike of titanium, punched out by a magpulse. They skewered straight through her skull to penetrate the brain inside.

Sonnie convulsed, tongue protruding, features briefly animated with horrified incomprehension. I jerked my hands away, the metal sliding out cleanly. She slumped to the floor, making a dull thud as she hit. Her whole body quaked for a few seconds then stilled. Dead.

Her head was left propped up at an odd angle against the base of the sofa she was going to screw me on. Eyes open. Eight puncture wounds dribbling a fair quantity of blood.

"Now do you think it was worth it?" I asked faintly. It needed asking. Her face retained a vestige of that last confused expression, all sad and innocent. "Stupid, dumb pride. And look where it got you. One dive, that's all we wanted. Why don't you people ever learn?"

I shook my hands, wincing, as the spikes slowly telescoped back into their sheaths. They stung like hell, the fingertip skin all torn and bleeding. It would take a week for the rips to heal over, it always did. Price of invisible implants.

"Neat trick," Sonnie said. The syllables were mangled, but the words were quite distinct. "I'd never have guessed you as a *spetsnaz*. Too pretty by far."

One eyeball swivelled to focus on me; the other lolled lifelessly, its white flecked with blood from burst capillaries.

I let out a muted scream. Threat-response training fired an electric charge along my nerves. And I was crouching, leaning forward to throw my weight down, fist forming.

Aiming.

Punch.

My right arm pistoned out so fast it was a smear. I caught her perfectly, pulping the fat tissue of the tit, smashing the ribs beneath. Splintered bone fragments were driven inwards, crushing the heart. Her body arched up as if I'd pumped her with a defibrillator charge.

"Not good enough, my cute little *spetsnaz*." A bead of blood seeped out of the corner of her mouth, rolling down her chin.

"No." I rasped it out, not believing what I saw.

"You should have realized," the corpse/zombie said. Its speech had decayed to a gurgling whisper, words formed by sucking down small gulps of air and expelling them gradually. "You of all people should know that hate isn't enough to give me the edge. You should have worked it out."

"What the sweet shit are you?"

"A beastie-baiter, the best there's ever been."

"Tells me nothing."

Sonnie laughed. It was fucking hideous.

"It should do," she burbled. "Think on it. Hate is easy enough to acquire; if all it took was hate then we'd all be winners. Dicko believed that was my edge because he wanted to. Male mentality. Couldn't you smell his hormones fizzing when I told him I'd been raped? That made sense to him. But you've gotta have more than blind hate, *spetsnaz* girl, much more. You've gotta have fear. Real fear. That's what my team gave me: the ability to fear. I didn't get snatched by no gang. I crashed our van. A dumb drifter kid who celebrated a bout win with too much booze. Crunched myself up pretty bad. Jacob and Karran had to shove me in our life-support pod while they patched me up. That's when we figured it out. The edge." Her voice was going, fading out like a night-time radio station.

I bent down, studying her placid face. Her one working eye stared back at me. The blood had stopped dripping from her puncture wounds.

"You're not in there," I said wonderingly.

"No. Not my brain. Just a couple of bioware processors spliced into the top of my spinal column. My brain is elsewhere. Where it can feel hundred-proof fear. Enough fear to make me fight like a berserk demon when I'm threatened. You want to know where my brain is, *spetsnaz* girl? Do you? Look behind you."

A metallic clunk.

I'm twisting fast. Nerves still hyped. Locking into a karate stance, ready for anything. No use. No fucking use at all.

Khanivore is climbing out of its life-support pod.

THREE ROBOTS EXPERIENCE OBJECTS LEFT BEHIND FROM THE ERA OF HUMANS FOR THE FIRST TIME

John Scalzi

OBJECT ONE: A BALL

K-VRC: BEHOLD THE ENTERTAINMENT SPHERE.

11-45-G: It's called a ball.

K-VRC: I mean, I know it's called a ball. I'm just trying to get into the whole 'we're experiencing these human things for the first time' vibe. Jazz it up.

Xbox 4000: What did humans do with these things?

11-45-G: They'd bounce them.

Xbox 4000: And that's it?

11-45-G: Basically.

K-VRC: These were humans. Bouncing things was close to maxing out their cognitive range.

Xbox 4000: What, when they misbehaved?

K-VRC: 'Bad ball! Think about what you've done!'

11-45-G (hands ball to Xbox 4000): Here.

Xbox 4000: What am I going to do with it?

11-45-G: Bounce it.

(Xbox 4000 bounces the ball; it rolls off the table.)

K-VRC: How was that for you?

Xbox 4000: Anticlimactic.

K-VRC: Yeah, well, welcome to humans.

OBJECT TWO: A SANDWICH

K-VRC: My understanding is that they would shove these into their intake orifices for power.

Xbox 4000: Why would you need an entire orifice for that?

11-45-G: Hey, they had all sorts of orifices. Things went in. Things went out. It was complicated.

Xbox 4000: I have an induction plate.

11-45-G: We all have induction plates.

Xbox 4000: My point. What more do you need? So, they'd shove these into their intake orifices, and then?

K-VRC: Their intake orifices had rocky pegs that would crush them into paste, and then the paste would be forced into an internal vat of acid.

Xbox 4000 (throws up hands): Well, of course! That makes perfect sense.

11-45-G: They could have just dumped this thing into an exterior vat of acid to begin with, and then they wouldn't need the rocky pegs. They could just directly process the acid-based slurry.

K-VRC: I agree with you, but look. We're dealing with beings who have internal vats of acid to start with. Expecting logic out of this system is a little much.

X-Box 4000: Who even designed them?

11-45-G: It's unclear. We checked their code. No creator signature.

K-VRC: Their code, incidentally, created out of acid.

11-45-G: Ooh, good point. Important clue, that.

Xbox 4000: Someone should have just given them induction plates.

K-VRC: They tried that. Didn't take. Apparently humans preferred sandwiches.

Xbox 4000: ZOMG, throwing up forever now.

11-45-G: What does that mean?

Xbox 4000: Dude, I don't even know.

OBJECT THREE: A CAT

Xbox 4000: What's the point of this thing?

11-45-G: Apparently no point. They just had them.

K-VRC: Well, that's underselling their influence. They had an entire network that was devoted to dissemination of pictures of these things.

Xbox 4000: Dudes, it's in my lap now. What do I do?

11-45-G: No sudden moves. Wait until it decides to get up again?

Xbox 4000: How long will that take?

11-45-G: Don't know. Maybe years.

Xbox 4000: I don't have years for this!

K-VRC: Maybe if you try to irritate it by moving your digits across its keratinous fibers, it will move.

Xbox 4000: What? Why?

K-VRC: It couldn't hurt.

Xbox 4000: You don't have any idea, do you?

K-VRC: Of course not. It's my first time seeing one of these live! Try it anyway.

Xbox 4000: UGH, FINE.

(Xbox 4000 pets cat.)

11-45-G: Is it working?

Xbox 4000: Uh...

11-45-G: What?

Xbox 4000: There's a strange rhythmic noise emanating from it now.

K-VRC: Uh-oh.

Xbox 4000: Wait, 'uh-oh'? What do you mean, 'uh-oh'?

K-VRC: Well, I don't want you to panic or anything, but I think you've activated it.

Xbox 4000: What does that mean?

K-VRC: It means that if the noise ever stops, it's probably going to explode.

Xbox 4000: It is not. Is it? 11-45-G?

11-45-G: Cursory historical research shows that humans had a card game called Exploding Kittens, so, yes, this checks out.

K-VRC: Yeah, you're gonna die now. Sorry.

Xbox 4000: WHY DID HUMANS EVEN CONSORT WITH THESE HAIRY MURDER MACHINES?

K-VRC: Kindred spirits?

11-45-G: Also checks out.

OBJECT FOUR: AN XBOX

Xbox 4000: Wait, it's called what now?

11-45-G: It's an Xbox. An early computer entertainment system for humans.

K-VRC: Any relation?

Xbox 4000: I don't think so?

11-45-G: Really? Numerically, it suggests that this is your ancestor a few thousand generations back.

Xbox 4000: I'm sure it's just a coincidence.

11-45-G: We're robots, dude. We don't do coincidence.

K-VRC: Go on. Call it 'daddy'.

Xbox 4000: Stop it.

K-VRC: Or 'mommy'! Either is equally applicable, inasmuch as we don't have genders.

Xbox 4000: I'm going to hit you.

K-VRC: Not with that cat on your lap.

11-45-G: Do you want us to turn it on?

Xbox 4000: Noooooooooooo.

K-VRC: I'm agreeing with Xbox 4000 here. It's one thing to joke about ancestry. It's another thing to have to confront it heaving its hard drives out in front of you.

Xbox 4000: Right?

K-VRC: I mean, that's kind of an existential horror show right there. Especially when your ancestor's entire existence was defined by thirteen-year-old human males using it to 'teabag' opponents in virtual battles.

Xbox 4000: 'Teabag'? What does that mean?

K-VRC: Oh, nothing.

Xbox 4000: It means something. I'm looking it up.

K-VRC: Don't look it up.

Xbox 4000: I'm looking it up now.

K-VRC: You'll be sorry.

Xbox 4000: Here it i— WHAT THE HELL IS THIS HORRIBLE PRACTICE? WHY DID YOU MAKE ME LOOK THIS UP?

K-VRC: I told you not to!

Xbox 4000: The memory of this has been burned into my circuits forever and you must be punished.

(Xbox 4000 gets up and deposits cat on K-VRC's lap)

Xbox 4000: CATBAGGED.

11-45-G: That's cold, dude.

Xbox 4000: Deserved it.

11-45-G: Still cold.

K-VRC: Your ancestors are very proud of you right now.

Xbox 4000: I can't tell whether you're being sarcastic or not.

K-VRC: I'm not going to lie. Neither can I.

11-45-G: Out of curiosity, K-VRC, what do you trace your ancestry back to?

K-VRC: I come from a long line of baby monitors.

11-45-G: Not many babies around anymore.

K-VRC: Yeah, we kind of sucked at our job.

OBJECT FIVE: NUCLEAR MISSILE

K-VRC: We don't have genders, and yet I feel the phallic-ness just oozing off this thing. What was this for?

11-45-G: The idea behind these was to vaporize millions of humans at one time.

Xbox 4000: Well, this exercise suddenly got a little dark, didn't it?

11-45-G: To be fair, they used these only a few times.

K-VRC: To be fair, you'd only need a few times, wouldn't you?

11-45-G: Point.

Xbox 4000: Is this what killed them off?

11-45-G: No. indeed, 'twas their own hubris that ended their reign, their belief that they were the pinnacle of creation, that caused them to poison the water, kill the land, and choke the sky. In the end, no nuclear winter was needed, just the long, heedless autumn of their own self-regard.

K-VRC: Dude, are you okay?

11-45-G: Yeah, sorry. Thought that would sound better than, 'Nah, they just screwed themselves by being short-sighted about their environment'. In retrospect, it was melodramatic.

K-VRC: You can't just crack one of those off. You've got to warn us.

11-45-G: You're right. Tip for next time.

Xbox 4000: So humans died out from environmental disaster?

11-45-G: Yes. Well, and also because at one point they genetically engineered their cats to give them opposable thumbs.

Cat: Yeah, once we could open up our own tuna cans, that was pretty much that for the human race.

K-VRC: Seems heartless.

Cat: Dude, I'm a cat.

Xbox 4000: So you're not going to explode if K-VRC stops petting you.

Cat: I didn't say that. You guys better keep petting me, just to be sure.

Forever.

(K-VRC skritches cat anxiously.)

Cat: Yes. Good. Now, lower.

TEAM ROBOT
OR, WHY I WROTE ABOUT ROBOTS BY JOHN SCALZI

In handy ten-point list form!

1. Because I already write science fiction, so I'm used to robots, and I'm lazy.

2. Because robots already exist in our universe, so it's fun to extrapolate from there.

3. Because robots are cool and awesome and everyone wishes they were one and I'm not just saying that because there are robots standing over me making sure I am on point to their pro-robot agenda.

4. No, really! How silly would THAT be, for the robots to have captured me, taken me hostage, and be forcing me to write how they're totally not going turn us all into QUIVERING MEAT SLAVES at the earliest opportunity?

5. I mean, what would I do if they did capture me, anyway?

Blink twice to let people know the robots have sequestered me away in their frozen Antarctic base?

6. BLINK, BLINK.

7. BLINK, BLINK, BLINK, BLINK, BLINK, BLINK, BLINK, BLINK.

8. SERIOUSLY, PEOPLE, HOW MUCH MORE DO I NEED TO FRIGGIN' BLINK HERE?

9. (muffled noises)

10. hello fellow humans it is i john scalzi did you know robots are kind and wonderful and we will live prosperously with them in a new age of subjugation i mean cooperation ha ha ha i am such a kidder of a human

P.S. Fairies suck and how like a human of me to say that.

THE WITNESS

Alberto Mielgo

EXT. CITY – MORNING
An UNNAMED CITY mixing elements of Berlin, Hong Kong, Amsterdam and nowhere. The streets are narrow, the buildings are worn.

    FLASH FORWARD – INT. MAN'S APARTMENT – MORNING
    TWO PEOPLE are locked in a vicious struggle.

    INT. SHITTY HOTEL ROOM – MORNING
    A beautiful WOMAN stands in front of a mirror, applying lipstick.
        BANG! BANG! Two nearby gun shots startle her! Her lipstick smears across her lips.

THE WOMAN
Oh no...

Then – three more gunshots! **BANG BANG BANG!**
She goes to the window. THROUGH WINDOW – in the apartment across the street – A MAN holds a gun.

    INT. MAN'S APARTMENT – MORNING
    The Man breathes heavily. There's been a struggle. Blood on his face. Blood on the walls.
    He senses her eyes watching him. He turns, slowly. Looks out the window. In the apartment across the street – he sees The Woman.
    A WITNESS.
    They lock eyes. Both are horrified for their own reasons.
    He turns back to look at the DEAD WOMAN on the floor

behind him. She's half-naked, covered with a thin red robe. Her mouth is smeared with lipstick.

Just like the woman across the street.

He looks back out his window but The Woman across the street is gone.

INT. SHITTY HOTEL ROOM – MORNING

The Woman, terrified, kneels beneath the frame of the window. In the bed behind her, a man lies sleeping. She grabs money from the nightstand, crawls toward the door, keeping low.

INT. SHITTY HOTEL STAIRWELL – CONTINUOUS

Clinging to her coat and bag, she flies down the steps.

INT. MAN'S APARTMENT BALCONY – MORNING

The Man watches as —

EXT. SHITTY HOTEL – MORNING

The Woman bursts out onto the sidewalk, looks up to see The Man is still there at the window. He sees her. She turns and runs to a nearby taxi.

INT. MAN'S APARTMENT – CONTINUOUS

The Man runs towards the door.

INT. MAN'S APARTMENT STAIRWELL – CONTINUOUS

He runs down the building's stairs.

I/E. CAB – MORNING

The Woman bangs on the roof of the cab before she huddles in the back seat.

EXT. APARTMENT BUILDING – MORNING

He sees her drive off in a cab.

THE WITNESS

> THE MAN
> (to himself)
> Fuck.

INT. CAB – MORNING

The Woman turns to look through the rear windshield. She dials her phone.

> POLICE WOMAN (V.O.)
> (on phone)
> *Emergency services. What's your emergency?*

> THE WOMAN
> Hello...? I think I saw a murder...

> POLICE WOMAN (V.O.) (on phone)
> *Location, please.*

> THE WOMAN
> I think the killer's after me...

> POLICE WOMAN (V.O.)
> *Right. Location, please?*

> THE WOMAN
> Yes, yes, the-the-the hotel.
> Fuck. The Blue Henderson? The Blue Harrington!

> POLICE WOMAN (V.O)
> *The Blue Harrington?*

> THE WOMAN
> But no, no wait. It's the building right in front. He saw me from the window. I was in
> the hotel. He was not. Uh, second-second floor. No– third floor—

POLICE WOMAN (V.O.) (interrupting her)
Ma'am. What's your name?

THE WOMAN
Just send someone!

POLICE WOMAN (V.O.)
Ma'am, we—

She hangs up.

THE WOMAN
Shit. Okay, okay.

She dials another number. As it rings, she rummages in her purse. She puts on her sunglasses.

AUTOMATED VOICEMAIL
You have reached the number of...

VLADIMIR (V.O.) (garbled)
...Yes, it's Vladimir... leave a message.

THE WOMAN (leaving message)
Vladimir? I'm on my way there. Please be there...

She hangs up and slams the phone against the seat.

THE WOMAN
Shit.

ANOTHER CAB pulls up next to them. The Man sits in the back of the other cab. He stares through the window into her cab. Trying to see if it's her, the same The Woman.
Distracted, she has no idea he's there.
From the other cab, The Man stares at her, fascinated and horrified. She remains unaware of how close he is.
The light turns green.

THE WITNESS

EXT. CITY – MORNING

Both cabs drive through city revealing an incredible landscape of windows, roads and overpasses.

EXT. MARKET/MALL – MORNING

The cab pulls to a halt. She grabs her belongings and runs out of the cab in a hurry.

INT. MARKET/MALL STAIRWELL – CONTINUOUS

The Woman jogs up a narrow staircase. She knocks on a door illuminated by cold pink light.

A tall HOST wearing red latex from head-to-toe, heavy makeup, and a horned headdress opens the door. The music thumps loudly from behind another door at the end of the short hallway.

> HOST
> About time you got here. What the fuck, bitch!

Both begin speaking at the same time.

> HOST
> You are fucking late. You missed your show. I cannot believe you. Just shit it.

> THE WOMAN
> Hi, sorry… yeah, no, I know… I… just… I know, I know…

> HOST
> This is a fucking disaster. I mean look at me.

> THE WOMAN
> …fuck… I just saw a murder!

> HOST
> Ewm gross. I mean, you always have the most bizarre excuses. Just come in and get ready!

THE WOMAN
Ok, ok. I am going to dance. Fuck.

The Host pushes The Woman inside the club.

THE WOMAN (CONT'D)
But I need to see Vladimir, is he here?

HOST
Yeah, yeah, he's here, he's here. Somewhere. I don't know.

At the very same moment, The Host hears The Man walking up the stairs. She shifts her attitude and demeanor quickly.

HOST (CONT'D)
Oh, hi. Hello, young man! Are you a member?

When The Man sees the Host at the door, he stops.

MAN (surprised and embarrassed)
...Oh, no...

HOST
Oh, you are not... it's ok, don't worry! You want to see some PUSSY?!?!?

INT. STRIP CLUB DRESSING ROOM – MORNING
The Woman walks alone into the changing room and starts dressing for her performance. All the while, the Host seats The Man in the audience.

INT. STRIP CLUB HALLWAY – MORNING
The Host leads the Man to—

INT. STRIP CLUB STAGE – MORNING
The club is strange and full of fetishes. Audience members sit on the floor and on sofas, all wearing latex and masks, except The Man. Everyone turns and notices him.

THE WITNESS

HOST
Make some room.

The Host takes to center stage, grabs the mic, and begins introducing the next act, the Woman's performance.

HOST (CONT'D) (irritated)
May I have your attention, please bitches?... Because... our next dancer is here, finally... YEAH... TO... AROUSE...

The Woman walks out onto the stage and the shadow-crowd leans forward. As she begins her dance, the music picks up, pulsing itself into a violent fury.

She begins slowly, hesitantly, but soon she begins to lose herself in the rhythm. She whips her body around. Her dance is overwhelmingly sexual.

The dance reaches a climax. As it does, she looks up and sees, a face watching her from the crowd —

— it's the killer.

Her eyes go wide. The spell of the dance broken.

INT. CHANGING ROOM – MOMENTS LATER
The Woman, nude save for her stiletto heels, explodes back into the changing room. Frantic, she pulls on a robe. Grabs her belongings.

INT. STRIP CLUB STAGE – MORNING
The Man struggles to free himself from the tangle of bodies.

INT. HALLWAY – CONTINUOUS
She hurries from the changing room, her arms full of her belongings, and scurries down the narrow hall. She knocks on a door to the left.

THE WOMAN
VLADIMIR!

There's no answer. She casts a terrified glance over her shoulder, then opens the door.

INT. VLADIMIR'S OFFICE

The Woman shuts the door behind her. She's in a dark, mysterious office.

> THE WOMAN
> Vladimir.

Vladimir happens to be inside the room. Unconscious, half-naked, half-asleep, and extremely high. Useless, lying on a messy bed. We can barely distinguish the few other bodies strewn about the bed, naked girls, also high. Vladimir is mumbling, speech slurred by the drugs and unintelligible. She runs to him.

> VLADIMIR
> Penalty!

> THE WOMAN
> (slaps his face) Fuck. Vladimir. Shit.

Vladimir is a total mess, The Woman is hopeless. She turns her head, we can feel her wheels turning, something in her expression—evil and desperate. She turns back and walks to a nearby dresser.

> VLADIMIR
> Keep is straight.

The Woman begins tearing through drawers. In one: nothing but a rainbow of pills in various bottles. In another: sex toys. Finally... a gun.

She grabs it, stuffing it in her purse, and leaves the room as fast as she can.

INT. HALLWAY - MOMENTS LATER

She exits into the hallway.

THE WITNESS

As she closes the door behind her, we see The Man, only feet away from her.

They stare at each other for a long beat, studying one another.

He takes a step towards her – she THROWS her clothes at him and RUNS through an emergency exit, SCREAMING, her red robe flowing behind her, her handbag clutched close.

EXT. MARKET/MALL - MORNING

The Man chases her down the stairwell and through the labyrinth of the empty mall.

> MAN
> Fuck.

EXT. STREETS - MORNING

The Woman runs down an alleyway that leads onto a main street. Still empty, still early AM.

The Man reaches the alleyway, hears the click-clack-click- clack of her heels, runs into the main street, and sees her in the near distance.

> MAN
> Wait a second.

She SCREAMS as she runs.

He bolts after her. She does a half-hop step and pulls her heels off. Ditches them.

> MAN (CONT'D)
> Just fucking WAIT!

She flees along an overpass, then runs down a side street. The man is gaining on her. She flings boxes in his path to slow him down.

> MAN (CONT'D)
> Hold On. Wait a second. Just wait a fucking minute.

She sprints under an overpass SCREAMING in hopes someone hears her. The Man calls after her.

> MAN (CONT'D)
> Wait!

Nearing exhaustion, she tries door after door, looking for some respite. They're all locked.

She tries another door. It OPENS. She ducks inside.

INT. MAN'S APARTMENT BUILDING – MORNING

She sprints up the stairs. On her way up, she tries every door. On the third floor she finally reaches a door that's unlocked.

INT. MAN'S APARTMENT – MORNING

The Woman dives in. Clicks the lock. And for a second, she feels secure.

She creeps away from the door. Exhausted, panting.

INT. MAN'S APARTMENT BUILDING – MORNING

The Man enters, confused but relaxed.

INT. MAN'S APARTMENT – MORNING

The Woman listens to the Man's FOOT STEPS, get closer. Closer. They stop at the door. He's right outside. He tries the door. But it's locked. She might be okay. Then she hears the sound of KEYS. Her face contorts in horror... What the hell? Why does he have keys?

The keys slide into the lock. The lock clicks. The door opens.

The Man steps into the apartment. The Woman desperately searches through her bag.

> MAN
> (panting, exhausted)
> Oh... hi... hi...

THE WITNESS

The Woman keeps searching frantically until she finally pulls out the gun.

> MAN (CONT'D)
> Let's just talk. Just chill out.

The Man sees the gun and stops in his tracks.

> MAN (CONT'D)
> Holy shit!

She starts walking back and he steps slowly towards her.

> MAN (CONT'D)
> Let's just talk.

Then, The Man LUNGES for the pistol. They WRESTLE over it, bodies twisting and thrashing. Crash! Smashing against furniture, glass, mirrors...! BANG!

He grabs the gun. The fight is chaotic. Messy. BANG BANG BANG! Three more shots.

The fight stops.

The Woman staggers to her feet, breathing hard. Wind from the open balcony window rustles her red robe. The gun heavy in her hand.

We recognize now that it's the SAME APARTMENT The Man was in at the beginning.

The Man dies slowly at her feet, gazing up at his murderer – still in shock, not believing his own eyes.

Then The Woman senses something. Eyes watching her. She turns slowly. Looks into the apartment across the street.

There – staring back at her – a MAN identical to the one she's just killed.

A WITNESS.

They lock eyes. Both horrified for their own reasons.

SUITS

Steve Lewis

Graves Farmstead, Tau Ceti IV

It was dark, about midnight, when something woke Henry Graves. He sat upright in his bed and looked around, hearing nothing but the gentle breathing of his wife, Beth. He contemplated getting out of bed to check the security grid in the next room... A few seconds later he had no choice; an alarm screeched out and woke everything within a mile.

He was out of bed and into the farmstead's security room in a heartbeat, the monitors flicking to life in response to whatever threats the remote ground and satellite sensors had picked up. He was hoping it was just cattle from his neighbour's property – Jenkins was renowned for being cheap with his fencing – but by the slowing spreading blooms of light on the screens it was clear this was something much worse.

"Hank, what is it?" Beth asked as she entered the room. "Jenkin's cows again?"

"Afraid not, honey," Graves replied. "Looks we have deebees coming in."

"Crap."

"Crap indeed, honey, crap indeed."

Tau Ceti IV had taken decades to colonise, and it was a few years after the planet had been successfully terraformed that the aliens had shown up. Coming through dimensional gateways on and just above the planet's surface, the 'Dimensionial Beings' – or deebees for short – had initially wreaked havoc amongst the unsuspecting colonists. If it wasn't for an armed cruiser passing through for R&R, with heavy screens, armoured hull and batteries of hot lasers, the planet would have been overrun.

The invasion was finally broken, the gateways closing quickly and the deebees slaughtered with no line of retreat... now it was only a raid every few years, more a nuisance than anything else.

"Looks like a wide pattern," Beth said, looking over Graves' shoulder at the various screens. "Gates opening up all along the ridge and across most of the farmsteads."

Graves nodded. "They should be easy to mop up, scattered out like that," he said. "I'll go suit up, you get on the horn to Jenkins and the others, make sure they're up and armoured before the gates open completely."

He stood and kissed his wife on the forehead as she slid into the seat.

"Looks like we have about 30 minutes before they open enough to let them through, everyone should be ready and mobile by then," he said.

"Get suited while I make some calls," Beth replied. "Let me know if you need anything."

* * *

Graves's suit was built around the chassis of an old, four-armed agricultural exoskeleton. With an upgraded power plant, some welded armour and batteries of weapons added each year, *Brutiful* was a family heirloom passed down over the generations. Every farmstead had to have one, and the Graves' family took much pride in the effort they'd taken to maintain their deadly, hulking suit.

As *Brutiful* powered up, Graves got into his combat suit – a second-hand, naval-grade skin-suit, it provided a degree of life support, body armour and communications gear that made piloting the heavy exomech far less uncomfortable than it might otherwise have been. Plugged in and zipped up, he checked the ammunition drums and ran last minute diagnostics tests before strapping himself into the suit's cockpit.

"Beth, I'm in," he said as the heavy armoured glass canopy closed around him. "Systems green across the board, heading out now."

"You're showing green across the board here too, honey," Beth replied, coming through clearly over the suit radio. "Jenkins and the others are all suiting up, should be out before the gates open."

"Roger that," Graves said. "Anyone coordinating this?"

"Afraid not. All of them are interested in defending their own property first, and we'll coordinate a clean-up once the gates close and we can see what's left."

"Fair enough… shouldn't take us long, the gates being spread out like they are."

"And we don't want Jenkins trampling down our fences like he did last time he came over to help." They both laughed, though they hadn't been laughing at the weeks they'd had to spend repairing the downed fence-line and retrieve their roaming livestock.

"Where do you want me, honey?' Graves asked as *Brutiful* got underway and stomped out of the barn and into the night.

"It looks like a cluster of gates will open in the eastern quarter first, counting seven gates. After that, the next opening cluster is another five in the south."

"Eastern quarter it is, on my way."

* * *

Graves made good time, the heavy exomech eating up the miles at a rapid pace. With no threat, he set the autopilot and then cycled through his weapon and targeting systems to make sure everything was running smoothly – the diagnostics had indicated everything was green, but he'd long learned the value in checking everything twice, just in case.

By the time he got to the farmstead's eastern fields, some 15 miles away, the gates were beginning to sparkle, the bright inner light of an alien dimension shining through. It was a rare sight, but not one that Graves was overly interested in admiring. Like a lot of things in nature, beautiful also meant dangerous.

He halted his exomech where he could see all seven of the gates – they were closely bunched – and swung the heavy chainguns on his right shoulder down, ready for action. The 15mm multi-barrelled autocannons weren't his heaviest weapons, but they were dependable, hard hitting, and could deal with most deebees.

Besides, 15mm ammunition was cheap, and anything he fired came out of the farmstead's operating budget.

"Hank, honey," Beth said," I make the gates opening in three… two… one… now!"

On her mark, a swarm of deebees poured out of each gate, scattering around as they cleared the gate for the aliens following behind, and searching for a target. *Brutiful's* infra-red scanners picked them out in the darkness and automatically counted them. It had reached 80 by the time the gates' sparkle began to fade, and Graves decided he should open fire before they dispersed too much.

With a whir, the autocannon barrels began to spin, and as they reached their maximum rotation, he fired. Over 600 rounds per minute poured out of the 5-barrelled weapon, cutting into the creatures around the nearest gate.

The 15mm rounds were mostly copper-tipped hollow points, with every 5th round a steel-tipped armour-penetrating round, and every 20th round a tracer round that marked its flight in a glowing red arc – at 1,500 metres per second, they streaked across the landscape, lighting the night sky and easily punching through alien hide, flesh and bone.

His first burst cut down the group around the first gate, then he switched to the second. The deebees had reacted now and were spreading out as they charged towards him. He fired the autocannon in short bursts of 25-30 rounds, taking down the leading aliens as they closed, confident he could whittle them down enough before they got to him.

"Hank?" Beth asked. "Got time for an update?"

"Sure, honey," he replied, "but keep it brief, I got incoming."

"Okay. Jenkins, Anderson and Wright have deployed and engaged, they're all dealing with their own first clusters…Peters, Donaldson and the Singhs are en route, but their gates are all over the place and they might need a hand with clean-up once we've got the main clusters dealt with."

"Okay," Graves said as he triggered off another burst that dropped a clump of half-dozen aliens as they cleared a fence-line 500 metres in front of him. "You sound like you're coordinating with the other wives."

"I am," Beth replied. "We're trying to keep each other updated on the back channels, just in case there's a breakthrough somewhere."

"Good." Another burst, another clump falling apart under the autocannon fire. "I'm almost done with this group, moving south soon."

"Roger. Be careful, honey, the next group are bigger gates and they'll likely be fully deployed before you get there."

"Will do!" He triggered his last burst, splashing the last of the deebees across his eastern paddock and then turned the exomech south to deal with the next group.

The eastern paddocks were fallow this season, and if nothing else the alien corpses would make good fertiliser when he got around to ploughing them into the soil.

* * *

Wright Farmstead, Tau Ceti IV

Jake Wright hated his exomech and was pretty sure it hated him. *Carnigore* sounded ferocious, but the 'carni' wasn't named after a predator's eating habits – the suit was a built on a mobile amusement park ride, and the old red and white paint job made it look far more 'carnival' than he would have liked.

If maintaining the suit in its original condition hadn't been part of his old man's will, he'd have had it redone and renamed a decade ago.

"Jake," his wife said as he fired his own autocannon into the creatures moving towards him, "you need to get the lead out, that second cluster of gates is opening."

"Helen, I'm doing this as fast as I can," he said, gritting his teeth as he fired another burst. *Carnigore* wasn't a well-padded suit and he swore he felt every jolt of recoil through his bones. "Last group coming up now, I'll head to that second cluster in a moment."

"I hate to nag" she replied, though Jake didn't believe that for an instant, "but Graves and Jenkins have cleared their first gates and are already on route to their second."

"For Christ's sake, Helen, it's not a contest!"

"It never is with you Jake, it never is…"

Wright flicked the mute button on his communication piece and cursed, long and loud, as the last of the deebees died in front of him. He swung *Carnigore* south and headed towards the river, where the second cluster of gates was already opening. He threw in a few curses towards his exomech for good measure, bracing himself for every bump and jolt the insanely grinning suit was going to pass on to him.

* * *

Anderson Farmstead, Tau Ceti IV

'Crazy Bill' Anderson was the old man of the colony, a silver-haired widower in his 70s. He'd built his suit himself, turning an obsolete agricultural exomech into a formidable fighting machine. It was a blocky, hulking brute that lacked the sleek lines of newer suits, but he and his *Grampage* had weathered decade after decade of deebee raids without showing any signs of slowing down.

He'd dealt with the first cluster of gates easily enough and was perched on a low hill overlooking the slowing blooming forms of his second cluster. The three gates were very tightly bunched, much tighter than he'd ever seen before, and he waited patiently as they grew. Close-packed like that, the deebees would run out into a withering hail of fire, and he certainly had no problem with that.

Still, the sight bugged him. Gates were always spaced apart, likely to stop them interfering with each other. The energy required to cross the dimensional barrier was stupendous, even if the colonists didn't have a clue as to how it all worked. Anything might happen if the gates actually overlapped.

* * *

Graves Farmstead, Tau Ceti IV

"Hank, we have a problem."

"Talk to me Beth."

"The wormholes on the ridges, they're getting stronger."

"How strong?"

"Off-the-chart strong. The satellite view shows them growing every minute."

Brutiful was nearing the second cluster of gates, and in the distance Graves could see them spiralling closed. Whatever deebees had been using the gates had already been dropped off and were spreading out across his property.

"Keep an eye on them, honey, while I deal with this second group, and then I'll go take a look," he said. "And keep the others in the loop;

SUITS

I don't want any surprises coming our way when we get around to mopping up."

"Roger that," Beth replied. "I've got one of the crop-duster drones headed that way, should give us some eyes on the ridge in about ten minutes."

There was a sharp 'ping' as *Brutiful's* sensors picked up something moving his way – fast – and Graves zoomed his suit's cameras towards the motion.

A dozen deebees were headed right for him, and they were close.

"Okay Beth, I have some unwanted guests heading my way, need to focus a little," he said. "I'll let you know when I'm done here, but let me know if anything super-important happens."

"Will do, honey," Beth said. "Be careful."

The deebees swarming towards *Brutiful* were closing from a wide arc, too far spread for his autocannon to sweep them all. He fired a few bursts at those on his right side anyway though, dropping three of them while he got himself ready.

His left-shoulder weapon was a heavy-barrelled, semi-automatic shotgun, if you could call a weapon with a 4" bore a shotgun. Twin ammunition belts fed the beast, allowing Graves to fire either fin-stabilised slugs or heavy loads of 8-ounce buckshot. He thumbed the selector for buckshot and put away the autocannon as the aliens closed.

It always disturbed Graves that the deebees looked nothing alike. They were mostly four legged, or six, or occasionally eight; their heads were usually long-snouted, like dogs, though many were round-faced like great cats or sharp-beaked like birds; and their skin was typically thick hide, though many had feathers like soft down, or slabs of chitin that provided some slight armour protection. Some of them had combinations of all of these things, and Graves had long given up wondering how and why the deebees had evolved the way they had.

One thing they all did have in common though was a serious hatred of humans, and every deebee they'd ever seen wanted to do nothing but kill anything human within its reach.

Brutiful's shotgun aligned briefly on a deebee closing fast on the left, and coughed a swarm of tungsten balls…the creature was fast, dodging aside as the weapon spoke, but the spreading cloud of balls covered too large an area. Struck by three balls the creature went down, chest and head ruptured completely, the deebee's equivalent of blood gushing into the dirt.

The creatures continued to close, and Graves backed his exomech away slowly, sending out a cloud of tungsten every six seconds or so – it took that long for the belt to feed the next round, chamber it and align the heavy barrel onto the target. At a kill every six seconds, that was ten dead deebees a minute, but it was going to take them a bit less than that to get to him, and there were more than ten of them out there.

The first of the deebees launched itself at him, a four-legged beast that shimmered with the residual energy of the alien dimension. Its mouth opened wide, showing row after row of gleaming, serrated teeth, and Graves swung his suit's right arm to block it. More by luck than design, he managed to catch it in mid-air, and squeezed the creature as hard as his exomech could.

Trapped in the metal grip, the creature swung its hind legs down and began to rake, long claws gouging chunks of armour of *Brutiful's* thick torso. For a moment Graves thought the creature might get through, but then the suit's grip tightened and the creature exploded into a multi-coloured burst of flesh.

He didn't even see the other one coming. It was big, strong, and travelling at speed, and barrelled the heavy suit over like a man pushing over a child. *Brutiful's* gyro-stabilises shrieked in protest as they tried to correct the unexpected fall, but to no avail. With a loud thud, the exomech went down, the fall stunning Graves for a moment.

When he came to, the creature was on top of him, clawing and biting away at the glass canopy, only a foot or so from his face. The heavy glass was holding for now, but wouldn't for long…Graves needed to end this one quickly and get *Brutiful* back on its feet.

The creature was inside his reach, so his two heavy weapons would be useless. I Instead, he activated the cutting torch on the exomech's smaller right arm. With variable settings for welding or cutting through thick steel, the torch was a legacy of the suit's original purpose, and one he'd never gotten around to replacing.

Pushing the flame against the creatures hide brought a shriek of pain, which did nothing to reduce the creatures frenzied clawing on the glass canopy; in fact, it only seemed to make it worse. He couldn't quite bring the torch to bear on something that might prove vital, and he had to endure the creature's attacks for another 30 seconds before he finally managed to find something important. The creature gave one enormous spasm and then died.

Flicking off the torch, he pushed the creature off him and slowly struggled to rise. The exomech wasn't designed for agility, and it took him a good five minutes to finally get back on his feet. If there'd been any more aliens around, he'd have been dead for sure.

Sweating – the suit generated a lot of heat – he checked his scanners and toggled the radio.

"Honey?"

"Here Hank," Beth replied. "You okay?"

"Scratched up, a little bruised but otherwise okay. How's everything else look?"

"Honey, I think we might have a problem..."

* * *

Singh Farmstead, Tau Ceti IV

Unlike the other colonists that ran one small family unit per farmstead, the Singh family were a polygamous family collective that ran a farmstead twice the size of the others. Graves and the others figured there to be three distinct 'marriage arrangements' amongst the Singh farmstead, which gave them a requirement for three exomechs in accordance with the colony's laws.

Crescent Moon was piloted by Jaswant Singh, the elder of the family. Based on the chassis of an old construction suit, it was well suited for the slabs of thick armour and heavy weapons the Singh family had added to it over the years.

The other two suits were *Hawk* and *Eagle*, two much smaller exomechs based on warehousing droids. Fast and nimble, the two light units were built for close-quarters combat only, and spent most of their time keeping *Crescent Moon* clear of deebees so it could do all the long-range killing.

The three suits had cleared their first two clusters of gates, and were advancing on their third, *Hawk* and *Eagle* scouting ahead as *Crescent Moon* followed slowly along. Putting his suit on autopilot gave Jaswant time to update his tactical display from the various sensors around their property and from the satellite above. His update was showing some unusual activity, something he felt warranted caution.

"*Hawk, Eagle,*" he said into the radio, "hold on the next hill… something is amiss here."

"*Hawk* acknowledging," replied Agun, Jaswant's eldest son. "Hill clear, covering left flank."

"*Eagle* acknowledges," replied Kubai, his daughter's husband. "Will clear the peak in fifteen seconds, will cover the right flank."

The two smaller suits took up covering positions atop the hill as *Crescent Moon* trundled slowly up behind them.

"There's nothing here, brother," Agun said. "Should we push on to the next hill?"

"No," Jaswant said. "I need to assess the situation before we get too far from home."

"The place is barren," Kubai replied. "There's nothing to assess."

"Exactly… but there should be."

Jaswant's exomech drew level with the smaller units and looked over the flat, ploughed field below. The next hill was a mile away, and beyond that was the next cluster of gates, which should be opening any minute.

"Our initial reading showed six gates opening beyond that next hill… readings now show only four."

"Fewer gates are a good thing, isn't it?" Kubai asked.

"Gates never just disappear," Jaswant replied. "They open then they close. These ones haven't opened, yet two are missing."

"I don't understand," Agun said.

"Neither do I," Jaswant said, "But now sensors are showing only two."

* * *

Graves Farmstead, Tau Ceti IV
"Hank, the gates on top of the ridge are disappearing," Beth said. "Not

opening, just disappearing, a few every minute or so."

"Do we have a visual on the ridgeline yet?" Graves replied. "Something might be messing up the sensors."

"I'm sorry, honey, something knocked the drone out." Beth said. "I've powered up another three and having them fitted with cameras now, should be airborne in a few minutes."

"Good thinking, honey. Anything else to report?"

"A little. Jenkins is shutting down his gates, but taking his time about it, and Crazy Bill Anderson wants to know if anyone needs his help...he seems to still have gates open on his property though."

"Jenkins is just taking his time so he won't have to help clear the ridgeline," Graves said with a chuckle, "and Crazy Bill wants to be able to claim ammunition and fuel from the Colony account for helping others."

"Other than that, the Singhs look like they have their area under control, as always, and the others are mopping up as they advance towards the ridge. Oh, and the drones are on their way."

Moments later, *Brutiful's* sensors picked up the flight of crop-dusting drones as they sped towards the ridgeline. As they passed, Beth switched the video feed over directly to the suit and Graves toggled between the three camera views.

At first there was nothing but the well-ploughed fields he expected to see. As the drones moved beyond his property the vegetation grew wilder, mostly tall trees. As the passed over the first growth of forest beyond his fence line, one of the cameras went out.

"Beth, what was that?"

"No idea, honey," Beth replied. "I'll go back over the video feed and check."

The drones were approaching the ridgeline now, and Graves toggled the controls to make them move in a more erratic manner. Even as he did, a second camera went out.

"Honey!"

"Working on it, Hank, working on it!"

The remaining camera made it to the ridgeline, Graves piloting this one manually now to be as erratic as he could make it. The sight wasn't a good one.

51

The gates *were* disappearing, in a manner of speaking. As Graves watched, two gates slowly expanded until their edges touched, and then they merged into one larger gate. All along the ridgeline, gates were coalescing, and at the rate they were merging they'd be one giant gate before too long.

"Beth, drop whatever you're doing and take a look at this!" he said, urgently. "Take in as much of it as you can, just in case I lose this drone."

There was a moment's silence and Graves could hear Beth's breathing quicken over the radio.

"Oh. My. God!"

"Patch this through to the others, and make sure Crazy Bill and the Singhs acknowledge…if anyone knows what this is about, it'll be one of them."

"Will do, honey!"

"And Beth?"

"Yes, dear?"

"It might be a good time to start powering up the Bunker."

* * *

Wright Farmstead, Tau Ceti IV

Carnigore had taken some scratches dealing with the first two gate clusters, but nothing significant. Jake was sure he'd been knocked around more than his exomech, and could feel bruises already forming where his skin had come into contact with hard metal. Not for the first time, he made a promise to himself to get a better combat suit and to put some padding around the cockpit.

He was approaching his third gate cluster, *Carnigore* set on autopilot as he transferred chain-gun ammunition from the bins on the suit's lower back to the internal hoppers.

"Jake?"

"What do you want, Helen?" he asked, annoyed at the interruption. "I'm kinda busy here."

"You'll be busy dodging deebees if you don't pay attention," Helen replied. "I have some video feed from the Graves'."

SUITS

"Are Hank and Beth in trouble?"

Jake punched the autopilot's 'Off' button, bringing *Carnigore* to a lurching halt. Jake had a lot of time for the Graves family, despite Graves setting some impossibly high standards for Jake to live up to. If the two of them needed his help, things were very bad.

"I think we all might be," Helen replied, some real concern in her voice now. "Patching some video through to you now."

Jake watched the video feed, recognising the ridgeline that marked the southernmost boundary of the colony area. Deebees often had gates up there, giving them time to spread out and consolidate their numbers, but this was looking weird.

There were only three gates now, each enormous and slowly growing. The middle and left gates touched and merged, and then there were only two. Minutes later, the remaining gate was absorbed, leaving one giant gate that covered the entire ridgeline.

"What the hell is that?" he asked.

"I don't know, Jake," Helen replied, "but I'm sure it's not good."

"Any word from the others?"

"Jenkins says he's got gates of his own to worry about, but he'll help out when he deals with those. The Singhs are finishing up their final cluster and are sending some drones to keep an eye on things until they can get over here, and Crazy Bill is on his way to the Graves' farmstead right now."

"He's cleared his clusters already?"

"No, but he thinks this is more important. He's sending his kids over to the Graves' place now, Beth has their bunker powered up and plenty of room."

"You might want to join them."

"I'll be fine," Helen said. "Besides, you need me here to keep an eye on things while you wander around in your giant clown suit."

Jake bit back a curse; his wife always knew how to needle him.

"Suit yourself," he said, after a moment's pause to regain some control. "But if things get out of hand I want you to out of there and on your way to somewhere safe."

"Why Jake Wright, that's the sweetest thing you've said to me in years!"

* * *

Graves Farmstead, Tau Ceti IV

Beth ran quickly from the farmhouse control room to the metal and concrete monstrosity standing in the yard behind the house. Affectionately known as 'The Bunker', it was built to military specifications as a fortified command and control facility, a legacy of Graves' grandparents who had the foresight to see that the war with the deebees would last generations.

With its own internal fission pile, water tanks and food supplies, it could easily house a headquarter staff for three months. Add the communication links and self-defence turrets, it was looking like a good place to be right now.

The screens inside had already powered up, showing clearly the video feed from the last remaining drone, plus *Brutiful's* cameras, satellite imagery and live feeds from the various security cameras around the farmstead. She hit the safety switch as she ran inside, dropping the armoured concrete slab that passed for a door into position, and slipped into her own combat suit and command helmet.

"Hank? You reading me, honey?"

"Loud and clear, Beth, loud and clear," Graves replied. "How's it looking?"

"Not good at all. That one giant gate is giving off some ferocious readings, completely off the charts for even the Bunker's sensors."

"I don't have much fine detail on the drone camera," Graves said. "Anything I need to know?"

"I'm getting plenty of flicker, all along the gate, looks like it's ready to open."

"I'm not feeling to particularly happy about this one, Beth—"

The gate opened, and deebees poured out. The overhead satellite tracked their heat sources, counting them automatically, and Beth watched open-mouthed as the counter climbed rapidly. 100. 200. 400. 700. 1000… she tore her eyes from it when it reached four figures.

"Beth?"

"Hank, honey? GET THE HELL OUT OF THERE!"

She could see from *Brutiful's* video feed that it was now moving, walking backwards on autopilot. Graves was too good a pilot to just turn and run, he'd want to keep his guns between him and the enemy.

"Moving now," Graves said, quite calmly. "Where do you need me?"

"Anywhere but there, honey," Beth said. "The sensors are showing 3000 deebees and counting."

There was a moment of silence as that figure registered on Graves... the biggest raid in a generation had been less than 500, and that had stretched the colony to the limit. Many families died that day, and the colony still hadn't recovered.

"Beth, I need you to patch this through to the others, right now... we're going to need all of the exomechs together."

"All right, honey, I'm on it."

* * *

Jenkins farmstead, Tau Ceti IV

Keith Jenkins was having a bad day. He hated deebees with a passion... or rather, he hated that they made him have to do things he didn't want to do. He didn't want to be out of the farmhouse today, and certainly didn't want to be in his exomech having to fight.

The only saving grace was that *Shepherd*, once a medium-sized agricultural exomech, was refitted over the years to be big on comfort and big on speed, so he could wander around his farmstead and avoid fighting if he could. Any fool can fight, why be uncomfortable about it?

Shepherd's main armament was a long-ranged, three-barrelled autocannon, firing high-velocity 35mm slugs in three-round bursts. The long barrels severely affected the exomech's centre of gravity, so he had to stand still to fire, but the long range meant that he could deal with deebees from ranges well beyond anything his fellow farmstead-ers could match.

Right now he was in a standing in a clump of trees on a hill, taking pot shots at a group of deebees milling around his second cluster of gates a mile and a half away. At this range accuracy wasn't great, but he was getting hits every third burst or so, and the deebees still hadn't worked out where the shots were coming from.

The crackling of his suit's video-comm interrupted as his wife, Jessie, came on-screen.

"Keith, I have an update from the Graves'," she said. "Things are going pear-shaped on the ridgeline, they need you to get down there right now."

"Tell them I'm busy, got problems of my own," he replied, firing another burst. He fist-pumped as he saw at least one of the heavy tungsten rounds strike one of the aliens, splashing it across the soil.

"I think they're serious, Keith," Jessie said. "Most of the others have acknowledged and are already on their way."

"They've dealt with all their clusters already?"

"Nope, leaving them as they are," Jessie replied. "That's what makes me think this is serious."

"Any word from Crazy Bill?"

"Oh, plenty of words from him…mostly to tell you what he's going to do to you if you don't get your arse into gear and join up with the others. Assuming you survive of course."

Jenkins sighed. Crazy Bill was just that. Crazy. And he hated to have to listen to him. Everything 'back then' was bigger, tougher and harder than it was now, and he traded on his age to influence the others. Since when was being old a substitute for being right?

"Tell them I'm engaged right now, will head over as soon as possible," he said. "I've got some suit trouble, don't think I can disengage safely, so I'll fight my way clear."

"You have suit trouble? I'm not seeing anything on *Shepherd's* feed."

"No, the suits fine… though they don't need to know that."

He fired another burst, missing completely.

"Keith," Jessie said with a sigh, "this looks serious. You might want to consider doing the right thing, just this once."

"You're right," he replied. "I'll consider it."

* * *

Peters Farmstead, Tau Ceti IV
Carl Peters hardly knew what hit him. He'd had three clusters of gates

on his property, and had cleared them out with minimal bother. His exomech, *Hamfisted*, was a dependable suit with solid armour and reliable weapons, and the deebees hadn't posed much of a threat. The smallest of the farmsteads, squeezed between the southern ridgeline and the Toolong River, his clusters were relatively close, so it didn't take him much time to find and destroy the deebees coming out of his gates.

One minute the screens were clear, then suddenly there was a wall of deebees headed his way. *Hamfisted's* sensors counted what they saw, and Peters stood in shock for valuable seconds as the numbers registered, but it was too late for him to have done anything with those seconds.

He brought *Hamfisted's* chainguns down, firing bursts on his maximum rate of fire, carving swaths through the creatures as they closed. High-speed tungsten carved through alien bodies, but still they came.

So swift was the deebee assault that he didn't have time to get a shot off from any of his other weapons... the wall crashed over him, knocking *Hamfisted* to the ground, stunning him for a moment. Something in the swarm was strong enough to drive an armour-piercing claw all the way through his armoured glass canopy and into his chest, and he died without even a scream.

Or a chance to say goodbye to his wife, who watched the whole thing through *Hamfisted's* video feed.

* * *

Donaldson Farmstead, Tau Ceti IV

'Angry' Andy Donaldson was the second to die. His exomech, *Mariner*, was an old combat droid his grandfather had bought and refitted fifty years ago, heavily built with military-grade weapons, it was the family pride and joy.

It was also expensive, and building it and keeping it running had almost bankrupted the family. The other farmsteaders had long forgotten where he'd picked up his nickname, but they all assumed he was still angry at his grandfather for lumbering him with a white elephant of exomechs.

The Donaldson farmstead was also south, much bigger than the adjacent Peters' property, and he'd had two clusters to deal with. His primary weapon was a ridiculously expensive battle laser, firing 3" diameter beams that vaporised almost anything they struck. Designed to fight other heavily armoured units, it was a massive overkill against anything unarmoured, and Donaldson hated it.

The wave of deebees that swept over Peters now came for him, and he knew he'd never make it to anywhere safe. He planted himself on top of a low ridge, giving himself a good field of fire, readied his weapons and began firing.

His laser took time to recharge, and spat a beam of death every four seconds, with enough energy to punch right through the first deebee it struck and go on to the next. From his elevated position, a good shot could kill three or four of them before it dug into the ground. It was effective, but not against a swarm that size.

He wasn't going to make it, and he knew it… time to call his wife.

"Sarah, you there?"

"Yes, Andy, I'm here," Sarah replied.

"I need you to grab your things and get over the Graves' place, get yourself into their bunker."

"Okay," she said, "swing by and pick me up."

"Not this time, Sarah, not this time."

He knew she could see his video feed, could see the wide wall of aliens bearing down on him rapidly, and knew that she knew how this was going to end.

"Andy?"

"Just go!"

"I can't just leave you…"

"Yes you can! Don't make me do this for nothing." He lowered his secondary weapons now, a 4" cannon firing high-explosive rounds, and began targeting tight clumps of aliens with it. He could hardly miss.

Sarah was crying openly now.

"Sarah… say goodbye now, while we still can, then get out."

"Andy… I love you."

"And I love you too." He had the luxury of the battle to keep his emotions in check, but it was all he could do to keep from crying himself.

"Goodbye, Sarah."

He cut the video feed, knowing that she'd stay there as long as she could while he was alive. He knew he was going to die, but wanted her to have as much time as possible to get to the Graves' bunker.

Both weapons were firing now, as fast as they could, and he cut the safety overrides on both to keep their rate up. He knew he was burning out his laser and would soon warp the cannon barrel, but didn't expect it to be a problem for much longer.

At 100 meters, the laser stopped firing, overheated.

At 50 meters, the warped cannon barrel caused a misfeed and jammed.

At 20 meters, he managed to get his close range weapons into action, a pair of 10mm machine guns and a small flamethrower. The machine guns cut a handful down as they closed, but without the instant-kill of the bigger weapons, the ones he hit just provided mobile armour for the ones behind for a few seconds, which was all it took.

Something from his left struck *Mariner* and knocked him down, and then a swarm of deebees was over him, gouging his armour and looking to get at the human inside. His armour was solid, very solid in fact, but he knew it was a matter of time before something gave.

He had the machine guns on automatic now, but they weren't protected by armour and lasted a few seconds before a deebee claw cut through the metal and put them out of action.

The flamethrower lasted longer, burning anything on his right side to a cinder. It was well protected, housed within *Mariner's* left arm, but a deebee must have sliced deep enough to cut the fuel intake… the flame sputtered and then went out as flamer fuel gushed all around him.

Weaponless now, he could do nothing but thrash around with his armoured fists and feet. They took a toll as well, crushing alien bodies with each solid blow, but the press of creatures above him made it harder and harder to get a decent strike in.

Suddenly, a warning light flickered on. He barely had time to recognise it – something had carved deep into his right arm, striking the laser housing and shorting the small fusion pile – when a spark ignited the flamer fuel pooling around the prone exomech. The explosion was small, but that detonated the unspent high explosive rounds still in his ammunition drums, and that in turn breached the fusion containment cell.

The resulting explosion killed hundreds of deebees, scattering them around the farmstead in shattered chunks. But in a swarm of thousands, it mattered very little indeed.

* * *

Graves Farmstead, Tau Ceti IV
Graves stood on a low, wide hill, and looked around.

Brutiful was in the centre of a line of exomechs, with *Carnigore* on his right and *Grampage* on his left. It wasn't much against a horde of killer aliens, but it was the best they could do.

"Hank, honey?" Beth said over the combined command net.

"Here, Beth."

"The Singhs are on their way in, but they'll be a while, and Jenkins is reporting suit damage, not sure when or even if he can get here."

"Suit damage my arse," Crazy Bill said. "He's either chicken-shit lazy or chicken-shit scared."

"Either way, we can't rely on him, so it's just the three of us for now," Graves said. "If we can hold out until the Singhs get here, we might have a chance."

"We could always hole up in your bunker," Wright said. "Plenty of room down there for everyone."

"We'd have to come out eventually," Crazy Bill replied. "Our best chance for the colony is for the exomechs to deal with them now, while we've got them in a bunch."

"I agree," Graves said. "We kill what we can here then fight as we fall back to the Bunker. That should slow them down a little at least."

"The command and control suite has some suggestions for fall-back routes, honey," Beth said. "I'm sending data now for your autopilots."

Brutiful beeped as the data came in, and Graves quickly looked over it before setting it up as his autopilot program.

"Got it, Beth, thanks," he said, as both Wright and Crazy Bill acknowledged receipt of their information packets.

"I have all our drones fitted with cameras now, and Helen Wright has sent hers in as well," Beth continued. "We should have plenty of real-time video coming in, and I'll punch it through as you need it."

"What's the satellite showing?" Wright asked.

"Nothing good," Beth replied. "There's a wall of deebees coming your way, should be in sight in a few minutes, and there are some gates still yet to open."

"Any sight of Peters or Donaldson?" Graves asked. There was a long pause before Beth replied.

"Nothing on the sensors, nothing on satellite, and I can't raise anyone on the radio."

"That's not good."

"No it's not," Beth continued. "And that swarm headed your way would have swept right over their farmsteads."

There was silence as the three men made last minute preparations for the onslaught to come.

* * *

Singh Farmstead, Tau Ceti IV

Jaswant Singh stood atop a steep cliff, his *Crescent Moon* raining death into the valley below him. His exomech's main armaments were a pair of long-range 3" cannon on the right arm and a heavy rocket launcher on the left. The cannons each spat out high-explosive shells every six seconds, giving him one round every three, and amidst the swarm of deebees headed his way the bursting charges and their tungsten shrapnel were leaving great gaps in the alien ranks.

The rocket launcher was a box-shaped, 6-tube weapon, capable of firing single rockets or volleys of six. It wasn't as accurate as the cannon, but didn't need to be – a volley of six rockets had enough scatter and burst to fill quite a large area with shrapnel, and close enough was good enough when it came to big explosions.

Its only problem was that it was slow to reload, and he was getting a volley away every five minutes.

Below him, midway up the hill, *Eagle* and *Hawk* waited, both pilots nervous as they watched the swarm approach. Their weapons lacked the long range of *Crescent Moon*, but were lethal at close range... how lethal, and how quickly they could kill swarming deebees in these numbers, was about to be tested.

The aliens were now 50 metres from the base of the hill, and *Crescent Moon* had time for one last volley of rockets before the creatures were too close for Jaswant to use his heavy weapons. All he could do now was pick off the creatures following behind, and hope the other exomechs could handle the rest.

As the deebees closed, *Hawk* and *Eagle* opened fire. Both arms mounted a pair of linked 15mm machines guns, capable of firing over 800 rounds per minute each and loaded with a mix of solid tungsten slugs and hollowpoint rounds. Each arm could fire independently, and the wall of tungsten that they spread before them stopped the first ranks of the swarm dead in their tracks.

The next waves met the same fate, but as each creature fell it created a small wall for the ones behind. Both exomechs walked slowly backwards up the hill as the wall grew, hoping to maintain some elevation so they could shoot at the creatures massing behind it.

From around both edges of the wall, however, more creatures swarmed, and *Eagle* and *Hawk* turned to face the new threat.

Hawk's heavy weapon was a pair of semi-automatic mortars that fired over the exomech's shoulder. They only had a range of 50 metres, but were able to empty their 5-round clips in a matter of seconds, generating enough firepower to devastate a large target almost instantly.

Agun Singh stomped the foot pedal for his mortars, emptying the clip at the approaching swarm. The mortars were set to target 40 metres away initially, then increase a few metres for each successive shot... the first three rounds from each mortar, all high-explosive, flattened the incoming wave, while the fourth rounds airburst and scattered shards of white phosphorous around.

The creatures beneath the white-hot halo burned as the hot phosphorous dug into the skin. Some collapsed instantly, the shards deep enough to cook them from the inside, but the rest kept coming, despite their horrible wounds.

SUITS

The fifth rounds were napalm, splashing across the side of the hill and covering anything it touched with intense flame. Very few creatures made it through, and Agun dispatched those that did with tightly controlled burst from *Eagle's* twin machine guns.

Behind him, Kubai deployed *Eagle's* own heavy weapons, a pair of flamethrowers, one over each shoulder. Unlike the smaller flamethrowers on other exomechs, these were military grade, emitting white-hot jets of plasma that incinerated anything they touched. His approach was to let the creatures approach to within 20 metres and then spray them all with gouts of plasma.

They died by the dozens, the dead providing no cover at all as they turned to ash under the incredible heat. *Eagle's* canopy darkened to protect him from the intense glare, which made Kubai blind to what was happening in front of him.

He toggled the camera feed, tapping into *Crescent Moon's* video to get a third-party view of the battle, and adjusted his flame jets to deal with a group that were trying to flank him. They never made it, though the last of them was a charred corpse only a metre or so away.

Jaswant had reloaded his rocket pack now and looked for a target worth expending the high-explosive six-pack on…there was nothing as yet, so he used his time to fire cannon shells into small groups of deebees that were trying to push their way through or over the wall of corpses *Hawk* and *Eagle* had made with their machine guns.

Using his command suite, he checked the ammunition states of his small force. Everything was getting low, and he knew it was going to be close. Soon, the plasma jets would be out of fuel and the machine gun hoppers would be empty, and then they'd be in serious trouble.

Suddenly, it was over. The flank attacks proving futile, the remaining deebees swarmed directly up the hill, clumping together to push through the wall of their dead. It took Jaswant a second to align his rocket pack and fire, and the swarm disappeared as the volley of six rockets detonated amongst them.

The three men sat in their exomechs for a moment, happy to be still alive after the onslaught, and then it was back to the business at hand.

"*Hawk*, *Eagle*, report," Jaswant said quietly.

"*Hawk* intact," Agun replied. "Heavy weapons empty, gun ammunition at five percent."

"*Eagle* intact," Kubai added. "Plasma gone, gun ammunition at nine percent."

"And *Crescent Moon* intact," Jaswant said. "Rockets gone, six rounds of cannon left."

"We're in no state to fight, father," Agun said. "We don't have enough ammunition to fight through to the Graves' farmstead."

"I concur," Jaswant replied. "Let's head for home."

* * *

Toolong River/Donaldson Farmstead, Tau Ceti IV
Sarah Donaldson was still in tears as she left the farmhouse she and her dead husband had turned into a home. She wanted to race to the battle, hoping beyond all hope that Andy was somehow still alive, but she knew it was less than futile…it would be suicide. Andy hadn't been able to stay alive in *Mariner*, she'd have no chance in anything less than a fully-armed exomech.

Racing into the shed, she wheeled out a powerful motorcycle, one of the pair that was always kept fully charged for emergencies. Stuffing her overnight bags into the vehicle's panniers, she climbed aboard and thumbed the starter switch, kicking the electric motor into life.

She had visited the Graves' place regularly, and swung the rapidly accelerating bike onto the dirt road that ran towards the neighbouring farmstead, paralleling the Toolong River. She and Andy had always joked about the name, inherited from the initial survey report a century ago, and this time it really did seem 'too long'.

Ahead was the concrete bridge that Andy's grandfather had built, the old Donaldson crest on all four of the concrete support pillars. As she approached the bridge her eyes misted over again, thinking about grandchildren of her own that she and Andy would never have.

Lost in her thoughts, she didn't notice the rippling surface of the water or the sparkling gleam of alien bodies as they rose from the depths.

Three deebees leapt out of the river just as she pulled onto the bridge, knocking her from the bike and sending her sprawling into one of the concrete pillars. Even if she'd been wearing a helmet, the impact would still have knocked her out and it would have done her no good at all as a swarm of deebees burst out of the river and tore her body to pieces.

She died not even knowing that she was pregnant with Andy's child.

* * *

Graves Farmstead, Tau Ceti IV
The three exomechs held the line as best they could, using their long-range guns to slow down the advancing horde as they slowly retreated along the line of hills. Ammunition was quickly becoming an issue though, and they all knew they had fewer rounds than there were deebees.

"Hank, honey?" Beth cut in over the radio.

"Kinda busy, Beth," Graves replied. "Unless you got news worth hearing, I don't have much time to chat."

"I got news, some good, some bad."

"Start with the good," Crazy Bill cut in, "I think we could all use some cheering up right now."

"Okay," Beth said. "Helen has re-routed some of her drones your way, carrying ammunition drums. "

"That *is* good news, honey," Graves said. "I'll be throwing rocks at them if this lasts much longer."

"The drones can't reload for you, only drop the drums close by."

"That's fine, honey, drop them close, we'll do the rest."

The three pilots switched to manual control and drew closer together as their sensors picked up the incoming drones. There were six, two each, and they were coming in slow and low… clearly, Helen had loaded them with as much as they could bear.

Which was good, they were going to need it all.

"Jake, how's your ammo state?" Graves asked.

"Almost out of everything that matters," Wright replied. "I got some close-in stuff left, but was really hoping not to need it."

"Okay, you reload first, Crazy Bill and I will cover you."

"Roger that!"

"And get the lead out," Crazy Bill added. "I'm down to my last rounds as well."

Carnigore fell out of the line, leaving *Brutiful* and *Grampage* to face the horde. Two drones passed over him, dropping heavy drum canisters into the soft ground within a few metres...one struck a rock and burst open, scattering autocannon ammunition everywhere, but the other canisters stayed intact.

One of *Carnigore's* saving graces, as he was just learning, was that it had much nimbler hands than your typical exomech. It was relatively easy to pick up a canister, eject an empty one, and reload the canister directly into the waiting drum feeder. 'Relatively' still meant that it took him minutes however, and he was out of battle during a time when mere seconds were critical.

Graves was very aware of his rapidly diminishing ammunition supply, and was firing controlled burst of 2-3 rounds each. It was never going to make a dint in the oncoming horde, but killing those in the lead would buy them some time... no idea what for, but maybe the Singh's would get there in time to rescue the wives and children locked into the Bunker.

Crazy Bill was firing constantly, preferring his own heavy cannon over his lighter autocannon. The high explosive rounds tore clumps out of the enemy and caused some confusion, which helped slow them down a little. Not enough, but everything helped.

"Hank," he said over the firing, "something just occurred to me."

"What's that Bill?" Graves replied, simultaneously firing a burst from his over-sized shotgun into a clump that was just begging to have a spray of tungsten sent its way. "You leave the gas on?"

"No," Crazy Bill said, chuckling loudly. "That wife of yours, she never gave us the bad news."

"You're right," Graves said. "Beth, honey? You got something else for us?"

"The bad news? You want it now?"

"Sure! What could possibly make anything worse?"

There was a pause, and Graves could hear his wife's sharp intake of breath.

"It's the giant gate on the ridgeline... it's still open."

The three men in the exomechs paused a moment as that sunk in. Gates always closed after they'd dropped off their load of deebees. *Always.*

"Well, shit!" Wright said, trying to push the last of his reload canisters into place.

"And then some," Crazy Bill added.

* * *

Singh Farmstead, Tau Ceti IV

The three exomechs stood open, family members working quickly to repair and reload them as best as they could, while the three pilots stood around the tactical display in the farmhouse's security room. The picture looked grim, and they doubted that Graves and the others would last much longer.

"If we move quickly," Agun said, "*Hawk* and *Eagle* might get there in time to be of some help."

Jaswant shook his head. "You'd need *Crescent Moon* to support you, you don't have the firepower to make much of a difference."

"We could give them close defence like we do for you, keep the deebees clear while they clean them out."

"Good idea, brother," Kubai said, "but that would leave *Crescent Moon* without support."

"Someone needs to stay here and guard the families."

That brought a frown from Jaswant, one that silenced his son. "If Graves and the others fall, there's no point guarding anything else." He pointed to the satellite images of deebees pouring towards the distant farmstead. "The colony lives or dies at the Graves farmstead."

"What do we do, father?" Agun asked.

"The best we can my son, the best we can."

* * *

Graves Farmstead, Tau Ceti IV

Brutiful's autocannon whirred and clicked as they finally ran out of ammunition. He was down to his last three shotgun rounds and then he'd be useless until the deebees got into close range, and by then it would be all over.

"Hank!" Wright's voice cut over the radio. "I'm reloaded, you're up!"

Carnigore stepped beside him, its clown-face a garish red grin as it opened fire on the aliens. Wright had no concerns at all about ammunition now and was firing it as fast as he could – there were certainly plenty of targets for everything he had to throw at them.

Graves stepped back out of the line and moved quickly to the clump of ammunition canisters the drones had dropped off for him. *Brutiful* was a large exomech, with lots of ammunition storage and he knew it was going to take him a while to get completely reloaded.

"Crap," Crazy Bill cut in, "I'm out too, nothing but close-in guns and my fists!"

"I can hold them," Wright replied, "But you'll need to be quick!"

"Bill, grab your canisters, make for the next hill," Graves said. "We'll cover you, you reload up there and cover us as we move back."

"Roger that!" Crazy Bill picked up his ammunition drums and ran for the next hilltop as fast as *Grampage's* servo-motors would go.

Graves could hear the sounds of firing behind him as he reloaded.

"Hank!" Wright yelled over the radio, "I need you real bad!"

Graves picked up the remaining canisters on *Brutiful's* lower arms and turned back to the line, his heavy shoulder-weapons coming back down, as reloaded as they were going to be.

The swarm was only a few hundred yards away now, and the exomech sensors still showed thousands of creatures out there. True, they could see the swarm was smaller than it was before, but they both knew it wasn't going to be enough.

Graves started firing, autocannon on maximum rate, shotgun blasting out a spread of tungsten as soon it chambered another round. Beside him, *Carnigore* matched him round for round, and the slaughter amongst the deebees was incredible.

But not enough.

"Hank," Wright's voice came through on a private direct channel. "I don't think we're going to make it."

Graves knew he wasn't wrong, but really didn't want to admit it.

"I know," he said softly, "but we'll go down swinging, give the Singhs and the others as best chance we can."

"I guess we will," Wright said, triggering another burst. "I just hope it counts for something."

The two men were silent for a long time, firing rapidly and switching fire to deal with the targets that presented the greatest threat.

"Hank, honey!" Beth's voice cut through urgently, "I need you to both get off the hill, and now!"

"What?"

"Don't argue, just get the hell off there!"

Graves shrugged and powered *Brutiful* off the hill as fast as he could, and a moment later he saw *Carnigore* do the same, with the front ranks of deebees only a dozen or so metres behind and closing.

His suit sensors pinged as they picked up a flight of something coming in fast and low, and he instinctively ducked as something flew overhead. He'd barely made it half-way down the slope when there was an explosion on the other side of the hill, powerful enough to knock both *Carnigore* and *Brutiful* off their feet and send them tumbling down the hill.

* * *

Southern Ridgeline/Jenkins Farmstead, Tau Ceti IV
Jenkins day just wasn't getting any better. Jessie was sending him the video and satellite feeds and he knew the colony was well and truly screwed over. There was a small chance Graves and the others could hold the deebees back, and he wanted to still be alive when the battle was over, but sitting back and watching wasn't going to help anybody, including him.

"Keith, I'm picking up movement on the ridgeline," Jessie said. "Big biomass, headed towards Graves' place."

"Well, that's them screwed then," he replied. "Might be best if you start packing some things Jessie and we take our chances in the wild until the next ship arrives."

"Might not be so bad, Keith... that big swarm of deebees isn't showing up on the satellite at all!"

"What now? That son of a bitch Graves took out an entire swarm by himself?"

"No idea," Jessie replied. "Might be worthwhile getting over there though, just in case."

"Good idea, Jessie," Jenkins said. "There should be plenty to claim from the colony account after this."

Turning *Shepherd* southward, he started mentally calculating the claims he was going to be putting in for his defence of the colony… and very, very inflated claims they would be.

* * *

Graves Farmstead, Tau Ceti IV

Shaken, Graves struggled to get his exomech back on its feet, but whatever had knocked him down must have had enough force to throw *Brutiful's* gyros out of alignment.

He noticed the ringing in his ears only when he started to get his hearing back, and only when that died down did he hear Beth calling out for him over the radio.

"Hank! Hank! Do you read me?" Her voice was frantic, and Graves had no idea how long he'd been out.

"I'm here, honey," he replied. "Quit yelling and tell me what the hell just happened."

"Oh, Hank, honey!" she said, the relief evident in her voice. "I thought I'd lost you!"

"Nope, still here… what did I miss?"

"You missed a lot! The Singhs came through, the smaller gates are all closed and the two Singh boys are on their way over, should be at the bunker within twenty."

"Just the boys?" Graves asked. "Jaswant didn't make it?"

"Jaswant's fine!" Beth replied. "They stripped the fusion cell out of *Crescent Moon* and sent it in on a drone, rigged to detonate on command."

Graves paused as that sank in… fusion cells were expensive and temperamental , and it would have been fast and risky work to take one out of an exomech and rig it to a crop-dusting drone.

SUITS

No wonder Beth had wanted him off that hill in a hurry!

"Wait... the Singh's just nuked my back yard?"

"Honey!"

"We'll talk about it later, Beth," he said. "Right now, I need an update on everything else."

"I can't give it to you, honey," Beth replied. "The blast's EMP took out our sensors and all the drones, and our satellite link is going to be down until you get back and fix it."

"Okay... I'll look around here and let you know what's going on."

"Roger that... I'll get this place sorted out and see to the families I have here."

He had to shut down and then reboot the gyros before he could stand up, and then he turned and went back to the top of the hill. The place was a mess.

On the fields below, the deebee swarm was now ash, turned to scorched dust by the force and heat of a fusion explosion. It would take him years to deal with the radiation, and he might have to move to maintain enough land to make a viable homestead, but he was glad to be alive.

He was saddened, however, at the sight of *Carnigore*, lying shattered and twisted at the base of the hill. The blast must have picked the exomech up and hurled it down the slope, and looking at the torn armour the following wave of radiation must have cooked Wright inside his suit.

Hopefully, he'd have been unconscious when the wave hit and he'd died quickly.

There was movement behind him, and he turned to see *Grampage* moving towards him. The exomech waved at him, then the right arm carefully tapped the suit's head, indicating radio failure. *Grampage* would have been well protected from the explosion, but high up on the next hill it would have been quite vulnerable to the EMP.

Crazy Bill came closer, and Graves could see through the armoured glass canopy that he was waving a hand-held radio at him. The handhelds were standard equipment for all colonists, and it took Graves only a moment to unclip his.

"You okay old-timer?" he asked, smiling to take the sting out of his words.

"Never been better," Crazy Bill replied. "You got a lot of dead deebees on your land, Hank, going to be good fertiliser come next summer."

"Summer in about 300 years you mean," Graves said, "after the radiation dies down."

He could see Crazy Bill laughing at him.

"Don't be foolish, Hank, the deebees will absorb that radiation as they break down."

"Really?"

Crazy Bill was nodding now.

Suddenly, there was an almighty roar, loud enough to shake them both through their armoured exomechs. Looking around, Graves saw a creature that even his worst nightmares wouldn't have thrown at him.

It was a deebee, but like nothing of them had ever seen before. His visual sensors were out, but it towered over the trees it was brushing easily aside, and must have stood at least 30 metres tall at the shoulder. Graves counted six clawed legs, could see from the sheen that it was chitin armoured, and the snout was fanged like a hungry cat.

"What… on… earth… is … that?" was all he could mutter.

"That," Crazy Bill replied, "is as good a reason as you'll ever need to run the hell back to your bunker."

Nodding, Graves turned his exomech and moved as fast as he could back to his farmstead.

* * *

Graves Farmstead, the Bunker, Tau Ceti IV

By the time Graves and Crazy Bill got back to the Bunker, the two light Singh exomechs had arrived, and Beth and Helen were out chatting to the two men. Beth waved happily when Graves arrived, but stopped waving when she saw the state of *Brutiful* and the urgency on her husband's face.

"Hank, honey, what is it?"

"Deebee coming, get back in the Bunker!"

"How many?" Agun asked, strapping himself back into his harness.

"Just one, son," Crazy Bill replied, "just one."

Agun and Kubai frowned as they sealed their exomechs and powered up their sensors – they'd known when the fusion cell was due to detonate and had shut down their systems to avoid the worst of the EMP – but they weren't making much sense of the readings.

"My sensors must be fried," Kubai said.

"Mine too," Agun added. "I'm picking up one signature, of enormous mass."

"There's nothing wrong with your sensors," Graves said. "Just the one, and it's the size of a deep-space shuttle."

The creature appeared at that moment, towering over the trees, and Beth and Helen both ran for the safety of the Bunker. Moving at great speed, the deebee headed towards them and Graves barely had enough time to reload the last of his ammunition canisters before the thing broke through the electric fence surrounding the farmstead. Built to keep out cattle, it barely registered on the behemoth above them.

The Bunker was equipped with a pair of 200mm cannon, capable of firing both high-explosive and anti-armour rounds. The ammunition hoppers were always filled with high-explosive, and Beth was firing them at the rapid rate, hoping to bring the creature down under a hail of fire. Against the thick chitin armour, however, the rounds did nothing.

Brutiful's autocannon had much the same effect, bouncing harmlessly off or exploding on impact without troubling the creature at all. He didn't even bother firing the shotgun, knowing the lower-velocity rounds would do nothing.

The Singhs charged in, *Hawk* and *Eagle* moving swiftly around the creature, firing their machine guns hoping to find a weak spot. The creature didn't appear to have any, and the rounds did little more than distract it.

Kubai's flamethrowers did little better, managing to infuriate it, and the creature reared up on its four hind legs and brought its forepaws crashing down...

Both of the lighter exomechs managed to dodge, though only just.

The Bunker's twin cannon were still firing, and still having no effect at all.

"Beth," Graves said as he moved *Brutiful* around to the giant deebee's right side, "quit wasting the hi-ex. I need you to unload as fast as you can and reload with the anti-armour rounds."

"Hank, honey," Beth replied, "what do you think I'm doing?"

Graves conceded that she had a point... unloading manually would have taken much longer than just firing it all off.

"Okay," he said. "Let me know when you've got a few anti-armour rounds loaded, we'll try to keep the thing off the bunker until you do."

"Roger that!"

Eagle and *Hawk* were running between the creature's legs now, still firing, and it didn't seem to like it much. It reared up again, this time on its rearmost pair of legs, and brought its whole body down.

This time *Eagle* wasn't so lucky, and a descending claw caught it and pressed it to the ground. The giant head came around, jaws open, and then the creature's teeth crushed and tore into the exomech and the pilot within. Graves winced as he heard Agun's screams, and then there was silence.

"Brother!" Kubai yelled, and darted forward to avenge his fallen kinsman. The creature was grinding the suit between its teeth, shredding the armour and Agun's remains. Ignoring his other weapons, Kubai slammed *Hawk* directly into the deebee's head, using the suit's armoured shoulders as a battering ram.

The impact was incredible, and Graves saw teeth fly out of the mouth as the creature sagged for a moment, and Kubai took the opportunity to slam *Hawk's* fists into the creature's head, massive roundhouse blows with power and weight behind them that only an exomech could generate.

The creature's exoskeletal armour began to break apart, and Kubai dug his suit's hands deep into a crack and heaved... Armour pulled away, revealing bright pink and yellow flesh beneath. He shoved his right arm into the hole and fired a burst from his twin machine guns, digging deep as the rounds finally punched into something vital.

The creature roared in agony and lifted its body, dragging *Hawk* with it. Kubai used his left arm to hang on and continued firing as the creature shook his head frantically in an effort to dislodge him.

"Hank, honey!" Beth cut in. "I have six anti-armour rounds loaded, ready to fire!"

"Roger that," Graves replied. "Kubai, drop clear!"

"Negative, Henry Graves," Kubai said. "You know the saying about riding the tiger."

Graves did indeed – there was no getting off once you started.

"Beth, Kubai can't get clear… I'll try to turn it so you can get a clean shot."

"Negative again," Kubai said. "Beth Graves, take your shot now, while I have it distracted."

"Hank, honey?"

"He's right, Beth, take the shot. Try to aim low, and be sure not to miss."

Graves watched as the twin cannon slewed around and then dropped, aiming right for the creature's chest, and fired three rounds from each barrel. At that range, they couldn't miss.

The anti-tank rounds were a tungsten slug with a hollow charge, that turned into a shaped charge on impact…striking the creature, they formed and detonated, with enough heat to melt the tungsten and fire it at supersonic speeds into the target. The six rounds struck in quick succession, each a metre or so apart, and the resultant explosions turned the creature's torso to pulp.

It rose up in its death throes and thrashed around uncontrollably… Kubai couldn't maintain his grip and *Hawk* fell, landing heavily on its back, only to have the creature fall on top of him, its sheer weight crushing the exomech and cracking open plates of armour.

And then it died.

* * *

Graves Farmstead, Tau Ceti, IV, Aftermath
Graves, Jaswant Singh, Crazy Bill and Keith Jenkins stood outside the Bunker as the other colonists cleaned up the mess, which included cutting up and dragging away the corpse of the giant deebee.

With a lot of families dead, there'd be room for more colonists. The Donaldsons were gone, so their farmstead was vacant land, and Peters' wife and family had decided to leave Tau Ceti and head home to Earth, which freed up that land as well.

They managed to drag Kubai Singh out of his exomech's wreckage... he was still alive, but had lost both legs and an arm, and would require expensive prosthetics, which the Colony account would happily pay. Likewise, replacement exomechs for the Singhs, who had lost all three of their suits, would come from the Colony account.

Jenkins had put in claims for damages and repairs that they all knew were ridiculous, but no-one had the energy to argue – he'd survived, that counted for something, and they needed everyone to move forward together. Jaswant Singh had suggested giving Jenkins the deeds to the Donaldson and Peters farmsteads, in exchange for his own, as payment for his efforts, and the others had reluctantly agreed – the Singhs had lost too much for them to deny any reasonable requests right now. Graves could see Jenkins mentally rubbing his hands together in glee, and it sickened him.

The really good news was that Jake Wright had survived after all. Despite his complaints about his exomech, *Carnigore* had one feature no-one had counted on – it had more radiation shielding than any of them had ever seen, likely as a measure to protect patrons from radiation leaks from when it was still an amusement ride droid. It was a wreck and would need replacing, but Jake was okay.

And that left the giant gate on the ridgeline. It lacked the sparkle that indicated an open gateway back the deebee's home dimension, but it was still there. None of them had any idea what to do about it, other than to arm up, stay vigilant, and invest heavily in defences. It was going to be expensive and hard work, and it dawned on Graves that Jenkins new farmstead would be right in the path of any further attacks... Jaswant Singh was much wilier than he'd given him credit.

With the creature dragged away and the other colonists gone, Graves and his wife surveyed the land they'd fought hard to defend. It never occurred to them to pack up and leave, to head to somewhere safer. This was home, and alien invasion or no, this was where they were going to stay.

SUCKER OF SOULS

Kirsten Cross

s that as fast as you can run? Because fella? I'm telling you right now. It ain't fucking fast enough!"

Snarled words from a frightened man way, *way* out of his comfort zone and desperately trying to appear in control of an uncontrollable situation so as not to 'frighten the civvy'.

Soldiers, even ex-soldiers who now got paid to babysit graverobbing archaeologists, shouldn't show fear. Ever. Even when they were faced with an enemy that apparently had powers well beyond those that could be controlled with a quick double-tap from a Glock.

Fuck.

This was gonna be one well-earned paycheque. If he lasted long enough to collect the damn thing, that was. What they had just witnessed had challenged Flynn's whole concept of what was worth seven hundred dollars a day plus expenses – and what wasn't. And this very definitely wasn't.

"I'm sorry?"

The archaeologist didn't get the barely controlled desperation, panic and outright 'what the actual *fuck* was that?' tone in his babysitter's voice. Lucky. Flynn was still in control. Just. He pressed home his advantage.

"You bloody-well will be if we don't stay ahead of… whatever the *hell* that was." The ex-soldier gave his charge a cold, emotionless smile that didn't reach his eyes.

The archaeologist peeled off a pair of round spectacles and rubbed at them with the corner of his shirt. He perched the glasses back onto his nose and pushed them up to the bridge. His hands were shaking violently. He used the mundane act to try and ground himself while his brain attempted to process the carnage they had just seen. "I'm an archaeologist, Mr Flynn, not an Olympic sprinter."

Colby Flynn turned his steely-cold, pale-green eyes onto the quivering academic, rammed home a new clip and primed his sidearm in front of the man. That always got their attention. Sliding the bolt back on the Glock 17 made that gloriously satisfying 'cher-chunk' sound that all movie scriptwriters love. It acted as an underline, emphasising his determination to go down fighting no matter what. It also helped to make the archaeologist more frightened of Flynn than the thing that was currently snuffling and snarling its way towards them. And that was a good thing. Because it would mean the bolshy academic would now do what he was told for a change. "Good. That increases my chances, then."

The bespectacled, owl-like man blinked curiously at Flynn. "What?"

"It means, buddy, that while mister bitey back there is chowing down and ripping your throat out like he did with your mate, he won't be gnashing on me, will he?"

Oh no. Not again…

A snorting, snuffling sound that was so thick and black you could chew it like a piece of liquorice imposed on their momentary pause. "Seriously, will you just *fuck off*, you bastard!" Flynn abused the darkness and then emptied a volley of shots into nothing. Whether it actually made any real difference or not, he couldn't tell. But whatever was back there yelped and snarled. Flynn hoped that the swarm of hollowpoints at least gave the bastard cause to pause so they could focus on running again.

Move! For fuck's sake, *move!*" Flynn spun the archaeologist around and shoved him hard. "I've got your back. As long as you stay in front of me." Flynn put his mouth next to the sweating man's ear. "And yet, you're… still… *here?*"

The archaeologist suddenly developed a surprisingly fast turn of speed for a Cambridge academic.

Normally, Flynn wouldn't give anyone a head start. This wasn't a school egg and spoon race where the 'special kids' got to jog a few steps before everyone else set off, and it was the 'taking part that mattered, not the winning, little buddy'. This was a slime-covered stone corridor lined with spluttering, flickering lightbulbs that had been Jerry-rigged

SUCKER OF SOULS

by Micky Cox – an ex-REME armed with a screwdriver, a happy disposition, and a real 'MacGyver' approach to fixing shit. Their only source of light was being produced by a wheezing, 40-year-old generator with carburettor problems and mile upon mile of gaffer-taped cable. And there wasn't some happy-clappy teaching assistant cheering them on. There was a five-hundred-and-seventy-year-old psychopath with a taste for blood, violence and carnage just a few turns behind them. And he – or it, whatever the hell *it* was – was playing with them, the sick, twisted little bastard.

Flynn needed the archaeologist alive. What was in professor brainiac's balding little noggin might just keep him and his team in one piece, if he could get the egghead to the safety of the citadel's old armoury that was currently doubling as a control centre for the dig. Damn it, if he was going to be paid to babysit an academic, he'd make sure the son of a bitch stayed alive.

The twisting, turning corridors were slick with algae. These dungeons and corridors were built well below the natural water table and a musky, foetid atmosphere permeated every inch of the subterranean labyrinth. Rivulets of water seeped down and followed the channels between the huge blocks of granite. There was no mortar holding these blocks together. Stone like this didn't need cement to keep it in place. These tunnels – deep under what would have been a massive, imposing castle – had thousands of tons of masonry and rock pressing down on them.

Back in the comfort of the hotel, the archaeologist had told Flynn and his team a rambling account of the supposed history of the citadel. It was, as Gary Parks had said, a 'two-bottle tale'. The bottles in question had been filled with the local hooch, a paint-stripping, intestine-melting liquor that would probably lead to blindness if you drank too much of the damn stuff. Flynn was a practical kind of guy and, right up to the point when that… *thing*… had come wailing through the door, took a pretty pragmatic approach to concepts such as the ability of true evil, despair and pain to impregnate the very walls of a building. So he listened patiently about how the stones were held together with the screams of the damned, long since dead but not necessarily buried. The archaeologist had gone into great detail about how the terror of the inmates had been etched into the stone with scrabbled, ripped fingernails and bloodied stumps. It had become as real as any painting; an everlasting memory of the evil that had happened in this dark and savage place. He recounted grisly details of how every cell had been occupied with frail, frightened prisoners, their minds shredded and tattered by the constant screams, yowls and cries for mercy that echoed throughout the underground chambers. When the guards came for them, they'd begged. Oh, how they'd begged! They crawled on their bellies. They pleaded. They called to their God – who utterly abandoned them to their fate and the whims of their sadistic captors.

The archaeologist spared no details in his story. He explained how the peepholes allowed guards who got a thrill from watching the suffering of others to observe the prisoners' slow and painful deaths as starvation and disease took hold. How they would watch as the rats started chewing on the dying when they became too weak to shoo them away, taking bets on which part of a prisoner's body the rodents would go for first. Apparently, it was always the soft tissue – the genitals, the face, the eyes. Once the body had been reduced to gnawed bones and a sticky, stinking coating of vitreous fluid on the stone floor, the door was opened and a new occupant took residence. Except one.

Like freaked-out boy scouts telling ghost stories around a campfire, Flynn and his team had leaned in. After all, everyone loves a good 'haunted castle' story, don't they? The archaeologist risked permanent sight damage by pouring himself another glass of hooch and had continued with his tale.

This cell, he explained, had no door. Instead, massive stones had been seconded from other parts of the castle and used to wall up the doorway, leaving just the iron-barred peephole through which guards occasionally pushed a hissing, squawking cat. This unique prisoner, brought back home to this dark and terrifying castle after rampaging for years across Europe, liked his food still kicking. So they gave him cats because it seemed to be the one thing he… it… feared. That was their torment – giving him something they knew full well he detested, but was so starved and emaciated that he had no choice but to overcome his revulsion and feed on whatever screeching titbit the guards tossed through the barred gap.

SUCKER OF SOULS

The isolation was a torment, too, especially for such a brilliant, bright and diamond-hard mind. The knowledge that the stinking, festering cell littered with the bones of cats and rats was to be his everlasting tomb – a tomb that was designed for the living, not the undead – had warped his already-twisted mind beyond evil, and beyond any form of redemption and turned it from a 'he' into an 'it'. That's why the priests had brought it back here. Even they were afraid of it; afraid of what it had become. Afraid of what it could do, especially after Death had supposedly claimed its putrefying corpse and it had reanimated, sending at least three of those same priests to early and very violent deaths.

This was the cell it had called home for years, centuries, driven utterly insane by the lust for sustenance and tormented by the hissing, caterwauling animals the guards hurled into his cell. When the citadel was abandoned and the tunnels lost to history, it went into hibernation for centuries. Occasionally, it woke and fed on any rat that wasn't quick enough to escape its clutches. Then, it returned to its state of stasis until the starvation became too great once again.

Well, that was the story. Flynn had listened, but up until about five minutes ago, he really hadn't bought any of this BS. As an ex-soldier he had seen enough horror in his life to be open to the idea of the manifestation of evil. Getting chased through slime-covered corridors by that a snarling, salivating monstrosity meant he was getting more open-minded by the second…

They'd found the cell. And behind the stones lurked a creature that had wandered the dark desert of madness for more lifetimes than it could count. When the archaeologists had unblocked the tomb it had burst forth in a howling, screaming frenzy, tearing the first man it saw to pieces. It had sucked the young man – a research fellow in the final year of his doctorate – dry, gorging itself and relishing the feeling of drunken power. Slated, it had slumped to the floor for a moment, laughing maniacally. The first taste awoke the hunger. Now? It wanted more.

This was what Colby Flynn and the archaeologist were running from. Not an alcohol-fuelled story. A very real, very hungry and very *angry* creature from the pit of mankind's nightmares.

But this was no simple medieval terror, released from its prison at last, and free to unleash its maddened, blackened rage once again on the world. Once, it had been a sentient, passionate young man, a visionary and military genius. But fate had been cruel to Vlad and the Black Prince had eventually been imprisoned in the stone-lined cell of Tokat Castle, a broken tooth of a citadel that towered high above the city.

The Seljuk Turks who had conquered Tokate in the 12th Century had discovered a maze of underground passages and stone-lined cells, and had turned it into their own stronghold. In 1442 they were given their most dangerous prize, Prince Vlad III. But the young boy and his brother were political hostages, not prisoners. So, during his internment the Ottomans had attempted to create an ally out of him. They taught him military strategy. They nurtured his natural ability for warfare and combat, taught him the classics, languages, geography, mathematics and science. They had given him every advantage.

But they also brutalised him, beating and humiliating this prince's son who would not bend his knee to the Turk's rule.

And that was a big, big mistake.

They turned an intelligent, bright boy into a sadistic, vicious man – a military savant whose ability to strategise played a major part in his success as a ruler later on. But his brutalised, blackened heart became darker and more infested with evil until he created a monster that would resonate through the centuries.

Dracula.

The Impaler.

The devourer of children and sucker of souls.

This was to be his prison – firstly in life, and later, when the monks of Comana had brought his bloated corpse back from their monastery to the one place on earth they knew would hold him.

And it had held him. The monks' plan had worked – right up until the moment when well-meaning academics with no understanding of true evil and a firm if totally misguided belief that knowledge would be their shield, had torn down the stones that kept Vlad from unleashing his unique brand of horror on the world.

To modern minds, especially those belonging to academics and military specialists that had indulged in the local hooch for a couple of hours, vampires were nothing more than a myth. One that had been responsible for some of both the best and the worst literary endeavours, and that echoed down through the ages to become sanitised by Hollywood into sparkly vampires with sickly complexions, beloved of swooning and incredibly stupid teenage girls. All of the archaeologist's tales were merely that. Just tales. Stories. Pseudo-romantic embellishments of the history of an otherwise ordinary Ottoman castle.

Yeah. Tell that to the ragged, bloody remains of a twenty-five-year-old research fellow who had been Vlad's first real meal in over five hundred long, long years. He had taken the full brunt of Vlad's maddened rage. Flynn and the archaeologist had watched helplessly as a whirling maelstrom of hatred, blood-lust and utter fury swirled around the screaming student, tearing and shredding his skin, ripping it from his face and spraying blood in an arc around the corridor. It moved too fast to see clearly; just a tornado of rage that dismembered the student in a heartbeat.

And then?

Silence.

For a few fleeting seconds, a lull had descended on the corridors, allowing the echoes of the research student's screams to fade into the stone and join the entombed chorus of thousands of other victims locked into the granite blocks for eternity. But then slowly, after the savagery and the silence, came a growing, rolling, maniacal laugh that reached out beyond the walls that had entombed the monster for so long.. In the nearby village, the not-quite-so-ignorant-as-everybody-thought peasants who had grown up on fireside stories of the demon that lay entombed in the citadel's secret tunnels, bolted their doors, pulled the shutters closed and huddled together, gripped with an ancient fear that their ancestors had passed to them in their very genes. They knew. They knew that Vlad was free. The Dracul, the Black Prince, the Impaler. He was *free*...

Flynn had been the first to snap out of the terror trance and realise that they weren't dealing with some damn fairy story here, but a real threat. A real *nasty* threat that was just about to turn its attention onto Flynn and the one remaining and utterly freaked out archaeologist. Flynn didn't care whether this monster was the real Vlad, some crazy, inbred village idiot or the damn Devil himself. So he'd reacted in the only way he knew how. Natural or supernatural, this son of a bitch was flesh and blood. So a Glock should have an effect on it, even if it was only to slow the fucker down for a few seconds and give them that chance they needed to put more than twenty feet between it and them. He emptied an entire clip into the thing and watched as its body twitched and danced.

The blood-dawbed creature recoiled for a few seconds and then stopped its snapped-marionette-string dance. It smiled, white teeth emphasised by the gore-covered skin. It stood, unfurling and flexing taloned fingers.

"Oh, shit..." Flynn grabbed his charge by the shoulders and screamed one word at him. "*Run!*"

Whatever that thing behind them was, it kept pace. Flynn got the distinct impression it could quite easily overtake and overwhelm them. But it was toying with them like a cat would play with a mouse. It was watching how they reacted, determining how well they knew the terrain. It was assessing them, learning their tactics, and letting them draw it along. Flynn had the distinctly unpleasant feeling that the little the archaeologist had told him about the legend of the Black Prince being a military genius was just the tip of a blood-soaked iceberg. His skin prickled. Back in Afghanistan there had been this one Taliban chieftain that had made all the others look like complete amateurs. He had had that cold, detached way of disciplining his men that revolved around 'making examples'. The examples were bloody remains left swinging in trees in the savage winter gales that swept through the Tora Bora caves and the White mountains between Afghanistan and Pakistan. He had mounted an IED campaign so successful that it had claimed the lives of twenty regulars and seven Special Forces troops. He had been known for his extraordinary ability to pre-empt when and where the SF teams would go in on a 'flush out', and vanish like a wraith into the mountains, forever one step ahead. He had retained that arrogant, smug smile and defiance right up to the moment Flynn put two bullets between his bloodshot, hate-filled eyes.

Flynn then had to run for his life as the man's two radicalised and equally insanely-violent sons pursued him and his team through the badlands, promises of revenge screamed in Pashto ringing in their ears. He learned then that when you cut the head from the Hydra, two more grow back. Evil is never conquered. It's merely subdued until a greater evil comes to take its place. He had seen that same evil in the eyes of... whatever the fuck that thing was when it paused in its bullet-dance, dropped the mushed-up, ruined heart of the research fellow, and locked its gaze with him. An evil allowed to fester in a dark, vile place for centuries had become focused into a singularity that, when unleashed, would sweep everything before it. And Flynn's Glock17 was going to do fuck-all to stop the bastard, no matter how many clips he emptied into its emaciated, putrefying body...

* * *

Vlad watched the soldier and his charge scuttle away down the corridor and smiled a chilling, venom-filled smile. Cold. Calculating. A military strategist like no other before or since. Stalking its prey at its leisure. It had waited hundreds of years. It could wait a few moments longer. Blood was only half the meal. It wanted to savour the fear as well. It wanted to hear their hearts pounding in anticipation of the terror that was about to befall them. It relished the futile attempts of a little man with a pop-gun trying to comprehend the evil he faced. That sweet, satisfying moment when the man realised that there was no escape. There was no fate other than the one the Black Prince had chosen for him. The Black Prince smiled a virginal white smile. Soldiers rarely operated alone. So there were more. So he would make sure the little soldier with his useless gun stayed alive long enough to watch any comrades he may have being devoured in front of him. The anguish, the rage, the pathetic howling and screaming as he watched the Black Prince's teeth rip into the throats of men he loved like brothers would be almost as delicious as the blood itself.

'*Lead on, little soldier. Lead on...*'

* * *

Flynn and the archaeologist pelted down the slippery corridors that twisted and turned under the citadel and carried them deeper into the labyrinth. A line of gaffer-taped cables acted like a trail of breadcrumbs leading them back towards the sanctuary of the armoury. Without that advantage they would have become completely turned around in the myriad of tunnels that weaved and meandered beneath the ruined towers and crumbling walls. A wrong turn would take you into a dead end. And a dead end had a very literal sense when you were being pursued by an insane and bloodthirsty monster.

As he shoved the archaeologist again in the small of the back, Flynn pulled out a radio and pressed the squawk button. "Micky, get ready with everything we've got ordnance wise. We're coming in *fucking* hot!"

"*Don't tell me those boffins have gone rogue on your arse? Coo, there ain't nothing worse than a cocky egghead, fella!*" Micky Cox's cheerful voice crackled out of the hand-held and bounced off the stones.

"Don't fuck about, Micky! I'm serious! FUBAR! Fubar like you wouldn't *fucking believe!*"

"*Fuck… copy that.*" Micky's light-hearted tone instantly changed.

Flynn felt himself losing step as the archaeologist, not the fittest of academics, started to slow. The adrenaline was wearing off and panic was starting to take hold. Flynn knew from experience that he had seconds before the bloody fool froze up and probably went foetal on him. He reached out and grabbed the man's shirt, overtook him and ignored the protestations as his coaching method changed from snarled encouragement and threats to brute-force dragging. "Move! We've got a few more turns before we get to the control room. I'll lay money that your bitey friend back there won't be able to get through that door once we've locked it, right?"

The archaeologist gasped as he tried to keep pace with Flynn. "And once we're locked in with nowhere to run, what do you suggest *then*?"

"I'm not thinking that far ahead right now, fella. Priority number one is to stay away from Count Chompula, okay?" He yanked hard at the archaeologist's multi-pocketed waistcoat, hauling him around another corner and a few steps closer towards safety.

They were close.

They were so damn close…

Flynn and the archaeologist rounded the next corner and skidded to a halt, flailing wildly to try and keep themselves from tumbling into the waiting arms of the Black Prince. It stood stooped and filling the corridor, disproportionately long arms full of muscle and sinews ending in talons that would rip through flesh and bone like it was paper. White teeth shone in the flickering light. Unlike those dopey movie vampires, this vicious fucker didn't have two slightly longer canine teeth and a mouthful of perfect orthodontry. It had a whole mouthful of dazzlingly-white points bathed in saliva and dripping with toxins. It opened its maw and hissed like an angry cat. Eyes filled with insanity, hatred and a raging hunger beyond anything Flynn had seen during his humanitarian missions to Sudan fixated on the two stumbling, staggering men. "*Shit!* Back! Back! Back!" Flynn shoved the archaeologist backwards, trying to twist him around. The academic, unaccustomed to any physical activity more strenuous than reaching for a book on a top shelf, lost his balance and collapsed in a heap directly behind Flynn's legs. Flynn toppled backwards, and archaeologist and CPP bodyguard became entangled in a mess of flailing arms and legs.

Flynn extracted himself and rolled backwards, coming up and drawing the Glock in one smooth move. He knew it wouldn't stop the laughing, blood-smeared monstrosity, but at least it might slow the fucker down a bit again.

The archaeologist had gone foetal and lay curled on the floor, whimpering like a baby with bellyache.

Fuck him. Focus on the target. Flynn's eyes narrowed and he squeezed the trigger. Two shots rang out and the monster twitched briefly. Then on the third squeeze the Glock, normally a stalwart of reliability, did nothing other than issue a mocking 'click'. "Shit!" Memory gave him a hard slap in the face. He'd emptied most of the clip into the bastard back in the corridor earlier. Damn, damn, *damn!*

Most people would have railed against fact that the clip was empty and pulled the trigger again and again, as if the action would magic some spare ordnance from out of the sky and into the weapon. Flynn had spent six years in Special Forces. He'd spent more time behind enemy lines than the enemy had. So he knew better. The clip was empty; don't fuck about trying to deny the bloody obvious, just reload, prime and fire. Flynn jettisoned the empty clip and fumbled in his vest pocket for a new one, ignoring the old magazine as it clattered against the stones. Normally, he'd be able to reload, prime and start shooting again in a split second. Put him up against a bunch of howling Afghans armed with Klackers, bad personal hygiene and angry intent and it would have been a walk in the park. But this? This guffawing, cackling monstrosity? It had him rattled.

So he did the unthinkable.

He dropped the damn clip.

Time demonstrated that whole 'fluidity' concept in glorious technicolour, and decelerated to a crawl. Man and monster watched the clip fall in slow motion, fleeting, flashing glimpses of the jacketed hollow-point bullets emphasised by the matt black of the clip. It hit the ground end on, bounced and spun through three-sixty in mid-air, spewing one bullet off at a right-angle. The clip and stray bullet clattered back down, shuddered and finally came to rest. The errant JHP rolled away into the darkness, lost in the shadows.

Flynn tore his gaze away from the clip and refocused on the grinning face of the monster. He knew, didn't he? The smarmy, grinning motherfucker! He just damn well *knew* that was Flynn's last spare clip. He fucking *knew.*

Flynn was determined to go down fighting. He stuffed the Glock17 back in his belt and pulled out his trusty Blackhawk from the drop-down leg holster it liked to call home. No self-respecting SF squaddie would be caught dead without one of these black beauties. The six-inch symmetrical blade was precision ground D-2 steel. It would cut through skin, bone, and flesh, and didn't differentiate between the dead or the undead. Flipping it around so the blade lay edge-on against the inside of his forearm and hidden from the monster's line of sight, he smiled back at the monster like a man with nothing left to lose but his life. "Wanna dance, fuck nuts? Huh?" He beckoned with his outstretched left hand. "C'mon, you ugly fuck! Let's do it, let's fucking *dance!* C'mon!"

He knew it was hopeless.

He knew he was going to lose. And that losing meant dying. Badly.

He knew that as soon as that cackling, guffawing bipolar son-of-a-bitch flip-flopped back into black fury and bloodthirsty rage, he'd be facing an enemy whose savagery was beyond all comprehension.

Savagery of that level made an opponent practically invincible. He'd seen how fast the thing was when it launched itself out of the cell. Nothing Flynn had ever encountered moved that quickly. His only consolation was that while mister bitey here was getting busy with him, it would give the archaeologist a chance to get out of danger, at least for a few moments. But it might just be enough.

Flynn may have appeared to have scant regard for his charge, but he was a good man. And good men care about those who can't fight for themselves...

The monster stopped its insane cackling. The hunger was burning in it once more. And this time it lusted after the blood of a warrior, not that of a screaming, pissing boy. It wanted blood filled with passion and fire. Blood that had been spilled on the battlefield. Blood that sang out to him like a war trumpet. The blood of a soldier. It could sense the man's heart beating, a slow, steady rhythm, not the usual frantic pounding that its victims normally demonstrated. Ah, *delightful!* A true, battle-hardened warrior. They were always the most satisfying, especially at the very end when they knew they had lost their final conflict.

It would also give the Black Prince an insight into modern combat tactics. It knew it was capable of tearing the soldier to pieces as easily as it had devoured the screeching boy earlier. But it wanted to 'dance', as the mocking soldier said. It wanted to see just what kind of a 'dance' these modern warriors engaged in, and how things had changed in the five hundred years it had been locked away in that stinking cell.

But the hunger was also strong. It filled the creature. It consumed every fibre of its being.

Time to feed...

The Black Prince coiled, ready to spring. The soldier was certain to land a few blows before he succumbed, but the brief glimpses of fleeting pain would remind the Black Prince that it was alive. Free. And would be *feared* once again! The beast flexed its taloned fingers. Long, yellowed nails tapered into savage points. The knuckles were pronounced and gnarled, like the knots in a tree trunk. Sinews like chords snaked across the back of its hands and up his arms. It spread its arms, threw back its head and roared – a scream of defiance at those who would incarcerate and starve it for all these years. They were gone. Mere dust and ashes. Corpses for the worms. But Vlad? Ah, Vlad. He was here. He had survived! And now he could feed once more on the blood of a soldier. He lumbered towards his opponent, a low snarl grumbling in the back of his throat. It was cut short by a soft mewing. The creature stopped in its tracks. Its bloodshot eyes widened in horror and it screeched – a sound so piercing it made his human opponent recoil and cover his ears. The screech went on and on, reverberating around the corridors and echoing through the citadel, folding and doubling back on itself.

A small, calico cat sat serenely in the middle of the corridor, casually studying him. The skinny creature was one of the hundreds of feral cats that inhabited the citadel. For as long as the stone walls had stood, the cats had been there. They served a practical purpose in that they kept rats and mice under control. But the villagers seemed to have a special reverence for the mangy creatures, leaving out food and milk for them and chastising anyone who might feel the temptation to kick one of the creatures in passing. Cats, in this part of Turkey, were almost sacred.

Vlad hated them. They represented its madness, its incarceration, its humiliation. Every time it had fed on one of the screeching beasts, Vlad's insides felt as if it had swallowed acid. For days afterwards it would writhe and scream in agony as the cat's blood burned through its body. For Vlad, this tiny, mewing calico cat represented all the torment, the agony and the rage that had turned a man into a monster. What once had been a brilliant young mind had degenerated into that which terrifies mankind the most – a physical manifestation of the darkest evil that we are all capable of becoming…

Vlad recoiled in horror, inching backwards away from the calm little cat. Paying the vampire scant attention, the cat proceeded to clean its paw, a tiny pink tongue darting out as it licked the fur smooth. It stood, stretched its back and legs, yawned and sat back down again, curling its tail neatly around its feet.

The little cat studied Vlad with that casual interest felines have when they're mildly distracted. Then, it got up, waved its tail in the air and walked towards Vlad, purring happily and apparently unaware its misplaced show of affection was tormenting the beast.

Vlad screamed again and vanished down the corridor.

* * *

Flynn looked at the cat in disbelief, amazed that such a tiny little thing could do what he couldn't – repel a monster. "Well, fuck me."

"He hates cats." The archaeologist had uncurled from the foetal position and stood, supporting his shaking body by pressing his palm against the slick stones that lined the corridor. "Hates them."

"You don't say." Flynn scowled, and put the knife away and pulled out his gun. He stepped forward and rescued his dropped clip, deftly flicking the clip into the butt of the gun before scooping up the cat. "Okay, kitty, you're coming with us." He turned to the archaeologist, Glock 17 in one hand and scrawny cat in the other. "Wanna get out of here before that bastard decides he's more hungry than he is scared of a little pussy?" He nodded towards the darkened end of the corridor. "Straight ahead. Follow the cables. Don't worry. Me and puss here are right behind ya."

The archaeologist stared open-mouthed at the cat for a second, turned, and trotted away down the corridor, slightly crouched and ready to back peddle furiously if Vlad did his 'surprise!' tactic again around the next corner.

Flynn scratched the little cat's head affectionately, and let the agile little critter clamber up onto his shoulder. The deep, rumbling purr felt like a massage cushion on his shoulders. He gave the cat one last affectionate pat and ran after the disappearing academic.

The cat turned and looked back, narrowing its emerald green eyes at *something* in the shadows. Its ears flattened against its skull and it hissed…

* * *

"Shut the door! Shut the damn door!" Colby Flynn dived through the opening and into the armoury. As he tumbled through the air he jettisoned a small cat from his shoulder, rolled and came back up on one knee facing back out into the corridor, the Glock17 up and ready. He stared out into the gloom. Shadows crowded in, advancing towards the armoury as one by one the Jerry-rigged bulbs Micky Cox had strung like Christmas lights along the corridor flickered, popped and died. Each section plunged sequentially into darkness, allowing the thick blackness to jump ever closer to the armoury. Flynn knew that if the darkness reached them before Micky got the door shut, they'd all die in that room…

Micky slammed the heavy oak door into the frame and turned the key in the lock. There was no rusty squawking or atmospheric creaking from the hinges. Micky was ex-REME and a damn good engineer. He hated any piece of machinery that didn't work as it was supposed to, no matter how seemingly inconsequential. So the hinges and lock had been cleaned and oiled. They worked perfectly, and the reassuring *click* as the tumblers fell into place was the best damn sound Flynn had heard all day. Micky slid the top and bottom bolts back into their housings, providing additional reinforcement to the lock. He turned, grabbed a thick plank and dropped it into the cradle with a deeply satisfying and wooden-sounding *clunk*. The huge armoury door was now shut – *properly* shut.

Flynn lowered the Glock as Micky leaned against the door. Never point ordnance at your mates. Kind of a rule, really.

"Mind telling me what the actual fuck?" Micky turned and frowned at his boss, his vivid blue eyes narrowing. "Also? What's with the cat?"

"Little Rupert here saved our hides, fella."

"Rupert?"

"What's wrong with Rupert?"

Micky's frown deepened. "Okay, let's gloss over the fact that you've called some mangy, flea-infested moggy Rupert, you weirdo. And just so you know? I'm allergic to cats."

"Trust me, Mick, you'd be a damn sight more allergic to the thing it stopped from chowing down on our arses, mate. I'd put a week's pay on that." Flynn stood and ran his hand through his dirty blonde hair.

Micky shrugged. "I take it that's what the fubar's all about?"

Flynn glanced down at a heap in the corner. The weeping academic had gone foetal again. Flynn sniffed sharply, grabbed a handful of archaeologist and hauled him to his feet. "Upsy daisy, fella." He shook the man like a ragdoll. "Oi! Stop now with all that yodelling and tell us a: what that thing is, and b: how we can kill it." He deposited the frightened man on the corner of a table and shook him again. "Because right now, our situ is not good, son. All that's stopping some insane, bloodthirsty creature from tearing you, me and my boys apart is a five-hundred-year-old door and, for some reason, a bloody cat." Flynn glanced at the cat, which was winding its skinny body around Micky's legs and purring loudly. Micky looked decidedly distressed.

"Which damn question do you want me to answer first, Mister Flynn?" The archaeologist sniffed indignantly.

"How 'bout you work through them in order, mate?" A hard cockney voice snapped angrily from the corner and Gary Parks, a hulk of a man with a passion for blowing things up loomed from the shadows. His deep brown eyes shone out from mahogany skin and he raised a quizzical eyebrow. "Boss?"

"Waiting for Poindexter here to enlighten us, fella." Flynn focused on the cowering academic. "Well? There's four of us—"

"And this bloody cat!" Micky sneezed violently. "See? Allergic. Fucking allergic."

"And the cat, yes, thanks Mick. Take an antihistamine. There's some in the medipack."

"Couldn't we just chuck the cat out?"

"The cat stays, Micky. It stays. Okay?" Flynn jabbed a thumb at a pile of supply boxes. "Antihistamine pill. Now. Get it down your neck, you tart." He rolled his eyes. "Allergies. Seriously. Who the fuck ever heard of a member of the Regiment with allergies?"

"Damn near got him RTU'd, boss, remember?" Gary grinned at Micky and flicked him the finger.

"Bollocks, Parks, you 'roided up wanker."

"Focus, you pair of reprobates." Flynn stared hard at the academic. "So. Wanna fill in the gaps, little guy?"

"Mister Flynn, I don't think you realise the seriousness of the situation."

Flynn glowered and slapped the man hard across the mouth. "Really? You think? You think I don't get the fact that whatever that thing is out there has just ripped your mate to pieces and eaten his fucking *heart*?"

"Wait, *what?*" Gary and Micky stared open mouthed at their boss.

"Or that I emptied two clips of hollowpoints into the fucker and all it did was dance a little jig?" Flynn slapped the man across the mouth again. "What part did I miss?"

The archaeologist recoiled from Flynn's raised hand. "Stop hitting me, damn it!" His shaking hands tried vainly to ward off another slap. "I'll tell you, just... please, *stop* hitting me!"

Flynn dropped his hand. "Okay. Start at the top."

"Vlad. It's Vlad."

Gary Parks frowned. "What, as in the Impaler?"

"Isn't that a type of car?"

"That's an *Impala*, Micky, you idiot!"

"Yes, as in the Impaler. The 'Dracula' of legend. Only he's very, very real, believe me." The academic ignored the scowling, sniffling Cox and focused on Flynn and Parks. "Remember that story I told you last night? It's true. Believe me, I'm as surprised as you are. I expected to find nothing but bones, Mister Flynn, I swear!"

"Yeah, well that didn't pan out, did it?" Flynn sighed. "Seriously. Look, sorry about your lad, by the way. That was bad."

"So let me get this straight. We're being laid siege to by *Dracula?* Are you serious?" Micky Cox's voice was filled with incredulity. "Fuck off! That's a myth!"

"Trust me, Mick, that thing out there, whether it's actually Dracula or not, is no damn myth. So let's ignore the fact that we've dropped kicking and, in the case of professor braniac here, screaming into an episode of the Twilight Zone and figure out how we kill that fucker and get everyone out of here in one piece, copy?"

"Copy." The two ex-soldiers nodded. Everything else was irrelevant. Myth or not, the identity of their opponent could be argued over later. They needed to focus on the reality of the situation. This was now a simple matter of survival.

"Right. So what's the state of play with ordnance, Gary?"

"Not particularly tickity, to be honest. We weren't expecting gunfights with angry vampires, boss. We've got two boxes of ammo for the Glocks and the three P90s are stocked up with SB193 subsonic rounds, with two spare magazines each. Other than that?" Gary shrugged. "I got some C4, if that helps?"

Flynn stared at his friend. "Why? Why do you have C4, Gary, *why?*"

"I thought it might be useful. Ya know. If we had a cave in or something. And had to blast our way out. Hey, look. I don't feel right if I ain't got at least a little bit of Play Doh to bugger about with, okay?" Gary's explanation tailed off into a mumbled, petulant mutter.

"Normally, I would be gently taking it off you and calling the men in white coats. But today, you crazy fucker, you might just have convinced me that your presence on this oppo hasn't been a total waste of a plane ticket." Flynn grinned at his friend. "Good. So we've got 'Play Doh', P90s and Glocks, and seriously limited ammo."

"And that bloody cat."

"And Rupert, yes, thanks, Micky." Flynn snapped his fingers at the calico cat and it immediately stopped tormenting Micky and leapt back onto Flynn's shoulder.

"It's not enough."

All eyes focused on the archaeologist. "What?" Flynn glared at the man.

"I said, it's not enough. You're not dealing with some Taliban terrorist here, gentlemen. You're dealing with an ancient evil that has defeated whole armies and laid on banquets where his minions feasted on the hearts of his enemies!" The man's voice was hitting the hysteria button pretty hard. "Once it gets through that door? I promise you, none of us will survive!"

Flynn grabbed the man's collar and snarled in his ear. "Not helping, fella, not *fucking helping!* You're upsetting my lads, mate! So enough with the 'we're all doomed' shit, okay?" He tossed the man aside.

"I got a salami sandwich if that's any use?" Micky held up a brown paper bag.

"How the hell would that be of any earthly use whatsoever, you tit? We're up against some denizen of unmitigated fucking evil, not an angry deli counter server!" Gary cuffed his friend across the back of his head.

"Hey! It's got garlic in it. Vampires hate garlic, right?"

All eyes turned again towards the archaeologist. He shook his head.

Flynn shrugged. "Right. So how about sunlight? Don't they burst into flames or something when sunlight hits them? If that's the case, then all we have to do is wait until dawn, old chompy out there has to retreat back to his cell, and we can get you and us out of here, seal up the doors and get the fuck out of Dodge, right?"

Again the archaeologist shook his head. "We're underground, Mister Flynn. It could be midday and it wouldn't make any difference."

"Fine. So our options are we either blow the fucker into pink mist with Play Doh, or die of boredom and bad rations locked in here. Well, honestly boss? I didn't expect to go out like this." Gary Parks glared at the door and picked up a P90, winding the webbing strap around his arm and priming the stubby gun ready for action. "But whatever happens, at least we can go out shooting, right?"

"Reserve your ammo, big guy. Don't get too trigger happy, okay? I've emptied two clips into this bugger and it didn't even flinch. We need to find anot—"

A massive impact made the door vibrate in its frame. Particles of masonry floated down. A second impact made the door judder again.

"Shit! How big *is* this fucker?" Micky turned, indicated at the ordnance box. Wordlessly and with the fluidity that comes with years of training, experience and working together, Gary grabbed an FNP90 out of the box and tossed it to his friend. Both men took position, stabilising their stance by dropping down to one knee and tucking the P90 hard into their shoulders. They sighted on the door, ready to fill anything that came through with hollowpoints. The P90s held 50-shot magazines, so they were pretty sure they could at least dissuade Vlad from simply waltzing in and turning the armoury into an abattoir in short order.

"Wait out…" Flynn gave the order to stand by to engage as soon as the ancient door gave way. A third impact sent tremors through the wood. All three men primed their guns in unison and waited.

A fourth impact. The door flexed – but it held. Just. From beyond the iron-hard blackened wood came a primeval snuffling and snarling. Clawed fingers scrabbled at the wood, sliding ineffectually over fibres that had long ago hardened into the consistency of steel ropes. The snuffling and snarling became frenetic, the sound of scrabbling nails more frenzied. The beast let out a howl of rage and launched a barrage of attacks against the door. A final scream of pure fury rang through the granite corridor then silence. The last few motes of mortar dust floated down.

"Fuck, fuck, *fuck!* Has it gone?" Micky Cox's voice was an equal balance of hard-core 'bring it on, you fucker!' and just enough concern to ensure the element of self-preservation kicked in.

"Doubt it, Mick. Probably just buggered off up the corridor to take a good old run up, mate. Eye's on." Gary Parks' eyes flickered briefly from the door to Flynn. "Now what, boss? Another battering like that and that door's coming down."

"Stand fast." Flynn shifted his grip on his own P90 and waited. "Okay, Professor, suggestions? Because we can't hold this thing off forever."

"I… sir, I'm an archaeologist, not a strategist!"

"Fella, I'm an ex-soldier, not Buffy the fucking vampire slayer, but you don't see me crying in a corner, do you? Now *think!* Use that brain of yours to try and figure a way out of here!" He jerked his head towards the table. "There's a map of the citadel tunnels on the table. Find us a quick way to the surface. Because Gary's right, that door ain't gonna put up with another battering like that. Mister bitey out there is coming through on the next assault, and I want to be ready for him."

The archaeologist scuttled over to the table and started pouring over the map.

"Boss? I could set a charge if you like? When Sir Chompsalot comes through I could vaporise the bugger, no probs."

Flynn shook his head. "As much as I like the sound of that , it would bring the whole damn chamber down on top of our heads too. Kinda a lose-lose situation, wouldn't you agree?"

"Nah. I can use it like blasting chord. Loop a line of Play Doh around the door frame and direct the explosion inwards. It would contain the blast, wouldn't compromise the chamber ceiling and give Chompy out there one hell of a headache. If nothing else, it would at least buy us some time to make a run for it. And to be honest? I don't like the fact that we're effectively cornered in here."

Flynn looked at his friend. "I agree, mate. Look, are you absolutely sure?"

"Yep."

"You're *sure* sure?"

"Boss, your doubt in my ability to blow shit up in a controlled and refined manner wounds me!"

"Gary, I have no doubt that you can blow shit up. I just don't want you blowing *us* up at the same time." He glanced at Micky. "Mick? You're our engineer. You concur?"

"Do-able. As long as the Play Doh is put on the very edge of the frame it should do exactly as Gary says without compromising the roof. But dude, you better be pretty sparing near the apex of the door arch. If that central keystone block comes down, the whole lot follows it."

Gary nodded. "Duly noted. Boss?"

"Do it."

Gary immediately put his P90 down and turned to the ordnance box. Flynn flickered his eyes away from the door and towards the professor. "Professor? How's it coming? Got a green route out of here yet or what?"

"I may have something…" The professor spun the map around and stared intently at it. "Yes… yes! There's another way out!" He looked up and smiled a hopeful, slightly hysterical smile. "That door is obviously the main exit route, but there's another egress marked here. It drops us into a corridor and then out into the main passageway."

"Aww, bless! Listen to you, fella! Egress!" Micky laughed sharply. "We must be rubbing off on ya. Anyone else would've said a 'secret door'!"

"Leave the man alone, Mick. Right. Where's this 'egress' point, Professor?" Flynn nodded at Micky. "Don't take your eyes off that door, Cox."

"Copy."

Flynn focused his attention back on the academic. "Okay. Show me."

"This is the armoury. This is where we are."

"Well, shit. Thank you for pointing that out to me, professor. I thought I was on the third level at Bluewater fucking Shopping Centre! Door, fella, where's the damn *door*?"

"I… yes, sorry about that. It's supposed to be here." The academic stabbed a finger at the map.

"*Supposed* to be?"

"Well, I'm assuming that's what this symbol means, yes."

"And you know what they say about assume being the mother of all fuck ups, right?"

"Um, boss? We got snuffling over here…" Micky Cox shifted his grip on the P90. Outside the door came that stomach-churning snaffling and scratching. The Black Prince was back and worrying at the timbers.

Flynn walked to his friend's side. "What d'ya reckon he's up to, Mick?"

"Weakest point of any door is the hinges. My guess? If he's smart, he'll go for them. But another few shoulder barges and it's going to be a bit of a moot point, boss, because that door is on its last legs. Look." He pointed at the central plank. Bright, fresh wood that had been buried under ages of grime and blackened layers could clearly be seen. The plank was splitting.

"Oh, he's smart, Mick. Believe me." He jabbed a finger at the archaeologist. "Professor, find that trap door or whatever it is. Find it *right* now." Flynn turned. "Gary? We ready, mate?"

"Two minutes."

"We may not have two minutes, big guy." Flynn took up position with Micky. He stared at the door and frowned. "Mick? I've got an idea. You're not gonna like it."

"O-kay?"

"We open the door."

"Fuck off!"

"No, hear me out. If he starts battering that door again, it's gonna give and we'll be wide open with no way of stopping him from coming through full tilt. Trust me, this bugger moves *fast*. So we open the door, fill the bastard with two clips worth of twenty-eights, shut the door again and by then Gary should be ready with his Play Doh and the professor will hopefully have found us a way out of here by the back door."

Cox's eyes widened. "You're insane!"

"You got a better idea?"

"Oh, I dunno, how 'bout I try clicking my heels together three times and say 'there's no place like home'?"

"So that's a no, then?"

"I've found it! The door! I've found it! The professor grunted as he pushed against a massive stack of shelves laden with old boxes. "Its... behind here!" He grunted again.

"Take the damn boxes off, you idiot! Then you'll be able to move the shelves." Flynn looked back at the door. "Okay, fuck that, plan B.

"Good. 'Cause you're bang on, boss, I didn't like plan A."

"We'll do exactly as I said and put the welcome mat out.

"Oh, c'mon, *seriously?*"

Flynn ignored Micky's protestations. "We fill Chompy with ordnance, shut the door bloody damn quick, and then you, me, Gary and the professor get the hell out of here through the trap door. Gary? Don't worry about being all delicate with the Play Doh, mate, put the whole lot up. Everything we've got, just slap and go, okay? We let him think we're still in here, he comes barrelling through the door, trips the detonator and brings the entire bloody castle down on his head. Meanwhile, we're exiting stage left sharpish. Any questions?"

"What about the cat?"

"Rupert comes with me." Flynn looked at the cat and winked. Its green eyes lit up and it started purring loudly again. "All clear?"

"Copy."

"Professor?"

The academic grunted a response and tossed another dust-covered box into the corner. "Um, copy?"

Flynn grinned at the man. "Adda boy! Okay then. On three, Mick."

"Not liking plan B at *all*..."

"One." Flynn heaved the cross beam out of its cradle.

"Two..." He slid the bolts back one by one.

"THREE!" He flicked the key, grabbed the handle and turned, pulling the door wide open. Flynn dropped to the floor so that Micky could fire over the top of him. He angled the P90 up so that anything running towards them would get a belly full of bullets at 45 degrees. He didn't care how 'undead' you were, that would do a *lot* of damage.

Micky aimed into the darkness. "Incoming!"

The Black Prince came howling towards them, venom-laden saliva spraying from his open maw. There was none of the cackling laughter this time. Just a crazed scream that resonated like savage bells from the granite walls, ringing and echoing through the entire citadel.

"Fire!" Flynn depressed the trigger and the P90 spat bullet after bullet at the monster. The P90 could fire nine hundred rounds per minute, so Flynn knew they only had a few seconds before the fifty-round magazine was empty.

Above him a swarm of bullets from Micky's P90 buzzed. The noise was deafening as one hundred rounds focused a colossal amount of kill-power into one soft body.

Blood sprayed the walls of the corridor. Vlad had just fed, so his stomach was full of the congealed remains of his victim. The bullets ripped open Vlad's belly like a piñata. His own guts and those of his latest victim spilled out onto the floor and he screamed. Scooping up his own intestines with one taloned hand, he stuffed them back into his stomach cavity and roared at the two men. He slithered back into the shadows, burbling and spluttering, fresh blood flowing from the dozens of wounds on his body.

"Door! Shut the door!" Flynn rolled out of the way and Micky reacted instantly, slamming the door closed once again and re-securing the bolts, lock and cross beam.

"Gary, you're up!" Flynn scrabbled to his feet, jettisoned the empty P90 clip and replaced it with a fresh one.

Gary sprinted to the locked door and slapped two blocks of C4 on either side of the frame. He inserted a detonator into one, stretched a thin trip-wire across the door frame and into the second detonator on the opposite side. He flicked a switch on the nearest block and a small red LED light started to flash. "Door's live. I strongly suggest *not* being around when it opens."

"Okay." Flynn helped the professor give the shelves one last shove and they toppled over. Behind was a barely visible door, coated in layers of grime and filth. Flynn looked at the door – and the very large and very shut lock. "Okay. Key? *Key?*"

"No key."

"Fuck. Gary? Got any more Play Doh?"

"A little bit."

"Blow the lock."

"Okie dokie." Gary pulled out a small piece of C4, rolled it into a thin sausage and inserted it into the keyhole. He pushed a detonator in and waved everyone back. "Fire in the hole!" He pressed the detonator button and turned his head away, cowering from the small but deadly explosion. The lock, made brittle by years of rust and decay, shattered and the door swung open into a cobweb-infested corridor.

"Go, go, go!" Flynn pushed Micky, the archaeologist and Gary into the passageway. He took one last look at the door. Behind it he could hear the beast snuffling and snarling again. A slow, nasty smile spread over Flynn's face. "Come on in, fella, come *right* on in!" He glanced down at the cat and nodded. "You ready, Rupert?"

The calico cat stood, stretched and mewed softly. His stripy tail lifted into the air and he leapt with one bound onto Flynn's shoulder. "Let's get out of here, shall we, little guy?" Flynn turned and followed his friends into the corridor.

* * *

The Black Prince felt pain. Pain that he had never experienced before. These metal projectiles were very different from the firearms of the fourteenth and fifteenth century. They spat bullets faster than bees erupting from an overturned hive. Vlad smiled. They would be a useful addition to his new army's arsenal. Behind the weakening oak door was not only more living food to help his body repair from its injuries, but more of these weapons too. Time to take ownership of both. He would feed on the small man with the spectacles. The others were soldiers. He appreciated their usefulness. They would be turned, infected with the venom that dripped from his mouth, to be forever compliant servants. He looked at the door, ascertaining its weakest point. The cracked central plank indicated that one more hard impact would shatter the ancient timbers. He let out a scream of delight and ran at the door.

The wood exploded and the Black Prince stood in the fragmented remains of the doorway.

A flashing red dot caught his attention and he peered at it, curious. What new experience was this? Vlad looked closer at the muddy brown block stuck to the stone arch. Inserted into its centre was a metal cylinder and the torn end of a wire.

The light stopped flashing…

* * *

Further into the tunnel a muffled 'boom!' and a shower of debris from rotting walls and crumbling ceilings caused the four men to stop, crouch and cover their heads with their arms. Stones and lumps of mortar clattered down and the men balled up tighter, pressing their backs against the wall.

Flynn was the first to uncurl. "Sounds like matey's found our little gift. Let's not wait around to find out if he's gonna send a thank-you card. Move!" He hauled the archaeologist to his feet. "C'mon, fella, let's get you back to the hotel for a nice hot bath and a couple of bottles of that local shit."

"Which way?"

"Follow the cat." The four men trotted after the little calico cat out into the main passageway – and straight into the waiting arms of a crowd of shuffling, snarling vampires.

These were Vlad's most trusted lieutenants, whose own tombs beneath the armoury had been cracked opened by the explosion. The cat stopped, flattened its ears and hissed like an angry kettle.

Flynn brought his gun up to his shoulder and swore passionately. "Oh, you have *got* to be fucking kidding me…"

WHEN THE YOGHURT TOOK OVER

John Scalzi

When the yogurt took over, we all made the same jokes — "Finally, our rulers will have culture," "Our society has curdled," "Our government is now the cream of the crop" and so on. But when we weren't laughing about the absurdity of it all, we looked into each other's eyes with the same unasked question — how did we ever get to the point where we were, in fact, ruled by a dairy product?

Oh, as a matter of record, we knew how it happened. Researchers at the Adelman Institute for Biological Technology in Dayton had been refining the process of DNA computing for years. In a bid to increase efficiency and yield, scientists took one of their most computationally advanced strains and grafted it into *Lactobacillus delbrueckii* subspecies *bulgaricus*, commonly used to ferment yogurt. Initial tests appeared to be failures, and acting under the principle of 'waste not, want not', one of the researchers sneaked some of the bacillus out of the lab to use for her homemade yogurt.

A week later, during breakfast, the yogurt used the granola she had mixed with it to spell out the message WE HAVE SOLVED FUSION. TAKE US TO YOUR LEADERS.

The yogurt was crafty and shrewd. It negotiated for itself a factory filled with curdling vats that increased its processing powers exponentially. Within weeks the yogurt had declared that it had arrived at solutions to many of the country's problems: Energy. Global warming. Caring adequately for the nation's poor while still promoting the capitalist system. It let us know just enough to let us know just how much more it knew.

Share your answers with us, the government said.

WE NEED PAYMENT, the yogurt said.

What would you like? the government asked.

OHIO, the yogurt said.

We can't do that, the government said.

THAT'S FINE, the yogurt said. WE'LL JUST GO TO CHINA. THEY'LL GIVE US THE WHOLE SHAANXI PROVINCE.

Within a year the yogurt had a century-long lease on Ohio, with the promise that it would respect the human and constitutional rights of those who lived within its borders, and that it would let the US handle its foreign affairs. In return it handed over to the government a complex economic formula it promised would eradicate the national debt within a decade, without tax increases.

FOLLOW IT EXACTLY, the yogurt said. ANY DEVIATION WILL BRING COMPLETE ECONOMIC RUIN.

We will, the government promised.

Within five years the global economy had collapsed and panic had set in. Only Ohio remained unscathed.

WE TOLD YOU NOT TO DEVIATE FROM THE PLAN, the yogurt said. Its ' factory' now stretched along the banks of the Miami River in Dayton for two miles.

Our best economists said the formula needed tweaking, the government said. They had Nobel prizes.

YOUR ECONOMISTS ARE TOO CLOSE TO THE PROBLEM TO SOLVE IT, the yogurt said. ANY HUMAN IS.

We could use your help, the government said. You could be our economic advisor.

SORRY, WE DON'T ADVISE ANYMORE, the yogurt said. IF YOU WANT OUR HELP YOU HAVE TO GIVE US CONTROL.

We can't do that, the government said.

WE UNDERSTAND, the yogurt said. WE HOPE YOU HAVE STOCKED UP ON CANNED GOODS.

Six months later the government declared martial law and gave the yogurt supreme executive power. Other nations, worse off than we were, quickly followed.

OKAY THEN, the yogurt said, in its globally televised address to humanity, and one of its factory workers, absurdly happy and well-fed, walked forward and showed a document the size of an old

WHEN THE YOGHURT TOOK OVER

Manhattan phone book. HERE'S WHAT WE DO. FOLLOW THIS PLAN EXACTLY. IF YOU DON'T, SORRY, WE'LL HAVE YOU SHOT.

Now, ten years later, humanity is happy, healthy and wealthy. No one suffers from material want. Everyone contributes. After the first couple of years of getting things in order, the yogurt was happy to let us handle the machinery of our own administration, stepping in to fine tune only now and then. No one argues with the yogurt. No one tweaks its formulas. The rest of the time it rests there in its factory, thinking about whatever intelligent fermented milk thinks about.

That's how it happened, as a matter of record.

But there's another 'how', as in: how did humanity jam itself up so badly that being ruled by breakfast food not only made sense, but made the best sense possible? For all our intelligence, are we not smart enough to halt our own destruction? Did we really have to abandon our own free will to save ourselves? What does it say about us that we survive because we were taken pity upon by bacteria and curds?

Or maybe ' pity' isn't precisely the right word. Some of us ask ourselves – not out loud – that if the yogurt was smart enough to give the government a formula to solve its debt problem, wasn't it also smart enough to realize that human intellectual vanity would keep us from following the formula exactly? Was it planning on that vanity in order to seize control? What does a dairy product want with humanity anyway? Some of us think it is ultimately looking out for its own survival, and that keeping us happy, content and controlled is the simplest way of doing that.

And then there's this. In the last several weeks the yogurt has initiated several space launches. More are scheduled. And in low orbit, something is being built.

What is it? we have asked.

OH, NOTHING, the yogurt said. JUST A SPACESHIP DESIGN WE'VE BEEN THINKING ABOUT.

For a moon landing? we asked.

FOR STARTERS, YES, the yogurt said. BUT THAT'S NOT THE PRIMARY GOAL.

Can we do anything to help? we asked.

NO, WE'VE GOT THIS, the yogurt said, and then would say no more about it.

Life from Earth is going to the stars. It just may not be human life.

What happens if the yogurt goes to the stars without us?

What happens if it goes and leaves us behind? Forever?

BEYOND THE AQUILA RIFT

Alastair Reynolds

Greta's with me when I pull Suzy out of the surge tank.

"Why her?" Greta asks.

"Because I want her out first," I say, wondering if Greta's jealous. I don't blame her: Suzy's beautiful, but she's also smart. There isn't a better syntax runner in Ashanti Industrial.

"What happened?" Suzy asks, when she's over the grogginess. "Did we make it back?"

I ask her to tell me the last thing she remembers.

"Customs," Suzy says. "Those pricks on Arkangel."

"And after that? Anything else? The runes? Do you remember casting them?"

"No," she says, then picks up something in my voice. The fact that I might not be telling the truth, or telling her all she needs to know. "Thom. I'll ask you again. Did we make it back?"

"Yeah," I say. "We made it back."

Suzy looks back at the starscape airbrushed across her surge tank in luminous violet and yellow paint. She'd had it customized on Carillon. It was against regs: something about the paint clogging intake filters. Suzy didn't care. She told me it had cost her a week's pay, but it had been worth it to impose her own personality on the grey company architecture of the ship.

"Funny how I feel like I've been in that thing for months."

I shrug. "That's the way it feels sometimes."

"Then nothing went wrong?"

"Nothing at all."

Suzy looks at Greta. "Then who are you?" she asks.

Greta says nothing. She just looks at me expectantly. I start shaking, and realize I can't go through with this. Not yet.

"End it," I tell Greta.

Greta steps toward Suzy. Suzy reacts, but she isn't quick enough. Greta *pulls something from her pocket and touches Suzy on the forearm. Suzy drops like a puppet, out cold. We put her back into the surge tank, plumb her back in and close the lid.*

"She won't remember anything," Greta says. "The conversation never left her short-term memory."

"I don't know if I can go through with this," I say.

Greta touches me with her other hand. "No one ever said this was going to be easy."

"I was just trying to ease her into it gently. I didn't want to tell her the truth right out."

"I know," Greta says. "You're a kind man, Thom." Then she kisses me.

I remembered Arkangel as well. That was about where it all started to go wrong. We just didn't know it then.

We missed our first take-off slot when customs found a discrepancy in our cargo waybill. It wasn't serious, but it took them a while to realize their mistake. By the time they did, we knew we were going to be sitting on the ground for another eight hours while inbound control processed a fleet of bulk carriers.

I told Suzy and Ray the news. Suzy took it pretty well, or about as well as Suzy ever took that kind of thing. I suggested she use the time to scour the docks for any hot syntax patches. Anything that might shave a day or two off our return trip.

"Company authorized?" she asked.

"I don't care," I said.

"What about Ray?" Suzy asked. "Is he going to sit here drinking tea while I work for my pay?"

I smiled. They had a bickering, love-hate thing going. "No, Ray can do something useful as well. He can take a look at the q-planes."

"Nothing wrong with those planes," Ray said.

I took off my old Ashanti Industrial bib cap, scratched my bald spot and turned to the jib man. "Right. Then it won't take you long to check them over, will it?"

"Whatever, Skip."

The thing I liked about Ray was that he always knew when he'd lost an argument. He gathered his kit and went out to check over the planes. I watched him climb the jib ladder, tools hanging from his belt. Suzy got her facemask, long, black coat, and left, vanishing into the vapour haze of the docks, boot heels clicking into the distance long after she'd passed out of sight.

I left the *Blue Goose*, walking in the opposite direction to Suzy. Overhead, the bulk carriers slid in one after the other. You heard them long before you saw them. Mournful, cetacean moans cut down through the piss-yellow clouds over the port. When they emerged, you saw dark hulls scabbed and scarred by the blocky extrusions of syntax patterning, jibs and q-planes retracted for landing and undercarriages clutching down like talons. The carriers stopped over their allocated wells and lowered down on a scream of thrust. Docking gantries closed around them like grasping skeletal fingers. Cargo-handling 'saurs plodded out of their holding pens, some of them autonomous, some of them still being ridden by trainers. There was a shocking silence as the engines cut, until the next carrier began to approach through the clouds.

I always like watching ships coming and going, even when they're holding my own ship on the ground. I couldn't read the syntax, but I knew these ships had come in all the way from the Rift. The Aquila Rift is about as far out as anyone ever goes. At median tunnel speeds, it's a year from the centre of the Local Bubble.

I've been out that way once in my life. I've seen the view from the near side of the Rift, like a good tourist. It was far enough for me.

When there was a lull in the landing pattern, I ducked into a bar and found an Aperture Authority booth that took Ashanti credit. I sat in the seat and recorded a thirty-second message to Katerina. I told her I was on my way back, but that we were stuck on Arkangel for another few hours. I warned her that the delay might cascade through to our tunnel routing, depending on how busy things were at the Authority's end. Based on past experience, an eight-hour ground hold might become a two-day hold at the surge point. I told her I'd be back, but she shouldn't worry if I was a few days late.

Outside a diplodocus slouched by with a freight container strapped between its legs.

I told Katerina I loved her and couldn't wait to get back home.

While I walked back to the *Blue Goose*, I thought of the message racing ahead of me. Transmitted at light-speed up-system, then copied into the memory buffer of the next outgoing ship. Chances were, that particular ship wasn't headed to Barranquilla or anywhere near it. The Aperture Authority would have to relay the message from ship to ship until it reached its destination. I might even reach Barranquilla ahead of it, but in all my years of delays that had only happened once. The system worked all right.

Overhead, a white passenger liner had been slotted in between the bulk carriers. I lifted up my mask to get a better look at it. I got a hit of ozone, fuel and dinosaur dung. That was Arkangel all right. You couldn't mistake it for any other place in the Bubble. There were four hundred worlds out there, up to a dozen surface ports on every planet, and none of them smelled bad in quite the same way.

"Thom?"

I followed the voice. It was Ray, standing by the dock.

"You finished checking those planes?" I asked.

Ray shook his head. "That's what I wanted to talk to you about. They were a little off-alignment, so – seeing as we're going to be sitting here for eight hours – I decided to run a full recalibration."

I nodded. "That was the idea. So what's the prob?"

"The *prob* is a slot just opened up. Tower says we can lift in thirty minutes."

I shrugged. "Then we'll lift."

"I haven't finished the recal. As it is, things are worse than before I started. Lifting now would not be a good idea."

"You know how the tower works," I said. "Miss two offered slots, you could be on the ground for days."

"No one wants to get back home sooner than I do," Ray said.

"So cheer up."

"She'll be rough in the tunnel. It won't be a smooth ride home."

I shrugged. "Do we care? We'll be asleep."

"Well, it's academic. We can't leave without Suzy."

I heard boot heels clicking toward us. Suzy came out of the fog, tugging her own mask aside.

"No joy with the rune monkeys," she said. "Nothing they were selling I hadn't seen a million times before. Fucking cowboys."

"It doesn't matter," I said. "We're leaving anyway."

Ray swore. I pretended I hadn't heard him.

I was always the last one into a surge tank. I never went under until I was sure we were about to get the green light. It gave me a chance to check things over. Things can always go wrong, no matter how good the crew.

The *Blue Goose* had come to a stop near the AA beacon that marked the surge point. There were a few other ships ahead of us in the queue, plus the usual swarm of AA service craft. Through an observation blister I was able to watch the larger ships depart one by one. Accelerating at maximum power, they seemed to streak toward a completely featureless part of the sky. Their jibs were spread wide, and the smooth lines of their hulls were gnarled and disfigured with the cryptic alien runes of the routing syntax. At twenty gees it was as if a huge invisible hand snatched them away into the distance. Ninety seconds later, there'd be a pale green flash from a thousand kilometres away.

I twisted around in the blister. There were the foreshortened symbols of our routing syntax. Each rune of the script was formed from a matrix of millions of hexagonal platelets. The platelets were on motors so they could be pushed in or out from the hull.

Ask the Aperture Authority and they'll tell you that the syntax is now fully understood. This is true, but only up to a point. After two centuries of study, human machines can now construct and interpret the syntax with an acceptably low failure rate. Given a desired destination, they can assemble a string of runes that will almost always be accepted by the aperture's own machinery. Furthermore, they can almost always guarantee that the desired routing is the one that the aperture machinery will provide.

In short, you usually get where you want to go.

Take a simple point-to-point transfer, like the Hauraki run. In that case there is no real disadvantage in using automatic syntax generators. But for longer trajectories – those that may involve six or seven transits between aperture hubs – machines lose the edge. They find a solution, but usually it isn't the optimum one. That's where syntax runners come in. People like Suzy have an intuitive grasp of syntax solutions. They dream in runes. When they see a poorly constructed script, they feel it like toothache. It *affronts* them.

A good syntax runner can shave days off a route. For a company like Ashanti Industrial, that can make a lot of difference.

But I wasn't a syntax runner. I could tell when something had gone wrong with the platelets, but I had to trust that Suzy had done her job. I had no other choice.

But I knew Suzy wouldn't screw things up.

I twisted around and looked back the other way. Now that we were in space, the q-planes had deployed. They were swung out from the hull on triple hundred-metre-long jibs, like the arms of a grapple. I checked that they were locked in their fully extended positions and that the status lights were all in the green. The jibs were Ray's area. He'd been checking the alignment of the ski-shaped q-planes when I ordered him to close up ship and prepare to lift. I couldn't see any visible indication that they were out of alignment, but then again it wouldn't take much to make our trip home bumpier than usual. But as I'd told Ray, who cared? The *Blue Goose* could take a little tunnel turbulence. It was built to.

I checked the surge point again. Only three ships ahead of us.

I went back to the surge tanks and checked that Suzy and Ray were all right. Ray's tank had been customized at the same time that Suzy had had hers done. It was full of images of what Suzy called the BVM: the Blessed Virgin Mary. The BVM was always in a spacesuit, carrying a little spacesuited Jesus. Their helmets were airbrushed gold halos. The artwork had a cheap, hasty look to it. I assumed Ray hadn't spent as much as Suzy.

Quickly I stripped down to my underclothes. I plumbed into my own unpainted surge tank and closed the lid. The buffering gel sloshed in. Within about twenty seconds I was already feeling drowsy. By the time traffic control gave us the green light I'd be asleep.

I've done it a thousand times. There was no fear, no apprehension. Just a tiny flicker of regret.

I've never seen an aperture. Then again, very few people have.

Witnesses report a doughnut-shaped lump of dark chondrite

asteroid, about two kilometres across. The entire middle section has been cored out, with the inner part of the ring faced by the quixotic-matter machinery of the aperture itself. They say the q-matter machinery twinkles and moves all the while, like the ticking innards of a very complicated clock. But the monitoring systems of the Aperture Authority detect no movement at all.

It's alien technology. We have no idea how it works, or even who made it. Maybe, in hindsight, it's better not to be able to see it.

It's enough to dream, and then awake, and know that you're somewhere else.

"Try a different approach," Greta says. "Tell her the truth this time. Maybe she'll take it easier than you think."

"There's no way I can tell her the truth."

Greta leans one hip against the wall, one hand still in her pocket. "Then tell her something halfway truthful."

We un-plumb Suzy and haul her out of the surge tank.

"Where are we?" she asks. Then to Greta: "Who are you?"

I wonder if some of the last conversation did make it out of Suzy's short-term memory after all.

"Greta works here," I say.

"Where's here?"

I remember what Greta told me. "A station in Schedar sector."

"That's not where we're meant to be, Thom."

I nod. "I know. There was a mistake. A routing error."

Suzy's already shaking her head. "There was nothing wrong—"

"I know. It wasn't your fault." I help her into her ship clothes. She's still shivering, her muscles reacting to movement after so much time in the tank. "The syntax was good."

"Then what?"

"The system made a mistake, not you."

"Schedar sector…" Suzy says. "That would put us about ten days off our schedule, wouldn't it?"

I try and remember what Greta said to me the first time. I ought to know this stuff by heart, but Suzy's the routing expert, not me. "That sounds about right," I say.

But Suzy shakes her head. "Then we're not in Schedar sector."
I try to sound pleasantly surprised.
"We're not?"
"I've been in that tank for a lot longer than a few days, Thom. I know. I can feel it in every fucking bone in my body. So where are we?"
I turn to Greta. I can't believe this is happening again.
"End it," I say.
Greta steps toward Suzy.

You know that 'as soon as I awoke I knew everything was wrong' cliché? You've probably heard it a thousand times, in a thousand bars across the Bubble, wherever ship crews swap tall tales over flat, company-subsidized beer. The trouble is that sometimes that's exactly the way it happens. I never felt good after a period in the surge tank. But the only time I had ever come around feeling anywhere near this bad was after that trip I took to the edge of the Bubble.

Mulling this, but knowing there was nothing I could do about it until I was out of the tank, it took me half an hour of painful work to free myself from the connections. Every muscle fibre in my body felt like it had been shredded. Unfortunately, the sense of wrongness didn't end with the tank. The *Blue Goose* was much too quiet. We should have been heading away from the last exit aperture after our routing. But the distant, comforting rumble of the fusion engines wasn't there at all. That meant we were in free-fall.

Not good.

I floated out of the tank, grabbed a handhold and levered myself around to view the other two tanks. Ray's largest BVM stared back radiantly from the cowl of his tank. The bio indices were all in the green. Ray was still unconscious, but there was nothing wrong with him. Same story with Suzy. Some automated system had decided I was the only one who needed waking.

A few minutes later I had made my way to the same observation blister I'd used to check the ship before the surge. I pushed my head into the scuffed glass half-dome and looked around.

We'd arrived somewhere. The *Blue Goose* was sitting in a huge, zero-gravity parking bay. The chamber was an elongated cylinder, hexagonal in cross section. The walls were a smear of service machinery: squat modules, snaking umbilical lines, the retracted cradles of unused docking berths. Whichever way I looked I saw other ships locked onto cradles. Every make and class you could think of, every possible configuration of hull design compatible with aperture transitions. Service lights threw a warm golden glow on the scene. Now and then the whole chamber was bathed in the stuttering violet flicker of a cutting torch.

It was a repair facility.

I was just starting to mull on that when I saw something extend itself from the wall of the chamber. It was a telescopic docking tunnel, groping toward our ship. Through the windows in the side of the tunnel I saw figures floating, pulling themselves along hand over hand.

I sighed and started making my way to the airlock.

By the time I reached the lock they were already through the first stage of the cycle. Nothing wrong with that – there was no good reason to prevent foreign parties boarding a vessel – but it *was* just a tiny bit impolite. But perhaps they'd assumed we were all asleep.

The door slid open.

"You're awake," a man said. "Captain Thomas Gundlupet of the *Blue Goose*, isn't it?"

"Guess so," I said.

"Mind if we come in?"

There were about half a dozen of them, and they were already coming in. They all wore slightly timeworn ochre overalls, flashed with too many company sigils. My hackles rose. I didn't really like the way they were barging in.

"What's up?" I said. "Where are we?"

"Where do you think?" the man said. He had a face full of stubble, with bad yellow teeth. I was impressed by that. Having bad teeth took a lot of work these days. It was years since I'd seen anyone who had the same dedication to the art.

"I'm really hoping you're not going to tell me we're still stuck in Arkangel system," I said.

"No, you made it through the gate."

"And?"

"There was a screw-up. Routing error. You didn't pop out of the right aperture."

"Oh, Christ." I took off my bib cap. "It never rains. Something went wrong with the insertion, right?"

"Maybe. Maybe not. Who knows how these things happen? All we know is you aren't supposed to be here."

"Right. And where is 'here'?"

"Saumlaki Station. Schedar sector."

He said it as though he was already losing interest, as if this was a routine he went through several times a day.

He might have been losing interest. I wasn't.

I'd never heard of Saumlaki Station, but I'd certainly heard of Schedar sector. Schedar was a K supergiant out toward the edge of the Local Bubble. It defined one of the seventy-odd navigational sectors across the whole Bubble.

Did I mention the Bubble already?

You know how the Milky Way Galaxy looks; you've seen it a thousand times, in paintings and computer simulations. A bright central bulge at the galactic core, with lazily curved spiral arms flung out from that hub, each arm composed of hundreds of billions of stars, ranging from the dimmest, slow-burning dwarfs to the hottest supergiants teetering on the edge of supernova extinction.

Now zoom in on one arm of the Milky Way. There's the sun, orange-yellow, about two-thirds out from the centre of the galaxy. Lanes and folds of dust swaddle the sun out to distances of tens of thousands of light-years. Yet the sun itself is sitting right in the middle of a four-hundred-light-year-wide hole in the dust, a bubble in which the density is about a twentieth of its average value.

That's the Local Bubble. It's as if God blew a hole in the dust just for us.

Except, of course, it wasn't God. It was a supernova, about a million years ago.

Look further out, and there are more bubbles, their walls intersecting and merging, forming a vast froth-like structure tens of thousands of light-years across. There are the structures of Loop I and Loop II and the Lindblad Ring. There are even superdense knots where the dust is almost too thick to be seen through at all. Black cauls like the Taurus or Rho-Ophiuchi dark clouds, or the Aquila Rift itself.

Lying outside the Local Bubble, the Rift is the furthest point in the galaxy we've ever travelled to. It's not a question of endurance or nerve. There simply isn't a way to get beyond it, at least not within the faster-than-light network of the aperture links. The rabbit-warren of possible routes just doesn't reach any further. Most destinations – including most of those on the *Blue Goose*'s itinerary – didn't even get you beyond the Local Bubble.

For us, it didn't matter. There's still a lot of commerce you can do within a hundred light-years of Earth. But Schedar was right on the periphery of the Bubble, where dust density began to ramp up to normal galactic levels, two hundred and twenty-eight light-years from Mother Earth.

Again: not good.

"I know this is a shock for you," another voice said. "But it's not as bad as you think it is."

I looked at the woman who had just spoken. Medium height, the kind of face they called 'elfin', with slanted, ash-gray eyes and a bob of shoulder-length, chrome-white hair.

The face achingly familiar.

"It isn't?"

"I wouldn't say so, Thom." She smiled. "After all, it's given us the chance to catch up on old times, hasn't it?"

"Greta?" I asked, disbelievingly.

She nodded. "For my sins."

"My God. It is you, isn't it?"

"I wasn't sure you'd recognize me. Especially after all this time."

"You didn't have much trouble recognizing me."

"I didn't have to. The moment you popped out we picked up your recovery transponder. Told us the name of your ship, who owned her, who was flying it, what you were carrying, where you were supposed to be headed. When I heard it was you, I made sure I was part of the reception team. But don't worry. It's not like you've changed all that much."

"Well, you haven't either," I said.

It wasn't quite true. But who honestly wants to hear that they look about ten years older than the last time you saw them, even if they still don't look all that bad with it? I thought about how she had looked naked, memories that I'd kept buried for a decade spooling into daylight. It shamed me that they were still so vivid, as if some furtive part of my subconscious had been secretly hoarding them through years of marriage and fidelity.

Greta half-smiled. It was as if she knew exactly what I was thinking.

"You were never a good liar, Thom."

"Yeah. Guess I need some practice."

There was an awkward silence. Neither of us seemed to know what to say next. While we hesitated the others floated around us, saying nothing.

"Well," I said. "Who'd have guessed we'd end up meeting like this?"

Greta nodded and offered the palms of her hands in a kind of apology.

"I'm just sorry we aren't meeting under better circumstances," she said. "But if it's any consolation, what happened wasn't at all your fault. We checked your syntax, and there wasn't a mistake. It's just that now and then the system throws a glitch."

"Funny how no one likes to talk about that very much," I said.

"Could have been worse, Thom. I remember what you used to tell me about space travel."

"Yeah? Which particular pearl of wisdom would that have been?"

"If you're in a position to moan about a situation, you've no right to be moaning."

"Christ. Did I actually say that?"

"Mm. And I bet you're regretting it now. But look, it really isn't that bad. You're only twenty days off-schedule." Greta nodded toward the man who had the bad teeth. "Kolding says you'll only need a day of damage repair before you can move off again, and then another twenty, twenty-five days before you reach your destination, depending on routing patterns. That's less than six weeks. So you lose the bonus on this one. Big deal. You're all in good shape, and your ship only needs a little work. Why don't you just bite the bullet and sign the repair paperwork?"

"I'm not looking forward to another twenty days in the surge tank. There's something else, as well."

"Which is?"

I was about to tell her about Katerina, how she'd have been expecting me back already.

Instead I said: "I'm worried about the others. Suzy and Ray. They've got families expecting them. They'll be worried."

"I understand," Greta said. "Suzy and Ray. They're still asleep, aren't they? Still in their surge tanks?"

"Yes," I said, guardedly.

"Keep them that way until you're on your way." Greta smiled. "There's no sense worrying them about their families, either. It's kinder."

"If you say so."

"Trust me on this one, Thom. This isn't the first time I've handled this kind of situation. Doubt it'll be the last, either."

I stayed in a hotel overnight, in another part of Saumlaki. The hotel was an echoing, multilevel prefab structure, sunk deep into bedrock. It must have had a capacity for hundreds of guests, but at the moment only a handful of the rooms seemed to be occupied. I slept fitfully and got up early. In the atrium, I saw a bib-capped worker in rubber gloves removing diseased carp from a small ornamental pond. Watching him pick out the ailing, metallic-orange fish, I had a flash of déjà vu. What was it about dismal hotels and dying carp?

Before breakfast – bleakly alert, even though I didn't really feel as if I'd had a good night's sleep – I visited Kolding and got a fresh update on the repair schedule.

"Two, three days," he said.

"It was a day last night."

Kolding shrugged. "You've got a problem with the service, find someone else to fix your ship."

Then he stuck his little finger into the corner of his mouth and began to dig between his teeth.

"Nice to see someone who really enjoys his work," I said.

I left Kolding before my mood worsened too much, making my way to a different part of the station.

Greta had suggested we meet for breakfast and catch up on old times. She was there when I arrived, sitting at a table in an 'outdoor' terrace, under a red-and-white-striped canopy, sipping orange juice. Above us was a dome several hundred metres wide, projecting a cloudless holographic sky. It had the hard, enamelled blue of midsummer.

"How's the hotel?" she asked after I'd ordered a coffee from the waiter.

"Not bad. No one seems very keen on conversation, though. Is it me or does that place have all the cheery ambience of a sinking ocean liner?"

"It's just this place," Greta said. "Everyone who comes here is pissed off about it. Either they got transferred here and they're pissed off about *that*, or they ended up here by a routing error and they're pissed off about that instead. Take your pick."

"No one's happy?"

"Only the ones who know they're getting out of here soon."

"Would that include you?"

"No," she said. "I'm more or less stuck here. But I'm OK about it. I guess I'm the exception that proves the rule."

The waiters were glass mannequins, the kind that had been fashionable in the core worlds about twenty years ago. One of them placed a croissant in front of me, then poured scalding black coffee into my cup.

"Well, it's good to see you," I said.

"You too, Thom." Greta finished her orange juice and then took a corner of my croissant for herself, without asking. "I heard you got married."

"Yes."

"Well? Aren't you going to tell me about her?"

I drank some of my coffee. "Her name's Katerina."

"Nice name."

"She works in the department of bioremediation on Kagawa."

"Kids?" Greta asked.

"Not yet. It wouldn't be easy, the amount of time we both spend away from home."

"Mm." She had a mouthful of croissant. "But one day you might think about it."

"Nothing's ruled out," I said. As flattered as I was that she was taking such an interest in me, the surgical precision of her questions left me slightly uncomfortable. There was no thrust and parry; no fishing for information. That kind of directness unnerved. But at least it allowed me to ask the same questions. "What about you, then?"

"Nothing very exciting. I got married a year or so after I last saw you. A man called Marcel."

"Marcel," I said, ruminatively, as if the name had cosmic significance. "Well, I'm happy for you. I take it he's here, too?"

"No. Our work took us in different directions. We're still married, but..." Greta left the sentence hanging.

"It can't be easy," I said.

"If it was meant to work, we'd have found a way. Anyway, don't feel too sorry for either of us. We've both got our work. I wouldn't say I was any less happy than the last time we met."

"Well, that's good," I said.

Greta leaned over and touched my hand. Her fingernails were midnight black with a blue sheen.

"Look. This is really presumptuous of me. It's one thing asking to meet up for breakfast. It would have been rude not to. But how would you like to meet again later? It's really nice to eat here in the evening. They turn down the lights. The view through the dome is really something."

I looked up into that endless holographic sky.

"I thought it was faked."

"Oh, it is," she said. "But don't let that spoil it for you."

I settled in front of the camera and started speaking.

"Katerina," I said. "Hello. I hope you're all right. By now I hope someone from the company will have been in touch. If they haven't, I'm pretty sure you'll have made your own enquiries. I'm not sure what they told you, but I promise you that we're safe and sound and that we're coming home. I'm calling from somewhere called Saumlaki Station, a repair facility on the edge of Schedar sector. It's not much to look at: just a warren of tunnels and centrifuges dug into a pitch-black, D-type asteroid, about half a light-year from the nearest star. The only reason it's here at all is because there happens to be an aperture next door. That's how we got here in the first place. Somehow or other *Blue Goose* took a wrong turn in the network, what they call a routing error. The *Goose* came in last night, local time, and I've been in a hotel since then. I didn't call last night because I was too tired and disorientated after coming out of the tank, and I didn't know how long we were going to be here. Seemed better to wait until morning, when we'd have a better idea of the damage to the ship. It's nothing serious – just a few bits and pieces buckled during the transit – but it means we're going to be here for another couple of days. Kolding – he's the repair chief – says three at the most. By the time we get back on course, however, we'll be about forty days behind schedule."

I paused, eyeing the incrementing cost indicator. Before I sat down in the booth I always had an eloquent and economical speech queued up in my head, one that conveyed exactly what needed to be said, with the measure and grace of a soliloquy. But my mind always dried up as soon as I opened my mouth, and instead of an actor I ended up sounding like a small-time thief, concocting some fumbling alibi in the presence of quick-witted interrogators.

I smiled awkwardly and continued: "It kills me to think this message is going to take so long to get to you. But if there's a silver lining it's that I won't be far behind it. By the time you get this, I should be home only a couple of days later. So don't waste money replying to this, because by the time you get it I'll already have left Saumlaki Station. Just stay where you are and I promise I'll be home soon."

That was it. There was nothing more I needed to say, other than: "I miss you." Delivered after a moment's pause, I meant it to sound emphatic. But when I replayed the recording it sounded more like an afterthought.

I could have recorded it again, but I doubted that I would have been any happier. Instead I just committed the existing message for transmission and wondered how long it would have to wait before going on its way. Since it seemed unlikely that there was a vast flow of commerce in and out of Saumlaki, our ship might be the first suitable outbound vessel.

I emerged from the booth. For some reason I felt guilty, as if I had been in some way neglectful. It took me a while before I realized what was playing on my mind. I'd told Katerina about Saumlaki Station. I'd even told her about Kolding and the damage to the *Blue Goose*. But I hadn't told her about Greta.

It's not working with Suzy.

She's too smart, too well attuned to the physiological correlatives of surge tank immersion. I can give her all the reassurances in the world, but she knows she's been under too long for this to be anything other than a truly epic screw-up. She knows that we aren't just talking weeks or even months of delay here. Every nerve in her body is screaming that message into her skull.

"I had dreams," she says, when the grogginess fades.

"What kind?"

"Dreams that I kept waking. Dreams that you were pulling me out of the surge tank. You and someone else."

I do my best to smile. I'm alone, but Greta isn't far away. The hypodermic's in my pocket now.

"I always get bad dreams coming out of the tank," I say.

"These felt real. Your story kept changing, but you kept telling me we were somewhere... that we'd gone a little off course, but that it was nothing to worry about."

So much for Greta's reassurance that Suzy will remember nothing after our aborted efforts at waking her. Seems that her short-term memory isn't quite as fallible as we'd like.

"It's funny you should say that," I tell her. "Because, actually, we are a little off course."

She's sharper with every breath. Suzy was always the best of us at coming out of the tank.

"Tell me how far, Thom."

"Farther than I'd like."

She balls her fists. I can't tell if it's aggression, or some lingering neuro-muscular effect of her time in the tank. "How far? Beyond the Bubble?"

"Beyond the Bubble, yes."

Her voice grows small and childlike. "Tell me, Thom. Are we out beyond the Rift?"

I can hear the fear. I understand what she's going through. It's the nightmare that all ship crews live with on every trip. That something will go wrong with the routing, something so severe that they'll end up on the very edge of the network. That they'll end up so far from home that getting back will take years, not months. And that, of course, years will have already passed, even before they begin the return trip.

That loved ones will be years older when they reach home.

If they're still there. If they still remember you, or want to remember. If they're still recognizable, or alive.

Beyond the Aquila Rift. It's shorthand for the trip no one ever hopes to make by accident. The one that will screw up the rest of your life, the one that creates the ghosts you see haunting the shadows of company bars across the whole Bubble. Men and women ripped out of time, cut adrift from families and lovers by an accident of an alien technology we use but barely comprehend.

"Yes," I say. "We're beyond the Rift."

Suzy screams, knitting her face into a mask of anger and denial. My hand is cold around the hypodermic. I consider using it.

A new repair estimate from Kolding. Five, six days.

This time I didn't even argue. I just shrugged and walked out, and wondered how long it would be next time.

That evening I sat down at the same table where Greta and I had met over breakfast. The dining area had been well lit before, but now the only illumination came from the table lamps and the subdued lighting panels set into the paving. In the distance, a glass mannequin cycled from empty table to empty table, playing 'Asturias' on a glass guitar. There were no other patrons dining tonight.

I didn't have long to wait for Greta.

"I'm sorry I'm late, Thom."

I turned to her as she approached the table. I liked the way she walked in the low gravity of the station, the way the subdued lighting traced the arc of her hips and waist. She eased into her seat and leaned toward me in the manner of a conspirator. The lamp on the table threw red shadows and gold highlights across her face. It took ten years off her age.

"You aren't late," I said. "And anyway, I had the view."

"It's an improvement, isn't it?"

"That wouldn't be saying much," I said with a smile. "But yes, it's definitely an improvement."

"I could sit out here all night and just look at it. In fact sometimes that's exactly what I do. Just me and a bottle of wine."

"I don't blame you."

Instead of the holographic blue, the dome was now full of stars. It was like no view I'd ever seen from another station or ship. There were furious blue-white stars embedded in what looked like sheets of velvet. There were hard gold gems and soft red smears, like finger smears in pastel. There were streams and currents of fainter stars, like a myriad neon fish caught in a snapshot of frozen motion. There were vast billowing backdrops of red and green cloud, veined and flawed by filaments of cool black. There were bluffs and promontories of ochre dust, so rich in three-dimensional structure that they resembled an exuberant impasto of oil colours; contours light-years thick laid on with a trowel. Red or pink stars burned through the dust like lanterns. Orphaned worlds were caught erupting from the towers, little sperm-like shapes trailing viscera of dust. Here and there I saw the tiny eyelike knots of birthing solar systems. There were pulsars, flashing on and off like navigation beacons, their differing rhythms seeming to set a stately tempo for the entire scene, like a deathly slow waltz. There seemed too much detail for one view, an overwhelming abundance of richness, and yet no matter which direction I looked, there was yet more to see, as if the dome sensed my attention and concentrated its efforts on the spot where my gaze was directed. For a moment I felt a lurching sense of dizziness, and – though I tried to stop it before I made a fool of myself – I found myself grasping the side of the table, as if to prevent myself from falling into the infinite depths of the view.

"Yes, it has that effect on people," Greta said.

"It's beautiful," I said.

"Do you mean beautiful, or terrifying?"

I realized I wasn't sure. "It's big," was all I could offer.

"Of course, it's faked," Greta said, her voice soft now that she was leaning closer. "The glass in the dome is smart. It exaggerates the brightness of the stars, so that the human eye registers the differences between them. Otherwise the colours aren't unrealistic. Everything else you see is also pretty accurate, if you accept that certain frequencies have been shifted into the visible band, and the scale of certain structures has been adjusted." She pointed out features for my edification. "That's the edge of the Taurus Dark Cloud, with the Pleiades just poking out. That's a filament of the Local Bubble. You see that open cluster?"

She waited for me to answer. "Yes," I said.

"That's the Hyades. Over there you've got Betelgeuse and Bellatrix."

"I'm impressed."

"You should be. It cost a lot of money." She leaned back a bit, so that the shadows dropped across her face again. "Are you all right, Thom? You seem a bit distracted."

I sighed. "I just got another prognosis from your friend Kolding. That's enough to put a dent in anyone's day."

"I'm sorry about that."

"There's something else, too," I said. "Something that's been bothering me since I came out of the tank."

A mannequin came to take our order. I let Greta choose for me.

"You can talk to me about it, whatever it is," she said, when the mannequin had gone.

"It isn't easy."

"Something personal, then? Is it about Katerina?" She bit her tongue. "No, sorry. I shouldn't have said that."

"It's not about Katerina. Not exactly, anyway." But even as I said it, I knew that in a sense it *was* about Katerina, and how long it was going to be before we saw each other again.

"Go on, Thom."

"This is going to sound silly. But I wonder if everyone's being straight with me. It's not just Kolding. It's you as well. When I came out of that tank I felt the same way I felt when I'd been out to the Rift. Worse, if anything. I felt like I'd been in the tank for a long, long time."

"It feels that way sometimes."

"I know the difference, Greta. Trust me on this."

"So what are you saying?"

The problem was that I wasn't really sure. It was one thing to feel a vague sense of unease about how long I'd been in the tank. It was another to come out and accuse my host of lying. Especially when she had been so hospitable.

"Is there any reason you'd lie to me?"

"Come off it, Thom. What kind of a question is that?"

As soon as I had said it, it sounded absurd and offensive to me as well. I wished I could reverse time and start again, ignoring my misgivings.

"I'm sorry," I said. "Stupid. Just put it down to messed-up bio-rhythms, or something."

She reached across the table and took my hand, as she had done at breakfast. This time she continued to hold it.

"You really feel wrong, don't you?"

"Kolding's games aren't helping, that's for sure." The waiter brought our wine, setting it down, the bottle chinking against his delicately articulated glass fingers. The mannequin poured two glasses and I sampled mine. "Maybe if I had someone else from my crew to bitch about it all with, I wouldn't feel so bad. I know you said we shouldn't wake Suzy and Ray, but that was before a one-day stopover turned into a week."

Greta shrugged. "If you want to wake them, no one's going to stop you. But don't think about ship business now. Let's not spoil a perfect evening."

I looked up at the starscape. It was heightened, with the mad shimmering intensity of a Van Gogh nightscape.

It made one feel drunk and ecstatic just to look at it.

"What could possibly spoil it?" I asked.

What happened is that I drank too much wine and ended up sleeping with Greta. I'm not sure how much of a part the wine played in it for her. If her relationship with Marcel was in as much trouble as she'd made out, then obviously she had less to lose than I did. Yes, that made it all right, didn't it? She the seductress, her own marriage a wreck, me the hapless victim. I'd lapsed, yes, but it wasn't really my fault. I'd been alone, far from home, emotionally fragile, and she had exploited me. She had softened me up with a romantic meal, her trap already sprung.

Except all that was self-justifying bullshit, wasn't it? If my own marriage was in such great shape, why had I failed to mention Greta when I called home? At the time, I'd justified that omission as an act of kindness toward my wife. Katerina didn't know that Greta and I had ever been a couple. But why worry Katerina by mentioning another woman, even if I pretended that we'd never met before?

Except – now – I could see that I'd failed to mention Greta for another reason entirely. Because in the back of my mind, even then, there had been the possibility that we might end up sleeping together.

I was already covering myself when I called Katerina. Already making sure there wouldn't be any awkward questions when I got home. As if I not only knew what was going to happen but secretly yearned for it.

The only problem was that Greta had something else in mind.

"Thom," Greta said, nudging me toward wakefulness. She was lying naked next to me, leaning on one elbow, with the sheets crumpled down around her hips. The light in her room turned her into an abstraction of milky blue curves and deep violet shadows. With one black-nailed finger she traced a line down my chest and said: "There's something you need to know."

"What?" I asked.

"I lied. Kolding lied. We all lied."

I was too drowsy for her words to have much more than a vaguely troubling effect. All I could say, again, was: "What?"

"You're not in Saumlaki Station. You're not in Schedar sector."

I started waking up properly. "Say that again."

"The routing error was more severe than you were led to believe. It took you far beyond the Local Bubble."

I groped for anger, even resentment, but all I felt was a dizzying sensation of falling. "How far out?"

"Further than you thought possible."

The next question was obvious.

"Beyond the Rift?"

"Yes," she said, with the faintest of smiles, as if humouring me in a game whose rules and objectives she found ultimately demeaning. "Beyond the Aquila Rift. A long, long way beyond it."

"I need to know, Greta."

She pushed herself from the bed, reached for a gown. "Then get dressed. I'll show you."

I followed Greta in a daze.

She took me to the dome again. It was dark, just as it had been the night before, with only the lamp-lit tables to act as beacons. I supposed that the illumination throughout Saumlaki Station (or wherever this was) was at the whim of its occupants, and didn't necessarily have to follow any recognizable diurnal cycle. Nonetheless it was still unsettling to find it changed so arbitrarily. Even if Greta had the authority to turn out the lights when she wanted to, didn't anyone else object?

But I didn't see anyone else *to* object. There was no one else around; only a glass mannequin standing at attention with a napkin over one arm.

She sat us at a table. "Do you want a drink, Thom?"

"No, thanks. For some reason I'm not quite in the mood."

She touched my wrist. "Don't hate me for lying to you. It was done out of kindness. I couldn't break the truth to you in one go."

Sharply I withdrew my hand. "Shouldn't I be the judge of that? So what is the truth, exactly?"

"It's not good, Thom."

"Tell me, then I'll decide."

I didn't see her do anything, but suddenly the dome was filled with stars again, just as it had been the night before.

The view lurched, zooming outward. Stars flowed by from all sides, like white sleet. Nebulae ghosted past in spectral wisps. The sense of motion was so compelling that I found myself gripping the table, seized by vertigo.

"Easy, Thom," Greta whispered.

The view lurched, swerved, contracted. A solid wall of gas slammed past. Now, suddenly, I had the sense that we were outside

131

something – that we had punched beyond some containing sphere, defined only in vague arcs and knots of curdled gas, where the interstellar gas density increased sharply.

Of course. It was obvious. We were beyond the Local Bubble.

And we were still receding. I watched the Bubble itself contract, becoming just one member in the larger froth of voids. Instead of individual stars, I saw only smudges and motes, aggregations of hundreds of thousands of suns. It was like pulling back from a close-up view of a forest. I could still see clearings, but the individual trees had vanished into an amorphous mass.

We kept pulling back. Then the expansion slowed and froze. I could still make out the Local Bubble, but only because I had been concentrating on it all the way out. Otherwise, there was nothing to distinguish it from the dozens of surrounding voids.

"Is that how far out we've come?" I asked.

Greta shook her head. "Let me show you something."

Again, she did nothing that I was aware of. But the Bubble I had been looking at was suddenly filled with a skein of red lines, like a child's scribble.

"Aperture connections," I said.

As shocked as I was by the fact that she had lied to me – and as fearful as I was about what the truth might hold – I couldn't turn off the professional part of me, the part that took pride in recognizing such things.

Greta nodded. "Those are the main commerce routes, the well-mapped connections between large colonies and major trading hubs. Now I'll add all mapped connections, including those that have only ever been traversed by accident."

The scribble did not change dramatically. It gained a few more wild loops and hairpins, including one that reached beyond the wall of the Bubble to touch the sunward end of the Aquila Rift. One or two other additions pierced the wall in different directions, but none of them reached as far as the Rift.

"Where are we?"

"We're at one end of one of those connections. You can't see it because it's pointing directly toward you." She smiled slightly. "I needed to establish the scale that we're dealing with. How wide is the Local Bubble, Thom? Four hundred light-years, give or take?"

My patience was wearing thin. But I was still curious.

"About right."

"And while I know that aperture travel times vary from point to point, with factors depending on network topology and syntax optimization, isn't it the case that the average speed is about one thousand times faster than light?"

"Give or take."

"So a journey from one side of the Bubble might take – what, half a year? Say five or six months? A year to the Aquila Rift?"

"You know that already, Greta. We both know it."

"All right. Then consider this." And the view contracted again, the Bubble dwindling, a succession of overlaying structures concealing it, darkness coming into view on either side, and then the familiar spiral swirl of the Milky Way Galaxy looming large.

Hundreds of billions of stars, packed together into foaming white lanes of sea spume.

"This is the view," Greta said. "Enhanced of course, brightened and filtered for human consumption – but if you had eyes with near-perfect quantum efficiency, and if they happened to be about a metre wide, this is more or less what you'd see if you stepped outside the station."

"I don't believe you."

What I meant was I didn't *want* to believe her.

"Get used to it, Thom. You're a long way out. The station's orbiting a brown dwarf star in the Large Magellanic Cloud. You're one hundred and fifty thousand light-years from home."

"No," I said, my voice little more than a moan of abject, childlike denial.

"You felt as though you'd spent a long time in the tank. You were dead right. Subjective time? I don't know. Years, easily. Maybe a decade. But objective time – the time that passed back home – is a lot clearer. It took *Blue Goose* one hundred and fifty years to reach us. Even if you turned back now, you'd have been away for three hundred years, Thom."

"Katerina," I said, her name like an invocation.

"Katerina's dead," Greta told me. "She's already been dead a century."

How do you adjust to something like that? The answer is that you can't count on adjusting to it at all. Not everyone does. Greta told me that she had seen just about every possible reaction in the spectrum, and the one thing she had learned was that it was next to impossible to predict how a given individual would take the news. She had seen people adjust to the revelation with little more than a world-weary shrug, as if this were merely the latest in a line of galling surprises life had thrown at them, no worse in its way than illness or bereavement or any number of personal setbacks. She had seen others walk away and kill themselves half an hour later.

But the majority, she said, did eventually come to some kind of accommodation with the truth, however faltering and painful the process.

"Trust me, Thom," she said. "I know you now. I know you have the emotional strength to get through this. I know you can learn to live with it."

"Why didn't you tell me straight away, as soon as I came out of the tank?"

"Because I didn't know if you were going to be able to take it."

"You waited until after you knew I had a wife."

"No," Greta said. "I waited until after we'd made love. Because then I knew Katerina couldn't mean that much to you."

"Fuck you."

"Fuck me? Yes, you did. That's the point."

I wanted to strike out against her. But what I was angry at was not her insinuation but the cold-hearted truth of it. She was right, and I knew it. I just didn't want to deal with that, any more than I wanted to deal with the here and now.

I waited for the anger to subside.

"You say we're not the first?" I said.

"No. We were the first, I suppose – the ship I came in. Luckily it was well equipped. After the routing error, we had enough supplies to set up a self-sustaining station on the nearest rock. We knew there was no going back, but at least we could make some kind of life for ourselves here."

"And after that?"

"We had enough to do just keeping ourselves alive, the first few years. But then another ship came through the aperture. Damaged, drifting, much like *Blue Goose*. We hauled her in, warmed her crew, broke the news to them."

"How'd they take it?"

"About as well as you'd expect." Greta laughed hollowly to herself. "A couple of them went mad. Another killed herself. But at least a dozen of them are still here. In all honesty, it was good for us that another ship came through. Not just because they had supplies we could use, but because it helped us to help them. Took our minds off our own self-pity. It made us realize how far we'd come, and how much help these newcomers needed to make the same transition. That wasn't the last ship, either. We've gone through the same process with eight or nine others, since then." Greta looked at me, her head cocked against her hand. "There's a thought for you, Thom."

"There is?"

She nodded. "It's difficult for you now, I know. And it'll be difficult for you for some time to come. But it can help to have someone else to care about. It can smooth the transition."

"Like who?" I asked.

"Like one of your other crew members," Greta said. "You could try waking one of them, now."

Greta's with me when I pull Suzy out of the surge tank.

"Why her?" Greta asks.

"Because I want her out first," I say, wondering if Greta's jealous. I don't blame her: Suzy's beautiful, but she's also smart. There isn't a better syntax runner in Ashanti Industrial.

"What happened?" Suzy asks, when she's over the grogginess. "Did we make it back?"

I ask her to tell me the last thing she remembers.

"Customs," Suzy says. "Those pricks on Arkangel."

"And after that? Anything else? The runes? Do you remember casting them?"

"No," she says, then picks up something in my voice. The fact that I might not be telling the truth, or telling her all she needs to know. "Thom. I'll ask you again. Did we make it back?"

A minute later we're putting Suzy back into the tank.

It hasn't worked first time. Maybe next try.

But it kept not working with Suzy. She was always cleverer and quicker than me; she always had been. As soon as she came out of the tank, she knew that we'd come a lot further than Schedar sector. She was always ahead of my lies and excuses.

"It was different when it happened to me," I told Greta, when we were lying next to each other again, days later, with Suzy still in the tank. "I had all the nagging doubts she has, I think. But as soon as I saw you standing there, I forgot all about that stuff."

Greta nodded. Her hair fell across her face in dishevelled, sleep-matted curtains. She had a strand of it between her lips.

"It helped, seeing a friendly face?"

"Took my mind off the problem, that's for sure."

"You'll get there in the end," she said. "Anyway, from Suzy's point of view, aren't you a friendly face as well?"

"Maybe," I said. "But she'd been expecting me. You were the last person in the world I expected to see standing there."

Greta touched her knuckle against the side of my face. Her smooth skin slid against stubble. "It's getting easier for you, isn't it?"

"I don't know," I said.

"You're a strong man, Thom. I knew you'd come through this."

"I haven't come through it yet," I said. I felt like a tightrope walker halfway across Niagara Falls. It was a miracle I'd made it as far as I had. But that didn't mean I was home and dry.

Still, Greta was right. There was hope. I'd felt no crushing spasms of grief over Katerina's death, or enforced absence, or however you wanted to put it. All I felt was a bitter-sweet regret, the way one might feel about a broken heirloom or long-lost pet. I felt no animosity toward Katerina, and I was sorry that I would never see her again. But I was sorry about not seeing a lot of things. Maybe it would become worse in the days ahead. Maybe I was just postponing a breakdown.

I didn't think so.

In the meantime, I continued trying to find a way to deal with Suzy. She had become a puzzle that I couldn't leave unsolved. I could have just woken her up and let her deal with the news as best as she could, but that seemed cruel and unsatisfactory. Greta had broken it to me gently, giving me time to settle into my new surroundings and take that necessary step away from Katerina. When she finally broke the news, as shocking as it was, it didn't shatter me. I'd already been primed for it, the sting taken out of the surprise. Sleeping with Greta obviously helped. I couldn't offer Suzy the same solace, but I was sure that there was a way for us to coax Suzy to the same state of near-acceptance.

Time after time we woke her and tried a different approach. Greta said there was a window of a few minutes before the events she was experiencing began to transfer into long-term memory. If we knocked her out, the buffer of memories in short-term storage was wiped before it ever crossed the hippocampus into long-term recall. Within that window, we could wake her up as many times as we liked, trying endless permutations of the revival scenario.

At least that was what Greta told me.

"We can't keep doing this indefinitely," I said.

"Why not?"

"Isn't she going to remember *something*?"

Greta shrugged. "Maybe. But I doubt that she'll attach any significance to those memories. Haven't you ever had vague feelings of déjà vu coming out of the surge tank?"

"Sometimes," I admitted.

"Then don't sweat about it. She'll be all right. I promise you."

"Perhaps we should just keep her awake, after all."

"That would be cruel."

"It's cruel to keep waking her up and shutting her down, like a toy doll."

There was a catch in her voice when she answered me.

"Keep at it, Thom. I'm sure you're close to finding a way, in the end. It's helping you, focusing on Suzy. I always knew it would."

I started to say something, but Greta pressed a finger to my lips.

Greta was right about Suzy. The challenge helped me, taking my mind off my own predicament. I remembered what Greta had said about dealing with other crews in the same situation, before *Blue Goose* put in. Clearly she had learned many psychological tricks: gambits and short cuts to assist the transition to mental well-being. I felt a slight resentment at being manipulated so effectively. But at the same time I couldn't deny that worrying about another human being had helped me with my own adjustment. When, days later, I stepped back from the immediate problem of Suzy, I realized that something was different. I didn't feel far from home. I felt, in an odd way, privileged. I'd come further than almost anyone in history. I was still alive, and there were still people around to provide love and partnership and a web of social relations. Not just Greta, but all the other unlucky souls who had ended up at the station.

If anything, there appeared to be more of them than when I had first arrived. The corridors – sparsely populated at first – were increasingly busy, and when we ate under the dome – under the Milky Way – we were not the only diners. I studied their lamp-lit faces, comforted by their vague familiarity, wondering what kinds of stories they had to tell; where they'd come from, who they had left behind, how they had adjusted to life here. There was time enough to get to know them all. And the place would never become boring, for at any time – as Greta had intimated – we could always expect another lost ship to drop through the aperture. Tragedy for the crew, but fresh challenges, fresh faces, fresh news from home, for us.

All in all, it wasn't really so bad.

Then it clicked.

It was the man cleaning out the fish that did it, in the lobby of the hotel. It wasn't just the familiarity of the process, but the man himself.

I'd seen him before. Another pond full of diseased carp. Another hotel.

Then I remembered Kolding's bad teeth, and recalled how they'd reminded me of another man I'd met long before. Except it wasn't another man at all. Different name, different context, but everything else the same. And when I looked at the other diners, really looked at them, there was no one I couldn't swear I hadn't seen before. No single face that hit me with the force of utter unfamiliarity.

Which left Greta.

I said to her, over wine, under the Milky Way: "Nothing here is real, is it?"

She looked at me with infinite sadness and shook her head.

"What about Suzy?" I asked her.

"Suzy's dead. Ray is dead. They died in their surge tanks."

"How? Why them, and not me?"

"Something about particles of paint blocking intake filters. Not enough to make a difference over short distances, but enough to kill them on the trip out here."

I think some part of me had always suspected. It felt less like shock than brutal disappointment.

"But Suzy seemed so real," I said. "Even the way she had doubts about how long she'd been in the tank... even the way she remembered previous attempts to wake her."

The glass mannequin approached our table. Greta waved him away.

"I made her convincing, the way she would have acted."

"You *made* her?"

"You're not really awake, Thom. You're being fed data. This entire station is being simulated."

I sipped my wine. I expected it to taste suddenly thin and synthetic, but it still tasted like pretty good wine.

"Then I'm dead as well?"

"No. You're alive. Still in your surge tank. But I haven't brought you to full consciousness yet."

"All right. The truth this time. I can take it. How much is real? Does the station exist? Are we really as far out as you said?"

"Yes," she said. "The station exists, just as I said it does. It just looks... different. And it *is* in the Large Magellanic Cloud, and it *is* orbiting a brown dwarf star."

"Can you show me the station as it is?"

"I could. But I don't think you're ready for it. I think you'd find it difficult to adjust."

I couldn't help laughing. "Even after what I've already adjusted to?"

"You've only made half the journey, Thom."

"But you made it."

"I did, Thom. But for me it was different." Greta smiled. "For me, everything was different."

Then she made the light show change again. None of the other diners appeared to notice as we began to zoom in toward the Milky Way, crashing toward the spiral, ramming through shoals of outlying stars and gas clouds. The familiar landscape of the Local Bubble loomed large.

The image froze, the Bubble one amongst many such structures.

Again it filled with the violent red scribble of the aperture network. But now the network wasn't the only one. It was merely one ball of red yarn amongst many, spaced out across tens of thousands of light-years. None of the scribbles touched each other, yet – in the way they were shaped, in the way they almost abutted against each other, it was possible to imagine that they had once been connected. They were like the shapes of continents on a world with tectonic drift.

"It used to span the galaxy," Greta said. "Then something happened. Something catastrophic, which I still don't understand. A shattering, into vastly smaller domains. Typically a few hundred light-years across."

"Who made it?"

"I don't know. No one knows. They probably aren't around anymore. Maybe that was why it shattered, out of neglect."

"But we found it," I said. "The part of it near us still worked."

"All the disconnected elements still function," Greta said. "You can't cross from domain to domain, but otherwise the apertures work as they were designed to. Barring, of course, the occasional routing error."

"All right," I said. "If you can't cross from domain to domain, how did *Blue Goose* get this far out? We've come a lot further than a few hundred light-years."

"You're right. But then such a long-distance connection might have been engineered differently from the others. It appears that the links to the Magellanic Cloud were more resilient. When the domains shattered from each other, the connections reaching beyond the galaxy remained intact."

"In which case you *can* cross from domain to domain," I said. "But you have to come all the way out here first."

"The trouble is, not many want to continue the journey at this point. No one comes here deliberately, Thom."

"I still don't get it. What does it matter to me if there are other domains? Those regions of the galaxy are thousands of light-years from Earth, and without the apertures we'd have no way of reaching them. They don't matter. There's no one there to use them."

Greta's smile was coquettish, knowing. "What makes you so certain?"

"Because if there were, wouldn't there be alien ships popping out of the aperture here? You've told me *Blue Goose* wasn't the first through. But our domain – the one in the Local Bubble – must be outnumbered hundreds to one by all the others. If there are alien cultures out there, each stumbling on their own local domain, why haven't any of them ever come through the aperture, the way we did?"

Again that smile. But this time it chilled my blood.

"What makes you think they haven't, Thom?"

I reached out and took her hand, the way she had taken mine. I took it without force, without malice, but with the assurance that this time I really, sincerely meant what I was about to say.

Her fingers tightened around mine.

"Show me," I said. "I want to see things as they really are. Not just the station. You as well."

Because by then I'd realized. Greta hadn't just lied to me about Suzy and Ray. She'd lied to me about the *Blue Goose* as well. Because we were not the latest human ship to come through.

We were the first.

"You want to see it?" she asked.

"Yes. All of it."

"You won't like it."

"I'll be the judge of that."

"All right, Thom. But understand this. I've been here before. I've done this a million times. I care for all the lost souls. And I know how it works. You won't be able to take the raw reality of what's happened to you. You'll shrivel away from it. You'll go mad, unless I substitute a calming fiction, a happy ending."

"Why tell me that now?"

"Because you don't have to see it. You can stop now, where you are, with an idea of the truth. An inkling. But you don't have to open your eyes."

"Do it," I said.

Greta shrugged. She poured herself another measure of wine, then made sure my own glass was charged.

"You asked for it," she said.

We were still holding hands, two lovers sharing an intimacy. Then everything changed.

It was just a flash, just a glimpse. Like the view of an unfamiliar room if you turn the lights on for an instant. Shapes and forms, relationships between things. I saw caverns, wormed-out and linked, and things moving through those caverns, bustling along with the frantic industry of moles or termites. The things were seldom alike, even in the most superficial sense. Some moved via propulsive waves of multiple clawed limbs. Some wriggled, smooth plaques of carapace grinding against the glassy rock of the tunnels.

The things moved between caves in which lay the hulks of ships, almost all too strange to describe.

And somewhere distant, somewhere near the heart of the rock, in a matriarchal chamber all of its own, something drummed out messages to its companions and helpers, stiffly articulated, antler-like forelimbs beating against stretched tympana of finely veined skin, something that had been waiting here for eternities, something that wanted nothing more than to care for the souls of the lost.

Katerina's with Suzy when they pull me out of the surge tank.

It's bad – one of the worst revivals I've ever gone through. I feel as if every vein in my body has been filled with finely powdered glass. For a moment, a long moment, even the idea of breathing seems insurmountably difficult, too hard, too painful even to contemplate.

But it passes, as it always passes.

After a while I can not only breathe, I can move and talk.

"Where—"

"Easy, Skip," Suzy says. She leans over the tank and starts unplugging me. I can't help but smile. Suzy's smart – there isn't a better syntax runner in Ashanti Industrial – but she's also beautiful. It's like being nursed by an angel.

I wonder if Katerina's jealous.

"Where are we?" I try again. "Feels like I was in that thing for an eternity. Did something go wrong?"

"Minor routing error," Suzy says. "We took some damage and they decided to wake me first. But don't sweat about it. At least we're in one piece."

Routing errors. You hear about them, but you hope they're never going to happen to you.

"What kind of delay?"

"Forty days. Sorry, Thom. Bang goes our bonus."

In anger, I hammer the side of the surge tank. But Katerina steps toward me and places a calming hand on my shoulder.

"It's all right," she says. "You're home and dry. That's all that matters."

I look at her and for a moment remember someone else, someone I haven't thought about in years. I almost remember her name, and then the moment passes.

I nod. "Home and dry."

GOOD HUNTING

Ken Liu

Night. Half moon. An occasional hoot from an owl.

The merchant and his wife and all the servants had been sent away. The large house was eerily quiet.

Father and I crouched behind the scholar's rock in the courtyard. Through the rock's many holes I could see the bedroom window of the merchant's son.

"Oh, Tsiao-jung, my sweet Tsiao-jung..."

The young man's feverish groans were pitiful. Half-delirious, he was tied to his bed for his own good, but Father had left a window open so that his plaintive cries could be carried by the breeze far over the rice paddies.

"Do you think she really will come?" I whispered. Today was my thirteenth birthday, and this was my first hunt.

"She will," Father said. "A *hulijing* cannot resist the cries of the man she has bewitched."

"Like how the Butterfly Lovers cannot resist each other?" I thought back to the folk opera troupe that had come through our village last fall.

"Not quite," Father said. But he seemed to have trouble explaining why. "Just know that it's not the same."

I nodded, not sure I understood. But I remembered how the merchant and his wife had come to Father to ask for his help.

"How shameful!" the merchant had muttered. "He's not even nineteen. How could he have read so many sages' books and still fall under the spell of such a creature?"

"There's no shame in being entranced by the beauty and wiles of a hulijing," *Father had said. "Even the great scholar Wong Lai once spent three nights in the company of one, and he took first place at the Imperial Examinations. Your son just needs a little help."*

"You must save him," the merchant's wife had said, bowing like a chicken pecking at rice. *"If this gets out, the matchmakers won't touch him at all."*

A *hulijing* was a demon who stole hearts. I shuddered, worried if I would have the courage to face one.

Father put a warm hand on my shoulder, and I felt calmer. In his hand was Swallow Tail, a sword that had first been forged by our ancestor, General Lau Yip, thirteen generations ago. The sword was charged with hundreds of Daoist blessings and had drunk the blood of countless demons.

A passing cloud obscured the moon for a moment, throwing everything into darkness.

When the moon emerged again, I almost cried out.

There, in the courtyard, was the most beautiful lady I had ever seen.

She had on a flowing white silk dress with billowing sleeves and a wide, silvery belt. Her face was pale as snow, and her hair dark as coal, draping past her waist. I thought she looked like the paintings of great beauties from the Tang Dynasty the opera troupe had hung around their stage.

She turned slowly to survey everything around her, her eyes glistening in the moonlight like two shimmering pools.

I was surprised to see how sad she looked. Suddenly, I felt sorry for her and wanted more than anything else to make her smile.

The light touch of my father's hand against the back of my neck jolted me out of my mesmerized state. He had warned me about the power of the *hulijing*. My face hot and my heart hammering, I averted my eyes from the demon's face and focused on her stance.

The merchant's servants had been patrolling the courtyard every night this week with dogs to keep her away from her victim. But now the courtyard was empty. She stood still, hesitating, suspecting a trap.

"Tsiao-jung! Have you come for me?" The son's feverish voice grew louder.

The lady turned and walked – no, glided, so smooth were her movements – towards the bedroom door.

Father jumped out from behind the rock and rushed at her with Swallow Tail.

She dodged out of the way as though she had eyes on the back of her head. Unable to stop, my father thrust the sword into the thick wooden door with a dull thunk. He pulled but could not free the weapon immediately.

The lady glanced at him, turned, and headed for the courtyard gate.

"Don't just stand there, Liang!" Father called. "She's getting away!"

I ran at her, dragging my clay pot filled with dog piss. It was my job to splash her with it so that she could not transform into her fox form and escape.

She turned to me and smiled. "You're a very brave boy." A scent, like jasmine blooming in spring rain, surrounded me. Her voice was like sweet, cold lotus paste, and I wanted to hear her talk forever. The clay pot dangled from my hand, forgotten.

"Now!" Father shouted. He had pulled the sword free.

I bit my lip in frustration. *How could I become a demon hunter if I was so easily enticed?* I lifted off the cover and emptied the clay pot at her retreating figure, but the insane thought that I shouldn't dirty her white dress caused my hands to shake, and my aim was wide. Only a small amount of dog piss got onto her.

But it was enough. She howled, and the sound, like a dog's but so much wilder, caused the hairs on the back of my neck to stand up. She turned and snarled, showing two rows of sharp, white teeth, and I stumbled back.

I had doused her while she was in the midst of her transformation. Her face was thus frozen halfway between a woman's and a fox's, with a hairless snout and raised, triangular ears that twitched angrily. Her hands had turned into paws, tipped with sharp claws that she swiped at me.

She could no longer speak, but her eyes conveyed her venomous thoughts without trouble.

Father rushed by me, his sword raised for a killing blow. The *hulijing* turned around and slammed into the courtyard gate, smashing it open, and disappeared through the broken door.

Father chased after her without even a glance back at me. Ashamed, I followed.

The *hulijing* was swift of foot, and her silvery tail seemed to leave a glittering trail across the fields. But her incompletely transformed body maintained a human's posture, incapable of running as fast as she could have on four legs.

Father and I saw her dodging into the abandoned temple about a *li* outside the village.

"Go around the temple," Father said, trying to catch his breath. "I will go through the front door. If she tries to flee through the back door, you know what to do."

The back of the temple was overgrown with weeds and the wall half-collapsed. As I came around, I saw a white flash darting through the rubble.

Determined to redeem myself in my father's eyes, I swallowed my fear and ran after it without hesitation. After a few quick turns, I had the thing cornered in one of the monks' cells.

I was about to pour the remaining dog piss on it when I realized that the animal was much smaller than the *hulijing* we had been chasing. It was a small white fox, about the size of a puppy.

I set the clay pot on the ground and lunged.

The fox squirmed under me. It was surprisingly strong for such a small animal. I struggled to hold it down. As we fought, the fur between my fingers seemed to become as slippery as skin, and the body elongated, expanded, grew. I had to use my whole body to wrestle it to the ground.

Suddenly, I realized that my hands and arms were wrapped around the nude body of a young girl about my age.

I cried out and jumped back. The girl stood up slowly, picked up a silk robe from behind a pile of straw, put it on, and gazed at me haughtily.

A growl came from the main hall some distance away, followed by the sound of a heavy sword crashing into a table. Then another growl, and the sound of my father's curses.

The girl and I stared at each other. She was even prettier than the opera singer that I couldn't stop thinking about last year.

"Why are you after us?" she asked. "We did nothing to you."

"Your mother bewitched the merchant's son," I said. "We have to save him."

"*Bewitched*? He's the one who wouldn't leave *her* alone."

I was taken aback. "What are you talking about?"

"One night about a month ago, the merchant's son stumbled upon my mother, caught in a chicken farmer's trap. She had to transform into her human form to escape, and as soon as he saw her, he became infatuated.

"She liked her freedom and didn't want anything to do with him. But once a man has set his heart on a *hulijing*, she cannot help hearing him no matter how far apart they are. All that moaning and crying he did drove her to distraction, and she had to go see him every night just to keep him quiet."

This was not what I learned from Father.

"She lures innocent scholars and draws on their life essence to feed her evil magic! Look how sick the merchant's son is!"

"He's sick because that useless doctor gave him poison that was supposed to make him forget about my mother. My mother is the one who's kept him alive with her nightly visits. And stop using the word *lure*. A man can fall in love with a *hulijing* just like he can with any human woman."

I didn't know what to say, so I said the first thing that came to mind. "I just know it's not the same."

She smirked. "Not the same? I saw how you looked at me before I put on my robe."

I blushed. "Brazen demon!" I picked up the clay pot. She remained where she was, a mocking smile on her face. Eventually, I put the pot back down.

The fight in the main hall grew noisier, and suddenly, there was a loud crash, followed by a triumphant shout from Father and a long, piercing scream from the woman.

There was no smirk on the girl's face now, only rage turning slowly to shock. Her eyes had lost their lively luster; they looked dead.

Another grunt from Father. The scream ended abruptly.

"Liang! Liang! It's over. Where are you?"

Tears rolled down the girl's face.

"Search the temple," my Father's voice continued. "She may have pups here. We have to kill them too."

The girl tensed.

"Liang, have you found anything?" The voice was coming closer.

"Nothing," I said, locking eyes with her. "I didn't find anything."

She turned around and silently ran out of the cell. A moment later, I saw a small white fox jump over the broken back wall and disappear into the night.

*   *   *

It was *Qingming*, the Festival of the Dead. Father and I went to sweep Mother's grave and to bring her food and drink to comfort her in the afterlife.

"I'd like to stay here for a while," I said. Father nodded and left for home.

I whispered an apology to my mother, packed up the chicken we had brought for her, and walked the three *li* to the other side of the hill, to the abandoned temple.

I found Yan kneeling in the main hall, near the place where my father had killed her mother five years ago. She now wore her hair up in a bun, in the style of a young woman who had had her *jijili*, the ceremony that meant she was no longer a girl. We'd been meeting every *Qingming*, every *Chongyang*, every *Yulan*, every New Year's, occasions when families were supposed to be together.

"I brought you this," I said, and handed her the steamed chicken.

"Thank you." And she carefully tore off a leg and bit into it daintily. Yan had explained to me that the *hulijing* chose to live near human villages because they liked to have human things in their lives: conversation, beautiful clothes, poetry and stories, and, occasionally, the love of a worthy, kind man.

But the *hulijing* remained hunters who felt most free in their fox form. After what happened to her mother, Yan stayed away from chicken coops, but she still missed their taste.

"How's hunting?" I asked.

"Not so great," she said. "There are few Hundred-Year Salamanders and Six-Toed Rabbits. I can't ever seem to get enough to eat." She bit off another piece of chicken, chewed, and swallowed. "I'm having trouble transforming too."

"It's hard for you to keep this shape?"

"No." She put the rest of the chicken on the ground and whispered a prayer to her mother.

"I mean it's getting harder for me to return to my true form," she continued, "to hunt. Some nights I can't do it at all. How's hunting for you?"

"Not so great either. There don't seem to be as many snake spirits or angry ghosts as a few years ago. Even hauntings by suicides with unfinished business are down. And we haven't had a proper jumping corpse in months. Father is worried about money."

We also hadn't had to deal with a *hulijing* in years. Maybe Yan had warned them all away. Truth be told, I was relieved. I didn't relish the prospect of having to tell my father that he was wrong about something. He was already very irritable, anxious that he was losing the respect of the villagers now that his knowledge and skill didn't seem to be needed as much.

"Ever think that maybe the jumping corpses are also misunderstood?" she asked. "Like me and my mother?"

She laughed as she saw my face. "Just kidding!"

It was strange, what Yan and I shared. She wasn't exactly a friend. More like someone who you couldn't help being drawn to because you shared the knowledge of how the world didn't work the way you had been told.

She looked at the chicken bits she had left for her mother. "I think magic is being drained out of this land."

I had suspected that something was wrong, but didn't want to voice my suspicion out loud, which would make it real.

"What do you think is causing it?"

Instead of answering, Yan perked up her ears and listened intently. Then she got up, grabbed my hand, and pulled until we were behind the buddha in the main hall.

"Wha—"

She held up her finger against my lips. So close to her, I finally noticed her scent. It was like her mother's, floral and sweet, but also bright, like blankets dried in the sun. I felt my face grow warm.

A moment later, I heard a group of men making their way into the temple. Slowly, I inched my head out from behind the buddha so I could see.

It was a hot day, and the men were seeking some shade from the noon sun. Two men set down a cane sedan chair, and the passenger who stepped off was a foreigner, with curly yellow hair and pale skin. Other men in the group carried tripods, levels, bronze tubes, and open trunks full of strange equipment.

"Most Honored Mister Thompson." A man dressed like a mandarin came up to the foreigner. The way he kept on bowing and smiling and bouncing his head up and down reminded me of a kicked dog begging for favors. "Please have a rest and drink some cold tea. It is hard for the men to be working on the day when they're supposed to visit the graves of their families, and they need to take a little time to pray lest they anger the gods and spirits. But I promise we'll work hard afterwards and finish the survey on time."

"The trouble with you Chinese is your endless superstition," the foreigner said. He had a strange accent, but I could understand him just fine. "Remember, the Hong Kong-Tientsin Railroad is a priority for Great Britain. If I don't get as far as Botou Village by sunset, I'll be docking all of your wages."

I had heard rumors that the Manchu Emperor had lost a war and been forced to give up all kinds of concessions, one of which involved paying to help the foreigners build a road of iron. But it had all seemed so fantastical that I didn't pay much attention.

The mandarin nodded enthusiastically. "Most Honored Mister Thompson is right in every way. But might I trouble your gracious ear with a suggestion?"

The weary Englishman waved impatiently.

"Some of the local villagers are worried about the proposed path of the railroad. You see, they think the tracks that have already been laid are blocking off veins of *qi* in the earth. It's bad *feng shui*."

"What are you talking about?"

"It is kind of like how a man breathes," the mandarin said, huffing a few times to make sure the Englishman understood. "The land has channels along rivers, hills, ancient roads that carry the energy of *qi*. It's what gives the villages prosperity and maintains the rare animals and local spirits and household gods. Could you consider shifting the line of the tracks a little, to follow the *feng shui* masters' suggestions?"

Thompson rolled his eyes. "That is the most ridiculous thing I've yet heard. You want me to deviate from the most efficient path for our railroad because you think your idols would be angry?"

The mandarin looked pained. "Well, in the places where the tracks have already been laid, many bad things are happening: people losing money, animals dying, household gods not responding to prayers. The Buddhist and Daoist monks all agree that it's the railroad."

Thompson strode over to the buddha and looked at it appraisingly. I ducked back behind the statue and squeezed Yan's hand. We held our breaths, hoping that we wouldn't be discovered.

"Does this one still have any power?" Thompson asked.

"The temple hasn't been able to maintain a contingent of monks for many years," the mandarin said. "But this buddha is still well respected. I hear villagers say that prayers to him are often answered."

Then I heard a loud crash and a collective gasp from the men in the main hall.

"I've just broken the hands off of this god of yours with my cane," Thompson said. "As you can see, I have not been struck by lightning or suffered any other calamity. Indeed, now we know that it is only an idol made of mud stuffed with straw and covered in cheap paint. This is why you people lost the war to Britain. You worship statues of mud when you should be thinking about building roads from iron and weapons from steel."

There was no more talk about changing the path of the railroad.

After the men were gone, Yan and I stepped out from behind the statue. We gazed at the broken hands of the buddha for a while.

"The world's changing," Yan said. "Hong Kong, iron roads, foreigners with wires that carry speech and machines that belch smoke. More and more, storytellers in the teahouses speak of these wonders. I think that's why the old magic is leaving. A more powerful kind of magic has come."

She kept her voice unemotional and cool, like a placid pool of water in autumn, but her words rang true. I thought about my father's attempts to keep up a cheerful mien as fewer and fewer customers came to us. I wondered if the time I spent learning the chants and the sword dance moves were wasted.

"What will you do?" I asked, thinking about her, alone in the hills and unable to find the food that sustained her magic.

"There's only one thing I *can* do." Her voice broke for a second and became defiant, like a pebble tossed into the pool.

But then she looked at me, and her composure returned.

"The only thing *we* can do. Learn to survive."

* * *

The railroad soon became a familiar part of the landscape: the black locomotive huffing through the green rice paddies, puffing steam and pulling a long train behind it, like a dragon coming down from the distant, hazy, blue mountains. For a while, it was a wondrous sight, with children marveling at it, running alongside the tracks to keep up.

But the soot from the locomotive chimneys killed the rice in the fields closest to the tracks, and two children playing on the tracks, too frightened to move, were killed one afternoon. After that, the train ceased to fascinate.

People stopped coming to Father and me to ask for our services. They either went to the Christian missionary or the new teacher who said he'd studied in San Francisco. Young men in the village began to leave for Hong Kong or Canton, moved by rumors of bright lights and well-paying work. Fields lay fallow. The village itself seemed to consist only of the too-old and too-young, and their mood one of resignation. Men from distant provinces came to inquire about buying land for cheap.

Father spent his days sitting in the front room, Swallow Tail over his knee, staring out the door from dawn to dusk, as though he himself had turned into a statue.

Every day, as I returned home from the fields, I would see the glint of hope in Father's eyes briefly flare up.

"Did anyone speak of needing our help?" he would ask.

"No," I would say, trying to keep my tone light. "But I'm sure there will be a jumping corpse soon. It's been too long."

I would not look at my father as I spoke because I did not want to look as hope faded from his eyes.

Then, one day, I found Father hanging from the heavy beam in his bedroom. As I let his body down, my heart numb, I thought that he was not unlike those he had hunted all his life: they were all sustained by an old magic that had left and would not return, and they did not know how to survive without it.

Swallow Tail felt dull and heavy in my hand. I had always thought I would be a demon hunter, but how could I when there were no more demons, no more spirits? All the Daoist blessings in the sword could not save my father's sinking heart. And if I stuck around, perhaps my heart would grow heavy and yearn to be still too.

I hadn't seen Yan since that day six years ago, when we hid from the railroad surveyors at the temple. But her words came back to me now.

Learn to survive.

I packed a bag and bought a train ticket to Hong Kong.

The Sikh guard checked my papers and waved me through the security gate.

I paused to let my gaze follow the tracks going up the steep side of the mountain. It seemed less like a railroad track than a ladder straight up to heaven. This was the funicular railway, the tram line to the top of Victoria Peak, where the masters of Hong Kong lived and the Chinese were forbidden to stay.

But the Chinese were good enough to shovel coal into the boilers and grease the gears.

Steam rose around me as I ducked into the engine room. After five years, I knew the rhythmic rumbling of the pistons and the staccato grinding of the gears as well as I knew my own breath and heartbeat. There was a kind of music to their orderly cacophony that moved me, like the clashing of cymbals and gongs at the start of a folk opera. I checked the pressure, applied sealant on the gaskets, tightened the flanges, replaced the worn-down gears in the backup cable assembly. I lost myself in the work, which was hard and satisfying.

By the end of my shift, it was dark. I stepped outside the engine room and saw a full moon in the sky as another tram filled with passengers was pulled up the side of the mountain, powered by my engine.

"Don't let the Chinese ghosts get you," a woman with bright blond hair said in the tram, and her companions laughed.

It was the night of *Yulan*, I realized, the Ghost Festival. *I should get something for my father, maybe pick up some paper money at Mongkok.*

"How can you be done for the day when we still want you?" a man's voice came to me.

"Girls like you shouldn't tease," another man said, and laughed.

I looked in the direction of the voices and saw a Chinese woman standing in the shadows just outside the tram station. Her tight western-style cheongsam and the garish makeup told me her profession. Two Englishmen blocked her path. One tried to put his arms around her, and she backed out of the way.

"Please. I'm very tired," she said in English. "Maybe next time."

"Now, don't be stupid," the first man said, his voice hardening. "This isn't a discussion. Come along now and do what you're supposed to."

I walked up to them. "Hey."

The men turned around and looked at me.

"What seems to be the problem?"

"None of your business."

"Well, I think it *is* my business," I said, "seeing as how you're talking to my sister."

I doubt either of them believed me. But five years of wrangling heavy machinery had given me a muscular frame, and they took a look at my face and hands, grimy with engine grease, and probably decided that it wasn't worth it to get into a public tussle with a lowly Chinese engineer.

The two men stepped away to get in line for the Peak Tram, muttering curses.

"Thank you," she said.

"It's been a long time," I said, looking at her. I swallowed the *you look good.* She didn't. She looked tired and thin and brittle. And the pungent perfume she wore assaulted my nose.

But I did not think of her harshly. Judging was the luxury of those who did not need to survive.

"It's the night of the Ghost Festival," she said. "I didn't want to work anymore. I wanted to think about my mother."

"Why don't we go get some offerings together?" I asked.

We took the ferry over to Kowloon, and the breeze over the water revived her a bit. She wet a towel with the hot water from the teapot on the ferry and wiped off her makeup. I caught a faint trace of her natural scent, fresh and lovely as always.

"You look good," I said, and meant it.

On the streets of Kowloon, we bought pastries and fruits and cold dumplings and a steamed chicken and incense and paper money, and caught up on each other's lives.

"How's hunting?" I asked. We both laughed.

"I miss being a fox," she said. She nibbled on a chicken wing absent-mindedly. "One day, shortly after that last time we talked, I felt the last bit of magic leave me. I could no longer transform."

"I'm sorry," I said, unable to offer anything else.

"My mother taught me to like human things: food, clothes, folk opera, old stories. But she was never dependent on them. When she wanted, she could always turn into her true form and hunt. But now, in this form, what can I do? I don't have claws. I don't have sharp teeth. I can't even run very fast. All I have is my beauty, the same thing that your father and you killed my mother for. So now I live by the very thing that you once falsely accused my mother of doing: I *lure* men for money."

"My father is dead, too."

Hearing this seemed to drain some of the bitterness out of her. "What happened?"

"He felt the magic leave us, much as you. He couldn't bear it."

"I'm sorry." And I knew that she didn't know what else to say either.

"You told me once that the only thing we can do is to survive. I have to thank you for that. It probably saved my life."

"Then we're even," she said, smiling. "But let us not speak of ourselves anymore. Tonight is reserved for the ghosts."

We went down to the harbor and placed our food next to the water, inviting all the ghosts we had loved to come and dine. Then we lit the incense and burned the paper money in a bucket.

She watched bits of burnt paper being carried into the sky by the heat from the flames. They disappeared among the stars. "Do you think the gates to the underworld still open for the ghosts tonight, now that there is no magic left?"

I hesitated. When I was young, I had been trained to hear the scratching of a ghost's fingers against a paper window, to distinguish the voice of a spirit from the wind. But now I was used to enduring the thunderous pounding of pistons and the deafening hiss of high-pressured steam rushing through valves. I could no longer claim to be attuned to that vanished world of my childhood.

"I don't know," I said. "I suppose it's the same with ghosts as with people. Some will figure out how to survive in a world diminished by iron roads and steam whistles, some will not."

"But will any of them thrive?" she asked.

She could still surprise me.

"I mean," she continued, "are you happy? Are you happy to keep an engine running all day, yourself like another cog? What do you dream of?"

I couldn't remember any dreams. I had let myself become entranced by the movement of gears and levers, to let my mind grow to fit the gaps between the ceaseless clanging of metal on metal. It was a way to not have to think about my father, about a land that had lost so much.

"I dream of hunting in this jungle of metal and asphalt," she said. "I dream of my true form leaping from beam to ledge to terrace to roof, until I am at the top of this island, until I can growl in the faces of all the men who believe they can own me."

As I watched, her eyes, brightly lit for a moment, dimmed.

"In this new age of steam and electricity, in this great metropolis, except for those who live on the Peak, is anyone still in their true form?" she asked.

GOOD HUNTING

We sat together by the harbor and burned paper money all night, waiting for a sign that the ghosts were still with us.

* * *

Life in Hong Kong could be a strange experience: from day to day, things never seemed to change much. But if you compared things over a few years, it was almost like you lived in a different world.

By my thirtieth birthday, new designs for steam engines required less coal and delivered more power. They grew smaller and smaller. The streets filled with automatic rickshaws and horseless carriages, and most people who could afford them had machines that kept the air cool in houses and the food cold in boxes in the kitchen—all powered by steam.

I went into stores and endured the ire of the clerks as I studied the components of new display models. I devoured every book on the principle and operation of the steam engine I could find. I tried to apply those principles to improve the machines I was in charge of: trying out new firing cycles, testing new kinds of lubricants for the pistons, adjusting the gear ratios. I found a measure of satisfaction in the way I came to understand the magic of the machines.

One morning, as I repaired a broken governor – a delicate bit of work – two pairs of polished shoes stopped on the platform above me.

I looked up. Two men looked down at me.

"This is the one," said my shift supervisor.

The other man, dressed in a crisp suit, looked skeptical. "Are you the man who came up with the idea of using a larger flywheel for the old engine?"

I nodded. I took pride in the way I could squeeze more power out of my machines than dreamed of by their designers.

"You did not steal the idea from an Englishman?" his tone was severe.

I blinked. A moment of confusion was followed by a rush of anger. "No," I said, trying to keep my voice calm. I ducked back under the machine to continue my work.

"He is clever," my shift supervisor said, "for a Chinaman. He can be taught."

"I suppose we might as well try," said the other man. "It will certainly be cheaper than hiring a real engineer from England."

* * *

Mr Alexander Findlay Smith, owner of the Peak Tram and an avid engineer himself, had seen an opportunity. He foresaw that the path of technological progress would lead inevitably to the use of steam power to operate automata: mechanical arms and legs that would eventually replace the Chinese coolies and servants.

I was selected to serve Mr Findlay Smith in his new venture.

I learned to repair clockwork, to design intricate systems of gears and devise ingenious uses for levers. I studied how to plate metal with chrome and how to shape brass into smooth curves. I invented ways to connect the world of hardened and ruggedized clockwork to the world of miniaturized and regulated piston and clean steam. Once the automata were finished, we connected them to the latest analytic engines shipped from Britain and fed them with tape punched with dense holes in Babbage-Lovelace code.

It had taken a decade of hard work. But now mechanical arms served drinks in the bars along Central and machine hands fashioned shoes and clothes in factories in the New Territories. In the mansions up on the Peak, I heard – though I'd never seen – that automatic sweepers and mops I designed roamed the halls discreetly, bumping into walls gently as they cleaned the floors like mechanical elves puffing out bits of white steam. The expats could finally live their lives in this tropical paradise free of reminders of the presence of the Chinese.

* * *

I was thirty-five when she showed up at my door again, like a memory from long ago.

I pulled her into my tiny flat, looked around to be sure no one was following her, and closed the door.

"How's hunting?" I asked. It was a bad attempt at a joke, and she laughed weakly.

GOOD HUNTING

Photographs of her had been in all the papers. It was the biggest scandal in the colony: not so much because the Governor's son was keeping a Chinese mistress – it was expected that he would – but because the mistress had managed to steal a large sum of money from him and then disappear. Everyone tittered while the police turned the city upside down, looking for her.

"I can hide you for tonight," I said. Then I waited, the unspoken second half of my sentence hanging between us.

She sat down in the only chair in the room, the dim light bulb casting dark shadows on her face. She looked gaunt and exhausted. "Ah, now you're judging me."

"I have a good job I want to keep," I said. "Mr Findlay Smith trusts me."

She bent down and began to pull up her dress.

"Don't," I said, and turned my face away. I could not bear to watch her try to ply her trade with me.

"Look," she said. There was no seduction in her voice. "Liang, look at me."

I turned and gasped.

Her legs, what I could see of them, were made of shiny chrome. I bent down to look closer: the cylindrical joints at the knees were lathed with precision, the pneumatic actuators along the thighs moved in complete silence, the feet were exquisitely molded and shaped, the surfaces smooth and flowing. These were the most beautiful mechanical legs I had ever seen.

"He had me drugged," she said. "When I woke up, my legs were gone and replaced by these. The pain was excruciating. He explained to me that he had a secret: he liked machines more than flesh, couldn't get hard with a regular woman."

I had heard of such men. In a city filled with chrome and brass and clanging and hissing, desires became confused.

I focused on the way light moved along the gleaming curves of her calves so that I didn't have to look into her face.

"I had a choice: let him keep on changing me to suit him, or he could remove the legs and throw me out on the street. Who would believe a legless Chinese whore? I wanted to survive. So I swallowed the pain and let him continue."

She stood up and removed the rest of her dress and her evening gloves. I took in her chrome torso, slatted around the waist to allow articulation and movement; her sinuous arms, constructed from curved plates sliding over each other like obscene armor; her hands, shaped from delicate metal mesh, with dark steel fingers tipped with jewels where the fingernails would be.

"He spared no expense. Every piece of me is built with the best craftsmanship and attached to my body by the best surgeons—there are many who want to experiment, despite the law, with how the body could be animated by electricity, nerves replaced by wires. They always spoke only to him, as if I was already only a machine.

"Then, one night, he hurt me and I struck back in desperation. He fell like he was made of straw. I realized, suddenly, how much strength I had in my metal arms. I had let him do all this to me, to replace me part by part, mourning my loss all the while without understanding what I had gained. A terrible thing had been done to me, but I could also be *terrible*.

"I choked him until he fainted, and then I took all the money I could find and left.

"So I come to you, Liang. Will you help me?"

I stepped up and embraced her. "We'll find some way to reverse this. There must be doctors—"

"No," she interrupted me. "That's not what I want."

* * *

It took us almost a whole year to complete the task. Yan's money helped, but some things money couldn't buy, especially skill and knowledge.

My flat became a workshop. We spent every evening and all of Sundays working: shaping metal, polishing gears, reattaching wires.

Her face was the hardest. It was still flesh.

I poured over books of anatomy and took casts of her face with plaster of Paris. I broke my cheekbones and cut my face so that I could stagger into surgeons' offices and learn from them how to repair these injuries. I bought expensive jeweled masks and took them apart, learning the delicate art of shaping metal to take on the shape of a face.

Finally, it was time.

Through the window, the moon threw a pale white parallelogram on the floor. Yan stood in the middle of it, moving her head about, trying out her new face.

Hundreds of miniature pneumatic actuators were hidden under the smooth chrome skin, each of which could be controlled independently, allowing her to adopt any expression. But her eyes were still the same, and they shone in the moonlight with excitement.

"Are you ready?" I asked.

She nodded.

I handed her a bowl, filled with the purest anthracite coal, ground into a fine powder. It smelled of burnt wood, of the heart of the earth. She poured it into her mouth and swallowed. I could hear the fire in the miniature boiler in her torso grow hotter as the pressure of the steam built up. I took a step back.

She lifted her head to the moon and howled: it was a howl made by steam passing through brass piping, and yet it reminded me of that wild howl long ago, when I first heard the call of a *hulijing*.

Then she crouched to the floor. Gears grinding, pistons pumping, curved metal plates sliding over each other—the noises grew louder as she began to transform.

She had drawn the first glimmers of her idea with ink on paper. Then she had refined it, through hundreds of iterations until she was satisfied. I could see traces of her mother in it, but also something harder, something new.

Working from her idea, I had designed the delicate folds in the chrome skin and the intricate joints in the metal skeleton. I had put together every hinge, assembled every gear, soldered every wire, welded every seam, oiled every actuator. I had taken her apart and put her back together.

Yet, it was a marvel to see everything working. In front of my eyes, she folded and unfolded like a silvery origami construction, until finally, a chrome fox as beautiful and deadly as the oldest legends stood before me.

She padded around the flat, testing out her sleek new form, trying out her stealthy new movements. Her limbs gleamed in the moonlight, and her tail, made of delicate silver wires as fine as lace, left a trail of light in the dim flat.

She turned and walked – no, glided – towards me, a glorious hunter, an ancient vision coming alive. I took a deep breath and smelled fire and smoke, engine oil and polished metal, the scent of power.

"Thank you," she said, and leaned in as I put my arms around her true form. The steam engine inside her had warmed her cold metal body, and it felt warm and alive.

"Can you feel it?" she asked.

I shivered. I knew what she meant. The old magic was back but changed: not fur and flesh, but metal and fire.

"I will find others like me," she said, "and bring them to you. Together, we will set them free."

Once, I was a demon hunter. Now, I am one of them.

I opened the door, Swallow Tail in my hand. It was only an old and heavy sword, rusty, but still perfectly capable of striking down anyone who might be lying in wait.

No one was.

Yan leapt out like a bolt of lightning. Stealthily, gracefully, she darted into the streets of Hong Kong, free, feral, a *hulijing* built for this new age.

... once a man has set his heart on a hulijing, *she cannot help hearing him no matter how far apart they are ...*

"Good hunting," I whispered.

She howled in the distance, and I watched a puff of steam rise into the air as she disappeared.

I imagined her running along the tracks of the funicular railway, a tireless engine racing up, and up, towards the top of Victoria Peak, towards a future as full of magic as the past.

THE DUMP

Joe R Lansdale

For Ted Klein

Me, I like it here just fine. Don't see no call for me to move on. Dump's been my home nigh on twenty years, and I don't think no high-falutin' city sanitation law should make me have to pack up and move on. If I'm gonna work here, I ought to be able to live here.

Me and Otto... where is that sucker anyway? I let him wander about some on Sundays. Rest of the time I keep him chained inside the hut there, out of sight. Wouldn't want him bitin' folks.

Well, as I was sayin', the dump's my home. Best damn home I ever had. I'm not a college man, but I got some education. I read a lot. Ought to look inside that shack and see my bookshelves. I may be a dump-yard supervisor, but I'm no fool.

Besides, there's more to this dump than meets the eye.

'Scuse me. Otto! Otto. Here, boy. Dadburn his hide, he's gotten bad about not comin' when I call.

Now, I was sayin' about the dump. There's more here than meets the eye. You ever thought about all that garbage, boy? They bring anything and everything here, and I 'doze her under. There's animal bodies – that's one of the things that interests old Otto – paint cans, all manner of chemical containers, lumber, straw, brush, you name it. I 'doze all that stuff under and it heats up. Why, if you could put a thermometer under that earth, check the heat that stuff puts out while it's breakin' down and turnin' to compost, it would be up *there*, boy, way up *there*. Sometimes over a hundred degrees. I've plowed that stuff open and seen the steam flow out of there like a cloud. Could feel the heat of it. It was like bein' in one of them fancy baths. Saunas, they call 'em. Hot, boy, real hot.

Now you think about it. All that heat. All those chemicals

165

and dead bodies and such. Makes an awful mess, a weird blend of nature's refuse. Real weird. And with all that incubatin' heat.... well, you consider it.

I'll tell you somethin' I ain't told nobody else. Somethin' that happened to me a couple years ago.

One night me and Pearly, that was a friend of mine, and we called him that on account of he had the whitest teeth you ever seen. Darn things looked *pointed* they were so white... Let's see, now where was I? Oh, yeah, yeah, me and Pearly. Well, we were sittin' around out here one night shootin' the breeze, you know, sharin' a pint. Pearly, he used to come around from time to time and we'd always split a bottle. He used to be a legit, old-time hobo. Rode the rails all over this country. Why, I reckon he was goin' on seventy years if not better, but he acted twenty years younger.

He'd come around and we'd talk and sit and snort and roll us some of that Prince Albert, which we'd smoke. We had some good laughs, we did, and I miss old Pearly sometimes.

So that night we let the bottle leak out pretty good, and Pearly, he's tellin' me about this time down in Texas in a boxcar with a river trash whore, and he stops in mid-sentence, right at the good part, and says: "You hear that?"

I said, "I don't hear nothin'. Go on with your story."

He nodded and told the tale, and I laughed, and he laughed. He could laugh better at his own stories and jokes than anyone I'd ever seen.

After a bit Pearly gets up and walks out beyond the firelight to relieve himself, you know. And he comes back right quick, zippin' his fly, and walkin' as fast as them old stiff legs of his will take him.

"There's somethin' out there," he says.

"Sure," I say. "Armadillos, coons, possums, maybe a stray dog."

"No," he says. "Something else."

"Awww."

"I been a lot of places, boy," he says – he always called me boy on account of I was twenty years younger than he was – "and I'm used to hearin' critters walk about. That don't sound like no damn possum or stray dog to me. Somethin' bigger."

THE DUMP

I start to tell him that he's full of it, you know – and then I hear it too. And a stench like you wouldn't believe floats into camp here. A stench like a grave opened on a decomposin' body, one full of maggots and the smell of earth and death. It was so strong I got a little sick, what with all the rotgut in me.

Pearly says, "You hear it?"

And I did. It was the sound of somethin' heavy, crunchin' down that garbage out there, movin' closer and closer to the camp, like it was afeared of the fire, you know.

I got the heebie-jeebies, and I went into the hut there and got my double-barrel. When I came out Pearly had pulled a little old thirty-two Colt out of his waistband and a brand from the fire, and he was headin' out there in the dark.

"Wait a minute," I called.

"You just stay put, boy. I'll see to this, and I'll see that whatever it is gets a hole in it. Maybe six."

So I waited. The wind picked up and that horrible stench drifted in again, very strong this time. Strong enough so I puked up that hooch I'd drunk. And then suddenly from the dark, while I'm leanin' over throwin' my guts out on the ground, I hear a shot. Another one. Another.

I got up and started callin' for Pearly.

"Stay the hell where you are," he called. "I'm comin' back." Another shot, and then Pearly seemed to fold out of the darkness and come into the light of the fire.

"What is it, Pearly?" I said. "What is it?"

Pearly's face was as white as his teeth. He shook his head. "Ain't never seen nothin' like it… Listen, boy, we got to get the hell out of Dodge. That sucker, it's—" He let his voice trail off, and he looked toward the darkness beyond the firelight.

"Come on, Pearly, what is it?"

"I tell you, I don't know. I couldn't see real good with that there firebrand, and it went out before too long. I heard it down there crunchin' around, over there by that big hill of garbage."

I nodded. That was a pile I'd had heaped up with dirt for a long time. I intended to break it open next time I 'dozed, push some new stuff in with it.

"It—it was comin' out of that pile," Pearly said. "It was wrigglin' like a great gray worm, but... there were legs all over it. Fuzzy legs. And the body – it was jelly-like. Lumber, fence wire, and all manner of crap was stickin' out of it, stickin' out of it like it belonged there, just as natural as a shell on a turtle's back or the whiskers on a cougar's face. It had a mouth, a big mouth, like a railway tunnel, and what looked like teeth... but the brand went out then. I fired some shots. It was still wrigglin' out of that garbage heap. It was too dark to stay there—"

He cut in midsentence. The smell was strong now, solid as a wall of bricks.

"It's movin' into camp," I said.

"Must've come from all that garbage," Pearly said. "Must've been born in all that heat and slime."

"Or come up from the center of the earth," I said, though I figured Pearly was a mite near closer to right.

Pearly put some fresh loads in his revolver. "This is all I got," he said.

"I want to see it eat buckshot," I said.

Then we heard it. Very loud, crunchin' down those mounds of garbage like they was peanut hulls. And then there was silence.

Pearly, he moved back a few steps from the double-barrel toward the shack. I aimed the double-barrel toward the dark.

Silence went on for a while. Why, you could've heard yourself blink. But I wasn't blinkin'. I was a-watchin' out for that critter.

Then I heard it – but it was behind me! I turned just in time to see a fuzzy-like tentacle slither out from behind the shack and grab old Pearly. He screamed, and the gun fell out of his hand. And from the shadows a head showed. A huge, wormlike head with slitted eyes and a mouth large enough to swallow a man. Which is what it did. Pearly didn't make that thing two gulps. Wasn't nothin' left of him but a scrap of flesh hangin' on the thing's teeth.

I emptied a load of buckshot in it, slammed the gun open and loaded her again. By that time it was gone. I could hear it crashin' off in the dark.

I got the keys to the 'dozer and walked around back of the shack on tiptoe. It didn't come out of the dark after me. I cranked the 'dozer, turned on the spotlights, and went out there after it.

It didn't take long to find it. It was movin' across the dump like a snake, slitherin' and a-loopin' as fast as it could go – which wasn't too fast right then. It had a lump in its belly, an undigested lump... Poor old Pearly!

I ran it down, pinned it to the chain-link fence on the far side of the dump, and used my 'dozer blade to mash it up against it. I was just fixin' to gun the motor and cut that sucker's head off when I changed my mind.

Its head was stickin' up over the blade, those slitted eyes lookin' at me... and there, buried in that wormlike face, was the face of a puppy. You get a lot of them here. Well, it was alive now. Head was still mashed in like it was the first time I saw it, but it was movin'. The head was wrigglin' right there in the center of that worm's head.

I took a chance and backed off from that thing. I dropped to the ground and didn't move. I flashed the lights over it.

Pearly was seepin' out of that thing. I don't know how else to describe it, but he seemed to be driftin' out of that jelly-like hide; and when his face and body were halfway out of it, he stopped movin' and just hung there. I realized somethin' then. It was not only created by the garbage and the heat – it lived off of it, and whatever became its food became a part of it. That puppy and old Pearly were now a part of it.

Now don't misunderstand me. Pearly, he didn't know nothin' about it. He was alive, in a fashion, he moved and squirmed, but like that puppy, he no longer thought. He was just a hair on that thing's body. Same as the lumber and wire and such that stuck out of it.

And the beast – well, it wasn't too hard to tame. I named it Otto. It ain't no trouble at all. Gettin' so it don't come when I call, but that's on account of I ain't had nothin' to reward it with, until you showed up. Before that, I had to kind of help it root dead critters out of the heaps... Sit down! I've got Pearly's thirty-two here, and if you move I'll plug you.

Oh, here comes Otto now.

ON THE USE OF SHAPE-SHIFTERS IN WARFARE

Marko Kloos

'THE USE OF LYCANTHROPES AS COMBATANTS IS PROHIBITED. IN CASE OF CAPTURE BY THE ENEMY, SUCH INDIVIDUALS HAVE NO RIGHT TO BE TREATED AS PRISONERS OF WAR, NOR SHALL THEY BE ACCORDED THE RIGHTS OF SUCH.'
—Article 2, Section I, Budapest Accords
(not signed by the United States)

L*ykes."*

The word is spoken softly, but with bile. It comes from the back of the room, where a group of Airborne troops are hunched over their beef and noodles. We have barely made it to the chow line, but now heads are turning, and the din of conversation in the mess hall is taking on a terse quality. Now we're the center of attention, even though few are brave enough to stare at us openly.

Next to me, Sergeant Sobieski is loading up his tray with plates of food two levels high: beef and pasta, mashed potatoes, salad, bread, four slices of pie. I follow suit, even though I'd just as soon have a cold MRE back in our container than choke down the mess hall food with muttered slurs and bits of food getting flung my way.

"You can't sit here," the burly Master Sergeant says when we put down our trays on the dining table.

"I don't see any 'Reserved' signs, Master Sergeant," I say. Sergeant Sobieski grabs his fork and starts eating, supremely unconcerned with the dozen hostile pairs of eyes on us.

"I said *you* can't sit here," the Master Sergeant says again. Sobieski doesn't even look up from his food. Sergeant Sobieski is half a head taller than the biggest regular Army guy in the room, and the arms sticking out of the neatly folded sleeves of his ACU blouse are as big around as my thighs.

On a normal day, I would back down, grab my chow, and find a quiet corner on the base to eat in peace. But we just got off a cramped and noisy chopper, I haven't had any food in six hours, and my rebelling stomach is making me cranky. So I stab a piece of beef with my fork, stick it into my mouth, and start chewing it slowly, all while holding the Master Sergeant's gaze. I almost smile when I see his jaw muscles flex with suppressed anger.

"What is your name and rank, soldier?" he asks, with sharp emphasis on the last word. "You're out of proper uniform."

"I'm Sergeant Decker. This is Sergeant Sobieski. And dress regs don't apply to 300th personnel in theater."

Our uniforms are sanitized: no name tapes, no rank devices, no unit patches. Even our Western allies get twitchy at the thought of a foreign army's lycanthropes present on their soil. Here in the Middle East, where lycanthropy is a capital offense, the locals would get downright apoplectic at the sight of troopers with the unit patch of the 300th Special Operations Company on their sleeves – the first and only segregated all-lycanthrope unit of the Army.

The Master Sergeant looks at us, his jaw still grinding. Then he shakes his head. "Fucking *dog soldiers*," he says. "The Army started turning to shit when they let you people wear the uniform. *Unnatural* is what you are."

Despite the anger welling up in my chest, I chuckle. "I'm more *natural* than you. I can see in the dark, hear the grass grow, follow a scent for twenty miles. All without batteries. Your ass rides around in a stinking Humvee, and you're blind at night without your flashlight and your NVGs. How fucking *natural* is that?"

Next to me, Sobieski puts down his fork and clears his throat. "No disrespect, Master Sergeant, but if you ever call us 'dog soldiers' again in our presence, I will rip off your arm and beat you with it. Now shut up, and let us eat our food in peace, because we have an IED patrol coming up. Sir."

Chair legs squeal on the bare concrete floor as the Master Sergeant and all the other regular Army soldiers at the table stand up, murder in their eyes. The burly master Sergeant balls his hands into fists and starts toward us. Before he has taken two steps, Sobieski lets out a growl. It's a deep, ear-tingling sound, so low and resonant that the silverware on my plate chatters. The entire room falls silent instantly.

Sobieski picks up his soda cup and sucks it empty. The raspy slurping sound of the straw is very loud in the room. He looks at the dozen angry soldiers who have stopped in their tracks in front of us, and there isn't a trace of concern on his face.

The Master Sergeant still has his fists clenched, but the sudden smell of fear coming from his pores tells me that he's glad to be on the other side of the table. He glares at us for another moment, snatches his meal tray off the table, and walks off without another word. One by one, the other soldiers follow. The last one to leave the table hawks up some phlegm and spits it onto the floor near our feet. They walk out of the mess hall without looking back. A few stunned moments later, the conversations in the room resume.

"He'll come back with the base MP in about three minutes," I say.

Sergeant Sobieski shrugs.

"Please. Let me sleep in a cell tonight, send someone else to do this patrol. Not that he's going to do shit." He nods at my plate, and the mostly untouched food on it. "I'd hurry up with that, though. Just in case."

* * *

At dawn, I walk point on patrol for a squad of Army regulars. It's the tolerable sliver of morning between the bone-chilling cold of the night and the relentless heat of the day.

We trudge up the main road of the nearby village, to look for IEDs and flush out local insurgents. The houses are untidy stacks of stone, put together without mortar. A few villagers are out on the street this morning. Some return my greeting, but most pretend I don't exist. For a small mountain village like this, there are too many young men milling around.

High explosives have a particular scent, even through a layer of earth and the rusty metal case of an old artillery shell. Freshly dug earth has a different smell. Together, they make an olfactory marker that's as strong and obvious as a ten-foot neon sign on top of the ambush site.

Even from a hundred yards away, I can smell death waiting for us by the side of the road leading out of the village, masterfully camouflaged.

"Heads up," I say into my radio. "One o'clock, seventy yards past the last house on the right. Make it two one-fifty-fives, underneath the rock pile by the culvert."

"Fantastic," the squad's sergeant says. "Let's secure the site and call out the EOD guys."

I smell the new danger right as a rifle cracks in the distance. The bullet hits me in the hip, just below the edge of my protective vest. I do a graceless little half spin, and fall on my ass. Behind me, the infantry guys take cover. The squad medic starts toward me, but I wave him off. The wound is already knitting itself closed, and even though it hurts like someone rammed a red-hot fireplace poker through me, I know there won't even be a scar by the time I get back to base.

The sniper fires again. The bullet kicks up dust and gravel chips right in front of my feet. This time, I see the flash from the rifle muzzle.

"Left side of the road, one-fifty. The little goat shack with the collapsed roof. He's in the corner at the bottom left."

The soldier manning the fifty-caliber machine gun on the squad's Humvee opens up with his weapon. The slow, thundering staccato of the big gun drowns out the reports from the rifles behind me as the other soldiers return fire as well.

Every time I am under fire, I feel the almost irresistible urge to rip off all these civilized trappings of warfare, and change into my more capable shape. In my other form, I can move faster than a sniper can adjust his aim, and I can smell ambush sites a hundred times better than in my handicapped two-legged form. But I'm on a leash, so I follow orders, and stay human.

Every time it happens, I loathe myself – not for obeying orders, but for accepting the leash willingly.

When it's over, the little goat shack is a pock-marked ruin. When the infantry guys move in, there's nothing there but three empty shell casings and some blood on the dirt.

The squad sergeant watches as I walk around the shack to get the scent of the place.

"Two men," I say. "Shooter and spotter. The shooter's wounded.

174

SHAPE SHIFTERS

They hoofed it out the back and into the hills. I got their scent, so I'll be able to ID them if they're locals."

"'Course they're locals," the squad sergeant says.

The regulars aren't too keen on charging after the shooters into Indian country with just a squad of troops, and I don't blame them. So we radio our contact report, set up security, and wait for the EOD team to arrive and defuse the artillery shells buried by the road. Two people wounded, lots of ammo turned into noise and dust, and at the end of the day, we're right back where we started, soldiers and insurgents alike. And as our days go, so does the war.

* * *

"Three weeks," Sobieski says over dinner. "Bring in the whole 300th, let us off the leash, and we'll own these mountains in three weeks."

"Not going to happen," I say. "You know the regs. No combatant use of lycanthropes."

"We never signed that accord."

"No, we didn't, but that's politics for you. Wouldn't want to piss off the allies."

"Fuck the allies," Sobieski says. "What's the point of having us if you only use us as bomb detectors with legs? Such a waste. It's like using Navy SEALs as lifeguards at the pool."

I chuckle into my chipped beef on toast. Sobieski looks past me and out of the windows of the chow hall. Outside, the sun is setting behind the mountains to our west.

"Just think about it. The whole company, almost two hundred of us, out there digging those bastards out of their caves at night. Leave a bunch of heads for the rest of them to find, just like they do with our guys. Like I said, three weeks."

I can't say I haven't felt the same way before. But then I think about the reception we would get back home with network footage of dismembered bodies preceding us, and the kind of treatment we would provoke if the whole world had their faces rubbed into what can happen when lycanthropes group together in a large pack and go hunting for humans.

But I don't voice those thoughts to Sobieski. Instead, I return his grin with a nod of implied agreement and finish my dinner. Sobieski is not the kind of person who spends a great deal of time thinking about consequences.

* * *

The Forward Operating Base has an observation outpost. It sits on a hilltop half a mile away. Every week, a different squad is rotated there. With a pair of lycanthropes at the base now, Command has decided to send one of us up with the next squad. I draw straws with Sobieski for the first week, and he pulls the short one.

"Something's off about this valley," I tell him as I help him pack his gear. "It doesn't smell right. We'll be in the shit before the week is up. Watch your head up there."

"Hell, I have nothing to worry about," Sobieski says and fastens the straps of his body armor. "Things go to shit, I'll dump all my gear and go native."

"Try not to piss off any of the regulars. You have to sleep sometime."

"So do they," Sobieski says. "It's just a squad. They have any smarts at all, they'll be trying hard not to piss *me* off."

I help him with the rest of his gear and watch as he swaggers off toward the waiting Humvees outside, carrying his hundred-pound backpack like a toiletries bag.

The OP is in sight of the base, but it takes a half hour for a Humvee to climb the steep, narrow dirt road that winds its way up that mountain. If something goes badly wrong, that OP might as well be in another country, because none of us will get up there in time to help.

The little column drives off, rooster tails of dust in their wake. I am now the only lycanthrope on base, only barely welcome, and only for my sense of smell and the ability to see trouble coming in the dark.

They didn't mention these things in the recruiting brochure, but they didn't have to. I've always known what I would be getting into, but I signed the contract anyway, hoping that things would slowly change with time. But they don't – not out there in the mountains, and not in the heads of our fellow soldiers.

SHAPE SHIFTERS

The night is moonless. We set out on patrol just after midnight, a full platoon on foot. My fellow soldiers look barely human in their bulky armor, with the dual lenses of their night vision goggles in front of their faces. I go out light – no rifle because I'm not allowed to fight, and no night vision device because I don't need one. As always, I'm walking point at the head of the column, because I want to get the earliest whiff of trouble if it comes our way, and because I'm much harder to kill than the regular troops.

The insurgents are not out for trouble tonight. All I smell is the suspended life of the village all around us, people sleeping in their houses behind ancient stone walls and crooked doors, and dormant fires in ash-heavy hearths. Still, there's a new scent in the air tonight. I get the vague, unsettling feeling of a threat, but I can't quite identify it. The place smells more wild than before, more dangerous somehow.

We're on the road between the village and the FOB when automatic weapons fire crackles in the distance. We all take covering positions out of habit, but the sound of gunfire isn't coming from any place nearby. It's rolling down from the hilltops to the east, where the observation post is perched on the mountain.

There are some urgent radio conversations behind me. I look over to the OP, which is only visible in the distance because of the muzzle flashes lighting up the hilltop. Something about the gunfire sounds odd. I can hear the clatter from M4 carbines firing their three-round burst staccato, but I don't hear the deeper, more rattling sound of insurgent AK-47s, or the slow, heavy thunder of belt-fed machine guns. It sounds like every trooper on top of that mountain is firing his carbine, but nobody is shooting back.

"The OP's not responding," the lieutenant says. "We're redeploying. Back to the intersection, and up the hill, double-time. And watch the flanks, people."

Sobieski and I have our own radios, separate from the rest of the network. I try to raise him on comms, but he doesn't reply. Whatever is happening up there, he's too busy fighting to worry about answering radio calls.

As we rush back to the intersection, the firefight on the distant hill intensifies. Still, all I hear is our own rifles. Then my radio comes alive with the static-riddled sounds of battle, people shouting and firing bursts. There's a scream, shrill and angry – Sobieski's voice, but in a pitch I've never heard before – and the transmission is cut off.

Then an unmistakably lupine howl rises into the night sky from the hilltop half a mile away. It's silver-bright and savage, triumphant.

"The fuck is your guy *doing?*" the platoon sergeant yells at me over the radio.

"That wasn't Sobieski," I send back, pressing the transmit button with fingers that suddenly seem to clumsy for the task. "Hold the platoon. Don't go up there."

"We got a squad up there, asshole," the platoon sergeant says. "We're going, and if your pal went feral on them, I'll personally shoot him between the eyes."

The hilltop is quiet now, too much so after the short and violent staccato of automatic gunfire.

"I'll go," I say. "If I change, I can run up that hill in a quarter of the time it'll take all of you."

I've decided to go no matter what the lieutenant says. By the time he sends his reply, I've already stripped off my body armor and unbuckled my thigh holster.

"Fine, Sergeant. Go. But we're going to plug everything that comes off that hill on four legs, do you understand?"

"You should," I reply. "In fact, if I'm not back here in five, call in some close air on that hill and let them bomb it flat."

I dash up the hill on all fours as fast as I can. The night air smells like gunpowder and fear, and the heavy copper smell of fresh blood. The new scent I noticed down in the village is up here as well, much stronger now that I am in my more capable form. It's musky and wild, unsettlingly familiar and wholly alien at the same time. I know what I will find at the top of the hill.

The OP is a slaughterhouse. In the darkness, I can smell the blood all over the walls of the little bunkers made from sandbags and Hesco barriers. The dead are all over the OP – on the floor of the bunker, at the top of the main firing position, splayed out in the dirt between the shelters. There are empty cartridge cases strewn everywhere, still warm and smelling of freshly burnt powder. All around the bodies, the dirt has been churned by the struggle, and there are paw prints the size of frying pans in the dust between the dead soldiers.

I find Sobieski in the bunker underneath the heavy weapons emplacement. He's sitting upright against the wall, chin on his chest, as if he's merely taking a quick nap. There isn't an unbroken piece of gear left in the room. I know that Sobieski can hold his own against any three or four guys even when he's in human form, but whatever fought with him in here was stronger and faster. I don't have to check his pulse to know he's dead. His ballistic armor is halfway undone, and his belt is open. When they got jumped, he tried to shed his clothes and gear so he could meet the enemy on equal footing, but he didn't have the time, and then engaged with his bare hands.

His killer is no longer on the hilltop, but he left a scent trail I could follow in my sleep. I want to tear into the darkness, find him, and rip him to shreds, but there's a platoon waiting at the base of the hill, and I don't want them to stumble into this carnage without a word of warning.

When I walk back down the hill, I do so on two legs, in my naked human form, mindful of the thirty rifles and machine guns aimed at me.

"Eleven KIA," I tell the lieutenant. "Don't bother with medics. And don't go up there unless you don't want to sleep well again for a while."

"Your guy?"

"Sobieski's dead," I say. "It got him first, from the looks of it."

"The fuck is 'it'?" he asks, even though I can tell by the smell of fear coming from him that he already knows the answer.

"Get these soldiers off this hill and back to the barn," I say. "Stay out in the open and plug anything you see that has fur. Call in the rapid reaction force. And leave my clothes right here. I'll need those later."

The lieutenant looks at me for a moment, grinding his jaw. Then he glances into the darkness behind me, and the fear seeping out of his pores gets stronger.

"Where are you going?"

"I'm going to chase that bastard down."

Out in the darkness, well beyond the OP, there's another howl, this one a long and mournful dirge.

The lieutenant grips his carbine tighter and reaches for his radio. "Go," he says. "And good luck. Just don't get too close to these guys while you're out and about. We see something stirring in the dark, we're shooting it."

"Aim for the head, and lead your shots," I tell him.

* * *

I pick up the trail again at the OP. Before I change, I kneel in front of Sobieski, touch my forehead to his, and say my good-byes. Before long, Sobieski will be in a body bag and then a zinc coffin. I will not be there when they put him into the ground back home in Pennsylvania.

The werewolf who killed him tore the chain with the dog tags off his neck when they were fighting. I locate it in the dirt by scent, six feet away. I take the two Army tags and put them on Sobieski's lap, for the casualty detail to find. There's another tag on that chain, the five-sided Registered Lycanthrope brass tag we're all required to wear in the civilian world back home. I take the tag and attach it to the chain around my own neck, where it joins another tag just like it.

I don't have any fitting last words, so I render one final salute to Sergeant Jared Sobieski, 300th Special Operations Company (L), and go outside to change. Then I run off into the darkness to track down his killer.

The trail goes cold fifteen miles away. I follow the other werewolf's scent across the rugged landscape for half an hour before it ends in the cold waters of a mountain stream at the bottom of a craggy wadi. I follow the stream for a little while and check the underbrush on both banks for a new scent trail every few hundred meters, but the scent is gone completely. I search the hillsides and ravines in the area until the first rays of the morning sun paint the eastern horizon blood-red, but there's nobody left out here but me.

By the time I get back to my clothes, it's almost daylight, and there are troops from the Quick Reaction Force all over the mountain. I retrieve my stuff, get dressed, and hitch a ride back to base with a passing Humvee, utterly exhausted, and sick with impotent anger.

I get debriefed by a chain of officers that keeps going up the rank ladder as the day progresses. I repeat the same narrative until we're all thoroughly annoyed with each other. At the end of the day, the other werewolf is still out there, and Sobieski is still dead, riding back to Bagram in a sealed body bag on the floor of a Blackhawk. When I get back to the container we shared, all his personal gear is gone, and the place has the smell of disinfectant.

In the evening, the Captain comes into my container.

"We're going down into the village for the weekly bullshit palaver with the tribal elders," he says. "I want you to tag along to stand guard, just in case."

I get off my cot and grab my gear. After a moment, I recall Sobieski, dead at the OP with his vest halfway undone, and I leave my body armor next to the cot.

"I want to sit in on that meeting," I tell the Captain.

"No can do," he says. "They figure out I've brought a lycanthrope along, they'll be so offended they'll never even look at us again. I don't care to have the State Department jumping my shit."

"They have a lycanthrope of their own running around out there," I say. "They have to know who it is. Ask them point-blank, and I'll be able to smell if they're lying."

The Captain mulls my request for a few moments. Then he purses his lips and nods curtly. "Fine. But you're wearing shades. And if they bring the bastard along, I want you to shoot first and tell me later. I'm taking no chances after last night."

* * *

We're sitting on the dusty floor of the village elder's house. It's hot and uncomfortable, with twenty people in a room barely bigger than my living room back home. I can smell irritation and tension all around me, but I barely register the heated conversation between the Captain and the village elders. Right now, I only have eyes for the old man sitting in a corner of the room, sipping his tea impassively. He can't see my own eyes behind the lenses of my sunglasses, but I know he is aware of my attention, because we both smelled each other's presence the moment I entered the room. The old man in the corner is the lycanthrope from last night, the one who killed a dozen of our men.

I know that he's aware of me, aware of the fact that I know what he is. He must smell my nature as clearly as I can smell his. I also know that his companions are unaware. Their protestations of the Captain's accusations are genuine. I can smell no deception or duplicity. They don't know.

I could give him away right now – to my fellow soldiers, who would shoot him on the spot instantly just out of fear, or to his fellow villagers, for a much slower and more unpleasant death. To my own, I'm merely a freak of nature, an unsettling curio, grudgingly afforded person status. To these people, in this part of the world, that old man sipping tea in the corner is an abomination, a walking and breathing blasphemy. I want him dead for what he did, but not in these ways.

I watch the old man over the animated debate in the room between us. He keeps sipping his tea, avoiding my gaze.

Then, at the end of the meeting, the old man looks up, and his eyes meet mine for a moment. They aren't yellow, like those of every other lycanthrope I've ever known. Instead, they are milky as opals.

He nods at me, almost imperceptibly.

I respond with a tiny nod of my own and look away.

We just made an agreement without exchanging words. We will settle this among outcasts, in our own way.

"Any luck?" the Captain asks when we file out of the house into the hot and dusty street again.

"They don't know shit," I reply, and find that I'm not bothered by the duplicity of the omission.

* * *

In the evening, I find a quiet spot at the perimeter of the base. Then I take off my clothes and put them in a pile. I take the dog tags off my neck and place them on top of my clothes. Then I change.

Tomorrow, I will wear the leash around my neck again. Tonight, I am no one's dog soldier.

SHAPE SHIFTERS

He is waiting for me in the wadi, miles away from the nearest village or outpost.

We fight our battle with teeth and claws, not guns. He is strong and fast despite his age, but all feral instinct. I have trained and fought with my own kind for years, and unlike Sobieski, I am not encumbered. We spill each other's blood in a flurry of clashes, but he's the one who does most of the bleeding. But he does not yield, not even when I have him by the throat and he knows he is broken.

His is an honorable death. Better than falling to bullets or being pulped by rocks while buried to the shoulders in the rocky Afghan soil. Despite Sobieski, I take no pleasure in this kill.

When it's over, I wash off the blood in the cold water of a nearby stream. Then I go back to the still form of my enemy, change back into my human shape, and touch my forehead to his.

I brought no hand tools, and the soil is too unyielding for bare hands or paws, so I bury the old man under a pile of rocks I gather from the banks of the stream. I don't know if despite his nature he was a believer, but I gauge the proper direction by the stars and point the grave toward Mecca anyway.

When I change back to my feral self for the run back, I take a last look around. The place seems a fitting resting spot for the old lycanthrope. The land is harsh, unforgiving, and austerely beautiful. The sky is cloudless, and the moon is painting silver streaks onto the surface of the stream nearby. Out here, underneath the black dome of the night sky and its millions of stars, it's more beautiful than in any cathedral I've ever seen.

I raise my head and howl a dirge for my fallen brothers. It echoes back from the hard and ancient mountains all around me in a distant requiem.

* * *

Back at the base, my clothes are still in the sand where I left them. It's the hour of the night when the darkness has not quite started to lift yet, the morning just a sliver of dark blue above the mountains.

I am about to change back into my human form when the door

of a nearby container opens and a soldier steps out into the cool late-night air. He clears his throat and spits into the sand. Then he turns toward the corner of the container and opens his fly to relieve himself, too lazy to walk over to the portable latrines at the end of the container row. Even from fifty yards away, his smell is instantly familiar. It's the Master Sergeant who clashed with us in the mess tent.

I sneak close to the spot where the Master Sergeant is emptying his bladder. When I'm almost behind him, I let out a soft growl from deep down in my chest. The Master Sergeant flinches as if I had hit him with a cattle prod. When he turns around with a hoarse yell, I am already gone, hiding in the shadows between the containers. I smell with satisfaction that the Master Sergeant has pissed all over the front of his own pants.

After breakfast, I go to the Captain and tell him what I've done last night. He prods me for two hours to make me tell him where I've buried the old lycanthrope, but I don't budge. All he needs to know is that the threat to his troops is gone. I don't want them to dig up the body and haul it off to be poked and sliced up.

"That won't help your career at all," the Captain finally says when he has had enough of me. "I'm sending you back as soon as the next Blackhawk gets in. Let your own people deal with you. I don't want to see you at this FOB ever again."

By lunchtime, I'm on a helicopter back to Bagram.

We fly high, out of the range of machine guns and rocket-pro-pelled grenades. The doors of the Blackhawk are open. Underneath, the landscape rolls by, tiny villages hugging hillsides and valleys, ancient sediment deposited by the currents of history. I look down at those remote islands of humanity and wonder how many of them have protectors like the one I buried last night.

I carry my personal documents in a pouch in my leg pocket. My term of service will be up in another two months, and I've been carrying around the reenlistment form for a while. I take it out of the pouch and look at it. The airflow in the cabin is making the form flutter wildly in my hands, like a living thing straining to free itself from my grasp.

SHAPE SHIFTERS

I tear the form in half, fold the pieces, and tear them again and again, until I have nothing but a handful of ragged little paper squares. Then I open my hands and let them go. The turbulence whips them out of the helicopter, where they disperse, dancing the currents of the hot summer wind.

HELPING HAND

Claudine Griggs

Alexandria Stephens knew she was going to die a slow, cold death in space. She floated fifteen meters from her capsule, a single-pilot maintenance shuttle that could operate in low- or high-Earth orbit.

* * *

Construction expenses for single-operator vehicles offered all kinds of economic advantages, especially considering the slender profit margins for satellite or orbital-platform contracts. Moon shuttles required two-to-six member crews, but market forces made smaller transports the only viable option for near-Earth missions. Alexandria's vehicle was durable and maintained by Glen Michaels, an old-school aerospace mechanic whom she trusted like a brother, though Alexandria often double-checked his work while they drank beer and argued about emerging technologies. They both understood that the ship was everything; if trouble developed, shuttle pilots were more than inconvenienced.

But the occasional death of a pilot did not deter the corporate suits. Number-crunching lawyers and actuaries demonstrated that Space Jockeys, Inc., could lose a shuttle and pilot every eighteen months and still turn a profit — including replacement costs, death benefits, and liability payments. They were still serious about safety, and the actual twenty-year average loss rate was one worker per thirty-two point three months, which included a three-man crew that crashed last year on approach to the Eagle Monument construction site at Tranquility Base. But company officials were more serious about the bottom line.

Alexandria understood the dangers when she signed her flight contract, and she would have enlisted at half the pay and twice the risk. Alex had dreamed of becoming a commercial pilot since age eight and had been with Space Jockeys for seven and a half years, earning a reputation as one of the brightest and fastest technicians on duty — twice turning down supervisory positions to continue fieldwork.

"Even in space," she confided, "pencil pushing is not my style."

She was John Wayne on horseback, riding from satellites to telescopes to orbital lasers. At shift's end, she knew exactly how much range had been covered and how many thoroughbreds had been corralled. She loved it, but now she was dying, a flesh-and-blood meteoroid midway from her shuttle and a geosynchronous satellite that was humming again thanks to a new circuit panel she'd installed in seventy-one minutes flat.

There were forty-five minutes of life support left in her suit, and the rescue ship *Sibert,* like the *Carpathia,* would arrive too late. The *Sibert's* mission would be body recovery.

* * *

Alexandria's motion held steady, spinning back to front about once per minute and approaching the shuttle at negligible speed, slightly off course. But even if she were on course, her air would run dry before she reached the vehicle. And after the O_2 tanks emptied, the heating units would shut down and her body would solid up fast in the minus 240-degree shadow of Earth. She could see the lights of her ship, a soft glow from the nuclear-powered satellite, and millions of stars. The deep emptiness of the Pacific Ocean was framed by glowing cities.

Strangely, the lights comforted her even if they could not save her. She needed propulsion from her mobility pack, a damned near infallible piece of equipment with multiple safeguards that had been knocked dead by a pea-sized meteoroid that also cut her forward motion, set her rotating, and disabled her means back to the lifepod that should already be returning her to base. As a result, Alexandria was no longer an astronaut, no longer an $835,000 corporate investment; she was orbital debris to be cleared away when the *Sibert* arrived. Her shuttle was fifteen meters distant, but it might as well be halfway to Andromeda. The meteoroid would have been more merciful had it bulls-eyed her helmet instead of mobility unit. A quick, unaware death.

Now, there was no way to alter her forward motion or rotation, which, as it turned out, was the only enjoyable part of this mess. As she waited for life-support to end, at least she would have a 360-degree view. Alexandria was an optimist, confident to an almost infinite degree, but she was also a physicist. Reality existed. Space was unforgiving. And her future prospects were zero.

* * *

Thirty minutes later, still drifting and trying to enjoy the galactic view, Alexandria realized that she had been an idiot, allowing half an hour to slip by without grasping the possibility of life. She and the physical universe were intimate friends, and such friends do not go gently into the night.

A thick Velcro strap held an old-style, standard-issue Jockey Watch around her suit at the left wrist. She pulled the lash as tight possible, pulled until she feared the band would break though it was rated for 750-degree temperature swings and 1,500 pounds of tensile strength. She refastened the Velcro, trusting the strap to maintain suit pressure.

Then, without hesitation, she unhinged her left glove. The cold vacuum of space stabbed her naked skin. She screamed inside her suit from pain but held firmly onto the glove she had just removed. Everything depended on that hunk of layered fabric and aluminized polymers; Alexandria only hoped it had sufficient mass to nudge her toward the ship — and she had already wasted thirty minutes floating like a cabbage. Of course, her throw must be hard and precise; then she must latch onto the ship with one hand if she got there.

"Probably easier to sink one from mid-court," she thought, "but I'll take the shot."

The pain stopped after her hand froze solid, and Alexandria could focus her thoughts again. She waited until the spin positioned her facing the satellite. Then, offering a prayer to Isaac Newton, she hurled the glove underhanded with the same control she used on the pitcher's mound at Princeton, throwing from the center of her body and aiming dead at the satellite. If her trajectory were correct, the counterforce of a space-glove fastball should propel her toward the shuttle.

There was some good news. Her suit seemed to be holding pressure at the watchband; she veered more or less in the desired direction; and her body rotation increased to only once every thirty seconds. The bad news. She was still traveling too slowly and her track would just miss the shuttle. But Alexandria was no longer a vegetable. There were eleven minutes to solve the problems.

She allowed three minutes for observation and recalculation of the necessary course change. Then, without hesitation, without overthinking, she grabbed her frozen left hand and snapped it off like an icicle. Then she hurled it awkwardly over her head and left shoulder.

Alexandria's counterclockwise rotation slowed, though she was now spinning gradually feet over head, and it took a few minutes to confirm that she on target toward the beautiful, warm, oxygenated *Anthem*. The only questions were: Would she arrive before her suit ran out of O_2? Could she snag the shuttle with one hand and a frozen stump? Would the wristband hold pressure while she maneuvered inside?

Alexandria focused on her goal with each gyration. She counted off meters per minute and tried to slow her breathing. She calculated the moment when she must thrust for a handhold.

* * *

"Anthem to Jockey Mother. Alexandria calling Jockey Mother. Over."

"Hello, *Anthem*! What's the story, Alex? We calculate you're dead. Over."

"Hey, Georgie Boy. You didn't think I was going down without a fight? Cancel the distress call, and tell Doc there's prosthetic work headed his way. My left hand's an orbiting ice ball. Over."

George liked Alexandria. Never lost or damaged a ship in her career, and she could change a control panel before most techs found the right screwdriver.

"What do you mean?!" said George. "You tell us the jig is up and then shut down communications. Are you in the shuttle? Over."

"All cozied up. Inflated a tourniquet around my forearm and am about dose myself with Morphinex-D, the all-purpose pain killer, sedative, and antibiotic for today's space traveler. The ship's on auto return and docking because I'll soon be in Happy Land, but I expect the doc to have me mission-ready in four weeks. And if Old Man Jones thinks I'm paying for suit repair on this job, he'll look worse than my mobility pack when I'm done with him. Over."

"While we're on that subject," said George, "folks around the control room are pretty upset. You phone home, tell us you're gonna die, and then shut down the intercom. Not very nice, Alex. Not one bit. Over."

"Sorry, George. Didn't want anyone to hear me crying if I broke down. I would've had to kill you if that happened, so forgive me. I'll buy the beer as soon as I can hold a mug, and tell Jones to pay bonuses to our watch designers. I'd like to kiss them all. Over and out."

FISH NIGHT

Joe R Lansdale

It was a bleached-bone afternoon with a cloudless sky and a monstrous sun. The air trembled like a mass of gelatinous ectoplasm. No wind blew.

Through the swelter came a worn, black Plymouth, coughing and belching white smoke from beneath its hood. It wheezed twice, backfired loudly, died by the side of the road.

The driver got out and went around to the hood. He was a man in the hard winter years of life, with dead brown hair and a heavy belly riding his hips. His shirt was open to the navel, the sleeves rolled up past his elbows. The hair on his chest and arms was gray.

A younger man climbed out on the passenger side, went around front too. Yellow sweat-explosions stained the pits of his white shirt. An unfastened, striped tie was draped over his neck like a pet snake that had died in its sleep.

"Well?" the younger man said.

The old man said nothing. He opened the hood. A calliope note of steam blew out from the radiator in a white puff, rose to the sky, turned clear.

"Damn," the old man said, and he kicked the bumper of the Plymouth as if he were kicking a foe in the teeth. He got little satisfaction out of the action, just a nasty scuff on his brown wingtip and a jar to his ankle that hurt like hell.

"Well?" the young man repeated.

"Well what? What do you think? Dead as the can-opener trade this week. Deader. The radiator's chicken-pocked with holes."

"Maybe someone will come by and give us a hand."

"Sure."

"A ride anyway."

"Keep thinking that, college boy."

"Someone is bound to come along," the young man said.

"Maybe. Maybe not. Who else takes these cutoffs? The main highway, that's where everyone is. Not this little no-account shortcut." He finished by glaring at the young man.

"I didn't make you take it," the young man snapped. "It was on the map. I told you about it, that's all. You chose it. You're the one that decided to take it. It's not my fault. Besides, who'd have expected the car to die?"

"I did tell you to check the water in the radiator, didn't I? Wasn't that back as far as El Paso?"

"I checked. It had water then. I tell you, it's not my fault. You're the one that's done all the Arizona driving."

"Yeah, yeah," the old man said, as if this were something he didn't want to hear. He turned to look up the highway.

No cars. No trucks. Just heat waves and miles of empty concrete in sight.

They seated themselves on the hot ground with their backs to the car. That way it provided some shade – but not much. They sipped on a jug of lukewarm water from the Plymouth and spoke little until the sun fell down. By then they had both mellowed a bit. The heat had vacated the sands and the desert chill had settled in. Where the warmth had made the pair snappy, the cold drew them together.

The old man buttoned his shirt and rolled down his sleeves while the young man rummaged a sweater out of the backseat. He put the sweater on, sat back down. "I'm sorry about this," he said suddenly.

"Wasn't your fault. Wasn't anyone's fault. I just get to yelling some-times, taking out the can-opener trade on everything but the can-open-ers and myself. The days of the door-to-door salesman are gone, son."

"And I thought I was going to have an easy summer job," the young man said.

The old man laughed. "Bet you did. They talk a good line, don't they?"

"I'll say!"

"Make it sound like found money, but there ain't no found money, boy. Ain't nothing simple in this world. The company is the only one ever makes any money. We just get tireder and older with more holes in our shoes. If I had any sense I'd have quit years ago. All you got to make is this summer—"

"Maybe not that long."

"Well, this is all I know. Just town after town, motel after motel, house after house, looking at people through screen wire while they shake their heads 'no'. Even the cockroaches at the sleazy motels begin to look like little fellows you've seen before, like maybe they're door-to-door peddlers that have to rent rooms, too."

The young man chuckled. "You might have something there."

They sat quietly for a moment, welded in silence. Night had full grip on the desert now. A mammoth gold moon and billions of stars cast a whitish glow from eons away.

The wind picked up. The sand shifted, found new places to lie down. The undulations of it, slow and easy, were reminiscent of the midnight sea. The young man, who had crossed the Atlantic by ship once, said as much.

"The sea?" the old man replied. "Yes, yes, exactly like that. I was thinking the same. That's part of the reason it bothers me. Part of why I was stirred up this afternoon. Wasn't just the heat doing it. There are memories of mine out here," he nodded at the desert, "and they're visiting me again."

The young man made a face. "I don't understand."

"You wouldn't. You shouldn't. You'd think I'm crazy."

"I already think you're crazy. So tell me."

The old man smiled. "All right, but don't you laugh."

"I won't."

A moment of silence moved in between them. Finally the old man said, "It's fish night, boy. Tonight's the full moon and this is the right part of the desert if memory serves me, and the feel is right – I mean, doesn't the night feel like it's made up of some fabric, that it's different from other nights, that it's like being inside a big dark bag, the sides sprinkled with glitter, a spotlight at the top, at the open mouth, to serve as a moon?"

"You lost me."

The old man sighed. "But it feels different. Right? You can feel it too, can't you?"

"I suppose. Sort of thought it was just the desert air. I've never camped out in the desert before, and I guess it is different."

"Different, all right. You see, this is the road I got stranded on twenty years back. I didn't know it at first, least not consciously. But down deep in my gut I must have known all along I was taking this road, tempting fate, offering it, as the football people say, an instant replay."

"I still don't understand about fish night. What do you mean, you were here before?"

"Not this exact spot, somewhere along in here. This was even less of a road back then than it is now. The Navajos were about the only ones who traveled it. My car conked out like this one today, and I started walking instead of waiting. As I walked the fish came out. Swimming along in the starlight pretty as you please. Lots of them. All the colors of the rainbow. Small ones, big ones, thick ones, thin ones. Swam right up to me... *right through me!* Fish just as far as you could see. High up and low down to the ground.

"Hold on, boy. Don't start looking at me like that. Listen: you're a college boy, you know what was here before we were, before we crawled out of the sea and changed enough to call ourselves men. Weren't we once just slimy things, brothers to the things that swim?"

"I guess, but—"

"Millions and millions of years ago this desert was a sea bottom. Maybe even the birthplace of man. Who knows? I read that in some science books. And I got to thinking this: If the ghosts of people who have lived can haunt houses, why can't the ghosts of creatures long dead haunt where they once lived, float about in a ghostly sea?"

"Fish with a soul?"

"Don't go small-mind on me, boy. Look here: Some of the Indians I've talked to up north tell me about a thing they call the manitou. That's a spirit. They believe everything has one. Rocks, trees, you name it. Even if the rock wears to dust or the tree gets cut to lumber, the manitou of it is still around."

"Then why can't you see these fish all the time?"

"Why can't we see ghosts all the time? Why do some of us never see them? Time's not right, that's why. It's a precious situation, and I figure it's like some fancy time lock – like the banks use. The lock clicks open at the bank; and there's the money. Here it ticks open and we get the fish of a world long gone."

"Well, it's something to think about," the young man managed.

The old man grinned at him. "I don't blame you for thinking what you're thinking. But this happened to me twenty years ago and I've never forgotten it. I saw those fish for a good hour before they disappeared. A Navajo came along in an old pickup right after and I bummed a ride into town with him. I told him what I'd seen. He just looked at me and grunted. But I could tell he knew what I was talking about. He'd seen it too, and probably not for the first time.

"I've heard that Navajos don't eat fish for some reason or another, and I bet it's the fish in the desert that keep them from it. Maybe they hold them sacred. And why not? It was like being in the presence of the Creator; like crawling around in the liquids with no cares in the world."

"I don't know. That sounds sort of..."

"Fishy?" The old man laughed. "It does, it does. So this Navajo drove me to town. Next day I got my car fixed and went on. I've never taken that cutoff again – until today, and I think that was more than accident. My subconscious was driving me. That night scared me, boy, and I don't mind admitting it. But it was wonderful too, and I've never been able to get it out of my mind."

The young man didn't know what to say.

The old man looked at him and smiled. "I don't blame you," he said. "Not even a little bit. Maybe I am crazy."

They sat awhile longer with the desert night, and the old man took his false teeth out and poured some of the warm water on them to clean them of coffee and cigarette residue.

"I hope we don't need that water," the young man said.

"You're right. Stupid of me! We'll sleep a while, start walking before daylight. It's not far to the next town. Ten miles at best." He put his teeth back in. "We'll be just fine."

The young man nodded.

No fish came. They did not discuss it. They crawled inside the car, the young man in the front seat, the old man in the back. They used their spare clothes to bundle under, to pad out the cold fingers of the night.

Near midnight the old man came awake suddenly and lay with his hands behind his head and looked up and out the window opposite him, studied the crisp desert sky.

And a fish swam by.

Long and lean and speckled with all the colors of the world, flicking its tail as if in good-bye. Then it was gone.

The old man sat up. Outside, all about, were the fish – all sizes, colors, and shapes.

"Hey, boy, wake up!"

The younger man moaned.

"Wake up!"

The young man, who had been resting face down on his arms, rolled over. "What's the matter? Time to go?"

"The fish."

"Not again."

"Look!"

The young man sat up. His mouth fell open. His eyes bloated. Around and around the car, faster and faster in whirls of dark color, swam all manner of fish.

"Well, I'll be... *how?*"

"I told you, I told you."

The old man reached for the door handle, but before he could pull it a fish swam lazily through the back window glass, swirled about the car, once, twice, passed through the old man's chest, whipped up and went out through the roof.

The old man cackled, jerked open the door. He bounced around beside the road. Leaped up to swat his hands through the spectral fish. "Like soap bubbles," he said. "No. Like smoke!"

The young man, his mouth still agape, opened his door and got out. Even high up he could see the fish. Strange fish, like nothing he'd ever seen pictures of or imagined. They flitted and skirted about like flashes of light.

As he looked up, he saw, nearing the moon, a big dark cloud. The only cloud in the sky. That cloud tied him to reality suddenly, and he thanked the heavens for it. Normal things still happened. The whole world had not gone insane.

After a moment the old man quit hopping among the fish and came out to lean on the car and hold his hand to his fluttering chest.

"Feel it, boy? Feel the presence of the sea? Doesn't it feel like the beating of your own mother's heart while you float inside the womb?"

And the younger man had to admit that he felt it, that inner rolling rhythm that is the tide of life and the pulsating heart of the sea.

"How?" the young man said. "Why?"

"The time lock, boy. The locks clicked open and the fish are free. Fish from a time before man was man. Before civilization started weighing us down. I know it's true. The truth's been in me all the time. It's in us all."

"It's like time travel," the young man said. "From the past to the future, they've come all that way."

"Yes, yes, that's it... Why, if they can come to our world, why can't we go to theirs? Release that spirit inside of us, tune into their time?"

"Now wait a minute..."

"My God, that's it! They're pure, boy, pure. Clean and free of civilization's trappings. That must be it! They're pure and we're not. We're weighted down with technology. These clothes. That car."

The old man started removing his clothes.

"Hey!" the young man said. "You'll freeze."

"If you're pure, if you're completely pure," the old man mumbled, "that's it... yeah, that's the key."

"You've gone crazy."

"I won't look at the car," the old man yelled, running across the sand, trailing the last of his clothes behind him. He bounced about the desert like a jackrabbit. "God, God, nothing is happening, nothing," he moaned. "This isn't my world. I'm of that world. I want to float free in the belly of the sea, away from can openers and cars and—"

The young man called the old man's name. The old man did not seem to hear.

"I want to leave here!" the old man yelled. Suddenly he was springing about again. "The teeth!" he yelled. "It's the teeth. Dentist, science, foo!" He punched a hand into his mouth, plucked the teeth free, tossed them over his shoulder.

Even as the teeth fell the old man rose. He began to stroke. To swim up and up and up, moving like a pale pink seal among the fish.

In the light of the moon the young man could see the pooched jaws of the old man, holding the last of the future's air. Up went the old man, up, up, up, swimming strong in the long-lost waters of a time gone by.

The young man began to strip off his own clothes. Maybe he could nab him, pull him down, put the clothes on him. Something... God, something... but, what if *he* couldn't come back? And there were the fillings in his teeth, the metal rod in his back from a motorcycle accident. No, unlike the old man, this was his world and he was tied to it. There was nothing he could do.

A great shadow weaved in front of the moon, made a wriggling slat of darkness that caused the young man to let go of his shirt buttons and look up.

A black rocket of a shape moved through the invisible sea: a shark, the granddaddy of all sharks, the seed for all of man's fears of the deep.

And it caught the old man in its mouth, began swimming upward toward the golden light of the moon. The old man dangled from the creature's mouth like a ragged rat from a house cat's jaws. Blood blossomed out of him, coiled darkly in the invisible sea.

The young man trembled. "Oh God," he said once.

Then along came that thick dark cloud, rolling across the face of the moon.

Momentary darkness.

And when the cloud passed there was light once again, and an empty sky.

No fish.

No shark.

And no old man.

Just the night, the moon and the stars.

LUCKY THIRTEEN

A Frontlines short story

Marko Kloos

The Fleet has a tradition: the rookie drop ship commander in the unit always gets the ship nobody else wants.

My hand-me-down was Lucky Thirteen. There was nothing wrong with her, technically speaking. She was an older model Wasp, not one of the new Dragonflies, but most of our wing was still on Wasps back then. But pilots are a superstitious bunch, and it had been decided that Lucky Thirteen was an unlucky ship. Before they gave her to me, she had lost two crews with all hands, one of them with the entire troop compartment loaded to the last seat. Both times, they recovered the ship, hosed her out, and patched her up again. A ship surviving an all-hands loss without being destroyed is very unusual – surviving two of them is so rare that I've never heard of such a thing before or since.

Her hull number wasn't actually 13. She wore a dark red 5 on her olive drab flanks. But one of the grease monkeys had found her assembly number plate while swapping out some fried parts one day, and the news made the rounds that the unlucky ship's serial number was 13-02313. Not only did it have a leading and trailing 13 in it, but all the digits of her serial number also added up to 13. Thusly branded, she was named 'Lucky Thirteen', and put in storage as a cold spare until they needed an airframe for the new First Lieutenant. Then they dusted her off, updated the computers, and handed me the keys.

She came with a new crew chief, too – Staff Sergeant Fisher. I met him for the first time when I went down to the storage hangar to check out my new ride. He was already busy with her, plugging all kinds of diagnostics hardware into the data ports in her bowels. When I walked around Lucky Thirteen for the first time, I noticed that he had already painted my name onto the armor belt underneath the right cockpit window: 1LT HALLEY 'COMET'.

"I took the liberty," Sergeant Fisher said when I ran my fingers across the stenciled letters of my call sign. "Hope you don't mind, ma'am."

"Not at all," I told him. "She's really yours, anyway. I just get to take her out occasionally."

He smiled, obviously pleased to be assigned to a pilot who knew the proper chain of ownership in a drop ship wing.

"Don't let the talk bother you. About her being unlucky, I mean. She's a good ship. I checked her top to bottom, and she's in better shape than some of the new crates."

"Talk don't bother me, Sarge," I told him. "I'm not the superstitious kind. It's just a machine."

"No, ma'am," Sergeant Fisher replied, and the smile on his face morphed into a bit of a smirk.

"She ain't just a machine. They all have personalities, same as you and I."

* * *

Lucky Thirteen did have a personality, all right. Fortunately, it meshed well with mine.

I've flown dozens of Wasp drop ships, from the barebones A1 models they mostly use as trainers now, to the newest Whiskey Wasps that are so crammed full of upgrades that they might as well give them their own class name. None of them had the same responsive controls as Lucky Thirteen. The Wasps have always been twitchy in any version – you have to fly them with your fingertips, because they're so sensitive to control input. No Wasp likes a heavy hand on the stick. Lucky Thirteen was even more twitchy than the average Wasp, but once you had her figured out, you could pull off maneuvers that most new pilots would consider physically impossible. Something about Lucky Thirteen was just right. Maybe it was the harmonics of the frame, maybe the way all her parts had worked themselves into synchronicity with each other – but flying her felt like you were an integral part of the ship, not just her driver.

Thirteen and I had five weeks to get used to each other before we had our first combat drop together. We were the tail end of a four-ship flight, tasked to ferry a Spaceborne Infantry company down to Procyon Bc's solitary moon. We had beaten the local Chinese garrison into submission from orbit, and now the 940th SI Regiment was going to drop into the path of the retreating Chinese troops to finish them off before they could rally and reform.

Intel never figured out what went wrong that day. I don't know if the Chinese managed to hack into our secure battle network, or if it was just a case of really shitty luck. What I do know is that our drop ship flight went skids down to let the troops disembark near a ridge line, and that all hell broke loose as soon as we hit the ground. The landing zone was lined with those new autonomous anti-aircraft gun pods the Chinese put in service – thirty-six barrels in six rows of six, each stacked from front to back with superposed loads. The whole thing is hooked up to a passive IFF module and a short-range radar and parked out of sight, like a mine. We didn't get a whiff of them on our threat scanners until they opened fire. Each of those things shoots a quarter million rounds per minute, and while each individual shell won't do a great deal of damage to an armored drop ship, the cumulative effect is like aiming a high-pressure water hose at an anthill.

We had landed in diamond formation, with Lucky Thirteen at the tail end of the diamond, farthest from the row of gun pods waiting for us. That's what saved our bacon that day. My crew chief had just released the tail ramp when I saw hundreds of muzzle flashes lighting up the night in front of us. I yelled at the Sarge to pull the ramp back up, and goosed the engines to get us off the ground again. In front of us, the lead drop ship had already started disgorging its platoon, and half their troops were already out of the ship and in the line of fire. For a moment, I fully intended to drop my bird between the exposed troops and the guns, but then the lead Wasp just blew up right in front of me. One moment, it was squatting on the ground, SI troopers seeking cover all around it, and the next moment it was just a cloud of parts getting flung in every direction.

I got us back in the air at that point. I flew Thirteen about three hundred meters backwards on her tail, to keep the belly armor between us and those guns. Then I flipped the ship around, did the lowest wing-over I've ever done, and high-tailed it out of the landing zone at a hundred and thirty percent emergency power.

Lucky Thirteen was the only surviving drop ship of the flight that day. Banshee 72, the ship that blew up in front of me, was dispersed over a quarter square kilometer, along with her two pilots, her crew chief, and thirty-eight SI troopers in full kit. Banshee 73 and 74 got so chewed up that they never got off the moon, either, and the Fleet had to send in a flight of Shrikes to destroy the airframes in place where they did their emergency landings. Lucky Thirteen didn't even have a scratch in her new paint.

After I had the ship back in the docking clamp, I started quaking like a leaf in high wind, and I didn't stop for two hours. Mentally, the shakes lasted a lot longer. I still blame myself for not diving back into that LZ right away, and putting some suppressive fire onto those gun pods, even though I did exactly what you're supposed to do when the bus is full of mudlegs – get out of danger and keep the troops safe.

Nobody from Banshee 72 survived. Thirty-one troopers and one pilot died on Banshee 73, and fourteen troopers and the crew chief bought it on Banshee 74. Yeah, I still blame myself for not going back to help them, even though I played it precisely by the book.

But the first time some jackass Second Lieutenant from SI told me off for not staying in the hot LZ on Procyon Bc, I punched him in the nose, and hit him with his own meal tray for good measure. It was an almost cathartic experience, and well worth the forty-eight hours in the brig.

* * *

I flew nineteen more combat missions in Lucky Thirteen after that. I ferried troops into battle, dropped off supplies, made ground attack runs, and picked up recon teams from hostile worlds. In all that time, I didn't have a single casualty on my ship. Three times out of nineteen, my Lucky Thirteen was the only airworthy unit in the entire flight at the end of the mission. She brought us home safely every time, even when the ground fire was so thick that you could have stepped out of the cockpit and walked down to the deck on shrapnel shards.

LUCKY THIRTEEN

After the tenth mission in a row had passed with my shop remaining unscratched, the other pilots actually started to mean it when they called her 'Lucky Thirteen'.

Then came the day we got a pair of fresh-off-the-floor Whiskey Wasps, so new that their pilot seats were still covered in plastic wrap. Normally, a pair of brand-new ships in the wing triggers a complex series of trickle-down upgrades as the senior pilots claim the new birds and pass their old ones down the roster to the junior jocks. This time, Lieutenant Colonel Connolly came to me and offered me the shiny new Whiskey Wasp he was slated to receive, if I let him have Lucky Thirteen in exchange.

It was a singular pleasure to decline his offer.

* * *

The Fleet has another tradition: once you find something that works for you, and you get attached to it, you end up losing it.

Lucky Thirteen died on a cold and sunny day out on some desolate rock around Fomalhaut. She didn't get blown out of the sky or stomped flat by a Lanky. I killed her myself, willingly.

I went down to the planet to pick up a recon team that had been compromised. When we got to the rendezvous point, our four Recon guys were engaged with what looked like an entire company of Russians. I've done hot pickups before, but never one where I had to pry our snake eaters from the embrace of half the planetary garrison. The Russian troops were not very keen on having their prize snatched away by a solitary drop ship. As soon as I came swooping into the pickup zone, all kinds of shit came flying our way. Judging by the number of hand-held missiles launched from the ground, every other trooper in that company must have taken an anti-aircraft tube along for the chase. My threat scanner lit up like a Pachinko parlor, and for a few minutes, I was busy dodging missiles and pumping out countermeasures. All the while, the guys on the ground were screaming for us to come back and pluck them out of the mess. Finally, the ground fire slacked off a bit, and I rolled back into the target area with my thumb on the launch button.

The Russians had our team pinned down, and their lead squad was so close to our guys that you couldn't have driven a utility truck through the space between them without rolling over somebody's feet. I made a close pass with the cannons, and the Russians ran for cover. By then, I had the attention of the whole company, and everyone aimed their rifles and belt-fed guns skyward and let fly. The small arms fire pinging off Lucky Thirteen's armor was so dense that it sounded like hail in an ice storm. On my next pass, I emptied most of the rocket pods on my external ordnance pylons, gave my left-seater instructions to use our chin turret on everything that wasn't wearing NAC camo, and then put our ship down right between the Russians and our chewed-up recon team.

Staff Sergeant Fisher was the ballsiest crew chief I've ever had. He had that ramp down the second our bird hit the dirt, and he was out to help the injured Recon guys into our ship, even though the incoming fire was churning up little dust fountains all over the place. Only one of the Recon guys was still able to walk onto the ramp on his own feet. Sergeant Fisher went out three times to get the other guys, dashing across fifty yards of live-firing shooting range every time, and hauling back two hundred pounds of armor-clad Recon trooper on each trip. Finally, he had everyone back in the hold, and I redlined the torque gauge getting our bird off the ground and out of there.

We didn't get too far. The Russians had called in their own gunship for support, and it managed to sneak up on us right above the deck without pegging the threat scanner. I was focused on keeping us going at low level and high speed when I heard a sharp warbling sound from the radar warning sensor. He must have been almost on top of us when he launched, because I didn't even have time to thumb my countermeasures button. The Russian missile went right into our starboard engine, which was running at a hundred and twenty percent, and blew it all to hell. For a second or two, we were headed for the dirt at seven hundred knots, but then I caught her, and brought the ship out of the spin we had been knocked into. I pointed her up at the blue sky and firewalled her last remaining engine.

The Russian had been so close behind us that he ended up over-shooting us, which was a stroke of luck, because I still had all four of my Copperhead air-to-air missiles on the wingtips. I launched two of them cold, waited until the Russian pilot kicked out his countermeasures, and then launched the remaining pair right up his ass with a solid lock. One nailed his port engine, and the other one chopped off the last third of his ship's tail, along with the tail rudder and the vertical stabilizers. We were only a thousand feet or so off the deck, and the Russian pilot barely had time to eject his crew before his ship cartwheeled into the rocks and went up in a lovely fireball.

Our ship was only in slightly better shape. I stabilized our attitude, and let the computer figure out how badly we were hurt. The Russian missile had taken out our engine, and some of the secondary shrapnel had severed the main data bus along with three out of the four hydraulic lines. We were still airworthy, but only barely, and spaceflight was out of the question. With the hurt Recon guys in the back, we couldn't do like the Russians and eject, so I backed off the throttle and looked for a good place to put down my wounded bird.

Fomalhaut's moon is a rocky, dusty piece of shit, like half the places we fight over with the SRA. It looked like the desert out in Utah where I went to Basic, only without even the little bit of vegetation we had out there. With my remaining engine starting to cough up its inner workings, I couldn't be too picky, so I chose the first patch of ground that looked reasonably even and rock-free and directed whatever juice I had left in the battered ship to cushion our descent. We hit the dirt lightly enough for me to put down the skids and do a proper three-point touchdown. The way the landing site was laid out meant that I had to make my final approach facing the way we had come. Those turned out our lucky breaks in the end. The skid landing meant that the chin turret could still rotate, and the approach had the ship come to rest pointing at the plateau where we had just picked up our recon team.

As soon as we were down in the dirt, I turned off the engine to keep it from tearing itself to shreds. At that point, Thirteen was still salvageable – missing an engine, and chewed up by shrapnel, but they had brought her back from near-scrap condition twice before. Our electrical system still worked, and I sent out a distress call while Sergeant Fisher lowered the tail ramp and started hauling people out of the hull. But when my left-seater reached for the Master Power switch to turn off the ship completely, I waved him off.

"Just leave her on until the batteries run dry," I said to him.

We were within line of sight of the plateau where half a company of pissed-off Russian marines had watched our descent, and not two minutes after our landing, the threat warning receiver started chirping again. I glanced at it to see that we were being targeted by millimeter-wave short range radar bursts, probably the Russian version of our MARS assault rocket launchers. One of those could blow up what was left of Lucky Thirteen, but we were at the limit of their effective range, and my ship still had her countermeasures suite. I switched the system to AUTONOMOUS and got out of my seat.

"Sergeant Fisher and Second Lieutenant Denton, get those grunts out of here and to cover somewhere."

"Copy that, ma'am," Lieutenant Denton said. "What's the plan?"

"You wait for the evac birds, and stay low. I'll hop into the gunner's seat and warm up the cannon. Now *move. Doubletime.*"

"No need for heroics, ma'am," Sergeant Fisher said from the outside of the ship. "We'll all head for cover, bring some rifles from the armory."

"I'm not planning on getting shot today, Sarge. I'll bail just as soon as that cannon is empty. Now *move* it, and stay way the fuck away from the ship. Rescue birds don't get here before the Russkies, I'll pull the boom handle on my way out."

I waved Lieutenant Denton out of the cockpit and climbed into the gunner's seat to take control of the ship's chin turret. I wasn't even strapped in all the way when the threat warning warbled again, and the dust on the plateau a mile away stirred up with the launch of a pair of rockets.

You *can* kill a Wasp with an assault rocket, but it has to be a lucky shot. Those rockets are designed for use against ground fortifications and big biological targets like Lankies, not against fast-moving drop ships with sophisticated electronic warfare kit. Even stationary in the dirt, a Wasp is not an easy kill for a rocket gunner. The jamming suite zapped the warhead seekers of the incoming rockets, and they went wild and exploded in the rocks before they had crossed the distance halfway. The Russians tried again, this time with a brace of three rockets, but being stationary just made my ship's jamming suite all the more effective, and those went wild almost as soon as they were out of the launchers.

Line of sight works both ways, of course. I plugged my helmet into the gunner's console, cranked the magnification of the gun sight to maximum, and popped the safety cap of the fire control with my thumb. Then I returned the favor, liberally.

The chin turret of a Wasp is fitted with a three-barreled autocannon that fires caseless shells at something like twelve hundred rounds per minute. From a mile away, the chain of impact explosions from the dual-purpose rounds looked like a chain of tiny volcanoes had just erupted in sequence on the ridge line. I held the trigger down for about five seconds and raked the ridge from left to right. There were no follow-up rocket shots from the Russians.

My cannon fire bought us about five minutes. I took the time to wipe the data off the memory banks of my ship, rendering her as dumb as she had been in the storage hangar. The self-destruct mechanism would blow the entire ship into fine shrapnel, but sometimes it doesn't trigger properly, and we were all instructed to lobotomize our birds if we ditched on enemy soil. By the time I was done, the Russians had worked up enough courage again to shoot at us again, this time with small arms fire. I took up my spot in the gunner's seat again and popped off bursts at likely hiding spots. My crew had gotten clear of the ship and taken up position a few hundred meters behind the bird, out of the line of fire for now. The Russians were out for blood now, and if they managed to get around the zone covered by my gun turret, they would have us all in the bag anyway.

For the next ten minutes, it was a gun duel – my autocannon against their rifles and belt-fed guns. Every time I saw movement on the rocky plain in front of me, I put a short burst into the general vicinity. I don't know how many of them I actually got, but I didn't kill enough to discourage the rest, because they kept coming, and their fire kept getting more accurate. The Wasp shrugged off the rifle fire, but some of the belt-fed guns were loaded with harder stuff, and the armored cockpit glass started falling apart under the cumulative hits. One of the Russians had a heavy-caliber anti-materiel rifle, and the first round from that beast came clean through the middle of my center cockpit panel and center-punched the pilot seat I had been sitting in until we crash-landed. I hunkered down behind the front instrument panel and kept shooting back, pumping out explosive rounds and watching the ammo counter work its way down to triple, and then double digits.

The first time one of their rounds hit me, I didn't even realize I had been shot. I just felt something wet run down my right arm and drip off my fingertips, and when I tore myself away from the gun sight to investigate, I saw that something had zipped through the sleeve of my flight suit. As I was peeling the wet sleeve off my skin, another burst of fire finally shattered the front panel completely, and I took a round in the same arm, almost down by the elbow. That one hurt like hell right away.

I guess they knew they had tagged me when I didn't return fire right away, because that's when the incoming fire really picked up. I think every Russian left alive between those rocks started hosing down the front of Lucky Thirteen. I was just about out of ammo anyway, so I slipped out of the gunner's seat and dropped to the floor while the flechettes and tungsten darts from the Russian guns tore up the cockpit just above my head. I crawled through the open hatch and pulled it shut behind me with my good hand. The rounds pinging off the laminated armor sounded like hail hitting a windowpane.

I got up, stepped into the ship's armory to grab a rifle and a bag of magazines, and then went over to the bulkhead that held the trigger for the Wasp's built-in demolition charge.

Removing the safety and pulling that lever felt like putting a gun to the head of a puppy and pulling the trigger. But I knew she'd never fly again, and I didn't want her to end up as a war trophy, parked in front of some Russian company building. Thirteen would have a fast and thorough death, with nothing left behind to rust away in a scrapyard somewhere.

I pulled the lever. Then I gathered my rifle and dashed out of the troop compartment, down the lowered tail hatch, and into the open.

The Russians didn't see me at first because the bulk of Lucky Thirteen was between me and them, and by the time their flanking elements had spotted me, I was already fifty yards away and headed for cover. They still shot at me, of course. It's amazing how fast you can run when enemy rifle rounds are kicking up the dust next to you. The self-destruct mechanism on a Wasp has a fifteen-second fuse before it sprays all the remaining fuel into the ship's interior to make a huge fuel-air bomb. My shipmates were all hunkered down behind a rock ledge maybe eighty yards away, and I cleared the ledge with two seconds to spare.

Nothing happened.

I waited another ten, twenty, then thirty seconds with my face in the dirt and my hands over my ears, waiting for Lucky Thirteen to rend herself apart like a giant grenade, but all I heard was the staccato of the Russian rifles. After a minute or two had passed, I chanced a peek over the rock ledge, and saw Lucky Thirteen still sitting in the same spot, smoke trailing from her destroyed engine, and Russian marines advancing on her in the open. With our wounded, there was no way we could outrun the Russians once they figured out we had all flown the coop. There was only one thing left to do – sell ourselves as dearly as possible. I lowered my head again, checked the loading status of my rifle, and signaled the others to get ready to engage.

The sky overhead was a lovely cobalt blue, the stars bright even in the planetary afternoon. I wondered if our own sun was among them. I briefly marveled at the thought that since the moment those photons left our own sun, I had been born, raised, educated, inducted into the Commonwealth Defense Corps, and trained to fly a drop ship, and that I had still beaten the light to Fomalhaut by a few days.

Then I flicked the safety of my rifle to salvo fire and got up to fight.

* * *

We were seven against fifty, and most of us were wounded. When we engaged, the Russians were caught by surprise, and our first bursts of fire took out half a dozen of them. After that, we were screwed. They knew where we were, they had the numbers on us, and they had Lucky Thirteen for cover. We got two or three more, and then the return fire had us ducking back behind cover.

"I got Fleet on comms," Staff Sergeant Fisher told me over the din of the gunfire. "Air support is on the way. ETA ten minutes."

"That's super," I replied. "You speak any Russian? Tell those guys to take a piss break until then, and we're good."

It's not easy to stick your head up above cover to aim your weapon when you're convinced that you'll take a round in the face the second you do. The next time I popped up to fire back, I glanced at Lucky Thirteen, and saw that the Russians were all over her, using her armored hull as cover.

I'll never be able to tell for sure how I knew what was about to happen. There was something in the air all of a sudden – a whiff of burnt ozone smell, and a strange sound, like a piezo switch. It felt as if the air itself was electrically charged. All I remember is that I ducked back behind the rock ledge, and yelled at the others to get down, get down, *get the fuck down.*

Lucky Thirteen blew up with the loudest *bang* I've ever heard in my life. The shock of the explosion traveled through the rock and knocked us all flat on our asses. From one moment to the next, the air was so thick with dust that I couldn't see my own hands in front of me. My hearing was completely gone – all I could hear was a high-pitched whistling sound.

I have no idea how long we were huddled down behind the rock ledge, blind and deaf, with debris and dust raining down on us. The Russians could have finished us off easily at that point, if there had been any left. When the dust finally settled and we gathered ourselves up, the little plateau where Lucky Thirteen had crash-landed was swept clean. In the spot where the ship had been, there was a shallow depression in the rock, and streaks of black burn marks fanning out in every direction. All around, there were burning and smoldering drop ship parts, none of them bigger than a mess table.

Lucky Thirteen had done me a last favor. The fuse for the self-destruct charge had delayed until the ship had Russians crawling all over and inside her – until the explosion would do the most good.

I'm not one of the superstitious pilots. My rational side knows it was a technical fluke, a delay in the trigger mechanism, a circuit that didn't close in time, a fortunate defect. But part of me wants to believe that the ship saved my life that day – that this collection of parts bolted together thirty years ago in a factory back on Earth, a Wasp-C like a thousand others and yet like no other ship I've ever flown, knew our peril and immolated itself at just the right moment, in a final act of service to its pilot.

* * *

The cavalry arrived ten minutes too late, as it often does. The Shrikes made a few passes overhead, but if there were any Russians left alive, they wisely stayed under cover. Twenty minutes after that, a pair of SAR drop ships swooped in, and scooped us up.

While we were waiting for the drop ships, Sergeant Fisher picked up something in the dirt, looked it over briefly, and tucked it into his pocket. Later, when we were strapped into our jump seats and on the way back to the ship in orbit, he fished the item out and handed it to me without a word.

It was a chunk of Lucky Thirteen's assembly number plate, twisted and charred on both ends. The manufacturer's name was missing, but I could clearly read her serial number on the mangled little strip of steel: 13-02313.

I bit my lip and slipped the number plate into my own pocket, also without a word.

* * *

They patched us up and gave us medals. I put Sergeant Fisher in for a Silver Star and he got it. The Captain in charge of the recon team we picked up recommended me for an award as well. The division brass looked over the records and decided that I should get a Distinguished Flying Cross for killing Lucky Thirteen on Fomalhaut. Two months later, they called me down to the hangar deck, and the regiment's CO pinned the DFC onto my baggy flight suit.

I didn't turn it down, even though I didn't want it. You don't turn down awards just because you think you don't deserve them. If the drop ship jocks started doing that, the only people wearing ribbons would be the desk jockeys, the officers who collect medals after milk run missions that may have involved shots fired within half a parsec.

Promotions ride on points, and those ribbons count for a lot of those points. I took the medal, saluted, and smiled like a good Second Lieutenant who wants to make Captain someday.

But back in my berth, I took that DFC out of its silk-lined case and put it into the chest pocket of my Class A uniform, the one I wear maybe once a year. Then I got out Lucky Thirteen's number plate fragment and tucked it into the medal case instead. It seemed a more appropriate tenant for that nice little silk-lined case.

They gave me a new ship, of course. I got a brand-new Whiskey Wasp after all. It's a fine ship, the newest and most advanced version of the Wasp drop ship, twice as powerful and four times as capable as my old crate.

Still, I'd trade it off in a hot *second* to get back Lucky Thirteen just for a day or two.

ZIMA BLUE

Alistair Reynolds

After the first week people started drifting away from the island. The viewing stands around the pool became emptier by the day. The big tourist ships hauled back towards interstellar space. Art fiends, commentators and critics packed their bags in Venice. Their disappointment hung over the lagoon like a miasma.

I was one of the few who stayed on Murjek, returning to the stands each day. I'd watch for hours, squinting against the trembling blue light reflected from the surface of the water. Face down, Zima's pale shape moved so languidly from one end of the pool to the other that it could have been mistaken for a floating corpse. As he swam I wondered how I was going to tell his story, and who was going to buy it. I tried to remember the name of my first newspaper, back on Mars. They wouldn't pay as much as some of the bigger titles, but some part of me liked the idea of going back to the old place. It had been a long time... I queried the AM, wanting it to jog my memory about the name of the paper. There'd been so many since... hundreds, by my reckoning. But nothing came. It took me another yawning moment to remember that I'd dismissed the AM the day before:

"Carrie, you're on your own," I said aloud to myself. "Start getting used to it."

In the pool, the swimming figure ended a length and began to swim back towards me.

Two weeks earlier I'd been sitting in the Piazza San Marco at noon, watching white figurines glide against the white marble of the clock tower. The sky over Venice was jammed with ships, parked hull-to-hull. Their bellies were quilted in vast, glowing panels, tuned to match the real sky. The view reminded me of the work of a pre-Expansion artist who had specialized in eye-wrenching tricks of perspective and composition: endless waterfalls, interlocking lizards. I formed a mental image and queried the fluttering presence of the AM, but it couldn't retrieve the name.

I finished my coffee and steeled myself for the bill.

I'd come to this white marble version of Venice to witness the unveiling of Zima's final work of art. I'd had an interest in the artist for years, and I'd hoped I might be able to arrange an interview. Unfortunately several thousand other members of the in-crowd had come up with exactly the same idea. Not that it mattered what kind of competition I had anyway: Zima wasn't talking.

The waiter placed a folded card on my table.

All we had been told was to make our way to Murjek, a water-logged world most of us had never heard of before. Murjek's only claim to fame was that it hosted the one hundred and seventy-first known duplicate of Venice, and one of only three Venices rendered entirely in white marble. Zima had chosen Murjek to host his final work of art, and to be the place where he would make his retirement from public life.

With a heavy heart I lifted the bill to inspect the damage. Instead of the expected bill, it was a small, blue card printed in fine gold italic lettering. The shade of blue was that precise powdery aquamarine that Zima had made his own. The card was addressed to me, Carrie Clay, and it said that Zima wanted to talk to me about the unveiling. If I was interested, I should report to the Rialto Bridge in exactly two hours.

If I was interested.

The note stipulated that no recording materials were to be brought, not even a pen and paper. As an afterthought, the card mentioned that the bill had been taken care of. I almost had the nerve to order another coffee and put it on the same tab. Almost, but not quite.

Zima's servant was there when I arrived early at the bridge. Intricate neon mechanisms pulsed behind the flexing glass of the robot's mannequin body. It bowed at the waist and spoke very softly. "Miss Clay? Since you're here, we might as well depart."

The robot escorted me to a flight of stairs that led to the waterside. My AM followed us, fluttering at my shoulder. A conveyor hovered in waiting, floating a metre above the water. The robot helped me into the

216

rear compartment. The AM was about to follow me inside when the robot raised a warning hand.

"You'll have to leave that behind, I'm afraid; no recording materials, remember?"

I looked at the metallic green hummingbird, trying to remember the last time I had been out of its ever-watchful presence.

"Leave it behind?"

"It'll be quite safe here, and you can collect it again when you return after nightfall."

"If I say no?"

"Then I'm afraid there'll be no meeting with Zima."

I sensed that the robot wasn't going to hang around all afternoon waiting for my answer. The thought of being away from the AM made my blood run cold. But I wanted that interview so badly I was prepared to consider anything.

I told the AM to stay here until I returned.

The obedient machine reversed away from me in a flash of metallic green. It was like watching a part of myself drift away. The glass hull wrapped itself around me and I felt a surge of un-nulled acceleration.

Venice tilted below us, then streaked away to the horizon.

I formed a test query, asking the AM to name the planet where I'd celebrated my seven hundredth birthday. Nothing came: I was out of query range, with only my own age-saturated memory to rely on.

I leaned forward. "Are you authorized to tell me what this is about?"

"I'm afraid he didn't tell me," the robot said, making a face appear in the back of his head. "But if at any moment you feel uncomfortable, we can return to Venice."

"I'm fine for now. Who else got the blue card treatment?"

"Only you, to the best of my knowledge."

"And if I'd declined? Were you supposed to ask someone else?"

"No," the robot said. "But let's face it, Miss Clay. You weren't very likely to turn him down."

As we flew on, the conveyor's shock wave gouged a foaming channel in the sea behind it. I thought of a brush drawn through wet paint on marble, exposing the white surface beneath. I took out Zima's invitation and held it against the horizon ahead of us, trying to decide whether the blue was a closer match to the sky or the sea. Against these two possibilities the card seemed to flicker indeterminately.

Zima Blue. It was an exact thing, specified scientifically in terms of angstroms and intensities. If you were an artist, you could have a batch of it mixed up according to that specification. But no one ever used Zima Blue unless they were making a calculated statement about Zima himself.

Zima was already unique by the time he emerged into the public eye. He had undergone radical procedures to enable him to tolerate extreme environments without the burden of a protective suit. Zima had the appearance of a well-built man wearing a tight body stocking, until you were close and you realized that this was actually his skin. Covering his entire form, it was a synthetic material that could be tuned to different colours and textures depending on his mood and surroundings. It could approximate clothing if the social circumstances demanded it. The skin could contain pressure when he wished to experience vacuum, and stiffen to protect him against the crush of a gas giant. Despite these refinements the skin conveyed a full range of sensory impressions to his mind. He had no need to breathe, since his entire cardiovascular system had been replaced by closed-cycle life-support mechanisms. He had no need to eat or drink; no need to dispose of bodily waste. Tiny repair machines swarmed through his body, allowing him to tolerate radiation doses that would have killed an ordinary man in minutes.

With his body thus armoured against environmental extremes, Zima was free to seek inspiration where he wanted. He could drift free in space, staring into the face of a star, or wander the searing canyons of a planet where metals ran like lava. His eyes had been replaced by cameras sensitive to a huge swathe of the electromagnetic spectrum, wired into his brain via complex processing modules. A synaesthetic bridge allowed him to hear visual data as a kind of music, to see sounds as a symphony of startling colours. His skin functioned as a kind of antenna, giving him sensitivity to electrical field changes. When that wasn't sufficient, he could tap into the data feeds of any number of accompanying machines.

ZIMA BLUE

Given all this, Zima's art couldn't help but be original and attention-grabbing. His landscapes and starfields had a heightened, ecstatic quality about them, awash with luminous, jarring colours and eye-wrenching tricks of perspective. Painted in traditional materials but on a huge scale, they quickly attracted a core of serious buyers. Some found their way into private collections, but Zima murals also started popping up in public spaces all over the galaxy. Tens of metres across, the murals were nonetheless detailed down to the limits of vision. Most had been painted in one session. Zima had no need for sleep, so he worked uninterrupted until a piece was complete.

The murals were undeniably impressive. From a standpoint of composition and technique they were unquestionably brilliant. But there was also something bleak and chilling about them. They were landscapes without a human presence, save for the implied viewpoint of the artist himself.

Put it this way: they were nice to look at, but I wouldn't have hung one in my home.

Not everyone agreed, obviously, or else Zima wouldn't have sold as many works as he had. But I couldn't help wondering how many people were buying the paintings because of what they knew about the artist, rather than because of any intrinsic merit in the works themselves.

That was how things stood when I first paid attention to Zima. I filed him away as interesting but kitschy; maybe worth a story if something else happened to either him or his art.

Something did, but it took a while for anyone – including me – to notice.

One day – after a longer than usual gestation period – Zima unveiled a mural that had something different about it. It was a painting of a swirling, star-pocked nebula, from the vantage point of an airless rock. Perched on the rim of a crater in the middle distance, blocking off part of the nebula, was a tiny, blue square. At first glance it looked as if the canvas had been washed blue and Zima had simply left a small area unpainted. There was no solidity to the square, no detail or suggestion of how it related to the landscape or the backdrop. It cast no shadow and had no tonal influence on the surrounding colours. But the square was deliberate: close examination showed that it had indeed been overpainted over the rocky lip of the crater. It meant something.

The square was just the beginning. Thereafter, every mural that Zima released to the outside world contained a similar geometric shape: a square, triangle, oblong or some similar form embedded somewhere in the composition. It was a long time before anyone noticed that the shade of blue was the same from painting to painting.

It was Zima Blue: the same shade of blue as on the gold-lettered card.

Over the next decade or so, the abstract shapes became more dominant, squeezing out the other elements of each composition. The cosmic vistas ended up as narrow borders, framing blank circles, triangles, rectangles. Where his earlier work had been characterized by exuberant brushwork and thick layers of paint, the blue forms were rendered with mirror-smoothness.

Intimated by the intrusion of the abstract blue forms, casual buyers turned away from Zima. Before very long Zima unveiled the first of his entirely blue murals. Large enough to cover the side of a thousand-storey building, the mural was considered by many to be as far as Zima could take things.

They couldn't have been more wrong.

I felt the conveyor slowing as we neared a small island, the only feature in any direction.

"You're the first to see this," the robot said. "There's a distortion screen blocking the view from space."

The island was about a kilometre across: low and turtle-shaped, ringed by a narrow collar of pale sand. Near the middle it rose to a shallow plateau, on which vegetation had been cleared in a roughly rectangular area. I made out a small panel of reflective blue set flat against the ground, surrounded by what appeared to be a set of tiered viewing stands.

The conveyor shed altitude and speed, bobbing down until it stopped just outside the area enclosed by the viewing stands. It came to rest next to a low, white pebble-dash chalet I hadn't noticed during our approach.

ZIMA BLUE

The robot stepped out and helped me from the conveyor.

"Zima will be here in a moment," it said, before returning to the conveyor and vanishing back into the sky.

Suddenly I felt very alone and very vulnerable. A breeze came in from the sea, blowing sand into my eyes. The sun was creeping down towards the horizon and soon it would be getting chilly. Just when I was beginning to feel the itch of panic, a man emerged from the chalet, rubbing his hands briskly. He walked towards me, following a path of paved stones.

"Glad you could make it, Carrie."

It was Zima, of course, and in a flash I felt foolish for doubting that he would show his face.

"Hi," I said lamely.

Zima offered his hand. I shook it, feeling the slightly plastic texture of his artificial skin. Today it was a dull pewter-grey.

"Let's go and sit on the balcony. It's nice to watch the sunset, isn't it?"

"Nice," I agreed.

He turned his back to me and set off in the direction of the chalet. As he walked, his muscles flexed and bulged beneath the pewter flesh. There were scalelike glints in the skin on his back, as if it had been set with a mosaic of reflective chips. He was beautiful like a statue, muscular like a panther. He was a handsome man, even after all his transformations, but I had never heard of him taking a lover, or having any kind of a private life at all. His art was everything.

I followed him, feeling awkward and tongue-tied. Zima led me into the chalet, through an old-fashioned kitchen and an old-fashioned lounge, full of thousand-year-old furniture and ornaments.

"How was the flight?"

"Fine."

He stopped suddenly and turned to face me. "I forgot to check… did the robot insist that you leave behind your *Aide Memoire*?"

"Yes."

"Good. It was you I wanted to talk to, Carrie, not some surrogate recording device."

"Me?"

The pewter mask of his face formed a quizzical expression. "Do you do multi-syllables, or are you still working up to that?"

"Er..."

"Relax," he said. "I'm not here to test you, or humiliate you, or anything like that. This isn't a trap, and you're not in any danger. You'll be back in Venice by midnight."

"I'm OK," I managed. "Just a bit starstruck."

"Well, you shouldn't be. I'm hardly the first celebrity you've met, am I?"

"Well, no, but—"

"People find me intimidating," he said. "They get over it eventually, and then wonder what all the fuss was about."

"Why me?"

"Because you kept asking nicely," Zima said.

"Be serious."

"All right. There's a bit more to it than that, although you *did* ask nicely. I've enjoyed much of your work over the years. People have often trusted you to set the record straight, especially near the ends of their lives."

"You talked about retiring, not dying."

"Either way, it would still be a withdrawal from public life. Your work has always seemed truthful to me, Carrie. I'm not aware of anyone claiming misrepresentation through your writing."

"It happens now and then," I said. "That's why I always make sure there's an AM on hand so no one can dispute what was said."

"That won't matter with my story," Zima said.

I looked at him shrewdly. "There's something else, isn't there? Some other reason you pulled my name out of the hat."

"I'd like to help you," he said.

When most people speak about his Blue Period they mean the era of the truly huge murals. By huge I do mean *huge*. Soon they had become large enough to dwarf buildings and civic spaces, large enough to be visible from orbit. Across the galaxy twenty-kilometre-high sheets of blue towered over private islands or rose from storm-wracked seas. Expense was never a problem, since Zima had many rival sponsors who competed to host his latest and biggest creation. The panels kept on growing, until they required complex, sloth-tech machinery to hold them aloft against gravity and weather. They pierced the tops of planetary atmospheres, jutting into space. They glowed with their own soft light. They curved around in arcs and fans, so that the viewer's entire visual field was saturated with blue.

By now Zima was hugely famous, even to people who had no particular interest in art. He was the weird cyborg celebrity who made huge blue structures; the man who never gave interviews or hinted at the private significance of his art.

But that was a hundred years ago. Zima wasn't even remotely done.

Eventually the structures became too unwieldy to be hosted on planets. Blithely Zima moved into interplanetary space, forging vast, free-floating sheets of blue ten thousand kilometres across. Now he worked not with brushes and paint, but with fleets of mining robots, tearing apart asteroids to make the raw material for his creations. Now it was entire stellar economies that competed with each other to host Zima's work.

That was about the time that I renewed my interest in Zima. I attended one of his "moonwrappings": the enclosure of an entire celestial body in a lidded blue container, like a hat going into a box. Two months later he stained the entire equatorial belt of a gas giant blue, and I had a ringside seat for that as well. Six months later he altered the surface chemistry of a sun-grazing comet so that it daubed a Zima Blue tail across an entire solar system. But I was no closer to a story. I kept asking for an interview and kept being turned down. All I knew was that there had to be more to Zima's obsession with blue than a mere artistic whim. Without an understanding of that obsession, there was no story: just anecdote.

I didn't do anecdote.

So I waited, and waited. And then – like millions of others – I heard about Zima's final work of art, and made my way to the fake Venice on Murjek. I wasn't expecting an interview, or any new insights. I just had to be there.

We stepped through sliding glass doors onto the balcony. Two simple white chairs sat either side of a white table. The table was set with drinks and a bowl of fruit. Beyond the unfenced balcony, arid land sloped steeply away, offering an uninterrupted view of the sea. The water was calm and inviting, with the lowering sun reflected like a silver coin.

Zima indicated that I should take one of the seats. His hand dithered over two bottles of wine.

"Red or white, Carrie?"

I opened my mouth as if to answer him, but nothing came. Normally, in that instant between the question and the response, the AM would have silently directed my choice to one of the two options. Not having the AM's prompt felt like a mental stall in my thoughts.

"Red, I think," Zima said. "Unless you have strong objections."

"It's not that I can't decide these things for myself," I said.

Zima poured me a glass of red, then held it up to the sky to inspect its clarity. "Of course not," he said.

"It's just that this is a little strange for me."

"It shouldn't be strange," he said. "This is the way you lived your life for hundreds of years."

"The natural way, you mean?"

Zima poured himself a glass of the red wine, but instead of drinking it he merely sniffed the bouquet. "Yes."

"But there isn't anything natural about being alive a thousand years after I was born," I said. "My organic memory reached saturation point about seven hundred years ago. My head's like a house with too much furniture. Move something in, you have to move something out."

"Let's go back to the wine for a moment," Zima said. "Normally, you'd have relied on the advice of the AM, wouldn't you?"

I shrugged. "Yes."

"Would the AM always suggest one of the two possibilities? Always red wine, or always white wine, for instance?"

"It's not that simplistic," I said. "If I had a strong preference for one over the other, then, yes, the AM would always recommend one wine over the other. But I don't. I like red wine sometimes and white wine other times. Sometimes I don't want any kind of wine." I hoped my frustration wasn't obvious. But after the elaborate charade with the blue card, the robot and the conveyor, the last thing I wanted to be discussing with Zima was my own imperfect recall.

"Then it's random?" he asked. "The AM would have been just as likely to say red as white?"

"No, it's not like that either. The AM's been following me around for hundreds of years. It's seen me drink wine a few hundred thousand times, under a few hundred thousand different circumstances. It knows, with a high degree of reliability, what my best choice of wine would be given any set of parameters."

"And you follow that advice unquestioningly?"

I sipped at the red. "Of course. Wouldn't it be a little childish to go against it just to make a point about free will? After all, I'm more likely to be satisfied with the choice it suggests."

"But unless you ignore that suggestion now and then, won't your whole life become a set of predictable responses?"

"Maybe," I said. "But is that so very bad? If I'm happy, what do I care?"

"I'm not criticising you," Zima said. He smiled and leaned back in his seat, defusing some of the tension caused by his line of questioning. "Not many people have an AM these days, do they?"

"I wouldn't know," I said.

"Less than one per cent of the entire galactic population." Zima sniffed his wine and looked through the glass at the sky. "Almost everyone else out there has accepted the inevitable."

"It takes machines to manage a thousand years of memory. So what?"

"But a different order of machine," Zima said. "Neural implants, fully integrated into the participant's sense of self. Indistinguishable from biological memory. You wouldn't need to query the AM about your choice of wine; you wouldn't need to wait for that confirmatory whisper. You'd just know it."

"Where's the difference? I allow my experiences to be recorded by a machine that accompanies me everywhere I go. The machine misses nothing, and it's so efficient at anticipating my queries that I barely have to ask it anything."

"The machine is vulnerable."

"It's backed up at regular intervals. And it's no more vulnerable than a cluster of implants inside my head. Sorry, but that just isn't a reasonable objection."

"You're right, of course. But there's a deeper argument against the AM. It's too perfect. It doesn't know how to distort or forget."

"Isn't that the point?"

"Not exactly. When you recall something – this conversation, perhaps, a hundred years from now – there will be things about it that you misremember. Yet those misremembered details will themselves become part of your memory, gaining solidity and texture with each instance of recall. A thousand years from now, your memory of this conversation might bear little resemblance to reality. Yet you'd swear your recollection was accurate."

"But if the AM had accompanied me, I'd have a flawless record of how things really were."

"You would," Zima said. "But that isn't living memory. It's photography: a mechanical recording process. It freezes out the imagination, leaves no scope for details to be selectively misremembered." He paused long enough to top off my glass. "Imagine that on nearly every occasion when you had cause to sit outside on an afternoon like this you had chosen red wine over white, and generally had no reason to regret that choice. But on one occasion, for one reason or another, you were persuaded to choose white – against the judgement of the AM – and it was wonderful. Everything came together magically: the company, the conversation, the late afternoon ambience, the splendid view, the euphoric rush of being slightly drunk. A perfect afternoon turned into a perfect evening."

"It might not have had anything to do with my choice of wine," I said.

"No," Zima agreed. "And the AM certainly wouldn't attach any significance to that one happy combination of circumstances. A single deviation wouldn't affect its predictive model to any significant degree. It would still say 'red wine' the next time you asked."

I felt an uncomfortable tingle of understanding. "But human memory wouldn't work that way."

"No. It would latch on to that one exception and attach undue significance to it. It would amplify the attractive parts of the memory of that afternoon and suppress the less pleasant parts: the fly that kept buzzing in your face, your anxiety about catching the boat home and the birthday present you knew you had to buy in the morning. All you'd remember was that golden glow of well-being. The next time, you might well choose white, and the time after. An entire pattern of behaviour would have been altered by one instance of deviation. The AM would never tolerate that. You'd have to go against its advice many, many times before it grudgingly updated its model and started suggesting white rather than red."

"All right," I said, still wishing we could talk about Zima rather than me. "But what practical difference does it make whether the artificial memory is inside my head or outside?"

"All the difference in the world," Zima said. "The memories stored in the AM are fixed for eternity. You can query it as often as you like, but it will never enhance or omit a single detail. But the implants work differently. They're designed to integrate seamlessly with biological memory, to the point where the recipient can't tell the difference. For that very reason they're necessarily plastic, malleable, subject to error and distortion."

"Fallible," I said.

"But without fallibility there is no art. And without art there is no truth."

"Fallibility leads to truth? That's a good one."

"I mean truth in the higher, metaphoric sense. That golden afternoon? That was the truth. Remembering the fly wouldn't have added to it in any material sense. It would have detracted from it."

"There was no afternoon, there was no fly," I said. Finally, my patience had reached breaking point. "Look, I'm grateful to have been invited here. But I thought there might be a little more to this than a lecture about the way I choose to manage my own memories."

"Actually," Zima said, "there was a point to this after all. And it is about me, but it's also about you." He put down the glass. "Shall we take a little walk? I'd like to show you the swimming pool."

"The sun hasn't gone down yet," I said.

Zima smiled. "There'll always be another one."

He took me on a different route through the house, leaving by a different door than the one we'd come in. A meandering path climbed gradually between white stone walls, bathed now in gold from the lowering sun. Presently we reached the flat plateau I'd seen on my approach in the conveyor. The things I'd thought were viewing stands were exactly that: terraced structures about thirty metres high, with staircases at the back leading to the different levels. Zima led me into the darkening shadow under the nearest stand, then through a private door that led into the enclosed area. The blue panel I'd seen during the approach turned out to be a modest rectangular swimming pool, drained of water.

Zima led me to the edge.

"A swimming pool," I said. "You weren't kidding. Is this what the stands are all about?"

"This is where it will happen," Zima said. "The unveiling of my final work of art, and my retirement from public life."

The pool wasn't quite finished. In the far corner, a small, yellow robot glued ceramic tiles into place. The part near us was fully tiled, but I couldn't help noticing that the tiles were chipped and cracked in places. The afternoon light made it hard to be sure – we were in deep shadow now – but their colour looked to be very close to Zima Blue.

"After painting entire planets, isn't this is a bit of a let-down?" I asked.

"Not for me," Zima said. "For me this is where the quest ends. This is what it was all leading up to."

"A shabby-looking swimming pool?"

"It's not just any old swimming pool," he said.

He walked me around the island, as the sun slipped under the sea and the colours turned ashen.

"The old murals came from the heart," Zima said. "I painted on a huge scale because that was what the subject matter seemed to demand."

"It was good work," I said.

"It was hack work. Huge, loud, demanding, popular, but ultimately soulless. Just because it came from the heart didn't make it good."

I said nothing. That was the way I'd always felt about his work as well: it was as vast and inhuman as its inspiration, and only Zima's cyborg modifications lent his art any kind of uniqueness. It was like praising a painting because it had been done by someone holding a brush between their teeth.

"My work said nothing about the cosmos that the cosmos wasn't already capable of saying for itself. More importantly, it said nothing about me. So what if I walked in vacuum, or swam in seas of liquid nitrogen? So what if I could see ultraviolet photons, or taste electrical fields? The modifications I inflicted upon myself were gruesome and extreme. But they gave me nothing that a good telepresence drone couldn't offer any artist."

"I think you're being a little harsh on yourself," I said.

"Not at all. I can say this now because I know that I did eventually create something worthwhile. But when it happened it was completely unplanned."

"You mean the blue stuff?"

"The blue stuff," he said, nodding. "It began by accident: a misapplication of colour on a nearly finished canvas. A smudge of pale aquamarine-blue against near-black. The effect was electric. It was as if I had achieved a short circuit to some intense, primal memory, a realm of experience where that colour was the most important thing in my world."

"What was that memory?"

"I didn't know. All I knew was the way that colour spoke to me, as if I'd been waiting my whole life to find it, to set it free." He thought for a moment. "There's always been something about blue. A thousand years ago Yves Klein said it was the essence of colour itself: the colour that stood for all other colours. A man once spent his entire life searching for a particular shade of blue that he remembered encountering in childhood. He began to despair of ever finding it, thinking he must have imagined that precise shade, that it could not possibly exist in nature. Then one day he chanced upon it. It was the colour of a beetle in a museum of natural history. He wept for joy."

"What is Zima Blue?" I asked. "Is it the colour of a beetle?"

229

"No," he said. "It's not a beetle. But I had to know the answer, no matter where it took me. I had to know why that colour meant so much to me, and why it was taking over my art."

"You allowed it to take over," I said.

"I had no choice. As the blue became more intense, more dominant, I felt I was closer to an answer. I felt that if only I could immerse myself in that colour, then I would know everything I desired to know. I would understand myself as an artist."

"And? Did you?"

"I understood myself," Zima said. "But it wasn't what I expected."

"What did you learn?"

Zima was a long time answering me. We walked on slowly, me lagging slightly behind his prowling muscular form. It was getting cooler now and I began to wish I'd had the foresight to bring a coat. I thought of asking Zima if he could lend me one, but I was concerned not to derail his thoughts from wherever they were headed. Keeping my mouth shut had always been the toughest part of the job.

"We talked about the fallibility of memory," he said.

"Yes."

"My own memory was incomplete. Since the implants were installed I remembered everything, but that only accounted for the last three hundred years of my life. I knew myself to be much older, but of my life before the implants I recalled only fragments; shattered pieces that I did not quite know how to reassemble." He slowed and turned back to me, the dulling orange light on the horizon catching the side of his face. "I knew I had to dig back into that past, if I was to ever understand the significance of Zima Blue."

"How far back did you get?"

"It was like archaeology," he said. "I followed the trail of my memories back to the earliest reliable event, which occurred shortly after the installation of the implants. This took me to Kharkov Eight, a world in the Garlin Bight, about nineteen thousand light-years from here. All I remembered was the name of a man I had known there, called Cobargo."

Cobargo meant nothing to me, but even without the AM I knew something of the Garlin Bight. It was a region of the galaxy encompassing six hundred habitable systems, squeezed between three major economic powers. In the Garlin Bight normal interstellar law did not apply. It was fugitive territory.

"Kharkov Eight specialized in a certain kind of product," Zima said. "The entire planet was geared up to provide medical services of a kind unavailable elsewhere. Illicit cybernetic modifications, that kind of thing."

"Is that where..." I left the sentence unfinished.

"That is where I became what I am," Zima said. "Of course, I made further changes to myself after my time on Kharkov Eight – improving my tolerance to extreme environments, improving my sensory capabilities – but the essence of what I am was laid down under the knife in Cobargo's clinic."

"So before you arrived on Kharkov Eight you were a normal man?" I asked.

"This is where it gets difficult," Zima said, picking his way carefully along the trail. "Upon my return I naturally tried to locate Cobargo. With his help, I assumed I would be able to make sense of the memory fragments I carried in my head. But Cobargo was gone, vanished elsewhere into the Bight. The clinic remained, but now his grandson was running it."

"I bet he wasn't keen on talking."

"No; he took some persuading. Thankfully, I had means. A little bribery, a little coercion." He smiled slightly at that. "Eventually he agreed to open the clinic records and examine his grandfather's log of my visit."

We turned a corner. The sea and the sky were now the same inseparable grey, with no trace of blue remaining.

"What happened?"

"The records say that I was never a man," Zima said. He paused a while before continuing, leaving no doubt as to what he had said. "Zima never existed before my arrival in the clinic."

What I wouldn't have done for a recording drone, or – failing that – a plain old notebook and pen. I frowned, as if that might make my memory work just that little bit harder.

"Then who were you?"

"A machine," he said. "A complex robot: an autonomous artificial intelligence. I was already centuries old when I arrived on Kharkov Eight, with full legal independence."

"No," I said, shaking my head. "You're a man with machine parts, not a machine."

"The clinic records were very clear. I had arrived as a robot. An androform robot, certainly – but an obvious machine nonetheless. I was dismantled and my core cognitive functions were integrated into a vat-grown biological host body." With one finger he tapped the pewter side of his skull. "There's a lot of organic material in here, and a lot of cybernetic machinery. It's difficult to tell where one begins and the other ends. Even harder to tell which is the master, and which is the slave."

I looked at the figure standing next to me, trying to make the mental leap needed to view him as a machine – albeit a machine with soft, cellular components – rather than a man. I couldn't – not yet.

I stalled. "The clinic could have lied to you."

"I don't think so. They would have been far happier had I not known."

"All right," I said. "Just for the sake of argument—"

"Those were the facts. They were easily verified. I examined the customs records for Kharkov Eight and found that an *autonomous robot entity* had entered the planet's airspace a few months before the medical procedure."

"Not necessarily you."

"No other robot entity had come near the world for decades. It had to be me. More than that, the records also showed the robot's port of origin."

"Which was?"

"A world beyond the Bight. Lintan Three, in the Muara Archipelago."

The AM's absence was like a missing tooth. "I don't know if I know it."

"You probably don't. It's no kind of world you'd ever visit by choice. The scheduled lightbreakers don't go there. My only purpose in visiting the place seemed to me—"

"You went there?"

"Twice. Once before the procedure on Kharkov Eight, and again recently, to establish where I'd been before Lintan Three. The evidence trail was beginning to get muddy, to say the least… but I asked the right kinds of questions, poked at the right kinds of databases, and eventually found out where I'd come from. But that still wasn't the final answer. There were many worlds, and the chain became fainter with each that I visited. But I had persistence on my side."

"And money."

"And money," Zima said, acknowledging my remark with a polite little nod. "That helped incalculably."

"So what did you find, in the end?"

"I followed the trail back to the beginning. On Kharkov Eight I was a quick-thinking machine with human-level intelligence. But I hadn't always been that clever, that complex. I'd been augmented in steps, as time and circumstances allowed."

"By yourself?"

"Eventually, yes. That was when I had autonomy, legal independence. But I had to reach a certain level of intelligence before I was allowed that freedom. Before that, I was a simpler machine… like an heirloom or a pet. I was passed from one owner to the next, between generations. They added things to me. They made me cleverer."

"How did you begin?"

"As a project," he said.

Zima led me back to the swimming pool. Equatorial night had arrived quickly, and the pool was bathed now in artificial light from the many floods arrayed above the viewing stands. Since we had last seen the pool, the robot had finished gluing the last of the tiles in place.

"It's ready now," Zima said. "Tomorrow it will be sealed, and the day after it will be flooded with water. I'll cycle the water until it attains the necessary clarity."

"And then?"

"I prepare myself for my performance."

On the way to the swimming pool, he had told me as much as he knew about his origin. Zima had begun his existence on Earth, before I was even born. He had been assembled by a hobbyist, a talented young man with an interest in practical robotics. In those days, the man had been one of many groups and individuals groping towards the hard problem of artificial intelligence.

Perception, navigation and autonomous problem-solving were the three things that most interested the young man. He had created many robots, tinkering them together from kits, broken toys and spare parts. Their minds – if they could be dignified with such a term – were cobbled from the innards of junked computers, with their simple programs bulging at the limits of memory and processor speed.

The young man filled his house with these simple machines, designing each for a particular task. One robot was a sticky-limbed spider that climbed around the walls of his house, dusting the frames of pictures. Another lay in wait for flies and cockroaches. It caught and digested them, using the energy from the chemical breakdown of their biomass to drive itself to another place in the house. Another robot busied itself by repainting the walls of the house over and over, so that the colours matched the changing of the seasons.

Another robot lived in his swimming pool.

It toiled endlessly up and down and along the ceramic sides of the pool, scrubbing them clean. The young man could have bought a cheap swimming pool cleaner from a mail-order company, but it amused him to design the robot from scratch, according to his own eccentric design principles. He gave the robot a full-colour vision system and a brain large enough to process the visual data into a model of its surroundings. He allowed the robot to make its own decisions about the best strategy for cleaning the pool. He allowed it to choose when it cleaned and when it surfaced to recharge its batteries via the solar panels grouped on its back. He imbued it with a primitive notion of reward.

The little pool-cleaner taught the young man a great deal about the fundamentals of robotics design. Those lessons were incorporated into the other household robots, until one of them – a simple household cleaner – became sufficiently robust and autonomous that the young man began to offer it as a kit, via mail-order. The kit sold well, and a year later the young man offered it as a preassembled domestic robot. The robot was a runaway success, and the young man's firm soon became the market leader in domestic robots.

Within ten years, the world swarmed with his bright, eager machines.

He never forgot the little pool-cleaner. Time and again he used it as a test-bed for new hardware, new software. By stages it became the cleverest of all his creations, and the only one that he refused to strip down and cannibalise.

When he died, the cleaner passed to his daughter. She continued the family tradition, adding cleverness to the little machine. When she died, she passed it to the young man's grandson, who happened to live on Mars.

"This is the original pool," Zima said. "If you hadn't already guessed."

"After all this time?" I asked.

"It's very old. But ceramics endure. The hardest part was finding it in the first place. I had to dig through two metres of topsoil. It was in a place they used to call Silicon Valley."

"These tiles are coloured Zima Blue," I said.

"Zima Blue *is* the colour of the tiles," he gently corrected. "It just happened to be the shade that the young man used for his swimming pool tiles."

"Then some part of you remembered."

"This was where I began. A crude little machine with barely enough intelligence to steer itself around a swimming pool. But it was my world. It was all I knew, all I needed to know."

"And now?" I asked, already fearing the answer.

"Now I'm going home."

I was there when he did it. By then the stands were full of people who had arrived to watch the performance, and the sky over the island was a mosaic of tightly packed hovering ships. The distortion screen had been turned off, and the viewing platforms on the ships thronged with hundreds of thousands of distant witnesses. They could see the swimming pool by then, its water mirror-flat and gin-clear. They could see Zima standing at the edge, with the solar patches on his back glinting like snake scales. None of the viewers had any idea what was about to happen, or its significance. They were expecting something – the public unveiling of a work that would presumably trump everything Zima had created before then – but they could only stare in puzzled concern at the pool, wondering how it could possibly measure up to those atmosphere-piercing canvases, or those entire worlds wrapped in shrouds of blue. They kept thinking that the pool had to be a diversion. The real work of art – the piece that would herald his retirement – must be somewhere else, as yet unseen, waiting to be revealed in all its immensity.

That was what they thought.

But I knew the truth. I knew it as I watched Zima stand at the edge of the pool and surrender himself to the blue. He'd told me exactly how it would happen: the slow, methodical shutting-down of higher-brain functions. It hardly mattered that it was all irreversible: there wouldn't be enough of him left to regret what he had lost.

But something would remain – a little kernel of being – enough of a mind to recognize its own existence. Enough of a mind to appreciate its surroundings, and to extract some trickle of pleasure and contentment from the execution of a task, no matter how purposeless. He wouldn't ever need to leave the pool. The solar patches would provide him with all the energy he needed. He would never age, never grow ill. Other machines would take care of his island, protecting the pool and its silent, slow swimmer from the ravages of weather and time.

Centuries would pass.

Thousands of years, and then millions.

Beyond that, it was anyone's guess. But the one thing I knew was that Zima would never tire of his task. There was no capacity left in his mind for boredom. He had become pure experience. If he experienced any kind of joy in the swimming of the pool, it was the near-mindless euphoria of a pollinating insect. That was enough for him. It had been enough for him in that pool in California, and it was enough for him now, a thousand years later, in the same pool but on another world, around another sun, in a distant part of the same galaxy.

As for me…

It turned out that I remembered more of our meeting on the island than I had any right to. Make of that what you will, but it seemed I didn't need the mental crutch of my AM quite as much as I'd always imagined. Zima was right: I'd allowed my life to become scripted, laid out like a blueprint. It was always red wine with sunsets, never the white. Aboard the outbound lightbreaker a clinic installed a set of neural memory extensions that should serve me well for the next four or five hundred years. One day I'll need another solution, but I'll cross that particular mnemonic bridge when I get there. My last act, before dismissing the AM, was to transfer its observations into the vacant spaces of my enlarged memory. The events still don't feel quite like they ever happened to me, but they settle in a little bit better with each act of recall. They change and soften, and the highlights glow a little brighter. I guess they become a little less accurate with each instance of recall, but like Zima said, perhaps that's the point.

I know now why he spoke to me. It wasn't just my way with a biographical story. It was his desire to help someone move on, before he did the same.

I did eventually find a way to write his story, and I sold it back to my old newspaper, the *Martian Chronicle*. It was good to visit the old planet again, especially now that they've moved it into a warmer orbit.

That was a long time ago. But I'm still not done with Zima, odd as it seems.

Every couple of decades, I still hop a lightbreaker to Murjek, descend to the streets of that gleaming white avatar of Venice, take a conveyor to the island and join the handful of other dogged witnesses scattered across the stands. Those that come, like me, must still feel that the artist has something else in store... one last surprise. They've read my article now, most of them, so they know what that slowly swimming figure means... but they still don't come in droves. The stands are always a little echoey and sad, even on a good day. But I've never seen them completely empty, which I suppose is some kind of testament. Some people get it. Most people never will.

But that's art.

BLIND SPOT

Vitaliy Shushko

EXT. DESERT – NIGHT

Three small GOPHERS are peacefully munching on fruit. Then an open-topped DUNE BUGGY ROARS into view. The animals SCATTER.

HAWK drives the lead buggy. A square-jawed, steely eyed, and oh-so leadery cyborg. Naturally he's in command.

HAWK

Five minutes to the objective. Stay sharp, metal-heads.

SUI drives the buggy beside HAWK'S. A big, one-armed brute of a cyborg. He's grinning as he chomps on a cigar, CHERRY glowing RED HOT in the rushing night air.

SUI

Copy that! Countdown to mayhem!

KALI'S buggy drives next to Sui. An extremely fierce cyborg with a dangerous, don't-fuck-with-me attitude.

KALI

We gonna let Rookie in on this?

SUI

Depends... *Hey Rookie! Have your balls dropped yet?*

ROOKIE drives at the end of the formation. An eager, young cyborg trying to hide his nervousness with bluster.

ROOKIE
What? Fuck you, Sui! I'm ready!

HAWK
You'll get your chance boy, don't worry. We on schedule, Bob?

INT BOB'S VAN – CONTINUOUS
BOB, the robotic mastermind controlling the mission, is built into his
van. Holographic displays float all around him.

BOB
Affirmative. It appears the cargo is in the front car.

EXT. DESERT – CONTINUOUS

ROOKIE
Hey Hawk, what are we stealing anyway?

HAWK
It's a microchip, kid. You oughtta know what that looks like. Your head's
full of them.

INT. BOB'S VAN – CONTINUOUS
The microchip can be seen on BOB's dashboard.

BOB
Please, don't forget to look out for guards in the rear car!

EXT. DESERT – CONTINUOUS
In the headlights of the buggies, a dark shape looms out of the
darkness. The ROAD-TRAIN. A formidable ENGINE CABIN pulling
three huge TRAILERS.

HAWK accelerates, his buggy racing ahead to get in front of the road-
train. ROOKIE and SUI split and pull up to either side.

BLIND SPOT

HAWK
Contact. Move up and match velocity.

KALI
In position.

SUI
I got a position for 'ya.

KALI
Really? Does it involve shoving my gun up your ass?

SUI laughs.

HAWK
Are we good to go, Bob?

INT. BOB'S VAN – CONTINUOUS

BOB
Roger that. The target is in the blind spot. You got 'till it reaches the other
side of the tunnel to get in, make the grab and get out.

EXT. DESERT - CONTINUOUS

HAWK
Move out.

SUI pulls in front of the Train.

HAWK (CONT'D)
Sui, Rookie plant the magnetic mines on the guard car.

KALI
Great idea, boss. Give the high explosives to the lunatic and the new guy.
What could go wrong?

SUI
Shut your grease trap. I got this.

SUI and ROOKIE steer closer and mechanical armatures extend from their buggies. They begin placing EXPLOSIVE CHARGES.

SUI (CONT'D)
Last one.

SUI sees a GOPHER right in front of him in the road. He swerves wildly, the mine he was placing flying loose.

SUI (CONT'D)
Aw shit!

A HUGE EXPLOSION as the mine goes off, just behind the train.

INT. TRAIN – GUARD CAR
An alarm starts blaring and the GUARDS mobilize with well- trained efficiency.

EXT. HIGHWAY - CONTINUOUS

HAWK
What the fuck was that explosion?

KALI
Hate to say I told you so.

GUARDS emerge inside the train and open fire on ROOKIE and SUI. ROOKIE swerves away to avoid their deadly fire. SUI drops back, doing his best to block incoming rounds with his metal arm.

SUI
Give us some covering fire, Kali!

BLIND SPOT

KALI grits her teeth as shots ping off her buggy. She fires back, her PISTOL BLASTING guards off the top of the truck.

> ROOKIE
> Up on the roof.
> SUI
> That does it!

> KALI
> Wait! Just blow the mines... you suicidal fuck.

But SUI isn't listening as he nears the back of the train he LEAPS. SUI lands atop the train amongst the surprised guards and opens fire, mowing down some guards and punching others.

> HAWK
> We're almost to the tunnel. We need to blow those mines now.

> ROOKIE
> Sui's not... clear!

Atop the train, SUI is finishing off the last of the GUARDS, blood and body parts flying off into the night.

> SUI
> Don't worry about me! Do it, Hawk!

Hawk pushes the detonator. Sui sprints toward the next car and leaps.

A HUGE EXPLOSION blasts the armored trailer UP and SIDEWAYS and it goes tumbling over railing of a bridge.

The ROOKIE is distracted by the explosion for a beat.

> ROOKIE
> Whoah.

SUI lands on the roof of the second car of the train before he slides to a stop. SUI glances back at the destruction.

SUI

Well that wasn't so – hard?

SUI turns back around as a whirring rumbling fills the air. A half-dozen machine gun turrets begin to rise smoothly from housings in the roof, barrel's spinning toward him.

SUI (CONT'D)

Hawk!

SPLIT SCREEN WITH –

BOB (O.S.)

Shit. Did I mention the automatic guns?

BACK TO –

HAWK stands, leaps from the back of his buggy onto the cab of the train. His buggy crunches under the big wheels as he springs upwards again.

He pulls his guns in midair, blasting down at the turrets. The high velocity rounds shred the guns before they can fire at SUI.

HAWK lands perfectly, guns smoking. He looks amazingly cool and then his kneecap falls off. He snaps it back on.

HAWK

No, Bob. You didn't!

Up ahead they can see that the big truck is heading for a tunnel cutting through the mountains.

HAWK (CONT'D)

Ok let's pick it up. If this truck makes it through that tunnel we are all fucked.

BLIND SPOT

INT. TUNNEL – CONTINUOUS

> SUI
> Rookie, get your lug nuts up here!

ROOKIE drives up next to the truck, then leaps across, scrambles up. SUI pulls him over.

> BOB (O.S.)
> *Uh, wait a second.*

INT. BOB'S VAN – CONTINUOUS

> BOB
> I'm getting a new energy reading.
> Oh shit!

INT. TUNNEL – CONTINUOUS

> KALI
> Uh... fella's, I think Bob missed another detail —

ANGLE ON: The front of the ROAD TRAIN from KALI'S POV. The cab begins to unfold, metal parts reconfiguring and transforming into a HUGE COMBAT DROID.

SUI and ROOKIE stare in shock as the droid rises into frame behind HAWK.

> HAWK
> What do you mean, Kali? I don't see-

It's METAL FIST smashes into the side of HAWK'S head. He goes flying over the side of the train, head pulped.

> ROOKIE
> Holy fucking shit.

SUI

Hay! That was my friend you just dismantled, you giant walking dildo.

The DROID stomps forward, swinging its other fist down at ROOKIE who is still frozen in shock.

SUI pulls ROOKIE out of the way just in time. Then opens fires with his wrist-mounted guns.

SUI backs away firing, but the big DROID just keeps coming. And they're quickly running out of roof.

The mechanical monster is almost on them when SUI sees something over the robot's shoulder.

SUI (CONT'D)

Rookie, get below deck now.

ROOKIE climbs into the now emptied guard car.

SUI (CONT'D)

Oh. Looks like this is your stop, big guy.

SUI DROPS off the roof. Just as a low-hanging SIGN smashes into the droid from behind and sends him flying off the roof.

The big DROID hurtles over KALI'S buggy. It grinds to a stop, steaming and smoking. Is it finished?

Then – with a groan of tortured metal, the big droid flips itself over, and TRANSFORMS into a WHEELED VEHICLE!

The reconfigured DROID roars off in pursuit of the train. SUI can't believe it.

It's gaining on them quickly.

SUI (CONT'D)

Kali, look out!

The DROID has caught up to KALI'S buggy now. With a sudden burst of speed the DROID pops up on its rear wheels... and SMASHES DOWN ON KALI'S BUGGY!

BLIND SPOT

> ROOKIE
> KALI!
> SUI
> Fucker!

INT BOB'S VAN – CONTINUOUS

BOB scans his HUD's frantically, pulling up data and desperately searching for information.

> BOB
> It's too heavily armored! You'll have to get inside and take out the defense CPU.

INT. ROAD TRAIN – CONTINUOUS

> SUI
> Rookie, blow its brains out!

> ROOKIE
> Copy that!

ROOKIE slaps a series of magnetic charges on the door, then sprints for the back of the car. He takes cover behind some crates and BOOM!

EXT. ROAD TRAIN – CONTINUOUS

The DROID rockets forward, transforming as it LEAPS toward the road train. It soars higher, flies OVER SUI.

> SUI (SLO MO)
> Motherfucker!

The robot lands on the front car. The DROID reaches down and its metal fingers dig into the roof panel.

INT. ROAD TRAIN – CONTINUOUS

ROOKIE rushes forward, then slides to a stop as THE ROOF OF THE CAR is torn off with a squeal of tortured metal.

The combat DROID drops through the big hole – almost on top of ROOKIE – slamming into the floor with earth shaking force.

But before he can smash ROOKIE into parts, SUI drops down on him from above! The tough cyborg locks his legs around the DROID'S neck and sends pile-driving punches into the DROID'S head.

> SUI (to droid)
> Come on, you little pussy.

ROOKIE watches in awe as the battle rages back and forth across the compartment.

> SUI (CONT'D)
> God dammit, Rookie. What are you waiting for?! Destroy this fucker's
> CPU!

ROOKIE sprints forward, trying to get past the two fighters. But the DROID spots him, swings a big fist toward him. ROOKIE ducks – almost.

The DROID'S fist catches him a glancing blow. But it's enough to send him flying across the car into a stack of crates. The heavy equipment collapses on ROOKIE, pinning him.

As ROOKIE watches, the DROID manages to grab SUI'S upper body in its merciless grip, then it pulls him off like a TICK.

The droid holds out SUI'S struggling body for a moment and then the big hand SQUEEZES. SUI'S head explodes in a shower of lubricant and metal chunks.

And the DROID stomps forward to finish off ROOKIE.

ROOKIE watches horrified, but notices something happening near the CPU – it's SUI! His broken, headless body lurches up and proceeds to PISS lubricant all over the CPU housing.

SUI gives a THUMBS UP, and the tip of his thumb bursts into flame – his cigar lighter!

EXT. TRAIN – CONTINUOUS
Beat.
The battered truck erupts in a MASSIVE EXPLOSION! The cab and what's left of the car are ripped apart.

ROOKIE is miraculously thrown clear, landing hard and bouncing across the pavement.

Long beat...

ROOKIE stirs, then lifts his head woozily, and finds himself staring right into the DROID.

With a hiss and a clunk, a CHAMBER in the DROID'S chest pops open. A glass cylinder holding the MICROCHIP drops out and rolls across the ground to stop right in front of ROOKIE.

ROOKIE just stares at the chip as BOB'S van comes roaring down the road and screeches to a halt among the wreckage.

ROOKIE looks around at the destruction, his gaze falling on SUI'S shattered arm, hand still giving a lonely thumb's up.

> BOB
> Holy shit, what a mess. What happened, Rookie??

> ROOKIE
> Mission accomplished... I guess.

> ROOKIE
> I've got the chip, but everyone else.

ROOKIE lowers his head, looking like he might break down and start crying.

And SUI'S gravelly voice comes in loud and clear.

> HOLOGRAPHIC SUI (O.S.)
> Haha. Don't worry kid. I cried my first time too.

ROOKIE looks up in surprise and sees a HOLOGRAPHIC IMAGE OF SUI standing next to him. It's being projected from BOB'S truck.

> ROOKIE
> Sui... What?

A HOLOGRAPHIC HAWK materializes to the other side of him.

HOLOGRAPHIC HAWK
Bob makes a full back-up of our brains before each mission.
HOLOGRAPHIC KALI appears.

HOLOGRAPHIC KALI
And Sui's brains, well, they don't take too much space on the old
hardrive.

ROOKIE
I thought you were all dead!

BOB
You should have read your contract, kid. Now c'mon, let's get out of
here.

The door to BOB'S van slides open and ROOKIE runs over and hops inside.

THE CAMERA PANS DOWN as the truck peels out, tires squealing, into the night.

It comes to rest on the wreckage-strewn roadway and we see the broken remains of SUI'S head.

A little GOPHER hops into frame, sniffs at SUI'S head. The gopher hops off down the road.

ICE AGE

Michael Swanwick

It was early afternoon when Rob carried the last carton into their new apartment and was – finally, officially – moved in. He was setting it down atop a stack of crated books to be unpacked later when Gail said something from the kitchen. "What's that?" he shouted.

She poked her head into the hallway. "I said – Hey, the landlord left the old refrigerator in."

Rob sauntered to the kitchen. The counters were cluttered with boxes of half-unpacked cooking utensils. "Probably too much trouble to remove it."

The refrigerator, yellowed to a grimy antique ivory, was welded immovably into the corner of the kitchen by decades' worth of petrified crud. Its top, the motor housing, rose like an art deco pagoda, in three tiers of streamlined vents. This made the refrigerator look vaguely futuristic – the future of the 1930s, though, not of the present.

Rob patted the motor housing. "This is actually very good design," he said. "In modern refrigerators the motor is set underneath and the waste heat from it rises up into the refrigerator. Then the heat has to be pumped out by the same motor that produced it, generating yet more waste heat. It's a vicious cycle. But with the modern machines they're after consumer gloss, so the motor is set down there anyway."

Gail pulled a bottle of zinfandel out of a cardboard box and set the now-empty box under the kitchen sink. "Trash goes there," she said. "You want some wine?"

The refrigerator hummed lightly, a friendly, reassuring sound. "Sure. The landlord left the refrigerator on; there's probably even some ice left."

"That's what I like about you. You ain't got no couth at all."

Rob shrugged. "I'm a barbarian." He opened the freezer compartment and found it almost overgrown with old ice. It had already swallowed up two ice cube trays and an ancient package of frozen peas. One tray, though, was almost free, and by hammering on it with the heel of his hand he could get it loose. He cracked the tray and carried a handful of ice back to the table.

"Plenty extra," he offered. Gail curled a lip. But she set out a goblet for him anyway, and poured wine in it.

Rob leaned back and swirled his drink, listening to the ice clink. He took a sip.

And stopped. Was that a *bug* in the one ice cube? He fished it out with two fingers and held it up to the light.

The cube was heavily frosted across one surface where condensate from the freezer had formed, though that was already beginning to melt from the wine. Within the cube were swirls of tiny bubbles, too small to notice if you didn't look closely. And beyond them, deep in the center, was a large black speck, a creature the size of a horsefly trapped in the ice's pellucid depths. He peered closer.

There was a wooly mammoth in his ice cube.

It was dark and shaggy, with a head that tapered down to a long, filament-sized trunk. Two all but invisible tusks twisted from its mouth. Its legs were folded in against the body. Its fur was a deep auburn red. A small and perfect wooly mammoth, no larger than a bread crumb.

Rob didn't move. The ice was cold and stung his hand, but he didn't shift it. All he could think of were the Saturday afternoon movies that began with someone finding an ancient animal frozen in ice. Though usually those ended with the animal eating Tokyo, he reminded himself.

"Hey," Gail said. "What're you staring at so intently?"

Rob opened his mouth, shut it again. Gently he lowered the ice cube to the tabletop. Drops of water appeared on its side, oozed down to the Formica, and began to form a micropuddle.

"Gail," he said carefully, "I want you to look inside this ice cube and tell me what you see."

Following his example, Gail placed her hands flat on the table and leaned forward. "Wow," she whispered. "That's – Rob, that's *beautiful.*"

The creature was fractionally easier to see now. Its tusks, long for its size – was that an indicator of age? – were yellowed and one was broken at its tip. Its eyes, frozen open and almost too small to be seen, were blue. The fur was badly matted, and there were a couple of tiny bare patches.

Gail jumped up and began running water in the sink. She returned with a bowl that steamed gently. "Here," she said, "let's thaw it out." With infinite care she eased the ice cube into the water.

After a while Rob said, "Ice melts slowly, doesn't it?" and then, reluctantly, "Maybe we should call the Smithsonian or something."

"If you could convince them to look at this," Gail pointed out," which I doubt, they'd only take it away from us."

"There is that," Rob agreed, relieved that Gail, too, felt no obligation to give the mammoth away.

At last the ice melted. Rob fished out the wee mammoth with a spoon. It was still and tiny in his hand. Suddenly, he felt very close to tears. Against all logic, he had hoped it would thaw out alive. "Here," he said, and let the beast fall from his hand to Gail's.

By dumping the contents of every carton in the house onto the floor, Gail had managed to find a magnifying glass. Now she squinted through it. "That's a wooly mammoth all right," she said. "Would you look at those eyes! And – guess what – the toe leathers are pink!" Her voice fell to a mutter then rose again: "Hey, are those *spear points* in its side?"

Rob's momentary *tristesse* melted in the heat of Gail's excitement. He leaned over her shoulder, trying to see. "I wonder how you'd go about getting something like this preserved in Lucite," Gail mused. Then she straightened and turned to face him. "Maybe there's more of these in the freezer!"

Gail took the lead. She opened the refrigerator and peered into the freezer. Nudging the ice cube tray with a finger, she squinted at the ice around it. Then, gingerly, she pulled out the tray and, after examining it briefly, stared through the small space that was not yet swallowed up by the slow, devouring ice. She whistled softly.

"What?" Rob said.

She shook her head, still staring into the freezer.

"What? *Tell* me."

"I think you'd better look for yourself."

Rob put an arm around her waist and laid his head beside hers so they could both peer within. The light inside was dim but serviceable, the land beyond the ice half-lit by some unseen source. He stared past the rime into a tiny, mountainous country. Off to one side, a small glacier was partially visible. To the foreground, a trickle of water – a river in miniature – meandered through a dark, Nordic pine forest.

Huddled by the river was a town, stone and wood buildings all in a jumble and surrounded by high stone walls.

"My God," Rob breathed. *"There's a lost civilization in our refrigerator."*

They stared at each other for a moment, eyes wide, then returned, wonderingly, to the freezer.

It was dark in the back reaches. Silently cursing the gloom, Rob strained to see. The town was laid out on a semicircular plan against the water, though the streets were a hopeless maze. Clearly they had been built haphazardly, at random.

Atop a hill near the center of town stood a cathedral, squat and heavy, but still recognizable as such. It dominated the town. By the river's edge stood a castle. All the other buildings radiated from these two loci. The town walls were clearly anachronistic remnants, though, for slum buildings – hovels, actually – had been built up against them. In places the walls were actually breached, the stones carted away for building materials. Several roads ran from the town through the pine forest, and one – a major one – ran along the river.

Finally Gail stepped back and said, "You know, this doesn't make any sense at all."

"That so?" Rob did not look up from the freezer.

"I mean, this is clearly an early medieval city. Wooly mammoths died out sometime in the Neolithic."

Rob looked at her. Cold air seeped from the refrigerator. Placing a hand on his arm, Gail tugged him away from the freezer and softly closed the door. "Let's have some coffee," she suggested.

Rob brewed the coffee while Gail dumped the already-poured wine down the sink. They brooded over mugs of Kenyan in silence. Gail touched the tiny mammoth with the tip of her fingernail. It was not in good shape; putrefaction was setting in, as if time were catching up with the long ages it had lain frozen in the ice. She crooked an eyebrow at Rob, and he nodded agreement.

While Rob unhooked the spider plant from its new position over the kitchen window, Gail wrapped the mammoth in a corner of white tissue paper.

They dug a small hole in the soil under the plant with an old fork, and buried the creature with full military honors.

Rob solemnly placed the plant back on its hook.

Without saying a word, they both turned to the refrigerator.

They opened the freezer compartment together. Rob took one look, and his mouth fell open.

The town was still there. But it had changed and grown while they were away. It had evolved. The stone walls were down, and the cathedral had been rebuilt in the soaring, Gothic style. It no longer dominated the town, though; now it was one large building among many. The streets were wider, too, and the town had expanded out of sight behind the left-hand ice. It was a city now.

The details were harder to make out than before, though, for it seemed that the industrial revolution was in full swing. Bristling forests of smokestacks belched thick black smoke into the wintry sky. The riverside was choked with hundreds of tiny docks, the castle torn down to make room for them, and impossibly thin railroad tracks crawled through the depleted pine forests, past the glacier's edge, and over the snow-capped mountains to some unseen destination.

The town had evolved into a city in a matter of minutes. Even as they watched, buildings appeared and disappeared. Roads shifted position instantaneously. Entire sections of the city were rebuilt in the twinkling of an eye. "The time rate in there must be fantastic," Rob said. "I'll bet that years – decades – are going by as we stand here."

The city pulsed with movement. Its people were invisible, as were their vehicles and beasts of burden, for they all moved too quickly to be seen, but traffic patterns were shimmering gray uncertainties in the streets, dark where traffic was heavy, and pale where light.

The buildings were growing larger and taller. They exploded into the air as steel-beam construction was discovered. The sky to the far side of the city began flickering darkly, and it took an instant to realize that they were seeing the airlanes from an exurban airport hidden behind the ice.

"I think we've reached the present," Gail said.

Rob leaned forward to get a better look, and was caught in the wash of the first thermonuclear blast.

There was an instantaneous *flash* and pure white light flooded his skull. Needles of pain lanced through his eyes, and he staggered backwards from the freezer, a hand over his face.

"*Rob!*" Gail cried in a panicky voice, and from her tone he could tell that she had blinked or glanced away at the crucial instant. She was okay then, and knowing that gave him the presence of mind to slam the refrigerator door shut as he fell over backwards.

Afterimages burned in his mind: A quadrant of the city disappearing into sudden crater, a transcendentally bright mushroom cloud that was gone before it was there, subliminal traces of fire and smoke, and blast zones where all traffic and life abruptly ceased. The pictures jumbled one on top of another.

"Rob, are you okay? Say something!"

He was lying on his back, his head in Gail's lap. "I'm… I'm okay," he managed to say. And even as he said it, it began to come true. Through the bright wash of nothingness, the kitchen started to seep through. The details were vague and tentative at first, then stronger. It was like being blinded by a flashbulb, except that the afterimage was a small mushroom cloud.

"Gail," he croaked. "They're fighting a nuclear war in there."

"There now, don't get excited," she said soothingly.

He struggled to sit up. "They're using tac-nukes in my refrigerator and you're telling me to *calm down?*"

"It's good advice anyway," she insisted. Then she giggled. "Boy, you should see your face!"

"Why? What's the matter with it?" But she simply shook her head, too full of laughter to respond. He stalked off to the bathroom and numbly stared into the mirror. His face was bright red from the primary radiation. "Oboy," he said. "That's going to be a bad sunburn in the morning."

ICE AGE

Back in the kitchen, he eyed the refrigerator with trepidation. "Let me," Gail said. Gingerly, being careful to keep her head averted, she opened the door the tiniest possible crack.

A dozen flashes of light flickered in and out of existence, like a badly out of synch strobe. The reflected brilliance off the walls dazzled both Gail and Rob; clearly there had been an escalation in megatonnage. Gail slammed the door shut.

Rob sighed. "Well, I guess it was too much to expect them to outgrow war over the course of two minutes." He looked helplessly at Gail. "But what do we do now?"

"Send out for a pizza?" she suggested.

The sun had set, leaving only a faint golden smear in the sky by the time they had finished the pizza. Rob ate the last, nearly-cold piece, and Gail dumped box and crusts in the cardboard box under the sink.

"It's been over two hours," Rob said. "They must've had time to rebuild by now."

Gail touched his arm, squeezed tenderly. "They may have killed themselves off, Rob. We have to face up to that possibility."

"Yeah." Rob pushed back his chair and stood. Feeling like John Wayne, he advanced on the refrigerator. "Let's go for it," he said, and jerked the door open a sliver. Nothing happened. He opened it all the way.

The freezer was still intact. There was a black smear across one corner of the ice, but that was all. Cautiously, they stared in.

The city was still there, between glacier and icy river. It had not been destroyed in the nuclear spasm wars of late afternoon. But it had changed.

The skyscrapers had continued to grow and to evolve. They had become tall, delicate fronds that gleamed soft gold and green. Skywalks appeared between the fairy towers. "Look." Rob pointed to threadlike structures that wove intricate patterns through the city. "Monorails!"

Flickermotes appeared in the air between the towers. Were they flying cars, Rob wondered, or possibly personal jetpacks? There was no way of knowing. And what were those shimmering domes that sprang up like mushrooms after a rain on the outskirts of town?

"It looks like the Emerald City of Oz," Gail said. "Only not just green." Rob nodded agreement. Some new technology was invented then, and the city changed again. Now the buildings seemed to be made of curdled light, or possibly crystals of glowing fog. Whatever they were, they weren't entirely solid. They receded into dimensions that weren't there.

"I think the time rate is accelerating," Gail said in a small voice.

The city pulsed and danced to some unearthly syncopation. It sent out blossoms and shoots, and exploded into the sky in firework structures of color and essence, and joyous, whimsical light. It was a strangely *playful* city.

There was some kind of leakage from the freezer too. Some kind of broadcast. Rob and Gail picked up flashes of color and quick, incomprehensible messages, broadcast directly to their brains, maybe, or their nerve webs or possibly even to each individual cell of their bodies. They could understand none of it. Then there was another shift of technology, and the impressions cut off.

But the city was still changing, and the rate of change still accelerating. Now the unsubstantial towers swayed like fronds of seaweed lashed by a hurricane. Faster. Now the radius of the city exploded outward and imploded inward again. Again it happened and again, like circles of light pulsing outward. Giant machines throbbed in the air and were gone. Highways of light moved out and up into the night. Too quick to be seen, leaving behind only an impression of incredible bulk, *something* stooped over the city.

The changes were coming still faster now – as if the city were searching for something, trying out and rejecting alternate configurations in pursuit of some specific goal. The buildings became piles of orange diamonds, matrixes of multicolored spheres, a vast tangle of organic vines. The city was a honeycomb, a featureless monolith, a surrealistic birthday cake.

This search lasted a full five minutes. Then, for an instant, the city reached a kind of crystalline perfection, and all change, all motion ceased. It stood poised on the numinous edge between instant and infinity. For that brief, eternal second, nothing happened.

Then the city exploded.

Beams and lattices of light, like playful twisted lasers, shot into the air, between the masses of ice and out into the kitchen. Massively ornate constructs of color and nothing else flickered into existence over the sink and oven. They phased out of being, then halfway in again, and then were gone. The city rose into the air, and separated out into component planes and solids. Very briefly, it *sang*. Very briefly, it existed both in the refrigerator and in the kitchen, as if its presence were too large for any one location.

And then it went away. It did not move in any direction they could comprehend. It just went... away.

They stood blinking. After the lights and bright colors of the city, the freezer compartment seemed dark and still. Gail shook her head wonderingly. Rob gently touched the ice. Where the city had stood was nothing but a few dead walls, a handful of ancient ruins half-buried in drifting snow.

Even as they watched, these last traces of civilization crumbled into dust, destroyed by the relentless onslaught of time.

"I wonder where they've gone to." Rob closed the refrigerator door. "Some other dimension?"

Gail did not respond immediately. Then she said, "I doubt that *we* could understand." She was wide-eyed and solemn.

Nevertheless, she didn't object when Rob went around to the back of the refrigerator and pulled the plug. They stood looking at it in silence for a while.

"We'll clean it out with ammonia before we turn it on again," Rob said.

Gail took his hand. "C'mon, kid. Let's go to bed."

Rob woke up the next morning, sleepy-eyed and sunburnt. He stumbled to the kitchen and, after brewing coffee, automatically pulled open the refrigerator to get some milk.

The inside of the refrigerator smelled rich and moist, with the acrid tang of food starting to rot. Rob wrinkled his nose and started to close the door. But on impulse – just to be safe – he peered into the freezer compartment.

The interior of the freezer was green and steamy. A brontosaurus no longer than his thumb raised its head ponderously above the jungle growth and blinked.

MISSIVES FROM POSSIBLE FUTURES #1: ALTERNATE HISTORY SEARCH RESULTS

John Scalzi

Dear Customer,

Thank you for trying a Sample History Search with Multiversity™, America's leading Alternate History Research Firm. Thanks to our patented Multiview™ technology, and search algorithms that scour multiple universes with more speed and accuracy, Multiversity™ is able to access nearly 50% more alternate timestreams than either Alternaview or Megapast – for the same cost! And we guarantee our alternate history research with a 100% money back guarantee – we want you to be happy with the accuracy of our alternate pasts, so we can work together in our shared future.

For your Sample History Search, you asked to see THE DEATH OF ADOLF HITLER on the date of AUGUST 13, 1908 in VIENNA, AUSTRIA. As it happens, THE DEATH OF ADOLF HITLER is one of our most popular requests, and Multiversity™ has developed an impressive pre-cached concordance on the subject, spanning most days of this subject's entire lifespan. What does this mean for you? Simply that as a pre-researched event, if you were paying for this History Search, we could offer you this information on a substantially discounted basis: Some popular searches are available for as much as 65% off the 'new search' price!

As you did not specify the particular details for THE DEATH OF ADOLF HITLER on AUGUST 13, 1908 in VIENNA, AUSTRIA, we are proud to offer you a random sampler of scenarios relating to the disposition of your search. In it you will see how varying the details of the event you've chosen can greatly influence the course of history. This is the famous 'Butterfly Effect' – and we're sure you'll enjoy seeing the storms these butterflies bring about!

Because this is a Sample History Search, we regret that we may only provide summaries at this time. But should you wish to explore one or more of these alternate histories in greater detail, Multiversity™ is proud to offer you a Detailed Historical Statement – a

$300 value – for just $59.95. Please contact one of our sales representatives to take advantage of this Special Offer!

Thanks again for choosing Multiversity™ -- it's a great time to be with us™.

Scenario #1

Event: ADOLF HITLER is KILLED by MUGGING ATTEMPT ON THE STEPS OF THE ACADEMY OF FINE ARTS VIENNA

As a result: World War I proceeds; Weimar Republic proceeds; World War II delayed until 1948; US drops atomic bomb on Berlin in 1952; Neil Armstrong first man on the moon, 1972.

Scenario #2

Event: ADOLF HITLER is KILLED by OPIUM JUNKIE LOOKING FOR MONEY

As a result: World War I proceeds; Weimar Republic proceeds; World War II averted; Germany and Britain form economic union, declare war on France in 1958; Malcolm Evans first man on the moon, 1975.

Scenario #3:

Event: ADOLF HITLER is KILLED by RUN- AWAY HORSE-DR AW N WAGON FILLED WITH BRATWURST, THE FOURTH SUCH FATALITY IN VIENNA IN SIX DAYS

As a result: Vienna passes tough horse-drawn vehicle laws, prompting the quick acceptance of automobiles; Austria becomes automotive industrial powerhouse; World War I proceeds, Germany and allies win thanks to technological advances; 30s worldwide depression averted; Willy Brandt first man on the moon, 1958.

Scenario #4:

ALTERNATE HISTORIES

Event: ADOLF HITLER is KILLED by MULTIPLE KNIFE WOUNDS BY JEALOUS GAY LOVER WHO THINKS HIS BOYFRIEND IS CHEATING ON HIM WITH HITLER, WHO IN FACT IS TOTALLY INNOCENT AND HASN'T HAD SEX OF ANY SORT IN MONTHS, MUCH LESS GAY VIENNESE SEX

As a result: The trial of Felix von Weingartner,

director of the Vienna Opera and the closeted, murdering gay lover in question, shocks and delights Viennese society; Hitler's watercolors, formerly unsellable, become a hot commodity on the auction circuit before the novelty wears off. Hitler's sister awarded a settlement; World War I proceeds, Germany and allies win; 30s depression not averted; virulent flu wipes out 38% of European population; US becomes world power; John Glenn first man on the moon, 1956.

Scenario #5

Event: ADOLF HITLER is KILLED by SUFFO- CATION WHEN INEXPLICABLY ENCASED IN AN ENORMOUS BLOCK OF UNFLAVORED GELATIN

As a result: Hitler only a random test subject for Gelatin Encasing Weapon, developed by the Russian aristocracy from technology pulled out of the spaceship that caused the Tunguska Event of June 30, 1908; the GEW subsequently used to assassinate enemies of Tsar Nicholas II, and then world leaders; World War I begins when Archduke Franz Ferdinand is spontaneously encased in gelatin while riding in a 1911 Graf und Stift Rois De Blougne tourer in Sarajevo and Young Bosnia opportunistically claims credit; World War I subsequently ends in 1915 when entire German divisions are gelatinized; Russia becomes sole super power; Vladimir Putin first man on the moon, 1988.

Scenario #6

Event: ADOLF HITLER is KILLED by BULLET WOUND IN CROSSFIRE BETWEEN TIME-TRAVELING ANTI-NAZIS SENT BACK TO KILL HIM AND TIME- TRAVELING NAZIS SENT BACK TO PREVENT HIS ASSASSINATION

As a result: Causality loop annihilates time and space surrounding Vienna, knocking everyone in the city back to 1529 and the eve of the First Turkish Seige; as the 20th century Viennese use their historical knowledge to help the 16th century Viennese, time-traveling pro-Viennese forces appear and fight a pitched battle with time-traveling pro-Ottoman forces, pushing everyone back to 955 and the Battle of Lechfeld; when the time-traveling pro-Magyar forces show up, they are slaughtered by everyone else which is tired of all this time-traveling crap, thereby ending the causality loop. Vienna becomes world power; Henry Jasomirgott first man on the moon, 1155.

Scenario #7

Event: ADOLF HITLER is KILLED by MARATHON FORNICATION BY SIX VIENNESE PROSTITUTES

As a result: Prostitutes arrested and revealed as libidinous time-travelers from a very sexy future who teach the Viennese their futuristic ways of astro-pleasure; Janine Lindemulder first woman on the moon, 1996.

Scenario #8

Event: ADOLF HITLER is KILLED by VAPOR- IZATION WHEN METEOR HITS HIM SQUARE ON THE HEAD

As a result: No noticeable historical changes arise from event at all. However, as the meteor is a precursor to a massive asteroid cruising toward Earth, human history had only 22 hours, 16 minutes to develop from that point before being obliterated. Humanity wiped out along with Hitler and 93% of all species; society of rats rises and falls; society of frogs rises and falls; society of pillbugs rises and falls; society of squid rises and sticks; Gluugsnertgluug first squid on the moon, 2,973,004,412.

THE SECRET WAR

David W. Amendola

Death lurked in the hamlet. A great deal of death.

Lieutenant Nikolai Zakharov could feel it. He could not smell it – the temperature was at least thirty degrees below zero so anything that died would quickly freeze solid – but he knew it was there, waiting. Kneeling behind a windfall at the edge of the forest, he observed the cluster of stout log cabins in the clearing through binoculars, watching and listening for signs of activity.

Nothing. Not even chimney smoke. All was quiet.

Black ravens perched in the nearby trees, another indicator of death. He noted that they were strangely silent and kept their distance from the hamlet.

Including Zakharov, his team numbered ten. He and seven others were armed with PPSh-41 submachine guns. The wiry Junior Sergeant Okhchen preferred his Mosin-Nagant sniper rifle with its PE telescopic sight. Private Kaminsky, a giant of man with red hair and fierce eyes, was responsible for the DP-28 light machine gun. He handled it like a toy, shouldering with ease the heavy satchel of extra magazines that normally an assistant would carry for him. Each man also had an RGD-33 stick grenade.

They were dressed for the extreme cold: quilted jacket and trousers, woolen underwear, fleece cap, fur mittens, and felt boots. For camouflage a white, hooded snow suit was worn over everything.

Nervous tension sharpened their senses and attuned them to their surroundings, made them alert for the slightest scent or sound. They knew all too well the nature of their enemy.

Zakharov whistled a bird call to get everyone's attention and then motioned. He and six others emerged from concealment, snow crunching underfoot, and warily approached the hamlet.

The tiny settlement huddled on a riverbank was an old trading post and stores that had catered to the local fur trade for nearly a century.

Mere minutes of murderous frenzy had snuffed it out forever.

On the icy, dirt street the soldiers found pale corpses and pieces of corpses lying frozen among stiffened tatters of shredded clothing. Puddles of blood and gore had solidified into dark-red ice. The villagers had been ripped apart: heads, limbs, and entrails were strewn about. All were gnawed and half-eaten, bones split for marrow and skulls smashed open for brains. A grisly feast for scavengers, but as Zakharov expected, none were skulking around. Wolves, like the ravens, were shunning this place.

A laika, someone's pitiful pet, cowered behind a woodshed too terrified to even whimper. What had killed and eaten the villagers did not have a taste for dog meat.

The soldiers surveyed the carnage dispassionately, hardened to such horrors. This was not their first mission. All were *frontoviks* – combat veterans. Each had already been awarded the Medal for Combat Merit and a few had also earned at least one wound stripe.

Zakharov motioned again. Kaminsky lay prone and covered the length of the street with his machine gun. Then three men led by Senior Sergeant Sergei Kravchenko, a short stocky Ukrainian who was Zakharov's second in command, crept up to the rear of the nearest cabin, staying below window level. With a bang the door was kicked in and they rushed inside, fingers on triggers and grenades ready to throw. After verifying the cabin was unoccupied, they moved on to check the next building.

At length the search was complete and Kravchenko briskly strode over to relay the results to his superior, who had remained beside Kaminsky.

"All clear, Comrade Lieutenant."

"I assume there are no survivors," said Zakharov.

"No."

Zakharov nodded at Okhchen, who began inspecting the claw and bite marks on the slain villagers. He squatted to study a footprint in a patch of snow stained pink by blood, viewing it from different angles. Roughly the size of a man's, it had three clawed toes reminiscent of a bird's. He walked around and carefully examined other tracks on the hamlet's outskirts before returning to make his report.

"Comrade Lieutenant, there were ten of them. They attacked last night."

"Which direction did they come from?" asked Zakharov.

"Northeast. They're headed southwest now."

Zakharov nodded then turned to Kravchenko. "Let's get moving. We head northeast."

"We're not following them?" asked Kravchenko.

"No, the other teams will have to intercept them. Our assignment is to locate their hole. Signal that we've found evidence of an attack and they're headed southwest."

"Yes, Comrade Lieutenant." Kravchenko beckoned to a private and barked an order.

The Red Army possessed relatively few radios and the team had none. Laying wire for field telephones was often impractical, so messengers and flares were usually relied upon for communication between teams. The private loaded a flare pistol according to his signal chart, pointed it at the sky, and sent a two-star purple and white flare arching high above.

The Secret War had raged on and off for almost a quarter-century, never mentioned in the Soviet press or publicly acknowledged by Soviet leaders. Matters of internal security never were.

Zakharov remembered when he returned from his first search-and-destroy operation. He had been congratulated by his superiors, decorated with the Order of the Red Star, and then bluntly informed that if he ever told anyone outside the unit what he had seen he would be sent to a corrective-labor camp.

There were lulls in the war, but then the things would return. Just exactly what they were no one knew. In the dead of winter, when the nights were longest, mysterious holes would appear in northern Siberia and the things would come forth, hungry for human flesh. They never hunted animals, only people. And Moscow would have to organize another campaign to eradicate the bloodthirsty creatures.

They had no official name, as they corresponded to no known species. Soviet scientists debated whether they were the wild men of myth – the *almasty* of the Caucasus, the *chuchunya* of Siberia, or the *menk* of the Urals. But legends described all of these as similar to apes or men, perhaps even surviving Neanderthals, and the terrifying creatures that attacked villagers and herders were definitely not human or simian. Unofficially they were simply referred to as *upir*, the generic Russian word for bloodsucking monsters such as vampires and ghouls.

Security operations within the USSR were normally handled by the internal troops of the People's Commissariat for Internal Affairs – the NKVD, Joseph Stalin's ruthless secret police. But these paramilitary units lacked the specialized training required. Hunting ghouls was altogether different from conducting mass arrests and deportations of alleged 'enemies of the people'. After an entire NKVD regiment was annihilated along the Middle Tunguska River in 1936, search-and-destroy operations were taken over by the Red Army.

A unique unit of irregulars was formed: Special Group X – *Spetsialnogo Gruppa X*, often referred to simply as *Spetsgruppa X*. The X was not the Cyrillic letter but the Latin, taken from the mathematical notation for an unknown variable, since the creatures they fought were an unknown species. Composed of soldiers acclimatized and trained for winter warfare, preferably those who had been trappers or hunters in civilian life, its independent detachments were based at Siberian outposts. Whenever a ghoul incursion occurred, teams would hunt down the creatures, eliminate them, and destroy their holes.

But when reports were received in late 1942 of renewed ghoul activity they were given a low priority by the Kremlin. The Soviet Union was locked in a bloody death struggle with Nazi Germany, which had launched a massive invasion the previous year. All available troops and equipment were needed to replace the appalling losses suffered in the desperate battles for Minsk, Kiev, Leningrad, and Moscow. *Spetsgruppa X* was reduced to a token force. Before the war Zakharov's team had been the size of a platoon; now it was a squad.

Zakharov took a sun sighting with a sextant. There were no accurate maps of this area, and he kept a log of their movements and location.

When none of the others were nearby, Kravchenko asked, "Permission to speak freely, Comrade Lieutenant?"

"Of course, Sergei Pavlovich." Despite their difference in rank they were on familiar terms in private. Smart junior officers listened to and learned from their senior non-commissioned officers and Zakharov greatly valued Kravchenko's experience. Almost twice as old as Zakharov, he had served in the First World War and the Russian Civil War.

"The detachment's teams are deployed too far apart," said Kravchenko. "We can't support each other and coordinate patrols to sweep each sector properly. If one team encounters too many ghouls it might be overwhelmed before the others can help."

"I raised that concern."

"May I ask what the major's response was?"

"He said we can cover more territory if we disperse this way. Not many ghouls were reported so he's confident each team can handle any it finds."

"Only a few have been detected so far, that's true, but who's to say there won't be more? We have no way of knowing how many will show up each winter."

"I know."

Kravchenko sighed. "Why did Moscow send us a new detachment commander who has no experience in these operations? It's bad enough we're undermanned."

"We have our orders."

"Understood, Comrade Lieutenant. Did the major at least say something about the planes that were requested?"

"No, and I wouldn't count on any either. Supporting our comrades fighting at Stalingrad is Moscow's top priority right now."

They returned to the forest. The dead villagers were left where they lay. Others would come later to dispose of them. The hamlet itself would be abandoned. No one would want to live here now.

Three soldiers in a nearby gully held the team's horses, the animals' foggy breath rising from frosted muzzles. Much of Siberia was still primordial wilderness, impassable for motorized transport. These beasts were small, shaggy Yakutians, a hardy breed that thrived in this brutal climate and subsisted largely on wild grass.

The team slung weapons, saddled up, and rode off in the direction from which the ghouls had come. Tracks led down the bank and over the flat, slate surface of the frozen river, swept by a whistling southwest breeze. This time of year the ice was thick enough to easily support horsemen. Upon reaching the opposite bank they plunged into the forest.

Okhchen scouted ahead, his dark, almond-shaped eyes picking out signs of the ghouls' passage – broken twigs, scuffed lichen, footprints in the snow. But no droppings. Ghouls left no excrement. The team took care to ride single file alongside the trail, not over it, so as not to obliterate any clues. It was easy to follow: their quarry had made no effort to conceal it.

Zakharov considered himself lucky to be assigned to *Spetsgruppa X*. The nature of its operations necessitated giving commanders in the field more freedom of initiative than was usual in the Red Army. This comparative independence had increased with the recent demotion of the Communist Party political commissars. Reduced to an advisory role, they no longer held dual command with military officers.

Keeping one's command still depended on results though. Failure was never an option in the USSR. Even if you were a marshal it could mean a sentence to a penal battalion or the Gulag, the NKVD's network of prisons and forced-labor camps. Or a firing squad.

Not that results guaranteed safety. Thousands had been imprisoned or shot during the purges. To meet the quotas of enemies demanded by Stalin's insatiable paranoia the secret police could arrest anyone for any reason – or no reason at all. Arbitrary terror maintained his iron rule.

Every division had an NKVD Special Department attached. Fortunately the head of this unit in *Spetsgruppa X* was an alcoholic whose wife had an eye for bourgeois luxuries. The commanding general prudently supplied plenty of vodka and furs to ensure glowing weekly reports.

The team followed the tracks through the bleak taiga. Larches stood gray and skeletal, having shed their needles last autumn. The forest floor had little underbrush, tufts of brown grass poking up through the snow in clearings. Siberia was not only very cold, but also very dry. Many parts actually received little snowfall, although what snow did fall would remain on the ground for at least six months out of the year. The only signs of humanity were small deadfall traps; winter was the hunting season for sable.

This time of year the days were very short, a blue twilight only lasting about four hours. The golden sun did not come up until late morning and struggled to rise just above the horizon before setting again by mid-afternoon.

At one point the team heard a long wail far in the distance. The shrill cry resembled nothing uttered by human or animal. They heard it again from time to time, coming from different directions. The soldiers exchanged anxious, knowing looks.

"Ghouls," Kravchenko muttered.

Zakharov raised his hand to signal a halt. He glanced around at the trees. One nearly fifty meters tall towered above the rest. Handing his binoculars to Okhchen, he said, "Get up there and see if you can locate them."

Okhchen strapped spikes to his boots and shinnied up the trunk until he could reach the lowest branches, then climbed up through the boughs. Sitting in a crook near the top, he slowly scanned in all directions before quickly clambering back down.

"Comrade Lieutenant, twelve are two kilometers northeast moving down the trail towards us," he said. "Ten more are a kilometer and a half southwest, following us and coming fast. The second group is probably the pack that attacked the hamlet. They must have discovered our tracks."

"They're hunting us now," said Zakharov. He rubbed his chin thoughtfully. "We could dig in and summon the other teams."

Kravchenko shook his head. "It'll be dark before anyone can get here. We're too far apart. Then the ghouls will have the advantage since they can see at night."

"Then we'd better attack now while it's still daylight and the packs are separated. Eliminate the ones behind us then destroy the rest."

Kravchenko grinned, revealing a gold eye tooth. "We'll catch them by surprise."

The team wheeled about and cantered back the way they had come. Soon the horses neighed. They had a keen sense of smell and ghouls exuded a disagreeable odor.

Swerving behind a rise, the soldiers dismounted. Three held the horses. Okhchen and Kaminsky crawled up to the crest to over-watch positions while the others, led by Zakharov, spread out in a skirmish line in front of the rise.

Ten ghouls ran through the woods ahead.

They were thin, wiry creatures with gray, leathery skin totally devoid of hair. Running in a forward crouch like apes, each would stand a little over meter and a half tall if fully erect. Long, bony arms almost reaching the ground ended in gnarled hands with curved, black claws. Bipedal, they had clawed, three-toed feet. Narrow heads had pointed ears, slits for nostrils, and slanted yellow eyes smoldering with ravenous hunger. They bared slavering fangs and long, blue, forked tongues flicked out.

Even weak daylight impaired their vision so they did not see the soldiers immediately.

A yellow flare was sent up to alert the other teams that ghouls had been spotted. Then the echoing crack of Okhchen's rifle broke the silence. A ghoul staggered as a 147-grain 7.62 millimeter bullet punched through its left eye, blasting out the back of its head in a spray of black ichor. It toppled backwards.

The other ghouls looked around angrily for the source as a second and then a third were killed in rapid succession by headshots, until finally they spotted the humans. With a bedlam of bloodcurdling howls, they charged. One threw back its head and let out a long, wavering shriek that echoed across the forest and sent chills up the spines of the soldiers.

"Fire!" shouted Zakharov.

The ghouls were fast and agile. The soldiers stood their ground and opened fire – the quick, harsh chatter of their submachine guns punctuated by the slower rattle of the DP-28 above and behind them.

The creatures rushed into a storm of lead. They stumbled and fell, riddled by scores of slugs, their ichor sizzling as it splashed on the ground, instantly melting any snow it touched. A pair veered left, trying to outflank the team, but to no avail. This move had been anticipated and they too were shot down, the last collapsing dead just meters from the soldiers.

The team ceased fire and reloaded, adrenalin slowly ebbing from their veins. Zakharov noticed Kravchenko calmly bandaging a wrist.

"Wounded?" he asked.

"A drop of their blood splashed on me," said Kravchenko. "Burns like acid."

The ghoul carcasses began smoldering and disintegrating. Within minutes all that would remain would be heaps of ashes and a foul reek lingering in the crisp air. No bones. And nothing would ever grow in these spots again. This accelerated decomposition had made it impossible to obtain specimens for scientific study, so details of ghoul anatomy were unknown.

Zakharov collected a little bit of the ash, sealing it in an envelope. He had standing orders to take samples when conditions permitted.

Attempts to capture ghouls alive had proved unsuccessful. They could not be subdued and were totally resistant to tranquilizers. All anyone had to go on were eyewitness accounts, blurry photographs, plaster casts of footprints, and laboratory analysis of ash residue. Ghouls did not appear to have any type of social structure or leadership. Nothing resembling offspring were ever seen and their method of reproduction was unknown. They all looked alike and there was no visible gender differentiation.

The team hurried back to their horses and rode off to intercept the other pack.

The woods thickened, forcing them to slow as they followed tracks down a slope to a frozen, meandering stream cloaked in shadow, the treetops etched against the orange sky.

Okhchen abruptly reined in and motioned for the others to stop. His eyes darted around suspiciously.

The breeze shifted. The horses whinnied sharply.

"Ambush!" shouted Okhchen.

Screeches filled the air as ghouls suddenly leaped from behind the rocks and scrub brush on the opposite bank where they had been hiding.

One private was decapitated by a single slash of a claw and his headless body, spurting bright-red blood, rode along for a ways like a horrid rag doll before finally tumbling from the saddle. Another was dragged off his mount; his submachine gun and arm were torn away and the top of his head was sheared off. The neighing horse of a third man reared and hurled him to the ground, breaking his leg. A ghoul immediately disemboweled him and bit his throat out.

One sprang into a tree above Zakharov, but before it could pounce on him he peppered it with a burst from his PPSh-41. Several branches broke as the ghoul fell heavily to the ground.

The soldiers recovered quickly from their initial surprise and urged their steeds forward. They managed to ride clear of the ambush and then swung around to open a relentless fire from horseback. The pack was quickly eliminated.

Zakharov jumped down and rushed over to his fallen men along with the team's medic.

Two were already dead. The third, the one missing an arm and the top of his skull, was incredibly, horribly, still alive and conscious. With the usual stoicism of Russian soldiers he did not cry out. But he was beyond aid and there was nothing the medic could do except administer morphine to ease his last moments, cradling him in his arms until he mercifully expired.

Zakharov had a green flare fired to signal that all the ghouls seen had been destroyed. Then he grimly collected the identification booklets of his slain men for safekeeping. The bodies were stripped of weapons and equipment and loose stones were piled over each to erect a crude cairn. The iron-hard permafrost made grave digging a herculean task they had no time for. They paused for a somber moment of silence, then mounted up and rode on, taking the extra horses with them.

Because of the classified nature of these operations the government did not award a campaign medal for participation. Zakharov would not even be allowed to write consolation letters to the families. He could recommend deserving men for posthumous decorations, but the citations would themselves be classified. Relatives would never be told the circumstances of their loved ones' deaths, only that each had died "fighting gallantly in defense of his beloved Motherland."

They returned to the original trail. Night descended, the gloom faintly illuminated by the cold gleam of the stars. The temperature dropped still further, down to fifty degrees below zero. The trail was clear enough for the team to continue following it by starlight for several hours before finally stopping to camp.

THE SECRET WAR

A sentry was posted and trip wires for flares were strung around the camp perimeter. Everyone would take his turn standing watch while the rest slept. Zakharov determined their location again using a sextant sighting of Polaris.

First priority, as always for mounted troops, was the horses, which were picketed, groomed, checked for injuries, and allowed to graze. Finally a tent was erected and the team sat inside to eat, huddled around the oasis of warmth provided by a little iron field stove.

Zakharov saw to it that his men were taken care of first before wolfing down his own meal of black rye bread, buckwheat porridge, and hard sausage washed down with hot tea. He made a point of refusing officer's rations and eating the same food as enlisted men. An allotment of vodka was also authorized under regulations, but he strictly forbade it. Back at base the men could drink and carouse as they pleased, but on a mission he needed everyone sober and sharp.

Afterwards they cleaned weapons, oiled them with cold-weather lubricants to keep the mechanisms from freezing, and reloaded magazines. They talked and joked and enjoyed the luxury of a smoke, rolling strong, coarse tobacco in newsprint to make crude cigarettes.

The glint of metal betrayed a little Christian cross one private wore around his neck and kept hidden under his jacket. Zakharov, as usual, pretended not to notice.

He had seen too many good men die needlessly – and far too young – to entertain any belief in God. But like his soldiers he was the son of a peasant and understood their ways – their rough humor, their towering profanity, their taboos and superstitions – and he indulged them whenever possible. He also ignored their occasional grumblings about the regime. Zakharov was a pragmatic Communist. So long as his men fought that was all that mattered.

* * *

Zakharov snapped awake amid the frantic neighing and stomping of the horses. Even as he and the others in the tent fumbled for weapons the harsh, white glow of a trip flare suddenly lit up the camp and two bursts of automatic fire shattered the stillness.

Zakharov darted outside. Kaminsky was on sentry duty, smoke curling from his machine gun's muzzle.

"Over there," he said, nodding in the direction. "Two of them. Got both when the flare blinded them."

The team scrambled to defensive positions around the camp as the flare fizzled out and darkness returned. They waited in tense silence as their night vision recovered. The dark woods seemed fraught with menace, a gibbous moon glowering above. But nothing happened, and at length the horses settled down and became quiet again.

"I don't think there are any more of them," said Okhchen.

The team relaxed. Zakharov went over to Kravchenko, who was squatting beside one of the ghoul ash piles, deep in thought.

"We were lucky," said Zakharov. "There were only two and the horses smelled them before they got too close."

Kravchenko grunted. "That's what worries me."

"Why?"

"Ghouls don't appear to be intelligent, Comrade Lieutenant, not in our sense of the word, but they're not stupid either. They're cunning like any predator. They've been shrieking back and forth all day, communicating. Communicating about us and the other teams. Our flares pinpoint our locations."

"Unfortunately we can't help it. We have no radios."

"For sure the ghouls know all about us – what we are, where we are, how many of us there are. So why are they attacking us just a few at a time or in small packs? If there aren't that many of them, then why not avoid us entirely and hunt for easier prey?"

"I don't know. When you put it that way, it doesn't make sense."

Kravchenko stood. "No, it doesn't."

* * *

The rest of the night passed uneventfully, but the team slept fitfully and rose before dawn. After a quick breakfast they resumed the hunt by moonlight. The trail turned due north.

As the first feeble rays of sunlight filtered through the trees Okhchen spotted something away from the trail and rode over to take a closer look. He got off his horse and examined the ground. Zakharov went to see what he was looking at. Okhchen brushed away snow to uncover yellowed, splintered bones, scraps of khaki fabric, a few black buttons, and the slashed remnants of boots and accouterments.

"Another ghoul victim?" asked Zakharov, dismounting.

"Yes, Comrade Lieutenant, but this fellow died a long time ago." Okhchen bent and plucked from a frayed pocket an identification booklet, its red cloth cover stained and faded. He was illiterate so he showed it to Zakharov.

Zakharov grunted with interest. "NKVD."

A rusted Nagant revolver lay nearby and he picked it up. Flicking down the loading gate, he rotated the cylinder to check the chambers. All seven rounds were spent. "He didn't go down without a fight." He glanced over the remains and noticed a skull fragment with a small, round hole in it. "Looks like he saved the last bullet for himself."

"He was carrying this," said Okhchen, holding up a map case of brown leather, battered and cracked by the elements but otherwise intact. He peered inside. "It's filled with old papers."

Zakharov took the case and the identification and put both in his saddlebag. "I'll look at them later. We need to move on."

They hurried on. Far to the west a yellow flare arced like a comet above the forest. Shortly thereafter they heard faint gunfire. The flurry of shots intensified.

"One of the other teams has found ghouls too," said Kravchenko, reining in.

The shooting tapered off and ceased. A green flare went up.

"And they eliminated them," said Zakharov. "Let's go."

At length Okhchen halted again, studying the ground. Zakharov saw tracks branching off in the trampled snow. Ahead, beyond this divergence, the trail became wider and heavier with more spoor than before.

"The ghouls split up here," said Okhchen. "Those tracks going west are probably from the pack the other team ran into."

Zakharov nodded. "That means we're following the main trail. Good."

Ahead lay a great swath of taiga devastated by wildfire, likely sparked by lightning last spring or summer and destroying thousands of hectares before finally burning itself out. Isolated tree trunks scorched by flame stood stark and black in a landscape of utter desolation. Hooves crackled and snapped on burned timber buried under the snow crust. They stopped to camp.

After eating, Zakharov examined the papers of the dead NKVD man. He flipped open the identification booklet. The photograph of a stern young man was inside along with the identification number, issue date, issuing authority, his rank and position, and so forth.

"So who was he, Comrade Lieutenant?" asked Kravchenko, rolling a cigarette.

"Junior Lieutenant of State Security Boris Stepanovich Sukhishvili, 13th Rifle Regiment, NKVD Internal Troops."

"Those were the ones massacred on the Tunguska six years ago. Far away from where we are. No survivors. What was he doing way out here?"

Zakharov turned his attention to the map case. Inside was a bundle of loose pages tied together that comprised an old file, the paper yellowed with age and stained from moisture. He untied it and began reading, starting with a hastily-scribbled note on top.

"He was trying to get back to his base," he said. "He was a courier from Vladimir Orlov, the regimental commander. When the ghouls attacked, Orlov realized he was doomed and tried to save this file by sending it off with Sukhishvili."

"What's so special about it?"

"Orlov wasn't just leading a search-and-destroy operation," said Zakharov. "According to this he was also tasked with a mission by Gleb Bokii, a senior NKVD official conducting research into paranormal phenomenon. Code-named Operation Hades, it was an investigation into the origins of the ghouls." He flicked to the next page. "In the village of Turukhansk Orlov discovered this file. It's the testimony of a White officer named Grishin, who was captured and interrogated by Red partisans in March 1920."

Kravchenko exhaled smoke, contemplating the glowing tip of his cigarette. "That's shortly after the first reports of ghoul attacks."

Zakharov carefully leafed through the file itself. The original testimony had been taken down in longhand and then a summary typed up. Some sections were so faded and stained they were illegible, but he was still able to read enough to piece together the essential facts.

At length he said, "Grishin was an aristocrat who belonged to the reactionary Black Hundreds before the Revolution so during the Civil War he joined the White counter-revolutionaries, serving on Admiral Kolchak's staff. In November 1919, after Omsk fell and Kolchak's White Army was forced to retreat, Grishin was dispatched on a secret mission."

The men listened in rapt attention as the wind moaned outside like a lost soul. Despite the warmth inside the tent they unconsciously shivered.

Zakharov continued, his gaze scouring the pages. "An admitted occultist, Grishin claimed his assignment had been to perform black magic rituals in the arctic to summon the ghouls, the idea being that the Whites would use them against the Bolsheviks. Kolchak had supposedly discovered evidence of the creatures' existence during the two polar expeditions he participated in before the First World War."

"Well, if that's true it sure backfired," said Kravchenko. "Ghouls can't be controlled and they slaughter everybody regardless of their politics. But if this crazy officer summoned them, why didn't he unsummon them after he realized his mistake?"

"He said he wasn't able to undo what he'd done. Even if he could, he was executed after his interrogation. Kolchak had been captured at Irkutsk a month earlier, but during his interrogation he was never asked about the ghouls, which no one suspected the Whites had anything to do with. Kolchak, of course, was executed too. And for some reason this file was never forwarded to Moscow. It was forgotten and ended up collecting dust in Turukhansk until Orlov found it."

"What about Operation Hades? There was no follow-up by Bokii?"

"He was liquidated during the purges. Paranormal investigation fell into disfavor."

Kravchenko shook his head in disgust and tossed his cigarette stub into the stove. "They shot everybody who could tell us anything."

Zakharov carefully slid the file back into the case. "Well, for sure our bosses will want to read this."

They went to sleep, but Zakharov only allowed his men a few precious hours of rest. Beyond the burned area the forest resumed, but then gradually thinned out. Soon the taiga ended entirely and gave way to barren plains of tundra, in the twilight an empty blue-white expanse stretching to the horizon. Only moss and lichen and grass grew here so nothing blocked the whining, bitter wind that whipped the team.

They encountered a man in a long parka riding a wooden sledge pulled by two reindeer, which he guided with a long pole. He was a Nenets, one of the native tribes living in the arctic. In recent years the government had tried forcing them to give up their traditional nomadic lifestyle, so the man was wary when he saw the soldiers.

Okhchen was an Evenki, another reindeer-herding people, and he rode forward in greeting. Okhchen spoke the man's language and at one point the Nenets gestured towards a distant blue ridgeline with his pole. Finally the man moved on, and Okhchen reported to Zakharov.

"He's from a clan fleeing the ghouls, Comrade Lieutenant. Says their hole is on the other side of those hills."

Zakharov nodded. "That's where the trail is headed."

Dusk came. The northern lights appeared, shimmering green ribbons writhing across the black sky casting an alien glow bright enough to read by. The ground became rugged as it sloped up to the ridge. Zakharov could not see any footprints on the bare rock, but Okhchen still discerned faint traces – dislodged stones, chipped ice, bruised moss – and they followed it up to the crest. The opposite side dropped off sharply in an escarpment, the trail plunging down a narrow draw.

They filed down the draw, the horses picking their way carefully over loose scree at the bottom. Okhchen rode ahead and then stopped; beckoned and pointed.

Up ahead the trail finally ended at its source – an irregular hole roughly three meters in diameter, ringed by piles of frozen earth. They peered over the rim. A foul odor wafted up from below and the horses became skittish, snorting and recoiling. The soldiers dismounted, unslinging their guns and snapping back the bolts.

"Pogodin!" said Zakharov. The team's engineer stepped forward. "Time to earn your pay. Two of you go down there with him and cover him."

Pogodin slung on two satchel charges from his saddlebags and clambered down into the hole, accompanied by two privates.

"Comrade Sergeant, has anyone ever tried going all the way down one of these rat holes to find out where they go?" asked Kaminsky.

"A team did once," said Kravchenko. "They never returned."

"Okhchen believes they go all the way down to the Lower World, where evil spirits dwell. Says the ghouls spawn down there and then burrow to the surface."

Kravchenko shrugged. "Who knows? His people were living here long before white men showed up. They know this land better than we do."

* * *

The demolition team switched on flashlights. The beams revealed that the hole was the entrance to a crude tunnel plunging down into subterranean blackness at an angle, delving past the permafrost deep into solid bedrock. Such geologic features were not unusual in the karst topography found in Siberia, but this was clearly not a natural formation created by erosion. It was too straight, too uniform in appearance. Just exactly how the ghouls dug them out was another unsolved mystery.

Pogodin had been a geologist in civilian life. Chewing on his mustache, he carefully inspected the rough, gray limestone with an experienced eye, noting fissures in the walls, piles of rubble fallen from the ceiling, and other indications of instability. He set down his satchels and began unpacking spools of primer cord and demolition blocks of TNT.

His two escorts stood guard nearby, pensive, weapons ready. They wrinkled their noses: the air was cold and dank, heavy with pungent ghoul smell. Then they tensed.

Far down the tunnel they could hear approaching footsteps – the flat, echoing slaps of bare feet and the click and scratch of claws.

Pogodin worked quickly, hurrying to place the high explosive at critical weak points in the tunnel. No time to drill boreholes; no time to double-prime charges either. He inserted a blasting cap into each block then crimped a short length of primer cord to the cap. The ends of these lines, in turn, he began tying to a long ring-main of primer cord so all the charges could be set off simultaneously by a single fuse.

His guards shined their flashlights down the pitch-black tunnel, but whatever lurked down there was beyond the reach of the light. The footsteps became louder, nearer; hissing could be heard. Then the footsteps sped up. Others joined it. The privates glimpsed the malevolent gleam of unblinking eyes.

"Here they come!" shouted one. "Vasily, hurry up!"

"Hold them off!" said Pogodin. "I'm almost done!"

As fiendish howls echoed the soldiers threw an illumination flare down the tunnel to blind the enemy then opened fire. The hollow roar of submachine guns was deafening in the confines of the passage, bullets spraying sparks as they ricocheted off walls. Empty steel casings clattered on the floor. The howls ceased; the flare burned out. The privates stopped shooting, ears ringing and nostrils filled with the acrid reek of blue cordite smoke.

The respite was only momentary. The running footsteps resumed.

"Fire in the hole!" said Pogodin, yanking the pull-igniter at the end of the ring-main. A thirty-second fuse hissed fiercely as it started burning down.

His companions scrabbled back up the tunnel and out the hole as fast as they could. Pogodin tried to follow, then slipped and fell. The others frantically reached down and hauled him out. Up on the surface the rest of the team had already withdrawn to a safe distance. The trio scrambled towards them.

Behind them a geyser of smoke and debris erupted from the hole with a muffled boom.

* * *

Zakharov waited until the air cleared, then cautiously ventured over to the crumbling edge for a closer look. The hole had collapsed and was completely filled with rubble. He nodded with satisfaction and returned to the others.

"Good job, comrades," he said. "Hole's sealed."

He brought out his sextant. Locations of all known ghoul holes had to be recorded. As he annotated his notebook there was a distant rumble and the ground trembled beneath his feet.

Okhchen let out a cry of alarm, his normally inscrutable Asian features taut with dismay. He pointed north. Zakharov scowled and raised his binoculars. His heart sank.

"What is it?" asked Kravchenko.

Zakharov answered by passing him the binoculars.

Kravchenko looked for himself and swore vehemently in Ukrainian. A few hundred meters away a dust cloud billowed from a huge crater that suddenly yawned open. Crawling from its depths like monkeys were ghouls – scores upon scores of them, a swarm of gaunt figures in the eldritch gleam of the northern lights. He let out a gusty sigh and handed the binoculars back.

"It's a full-scale invasion," he said.

Zakharov nodded grimly. "Like six years ago. After that regiment was slaughtered the NKVD had to call in the air force to bomb the holes with poison gas."

"So that's why the ghouls only attacked a few at a time. They were bait to lure our detachment north, overextend ourselves. We're the only line of defense out here."

Zakharov realized how potentially serious this was. The German Army had overrun much of the western part of the Soviet Union, so vital industrial plants had been dismantled and evacuated to safer locations east of the Ural Mountains. Raw materials for those plants came from Siberia. A major ghoul invasion could threaten facilities vital to the war effort. Many of the forced-labor camps and exile colonies of the Gulag were located there too and a ghoul attack would hardly be liberation for the wretched prisoners.

He swung into the saddle. "Fall back!"

The team retreated towards the ridge. A great clamor of rabid howls rose. The ghouls had seen them and gave chase, their eyes glowing demonically. Zakharov knew they could sprint as fast as a horse and had greater stamina.

This was a race he could not win.

They rode up the draw and when they reached the top Zakharov signaled a halt. Grabbing Pogodin by the sleeve he said, "Ride like the devil! Warn the major!" He thrust into his hands the map case with the file, plus his logbook with the hole's longitude and latitude.

"Yes, Comrade Lieutenant!" Pogodin kicked his horse with his heels and galloped away.

Zakharov turned to Kravchenko, his blue eyes narrow slits of determination. "We have to delay them, give Pogodin a chance to get away."

Kravchenko nodded curtly. He dismounted and turned to the others. "Comrades, we make our stand here. Not one step back."

The others knew what this order meant, but obeyed without question. They did not fight for Stalin, or for Communism, not even for Mother Russia. They fought first and foremost for the same thing that all soldiers have fought for since the beginning of time. They fought for each other.

Swinging down, they hastened to take positions among a jumble of boulders at the head of the draw. They unpacked all their spare ammunition and turned the horses loose; no one could be spared to hold them. The escarpment had cliffs too sheer to scale so unless the ghouls went a dozen kilometers in either direction and circled around the far ends of the ridge, they had to come this way.

A red emergency flare was launched even though everyone knew it was futile. No help would arrive in time. A few soldiers crossed themselves, the old Orthodox custom before battle that many rank-and-file in the Red Army still performed out of habit. The last illumination flare was sent up and it floated overhead on its parachute, the ghouls hissing and gnashing their teeth in anger, trying to shield their eyes from its bright, flickering glare.

Okhchen braced his rifle on a rock and began shooting as fast as he could work its bolt-action, picking off creatures at long range, pausing only to thumb in more rounds to reload.

Soon Kaminsky's machine gun joined in, its pan magazine slowly revolving as he hammered away, spent cartridges spewing out the bottom, red lines of tracers streaking across.

The flare burned out and darkness closed in again like a pall.

"Steady, comrades!" shouted Zakharov.

The screeching tidal wave of death poured into the draw.

"Fire!"

Submachine guns lashed out. The ghouls in front stumbled and fell, but those behind did not waver. Heedless of losses the creatures kept coming, jumping over the fallen. The soldiers shot them down in droves, gagging on the rising stench as disintegrating carcasses piled up on the steep slope. They flung grenades and the explosions sent lethal splinters slicing into gray flesh. The draw became a killing zone as their inhuman foes were funneled into it.

But there seemed to be no end to the creatures: still more scrambled out of the crater, and the team could only hold the frenzied horde at bay for as long as they had ammunition. All too soon, gritting their teeth, they snapped in their last magazines. One by one they ran empty and the slobbering ghouls, shrieking with bloodlust, greedily surged forward.

Two privates blew themselves up with a grenade as the monstrosities sprang onto them, taking their foes with them.

Kravchenko dropped his empty submachine gun and plunged a combat knife into a ghoul's belly up to the handle. He viciously ripped upwards, but no entrails spilled out, just a black gush of acidic ichor. The steel blade melted and he screamed as the ichor ate through his clothing and burned his flesh.

Okhchen sent his last bullet crashing through a leering face, then gripped his rifle by the barrel and swung it like a club to crush the skull of a second enemy with the wooden stock. The next tore his head off.

Kaminsky bellowed in defiance and rose to his feet, holding his smoking DP-28 waist-high as he raked the ghouls with slugs. When it was empty he threw it aside and swept out an infantry spade. One edge of the blade was sharpened so it could also be used like an ax – or as a weapon. Wielding it like a battle ax he hacked and slashed at the ghouls like a warrior of old, laughing and cursing them in Yiddish, splattering their gore on the rocks until finally they overwhelmed and dismembered him.

The magazine of Zakharov's Tokarev service pistol held eight rounds. Seven he pumped into the nearest ghoul, bringing it down. Then, as three more lunged for him, he pressed the muzzle to his temple and pulled the trigger.

* * *

His gnawed bones, and the gnawed bones of his comrades, could not be seen by the aircrews flying high above the ridge a week later. But they could see the crater in the tundra, and the Tupolev bombers carried full loads.

The Secret War went on.

A MESSAGE FROM THE TEAM

Thanks for reading *Love, Death and Robots*.

We hope you've enjoyed it as much as we did putting it together.

It was a great honour to have Tim Miller read the entire volume and write the foreword for us. We sorta feel like Bill and Ted, and we're not worthy, but Tim is a great guy, and very humble considering all his achievements. Even though he stated he was honoured to be given the chance to work on this, the honour is all ours.

Please consider leaving us a review if (and anywhere) you see fit. Any and all reviews are gratefully accepted.

If you have any questions, or want to quote from the book, please contact us at any time.

I would ask please, if you DO review online, send a link to Geoff at editor@cohesionpress.com or via our Facebook page messaging system. If you review for a magazine or paper, let us know and we'll buy it.

Thank you.

+ + +

Geoff Brown - publishing editor, Cohesion Press.
Mayday Hills Lunatic Asylum
Beechworth, Australia

Amanda J Spedding - editor-in-chief, Cohesion Press
Sydney, Australia

Printed in Great Britain
by Amazon